The
Sudden
Metropolis

K. K. Poole

First Published in 2017
by GWL Publishing
an imprint of Great War Literature Publishing LLP

Produced in United Kingdom

ISBN 978-1-910603-44-4 Paperback Edition

GWL Publishing
Forum House
Stirling Road
Chichester PO19 7DN
www.gwlpublishing.co.uk

Image Credits:
Map images sourced from the collections of the State Library of
Western Australia and reproduced with the permission of the
Library Board of Western Australia, and MAP G9021.H2 (Gold) from the
National Library of Australia.

K.K. Poole was born in 1969. He is the son of Australian parents and was educated at Magdalen College School and St. John's College, Oxford. For three successive years he rowed in 'The Boat Race' against Cambridge.

After University, he taught science, coached rowing and gained a doctorate in epilepsy epidemiology before qualifying as a general practitioner in 2003. He is married with three sons.

Dedication

For my brother Sean
adventurer and dreamer
(1971-1989)

Acknowledgements

I would like to thank the following for their encouragement and support during the writing process: my wife Alison and friends Juliet Solomon, Henry Wells and Rob Deavall. To the GWL publishing team, especially Wendy Lawrance: your faith in me is greatly appreciated. Thanks also to the café staff at 'Attibassi' (now called the Forum) for putting up with me and my laptop for hours at a time.

I am grateful to Mr Bowerman of Waihi, New Zealand, who, after hearing my great grandfather had once been a Wesleyan (Methodist) Minister in Fiji, was enthusiastic enough to pass on some photocopied pages from a rather obscure source called 'The Cyclopedia of Fiji'. Unbeknown to me (or my father for that matter), it transpired that before Fiji the Reverend W.R. Poole had worked the Western Australian goldfields during the boom years at the turn of the twentieth century. Significantly, from 1902-03, one of his postings was in Kalgoorlie, the same city my brother visited in the summer of 1989 prior to an ill-fated cycling journey across the Nullarbor Plain. This small but seemingly providential coincidence provided me at last with the historical setting and the hope to re-tell my brother's story in the way I wanted.

Disclaimer

The Sudden Metropolis is a work of fiction. However, some of the characters, settings and situations are factual. Small liberties may have been taken with certain elements of these characters' lives, their whereabouts and the timings of events, for the purposes of telling the story.

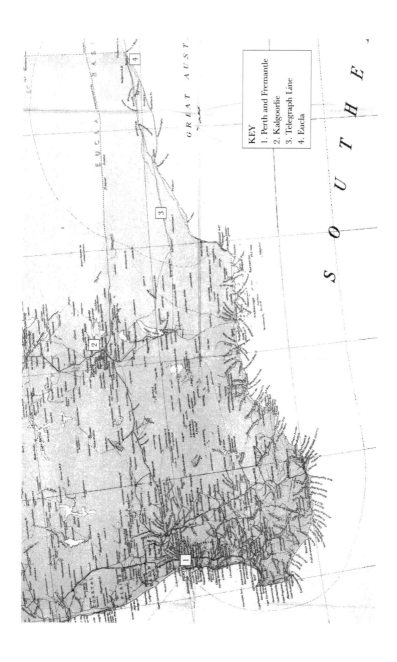

KEY
1. Perth and Fremantle
2. Kalgoorlie
3. Telegraph Line
4. Eucla

GREAT AUST.

EUCLA

SOUTHE

'Get gold, humanely if you can, but at all hazards, get gold.'

King Ferdinand of Spain, 1511

Chapter One

The Royal Victoria Military Hospital, Netley, Southampton
May 31, 1900

"… Lights out!"

A call, followed by the clank of a heavy switch, and my world was thrown into total darkness for another night.

'Lights out' was just one of the things about hospital life which reminded me of my boarding school; bells for mealtimes, prefect-like officious ward-officers strutting around telling you what to do, and then the teams of self-important doctors acting like school masters and telling the ward officers what to do in turn.

We patients even had a uniform of sorts; faded blue cotton suits with red ties, which gave off that institutionalised look. Around here they called it the 'hospital undress'. As a schoolboy I had been too young to know any better and had gone along with it, but now at the age of twenty-five, this supervised living was driving me half mad.

And at least in the school dorm I had been able to sleep. In this place, when I closed my eyes, the ticking of the ward clock got so loud it became amplified to Big Ben proportions. The only way to shut the damn thing off was to open my eyes again and stare out blindly into the darkness, awake and alert and haunted by what had happened in South Africa, only two months earlier.

The memories were still fresh.

As a doctor in the British Army I had dealt with a typhoid epidemic almost single-handed, looking after soldiers so weakened by the disease they could not even brush away the flies from their faces. That was the memory keeping me awake now. The insects had crawled across their eyes, up their nostrils, around their lips and inside their mouths, if they happened to be open, which in the gasping heat was more often than not. Great clusters of the bastards, moving freely and without impediment, their black bodies in stark contrast to the pallor of dying men, all gorging themselves on the film of sweat, tears and saliva.

Uninoculated, I had caught the disease myself and barely survived.

The one good thing about the whole episode was being reunited with my twin brother Freddie on the hospital ship home. Things had been worse for him; as a regular soldier he had not only contracted typhoid fever, but lost his right leg courtesy of a Boer bullet.

Anyway, to cut a long story short, the army had shipped us back to this bloody place to convalesce.

Freddie had the same insomnia as me and after lights out he would be awake too, reliving his own traumas. In the day it was easy to keep busy and push everything out of your mind, but at 'lights out' when things stopped and the silence fell, the memories would seep back in, like smoke from under a doorway.

Our solution was to escape to the hospital pier at night. Strictly forbidden of course, but we didn't care. Damn the rules. It was our secret act of defiance; half an hour of watching the water and sharing a cigarette made all the difference. Afterwards, the sought-after oblivion of sleep came a lot easier.

A door closed, signalling the night staff had finally decamped to the tea room. They would be smoking and playing cards in there for hours yet.

I sat on the edge of my bed ready to go.

Freddie's bed was right next to mine, three feet away.

"Hey…"

No response.

All I could hear was the deep breathing of sleep; not like him – most nights he was the one whispering across to me. He had been coughing a lot that day – the doctors on the morning round had all listened to his chest with their stethoscopes before concluding it was nothing serious. Now he was completely out of it and I judged it was best to let him rest up.

Tonight I was on my own.

Barefoot, I slipped out into the corridor of 'C Block', tiptoed down the cold stone stairs to the ground floor and climbed out of a window.

The one benefit of insomnia was good night vision: on the far side of the hospital lawn, silhouetted black against the purple night sky was the familiar row of Scots pines down by the waterline. Beyond the tallest of the trees was the pier.

It was creepy being alone – I wasn't used to it. Half way over the grass I sensed I was being watched and looked back, but I saw no movement, no life at all, just the brick monolith with its hundreds of windows all staring blankly back at me, like the opaque eyes of the men I had failed to save in South Africa.

Usually, whenever the boards of the pier rumbled under my feet, I would smile because I had come to associate the sound with freedom. Tonight was different though. That uneasy feeling – verging on fear – wasn't going away. Moments before it had been an imagined observer from the hospital building, now it was as if the trees themselves were watchers. Not just the pines on my shore but the whole crouching dark forest on the far side of Southampton Water as well.

Walking down the pier between these two opposing ranks of trees made me feel like a lone pawn advancing into the middle of a gigantic arboreal chess match, one in which I had no control of the final outcome. The world seemed somehow cruel tonight, uncaring and mean. That's how it felt. Like something bad was going to happen.

As I sat down on the bench at the end of the pier, a light rain began to fall.

The gentle hissing on the still waters was the same sound I heard whenever I was about to faint, lately a common occurrence because of the toll the typhoid fever had taken on my system. It was pleasant enough though, and my mind began to calm with the hiss. I closed my eyes and tilted my head back, savouring the soft rain on my face and the absence of the relentless, ticking ward clock.

Or was it absent?

Tick tock, Tick tock, TICK TOCK, TICK TOCK…

For a mad moment I thought the clock was hunting me down, before I recognised it as the sound of Freddie's crutches on the planks.

Throwing them down with a clatter, he hopped the last few feet over to the bench and collapsed next to me. Then he hoiked up some gruel from the depths of his lungs and spat it over the hand rail in a neat parabola.

"You didn't wake me," he said, a hurt edge to his tone.

"No… because you're not well. You shouldn't be out here with that cough, you know."

He shrugged.

"The docs gave me the all-clear on the ward round today, so it can't be that bad."

I didn't reply to that because I wasn't fully reassured; if the chaos in South Africa had taught me anything, it was that nothing in life was certain, least of all a doctor's lousy bloody opinion.

"Well, actually I'm glad you've come, because you have the tobacco."

"Yes, I do" he said, in a teasing manner, patting his breast pocket. "Yes indeed I do. I have the tobacco. I am the king, and you will have to make a formal request… I am a…"

"Christ Almighty, Freddie, are you going to talk all night or are you going to make us a smoke?"

"All right, all right… calm down…"

He opened a red tin on his knees, leaning over it to keep the rain out.

On the lid were the words 'SOUTH AFRICA 1900' and next to that a picture of the Queen's head. Originally, the tin had contained half a pound of chocolate – the Queen's New Year present to her troops in the field. After the chocolate was gone, the tins became useful containers. Sometimes, senior officers sent home a dead soldier's few possessions in them – letters, 'lucky' charms and the like. There must have been hundreds of these red tins scattered about England already, perched on mantelpieces in front rooms darkened by drawn curtains.

Freddie used his as a tobacco store.

Balancing a pinch onto a sheet of Rizla paper, he started rolling a cigarette. He did it with the quiet reverence of a vicar preparing communion, combined with the speed of an assembly-line worker – all in one smooth series of movements. Once lit, he flicked the match away and snapped shut the lid of the box. Then he took a drag and tilted his head back, the way I had done earlier, exhaling a rising plume of white smoke into the falling rain.

"Guess what?" he said.

"What?"

"We could be rich, you and I."

Oh God, I thought, *here we go again*.

He had got it into his head to join the Australian gold rush. All day long, he had been trying to badger me into going along with him.

I reached over, took his cigarette and closed my eyes as I smoked it. My fingertips started tingling. If only he would stop going on, then I could really relax.

He nudged me. "Hey… are you listening? Did you think about what I said earlier?"

My eyes were still shut. "Not yet."

"You know how they pay the doctors?"

"No."

"With gold. The doctors get gold nuggets this bloody big…"

I opened my eyes. Freddie was holding his thumb and index finger an inch apart.

"Can you believe that?" he said.

"Not really."

He examined his imaginary nugget for a second longer before snatching back his roll-up. "Give me that," he said, in mild irritation.

Freddie was frowning now, figuring out what to say next. Seeing him there, struggling with how best to employ his powers of persuasion, made me feel especially sorry for him, but not sorry enough to want to go to Australia.

"Listen, John," he said, sounding as rational as possible, "they need good doctors out there… and now we've both had the enteric, we'll be completely fine."

'Enteric' was another name for typhoid fever. After what I had been through, I never wanted to see another case of it again. I double-checked to see if he was joking; sometimes, with my brother, it was hard to tell.

I turned to him. "Let me get this straight… I fund this expedition by treating typhoid patients in some outback hospital and wait around until you make the find of the century. Does that about sum it up?"

He smiled. "Yes, that's exactly it."

That was my brother all right, the dreamer who lived his life out of the *Boy's Own* paper. Right there was the difference between us – the dreamer and the realist. For him, Australia was a land of gleaming riches, for me it was Captain Cook and a bunch of ex-convicts.

"I still can't see the draw, Freddie. Why the excitement about some yellow rock?"

He threw up his hands in exasperation.

"What the hell is the matter with you, John? You're so bitter."

He was right. I *was* bitter, bitter about gold most of all. Gold had caused the Boer War in the first place, the war turning us from idealistic sons of the Empire into typhoid-ridden shadows of our former selves. The way I saw it, gold was the reason we were getting soaked out on this god-forsaken pier at midnight in our bloody pyjama uniforms.

"Think of the odds, Freddie – hundreds, probably thousands, must fail for just one person to make their fortune. And you really think that the chosen one is going to be you? That you won't be just another luckless gold digger…"

I should have known that using reason would not work with him. He grabbed the nearest crutch up off the floor and stood, so that he was right in front of me.

"You'd change your tune if you saw a golden nugget glistening in the sun," he said. "You'd have gold fever, brother, not typhoid fever – you'd dance a bloody jig…"

He started to prance around on the boards, hopping back and forth on his good leg and glaring at me like a maniac. The make-believe nugget was back in his free hand: "Arrgggh… Look at this 'ere gold I found."

I smiled as he acted the pirate. It was good to see him like that, buoyed up with his old energy. He soon sat back down though, exhausted and out of breath.

"Promise me you'll think about it…"

"All right," I said, lying.

He didn't say anything else and we finished the rest of the cigarette together in silence, passing it back and forth between us.

Somewhere to the south, where the Solent merged with the English Channel, a ship's foghorn went off, drowning out the sound of the rain on the water.

I knew Freddie would keep on nagging, and that he had just parked the notion for a while, like he sometimes did with his half-smoked rollups, storing them away in his tin for another time. There was no way I was going to agree on this one though – my plan was to slot right back into my old Harley Street practice as soon as I was discharged. I couldn't wait to be out of the RAMC and back in London, in my civilian job. It was back to the high life for me, not some stinking dive in the Australian desert.

The rain started coming down harder and soon a bank of fog rolled in, completely blotting out Southampton Water and the far shore, where the edge of the New Forest hugged the land.

For another five minutes we sat there, smoking a second cigarette and getting drenched.

Freddie took a long last drag of the sodden cigarette and threw it over the railing; the same arc he had spat in twenty minutes before. Then he pulled his collar up around his neck for what little protection it gave him and slowly pushed himself up onto his crutches.

"Come on," he said. "Let's go back, I'm bloody freezing."
I got to my feet to join him.
Heads bowed, we started back down the pier.

Chapter Two

Something felt odd when I woke up and, for a while, I couldn't work out what it was.

From the bunk above, the Reverend Sean Rennie reached out for his glass of water which was hanging in its copper holder attached to the wall.

There were two beaker holders in our cabin, specially designed to always stay horizontal. For untold hours, I had watched our glass beakers swaying in sympathy with the ship's roll – in rough seas they would tilt right over and yet the water within remained perfectly level. They made me wish for an internal mechanism of my own to help set me level again.

Rennie's hand stopped short and hovered mid-air – he had noticed it too.

Everything was gently trembling – the bunks, the wood panelled walls of the cabin, even the water in the beakers. The ship's engines had taken on a deeper and lower tone. Finally, my brain clicked into gear: we were slowing down.

The slats on the top bunk buckled ominously as Rennie sat up in his bed. For two months now I had been living in fear of being buried by an avalanche of broken wood, mattress, bedding and the bulk of my room-mate. Not that he was a fat man; he was just big. Well over six feet tall, with the build of a blacksmith. How Rennie had ever attained his musculature was a mystery because from what I had seen on the voyage, he never exercised at all. As a trained man of science I would have to conclude he simply had 'good genes'. Rennie, on the other hand, would tell you it was 'God given'.

He had claimed the top bunk on the day of our departure by placing his black bible on the pillow, perhaps thinking that by sleeping up there he was one yard nearer to heaven.

Rennie tore open the porthole curtain, allowing shards of blinding sunlight to splinter into the cabin. Reflexively, I pulled my blanket over my head and shut my eyes, waiting for the porthole imprint on my retinas to fade to black.

"Land Ho," I heard him say. "Wake up, John."

I stayed hidden and listened to his morning routine; the loud creak as he swung off the bunk and then the heavy thump as his feet hit the floor. He padded over to the sink, turned on the tap and started slapping the shaving brush onto his chin.

Here it comes, I thought.

Right on cue, he launched into song, flat and out of key as usual:

"...Rule Britannia!

Britannia rule the waves!

Britons never, never, never shall be slaves."

I wondered if he mangled church hymns this badly.

He kept repeating the chorus, because he didn't know the rest. It didn't matter to him. Like his physicality, Rennie's optimism was a force to be reckoned with; it could fill a room with the same intensity as the Australian sun. And whether or not you wanted to, he would drag you along with him, just as I was being dragged from my sullen torpor now. I suppose his irrational optimism was a useful trait for someone tasked with convincing people a man had come back from the dead. I actually envied Rennie, for the simple fact that he seemed so damned happy the whole time.

I gave up pretending to be asleep and pulled back the covers.

Over at the sink he was singing and conducting with the razor in his right hand.

"…*Britons never, never, never, shall be slaves!*"

Then he stopped singing and started splashing his face in a sequence of mini baptisms, all the while repeating the phrase, "What a blessing!" as if each scoop of water was from the River Jordan itself.

Practically everything was a blessing for Rennie. One of his peculiar habits was to go into the galley after dinner and wash up the dirty pans. "What a blessing!" he would say, scrubbing away at the grease and burnt-on scraps of food with cheerful vigour. I would stand in the doorway, watching the chef and his team scratching their heads and looking at one another in confusion.

These were dirty pans and Rennie acted as if he really was enjoying cleaning them. Imagine what he would do if the Good Lord showed up on his doorstep unannounced. He would probably explode.

Catchphrases weren't Rennie's only eccentricity.

Once a week he would cut his own hair, snipping off any stray strands with a small pair of scissors. Despite this, or perhaps because of it, his hair was a mess; in fact in certain places you could even see the scalp underneath where he had cut it too short and made a divot.

In my opinion, it was only his position as a minister that saved him from public ridicule. Out on deck I had seen how the other passengers respected the dog collar no matter what the appearance of the wearer. "Morning Reverend," they would say, giving him the time of day. They all bowed their heads in prayer when he said grace at mealtimes too, out of an ingrained respect for the man of God. It was the uniform that did it. As a doctor, I knew how a white coat could cause a similar reaction in people, perhaps not quite bowing their heads in reverence, but almost.

Apart from the bald patches, the other results of Rennie's clumsy self-grooming were the nicks on his ears; an array of small scabs, all at various stages of healing. It was a safe bet he would injure himself at least once when he cut his hair and it didn't take him long this time.

"Oh confound it."

"When are you going to see a real barber?"

"Ah, the young doctor is awake," he said, changing the subject. He angled his head to get a better look at the damage in the mirror.

"There'll be a barber on shore who can cut your hair properly."

"Oh, come on, John, how hard can it be?"

"It looks pretty hard to me."

Rennie glanced round, still dabbing at the bloody ear with his handkerchief.

"You think Jesus went to a barber?" he said.

"How the hell should I know?" I paused for a moment. "Sean, do you think I would try and remove my own appendix?"

"Now you're just being obtuse, John."

"Oh, *I'm* the one being obtuse. I do apologise."

"Apology accepted." The bleeding had stopped now. He ran some water through his hair and slapped at his cheeks again. "Ah... What a blessing!"

Then he started sniffing like a beagle. He went over to the porthole and pressed his face right up against the glass so that it fogged up with his breath.

"I think I can smell wood smoke from the town, John... Australian wood smoke."

Groaning, I pulled the blanket back over my head again.

At first I thought we would become enemies.

As our ship had steamed through the Mediterranean, we had argued to the point of exhaustion. Religion versus Science: me interrogating him on the biblical inconsistencies with the geological record and he, in turn, gamely rebutting Darwin's theory of natural selection. "And where is this missing link of yours?" Rennie had said, doing monkey impressions in the ship's lounge in front of onlookers. No-one was interested in my reply – "Java man" – because they were all too busy laughing at the Minister pulling ape faces and tickling his armpits.

Somewhere between Suez and Ceylon though, when it was clear our entrenched opinions were just that, the arguments had moved away from the heavyweight issues to bickering about the small things, like an old married couple. It was the kind of light-hearted banter that helped me forget about everything else from before the trip and I welcomed the distraction.

It sounded like a drunken cocktail party in the lounge and it was only ten in the morning.

Through the noise of a hundred excited voices came yells from the ship's crew outside as they prepared for docking.

Rennie was in the chair next to me, feet up on his suitcase, head buried in his novel. He had been reading *The Count of Monte Cristo* for the entire voyage, interspersed with the Bible, of course.

Abruptly, he slammed the book shut. "Finished!"

"Congratulations."

A few moments later, he opened it up again.

"Listen to this, John – it's on the last page: *'Until the day when God will deign to reveal the future to man, all human wisdom is contained in these two words – wait and hope.'* I like that… Oh yes… I like that very much indeed."

"Wait and hope," I said to myself.

The phrase kept repeating in my head: *Wait and hope. Wait and hope,* and the words were still going round as the ship's engines were thrust into reverse and we finally shuddered to a halt up against the dock.

"One at a time ladies and gentlemen, please," said a red faced steward.

Rennie had gone and stood at the back of the pushing and shoving group, a good head and shoulders above them. When he moved forward to leave, they parted for him like the Red Sea.

I stayed in my chair, hiding from the reality waiting for me outside. The doubts were coming thick and fast now.

What had I been thinking, leaving London and all I knew?

Reluctant to join the exodus, I continued sipping hot tea and listening to the clanging of passengers' footsteps as they filed one by one down the metal gangway.

I was going to miss the ship. I had come to like its sounds and its loose routine, and the feeling of being surrounded on all sides by hundreds of miles of ocean, far from anywhere else.

The weeks at sea had been my true convalescence, far more restorative than the dire month at the Military Hospital in Southampton. You didn't have to think on board. Life was simple. To get fit again I had marched laps around the deck. Then I had done pull-ups on the overhead iron brackets by the lifeboats, with Rennie sat in a deckchair and keeping count like a sport's coach: "One, two, three… come on, John… one more…"

By the time the Australian coastline had appeared through the heat haze that morning, all remaining frailty from the typhoid fever had left me. Well, the physical frailty anyway.

The ship felt safe, so I continued to delay my exit, swirling the tea leaves in the bottom of my cup like a modern day soothsayer.

I began to daydream, travelling back to a cold day more than a decade before, when Freddie and I had been thirteen years old.

****

Boathouse on the River Thames, Oxford
January, 1888

"I swear it," Freddie was saying.

The other boy shook his head. "I don't believe you."

"I kept the bloody pieces. I'll show you if you want; they're in my study."

"Tell me again," the boy said. "Tell me *exactly* what happened."

By now the others were crowding around, leaning in close to hear, and so was I. Even though I had seen it happen, I liked the way my brother told the story.

Freddie sighed. "Crosbie catches me reading the *Boy's Own*. He comes over and tears it in two. Tells me, anything else I bring into class that isn't a Latin textbook will get the same treatment... so, the next lesson I take in last year's *Wisden*, just to see what would happen. I put it on my desk and wait. Crosbie comes over, takes a look at it and smiles. Then he picks it up and only bloody rips it in half... Like a wild animal he was... he even used his teeth!"

"That's impossible," the boy said.

The others were looking doubtful too.

"Is it true, Major?" the leader of the doubters said to me.

He was appealing to my trustworthy status as the older brother: Hunston 'Major' and Hunston 'Minor' – that's what we were called at school. As non-identical twins, I was the 'Major' by only five minutes, but those minutes could have been years when it came to the way people automatically saw me as the wiser one.

"It's true," I said, my expression solemn. "He tore it in half."

"Blimey..." the boy said, pleased to have been finally convinced.

Now they all started to believe.

We stood there shivering and watching our breath turning to fog in the clear January air. Out of the group waiting there at the boathouse, only Freddie and I had seen the episode, because we were the only ones in the bottom Latin set.

Crosbie hadn't used his teeth, but he had done it all right.

At first, when he had picked up the almanac, I had thought Crosbie was joking – we all had. The class had laughed, expecting him to admit defeat and get on with the lesson. But instead, his look had turned serious and he crossed some kind of line in his head. When he started to attack the *Wisden* our laughter ebbed away into an awed silence. There was a sharp cracking sound when he broke the spine over his knee, and that had been followed by a sustained period of violent animalistic wrenching. In the end, he dropped the two chunks onto Freddie's desk and said: "You should be reading almanacs about rowing, Minor, not ones about bloody cricket... I might have thought twice if you had brought that in..."

There was a reason for this remark: as well as teaching Latin, Crosbie was the Master in charge of the Boat Club.

The Boat Club was where the sporting rejects ended up; skinny boys, fat boys, boys with spectacles, mal-coordinated boys. There were half dozen of us waiting for Crosbie now, a motley crew who hated hockey and cricket or didn't care, or who did care but hadn't made either of the teams. Freddie and I fell into the 'didn't care' category, participating in both of those sports, but never quite seeing what all the fuss was about. We had never seen the attraction about rowing either, at least until now. The only reason we had decided to give it a go, was in order to train under the man who had destroyed the *Wisden*.

"So the monk really did it," the boy said, smacking his forehead in jest and getting a laugh from the others.

All the masters had nicknames. You didn't say the names directly to their faces of course, but they all knew what theirs were and I'm fairly sure most were secretly proud to have them.

I doubted this was the case for Crosbie, who was bald except for a rim of dark hair around the back of his head, like a monk's tonsure, and I didn't imagine he appreciated pupils smacking their foreheads and making fun of his baldness.

"Cave!" someone said in an urgent whisper.

Pronounced 'KayVee', it meant 'watch out'. Latin slang: we all used it. That was just how it was.

The laughing stopped abruptly.

Crosbie was ten yards away, parking his bicycle up against the side of the boat house. No one had heard him arrive. We watched in silence as he strode over towards us.

There was a definite 'edginess' about him, an air of menace in the way he looked and moved, almost as though he was spoiling for a fight. He bent down to pick something up and I thought for a surreal moment that he might be making a grab for one of the chickens pecking around in the long grass, in order to bite its head off. Instead, he picked up a rowing oar that was hidden there, one with different sized holes in its spoon like a piece of Swiss cheese.

"Afternoon, sir," said the boy who had been smacking his forehead, employing an ingratiation tactic which worked well with most masters. Crosbie blanked him and addressed us as one: "Shut your bloody mouths and watch."

He spoke in a halting staccato beat, as if his thoughts came to him in Latin and he had to translate them into English for everyone else's benefit.

Crosbie stepped into the 'bank tub', a floating platform in a stagnant siding of water alongside the boathouse. Tethered to two upright steel posts set into the bank to keep it stationary, it was like a punishment from a Greek myth; you could row forever and not move a single yard.

A rigger with an oarlock was bolted onto the tub on the waterside. Crosbie secured the oar into the rigger and sat down on the sliding seat, slotting his feet under the foot straps. Then he proceeded to row for a full minute, the only sounds the splash of the oar in the water and the metallic grinding of the posts holding the bank tub still. Water rushed through the holes in the spoon, frothing up the stagnant tributary.

It looked simple enough.

He climbed out of the tub and pointed at Freddie.

"You, boy… show me how it's done."

Freddie leapt into the tub, wedged his feet in, and started to race away. On the first stroke, the spoon dug so deep that he dredged up mud and the oar handle got stuck under his armpit. On my turn, I did the complete opposite, washing the spoon out of the water and falling backwards off the seat. By the time my minute was over, I was breathing hard. You had to be strong and fit for this lark, and your power had to be applied in a controlled way. Even on day one of our rowing training, I had an insight into how Crosbie had been able to rip the almanac in half.

The following week the group halved in size, and the week after that it halved again so that in the end, only Freddie and I were left.

Crosbie didn't seem at all bothered by the dwindling attendance rates.

He put us into single sculls and we became experts in the art of capsizing. We kept practising though; hours and hours of repetitive rowing strokes, and gradually we got the hang of it. By the end of the Hilary term we could scull up and down the river without falling in once. The basics mastered, we started to hone our skills, searching for ever more boat speed.

In the early-morning outings of Trinity term, the river would be shrouded in a low-lying mist, yet to be burnt off by the rising sun and in this other-worldly atmosphere, Freddie and I would leapfrog each other in our sculling boats – twenty strokes 'firm' and twenty strokes 'light' – shouting technical tips across the water to one another as we went along. On my turn to row light pressure, I would watch mesmerised as his boat bore down on mine, the bow nosing upwards gently with each boat surge. Freddie was the more stylish oarsman, the more natural 'boat mover', as Crosbie would say. Far from becoming disillusioned or dejected, seeing Freddie's mastery of the rowing stroke inspired me to keep working at my own technique, a fraternal sense of competition my driving force.

I liked the noise the bubbles made as they ran along the sides of the hull; sometimes, if you were going particularly well, they made a certain pitch of note, and when they sounded like that you were 'making the boat sing'.

We found an old double scull languishing behind the boathouse, a part of the school grounds called 'the boat graveyard' because of the dozens of dilapidated boats strewn around there, half hidden amongst the waist-high nettles. The double had a broken rigger and some other minor damage, the result of a collision with a river cruiser years before, but it was salvageable and we spent the whole long vacation repairing it; replacing the rigger, re-gluing each fractured strut and canvassing over the old rents and tears. We renamed it 'Wisden' in memory of the seminal event which had drawn us into the sport.

Five years later, in our last term at school – the Trinity term of '93 – Freddie and I finally peaked, winning pewter pots all over the summer regatta circuit.

Even if you weren't related, rowing a double scull for five years would make team-mates as close as brothers. As twins we barely needed to talk anyway, and by the end we were almost telepathic, moving together in the boat as one.

I always managed to get by at school, never drawing too much attention to myself and passing exams when I needed to.

Freddie was different. Our school was a like a sausage factory: if you were different you were cast into the slops.

Crosbie summed it up best: "Minor," he said to Freddie one time, "you have 'a French café' attitude to life." It was true – Freddie did seem almost *too* carefree. Even the way he walked seemed to be out of step with everyone else's solemn march towards the future. He had a slow-ish, particular kind of walk, knees slightly bent – a light-hearted sort of trudge. That bothered a lot of people. Aside from Crosbie, none of the schoolmasters liked him.

Having become a pariah by virtue of being different, Freddie set little stock in conventional academia and made no effort to 'play the game', rarely volunteering answers in lessons. His non-conformity finally reached breaking point in a chemistry lesson on the very last day of our final term, in early July 1893. Paradoxically, the episode occurred after he had volunteered an answer, and not only that, the correct answer.

There was an end of term test going on and the usual crowd of ingratiates were in their element, almost flirting with the master. The atmosphere in the room was a sickening warm fug of mutual admiration.

Freddie and I were sitting at the back; him doodling in his rough book, me thinking about that afternoon's scheduled rowing outing, the last of our schooldays.

I checked the clock by the blackboard – just a few minutes to go to the bell.

For the final question, the master drew a hexagon on the blackboard, some of the sides with two lines to indicate covalent bonds.

"Right then... name of molecule and its discoverer?"

The class were all shoving their hands up as if their very lives depended on it: "*Sir...Sir... Sir...*"

It was benzene and Freddie gave me a big grin because he knew the answer. After that year's benzene lesson, we had likened our rowing puddles to benzene rings.

"Hunston Minor… Is that you with your hand up?"

"Yes, sir."

"Let's hear it then…"

The master said this in a withering tone, setting off a wave of laughter in the class.

He was a muscular man of medium height, with shiny black hair that curled over his collar. He thought a lot of himself and always expected the class to laugh along with his jibes. As it happened, he was also the master in charge of the rugby team, and was therefore popular with the boys who played, which was the majority. It was said that as a younger man, he had been a very good player.

His mood – to use chemical parlance – was about as stable as sodium when dropped into water, in other words, not very. He would flip with minimal provocation, and those not in his 'mutual admiration club' were half terrified of him – Freddie and I included. In class, we were continually primed to expect a downturn and it made the lessons exhausting. In a bad mood he was vicious; renowned for pulling pupils up by their sideburns. You would try and ease the needle-like pain boring into your skull by tilting your head and standing on tiptoes but it wouldn't work because he simply pulled you up higher. It was a common sight in the school – a boy dangling helplessly like a tormented puppet in a pincer grip as he received his bloodless scalping.

His nickname was 'Sadist'.

"Benzene, sir… discovered by Kekule."

A look of genuine surprise appeared on Sadist's face.

"For once you are correct, Minor, but a cretin like you will not know *how* he discovered it. Anyone… anyone…?"

No one put their hand up this time.

Kekule had only given the anecdote a few years before, in a speech to the German Chemical Society. By sheer fluke I had overheard a group of picnicking chemists discussing the issue loudly on the riverbank of the Botanical Gardens. I had been in my single sculling boat at the time, practising a drill. One of them said that Kekule had dreamt of a snake eating its own tail, thus forming a ring. Freddie and I had integrated this knowledge into our rowing: "Make the snake rings!" we would say, as we powered down the river in our double scull. 'Snake rings'… it was a good call, and we always went faster when we said it.

Freddie's voice broke the classroom silence.

"I believe he dreamt a snake was eating its own tail… sir."

A hush fell over the room, everyone looking to the front for a visual cue.

Sadist was slightly pale now, his bluster gone. I could almost see the thought processes going on in his brain, specifically the two options presenting themselves – magnanimity or cruelty – and I saw which it would be long before he spoke. The bastard couldn't allow Freddie his tiny academic victory.

"Not bad for a decerebrate troll."

Raucous laughter – the prefects at the front laughed the loudest.

"Hilarious," Freddie said, loudly enough to be heard. The class laughed again, this time with him. So fickle, these identical receptacles, forged in the kiln of conformity, ready to switch allegiances at any moment if the circumstances demanded it.

Sadist beckoned my brother to approach the front with his index finger.

"Miiinooor…"

Nervous laughter now, as the class readied themselves for a good torture session. We all knew what was coming, Freddie included.

Wearily, Freddie stood up and made to move to the front, but then he shook his head, as if listening to some inner dialogue.

"Actually, sir, I don't think I will."

Time seemed to slow down from this point. I recall a collective gasp and the sight of the Sadist's face turning a bright crimson.

In moments he was storming down the gap between the desks towards us, his hand already raised, ready to grab Freddie's sideburns.

From the way it looked, he was going to be pulling very hard on this occasion.

Then, speaking through his gritted teeth, Freddie said: "Touch me and I'll knock you down," and there had been no sound at all in the classroom after that. This was way beyond what anyone knew – Freddie had entered a whole new realm of defiance.

Sadist stopped short. At eighteen years of age, Freddie was big enough to make his threat a viable one. My brother looked feral, his face the same as Crosbie's when he had torn into the *Wisden*: 'kill mode'.

As the seconds passed in the stand-off, I watched Freddie's future re-setting itself on a different course. That's how significant the moment felt.

"Get out," Sadist said at last in a quiet voice, visibly shocked and defeated.

Without stopping to gather up his books, Freddie left the classroom.

I would later find out that he kept going – leaving the building and walking out of the school gates, in effect expelling himself, saving the headmaster the bother and Sadist the satisfaction. Not that it really mattered – we had finished anyway. It was all 'academic'.

He caught the train back home that day, gathered up a few belongings and said goodbye to our father. And then he kept going. No joke – he travelled the world.

Occasionally, I would receive a letter from a distant shore, a jagged scrawl on some grubby pages. Sometimes mail would arrive from outposts so remote I had to look them up in an atlas. After a year, I bought a world map, hung it in my college room and stuck pins in it, charting his travels.

It was not until five years later, in 1898, that he finally came back to England and joined the army.

Freddie set his own standards and lived by them; he followed his own moral barometer and not the direction which society dictated.

Fremantle, Western Australia Colony
September 1900

The ship's steward shook me out of my daydream.

"Doctor Hunston?"

"Yes?"

"We're here, Doctor."

He was pointing over to the open steel door where sunbeams were streaming through into the gloom of the lounge. Apart from the two of us, the room was empty.

I sighed.

"This is it then."

"Pardon me, Doctor?"

"Oh, nothing…"

I put down my cup, and headed out.

The heat… Christ… Even South Africa hadn't been like this – it felt like I had opened an oven door in my face.

To look smart for the grand arrival I had worn my woollen flannel rowing blazer, a decision I was rueing by the time I reached the gangway. By then the sweat was flowing freely – sticking my shirt to my back and beading on my upper lip. I wiped at my face. Thirty feet below, the water slapped repetitively between the ship's hull and the wharf, giving a round of ironic applause at my clothing error.

Clad in his black suit, Rennie wasn't faring any better, I could see him down on the wharf tugging at his dog collar and frowning up at the heavens as if to say, 'you certainly work in mysterious ways'.

Next to him was a man holding up a sign: 'EGREMONT', it said.

It was the name of my new employer; the Egremont Mining Company.

The Egremont man was wearing a slouch hat, the kind the Australians had worn in South Africa, with the soft felt rolled up on one side. As the felt aged in the sun, it tended to bleach from brown to mustard yellow and the colour gave you a clue as to the wearer's length of service. This man's hat was pale mustard and he had a black patch over his right eye. No novice.

Stepping from the gangway onto the dockside, I staggered, my sea legs not used to the solid ground. The Egremont man looked at me and shook his head.

"You on the grog already, mate?"

"No, only tea."

From his trouser pocket he brought out a hip flask and held it out to me.

"Then you'd better get some of this down you."

He shook it impatiently.

"Go on then…"

Hesitantly I took it, undid the cap and drank a mouthful. The liquid burned its way down my throat and I struggled hard not to react.

I handed it back to him.

"Thanks," I said, my throat raw.

The Egremont man looked apologetically to Rennie.

"I hope you don't mind, Rev?"

"Not at all. It's not what goes into a man's mouth, but what comes out of a man's mouth that defiles him."

The Egremont man laughed, then winced and rubbed at his temple, as if struck by a sudden pain. When he noticed me staring, he flicked his index finger onto his eye patch so that it made a hollow 'toc' sound.

"Boers used me as target practice in South Africa. I like to think I stopped a few bullets… This one felt like a slap at the time. Hurts like buggery now. Anyway, the rum helps a bit."

He took a well-practiced swig from the flask, a quick tilt followed by the baring of his teeth as he swallowed, before screwing the cap back on and returning it to his pocket.

"Gentlemen," he said, as if restarting the welcome, "allow me to introduce myself. Name's Tom Dudley, mine manager at the Egremont. Welcome to Australia."

He drew out the word so it sounded like 'Austraaaayylllia'.

I had heard snippets of the accent before – from Australian soldiers out in South Africa – and it always made me think of roughly made furniture which hadn't been sanded down properly.

Dudley grinned and extended his hand. "G'day."

His grip felt strange and, with a shock, I saw he had no right thumb. No eye and no thumb – this man was missing body parts all over.

"Doctor John Hunston," I said, thrown by what I had seen.

He tugged the woollen lapel of my jacket.

"What's this fancy getup then?"

"It's a rowing 'Blues' blazer, Mr Dudley."

"Rowing, eh? Used to do a bit myself as it happens."

"Indeed?"

I was too hot and bothered to get into an in-depth rowing discussion and my distraction must have looked obvious. Sweat was streaming down my forehead.

"Thought it would be a bit colder, did you?" he said. "You can borrow a scarf if you want."

Dudley started laughing loudly at his own joke.

I blinked repeatedly. It was the white light that filled this place – it bounced off the sea, the metalwork of the ship and the galvanised roofs. Once, in a chemistry lesson, Sadist had lit a piece of magnesium ribbon in the school-yard and we had all stood around in a semi-circle, shielding our eyes from the blinding white flame. That's what this Australian light reminded me of.

Rennie was having the same problem, but chose to see it as some kind of blessing.

"'And suddenly there shined round about him a light from heaven'," he said, scrunching up his eyes into the glare. "Acts 9:3. Paul's conversion, Mr Dudley."

Dudley swatted away a fly lazily. "This isn't Damascus, mate."

He stopped smiling for a moment and his skin creases faded and the crow's feet around his good eye stood out pale against the tanned backdrop of his face.

"No, of course not," Rennie said, agreeing wholeheartedly.

Dudley laughed again. "Only messing with you, Rev…" he said. "I'm not just here for the overheating Doc, I'm here for you too, Rev. Rowe's an old chum of mine, and he asked me to pick you up. Hope you don't mind. He sends his apologies – but he had a service to conduct. Don't worry, you'll meet him soon enough… we'll be staying with him at the Perth Manse tomorrow."

Reverend George Rowe was basically the most senior Wesleyan in the colony. Even though they had never actually met, only corresponded, he was a mentor figure for Rennie, who considered him to be one of the few ministers out here who actually dared to work among the poorest of the poor and the sickest of the sick. By letter exchanges alone, Rowe had persuaded Rennie to come out to the goldfields once he had been ordained, and I had heard the story about a hundred times on the voyage south.

"I don't mind at all," Rennie said to Dudley. "I appreciate you doing this… a great blessing.'

Dudley clapped his hands together loudly.

"It's a pleasure. Anyway, for tonight I've got you gents a room here in Fremantle. Thought you both might like to take a look around… bit of sightseeing before our trip inland."

Sightseeing?

Old tin shacks bordered the docks and piles of logs lay stacked ready for export. Sprawled a few yards away were a dozen mail sacks. The whole place stank of rotting fish. What a dump. The only modern vessel in the port was our mail ship, its amber funnel out of place amongst the maritime forest of wooden masts, yards and furled sails. To get here, they would have taken the 'clipper route', rounding the Cape and skirting the Southern Ocean. We'd had it easy: a short cut through the Suez Canal, then the calm azure blue waters of the Indian Ocean.

"Ready gents?"

Rennie lifted his bags.

"Ready when you are, Mr Dudley."

"Call me Tom, boys. Sometimes I even answer to 'hey you'."

He slung the EGREMONT sign onto the mail sacks and started off towards the customs house on the other side of a railway line, Rennie in tow.

Dudley walked with a limp, his right leg stiff and awkward looking. 'Target practice' he had called it. The bullet count had just gone up to three.

I kept watching as they picked their way through the maze of luggage and ropes. It wasn't just the furnace making me sweat; the doubts were coming thick and fast now. Standing there on that sun-baked wharf, it was all I could do not to turn around and run back up the gangway.

A few hundred yards away, the crash of the ocean waves seemed to be agreeing: *'Go back. Go back. There is still time…'*

Then from out of nowhere, a great cackle of laughter rang out; 'OOOAAAHAHAHAHAHA', immediately joined by others, so that soon the whole port was filled with the unearthly cacophony. I was surrounded by a coven of witches all in on the same joke and they were laughing at me.

"For Christ's sake, Doc," Dudley said. "They're only bloody Kookaburras… native to these parts, unlike you."

He then said something to Rennie which I guessed might be an apology for having taken the Lord's name in vain.

Rennie waved over at me in encouragement, swinging his arm as if bowling a cricket ball backwards.

Finally, I set off towards them, but after a few yards had to stop. The heat was dismantling me. Setting down my bags, I wiped the sweat off my brow and swatted the flies away.

"You're going to fit right in, Doc… you already know the Aussie salute."

Dudley laughed and Rennie even joined in. This was getting embarrassing.

I took off my blazer and wedged it into the strapping around my suitcase. My shirt had become un-tucked and I left it free. I yanked off my tie, balled it up and stuffed it into my pocket. No need for club ties in a place like this.

That's where I had been – at my club, the 'Blue Boar' in London – when I had made the foolish decision to come out here.

Shaking my head, I picked up my Gladstone with one hand and suitcase with the other, and made my way through the debris towards the others.

I thought back to that day in the club and tried to console myself with the iron-clad certainty I had felt at the time.

Chapter Three

London
July, 1900

Fridays were supposed to be my busy days in Harley Street, but by mid-afternoon I was drowsing in my corner chair at the Blue Boar.

I simply had no stomach for it anymore; 'it' meaning just about everything – medicine, acquaintances, society in general. After what had happened in South Africa and at the Military Hospital, normal life now seemed like a pathetic joke.

During my morning surgery, an aristocratic gentleman in full morning dress had presented with a headache and, despite my attempts at reassurance, he had insisted on a neurological opinion over at Queen Square.

"Something must be done!"

His tone had been accusatory; as if it was my fault he had the headache in the first place.

"It really is just muscular tension," I had said to him. "You don't need a specialist. I can help you."

Evidently not a man used to coming up against obstacles, his reply had been a dressing down: "Now you listen here, young chappie… it's the likes of me that keeps the likes of you, and if it wasn't for us being ill, where would you be?"

To avoid developing a headache of my own I went ahead and made the referral, and then, for the second week in a row, cancelled my afternoon surgery and retreated to my club.

Outside, a thunderstorm was pounding the streets. The rain had come on with a sudden ferocity, as is sometimes the case after a week of glorious sunshine. It didn't feel like summer anymore, but that was England for you.

At the first clap of thunder, the pedestrians on Pall Mall had scattered and I made a dash for the last fifty yards, bursting into the atrium of the Blue Boar, out of breath but having missed the rain.

Since arriving, I had been idling in my corner by the window, dropping off to sleep and jerking awake whenever someone coughed or a piece of cutlery scraped against a plate.

A half-eaten ham sandwich was on the small table next to my chair.

These days, I could waste an entire afternoon just eating a sandwich. Today I was taking even longer than usual because I had used too much mustard, spooning it all over from the silver pot brought out by the waiter. Each bite made my nostrils catch on fire and I would pull a series of strange faces. An odd fellow in the corner, alternating between making facial contortions and sleeping like a drugged epileptic. God Almighty, what a fall.

The year before, when I was first in London as a fresh faced doctor from Oxford University, the members of the Blue Boar Club had avidly pursued me for membership. To be nominated you had to have seven seconders – seven! But for me that was easy: my high living friends from Oxford signed me up with seconders to spare. After downing the vodka-rum-gin-orange juice concoction in one go – the 'initiation' – I was solemnly declared a 'Blue Boar' and awarded the club tie.

The only rule was that you wore this tie, a dark suit and black shoes at all times. Otherwise, once you were in you could pretty much do as you liked. Mainly, that involved sitting around on leather sofas, reading the newspapers, smoking cigars and batting laconic remarks to one another across the room; generally acting as if you were a lot older than you actually were.

It was only after getting back from the war that the self-satisfaction pervading the place struck me for the first time; so much so, I was embarrassed I hadn't seen it before. But perhaps I had just chosen to ignore it and conform. After all, it was a lot easier to conform.

They were all so fucking dull. Everyone acted as if life was a great bore; even the way they moved was languid. To me they were now the Blue *Bores*. I had an inkling of how the Romans must have been just before the Visigoths closed in.

At first, a few of the members wanted to hear my war stories. The thing was though, my previous skills as a raconteur had rusted up and, within a few sentences, I would grind to a halt, like a nervous schoolboy at a poetry recital.

I could see them whispering to one another on their sofas, probably wondering why they had bothered to recruit me in the first place. Certainly not out of any concern for my state of mind.

They left me alone after that.

The irony was that before the war, I hadn't come in all that much. Now I came all the time – festering in my corner, taking hours to eat a sandwich, staring out of the windows, dozing.

I craved the sepia, dusty, church-like silence the club offered, not the companionship.

A copy of the British Medical Journal was open on my lap. Whenever I nodded off, it slipped onto the floor. The waiter would come over, pick it up and wake me by saying, "Excuse me, sir… your reading material."

It was gone three by the time I got around to reading an article about South Africa; of how in a fortnight in April, 377 men had died of disease, most of those from enteric fever.

Burdett-Coutts, a Times correspondent I had encountered in my field hospital, had been lambasting the medical arrangements in Bloemfontein and now the BMJ was attempting to counter the allegations, but it came across as whimpering self-justification and excuses.

I went over to the newspaper table and managed to dig out the previous week's paper from the pile, and found Burdett-Coutts's piece from 27th June. I could recall him poking around the place, scribbling away in his notebook; his face pale with horror at what he was witnessing.

His piece, *'Our Wars and our wounded'*, presented an accurate and graphic enough account:

'...hundreds of men to my knowledge were lying in the worst stages of typhoid, with only a blanket and a thin waterproof sheet (not even the latter for many of them) between their aching bodies and the hard ground, with no milk and hardly any medicines, without beds, stretchers or mattresses, without linen of any kind, without a single nurse amongst them, with only a few ordinary private soldiers to act as 'orderlies', rough and utterly untrained in nursing, and with only three doctors to attend on 350 patients... In many of these tents there were ten typhoid cases lying closely packed together, the dying with the convalescent, the man in his 'crisis' pressed against the man hastening to it. There was no room to step between them...'

The memories revived, I went back to glower in my corner seat.

I could see how it was going to pan out. To placate the outraged public and the baying press, the government would order an inquiry into the Bloemfontein typhoid epidemic and it would be a complete bloody whitewash.

Who was really at fault? There were a few heavyweight contenders if you wanted to play this game – the old duffers in the War Office for starters, the ones who had ignored the general medical consensus that all troops, medical officers and nurses receive compulsory inoculations before being sent overseas. This calamitous decision seemed to have passed everyone by; even Burdett-Coutts had missed it. The world was more interested in the inadequate provision of ratty blankets and condensed milk.

You could be sure the inquiry report would be a weighty tome, not unlike a *Wisden* Almanac, and full to overflowing with long rambling sentences: 'We do not consider that the great outbreak of enteric fever, or any considerable part of it, was due to preventable causes etc etc…' If they could get away with it, they would simply write: 'GO BACK TO SLEEP, BRITAIN. IT'S ALL UNDER CONTROL.'

Some out-of-touch relic would be running the inquiry, in fact it was a fair bet one of the more venerable Blue Boar club members would be chosen, perhaps one of the group who congregated at the far end of the lounge near the fireplace, like a herd of greying Wildebeest. The men in the War Office could sleep easy with the knowledge that the inquiry would be run by one of their own kind. No blame laid at their door, that's for sure.

Leaning back against the headrest of my chair I took some deep breaths, just trying to breathe freely without that catch of rage which seemed to be coming on a lot these days.

I stared up at the pictures on the mahogany-panelled wall, dozens of framed 'Spy' cartoons from *Vanity Fair*, the so-called 'Men of the Day'. Virtually every gentleman of any importance in England was on that wall. The picture closest to my corner seat had become familiar; its subject the most respectfully drawn of the series, without a red nose or pot belly. In recent weeks I had studied every detail, wondering who he was and why he was so important. Polished black boots with long spurs and standing legs wide apart, a riding crop wedged behind his back. He was looking to one side, his face in profile; you could see one half of a neatly trimmed moustache. The countenance was one of world domination – 'Empire'. Ever since I had taken up my corner seat residency this stalwart had been my silent companion and overseer. I almost regarded him as a friend.

My attention eventually drifted back to the BMJ.

I skimmed to the final pages, reading through the 'positions vacant' section. Here, the journal was full of dull advertisements for medical equipment: 'Double cyanide dressings & sulpho-chromic gut according to Sir Joseph Lister's latest instructions', 'Fannin & Co.'s clinical thermometers', 'Dr. Herschells's improved binaural stethoscope'. I was just about to doze off again when something caught my eye: a picture of a man in a khaki uniform and slouch hat, sitting astride a camel. A stethoscope around his neck. The backdrop was the distinctive outline of the Australian continent.

'MEDICAL OFFICER WANTED FOR THE EGREMONT MINING CO.
CITY OF KALGOORLIE, WESTERN AUSTRALIAN COLONY
APPLICATIONS VIA THE EMC OFFICES,
PICCADILLY, LONDON'

Scanning through the small print, the hairs on the back of my neck stood up; *'Candidates must be accustomed to the management of typhoid fever cases.'*

It wasn't a man in khaki, it was Freddie, and he was shouting at me from the page: 'Get up, you miserable bastard; get out of England… Here's your chance… It was the last bloody thing I ever asked you to do…'

I had the overwhelming sense that if I didn't heed this message from beyond the grave, then he would haunt me until I did. The decision surfaced from my subconscious like a breaching whale: my logical mind reluctantly having to acknowledge that the flesh and blood contraption it usually controlled had been taken over by this challenger from the deep. Red lights flashed on and off in my head, warning me that when this impulsivity had submerged again, I was going to regret it in a big way. For now though, the self-destruct button was fully depressed and I went with it – already in my mind I was on the outbound ship and the English coast was receding into the distance.

Using the journal to keep my head dry in the rain I marched straight round to the Egremont Offices on Piccadilly, cutting across Green Park, which was completely deserted because of the deluge. To my right, the lights of the Ritz stood out brightly in the gloom of the day. In my old life, I had often eaten there in its gilded dining room: a lunch, a dinner, sometimes even both in the same day, one rolling into the other.

Set back from the road and facing the park, the Egremont building was flashy and imposing, with a sweeping semi-circular driveway leading to an impressive pale stone façade.

A flurry of men in top hats were exiting the fast revolving front door with a confidence suggesting they were sure of both their immediate and long-term destinations. For the first time in weeks I was feeling the same way, so I stepped into the spinning portal too, and a moment later was spewed out into a lobby with a vaulted stone ceiling and glittering chandeliers.

A doorman in a gold-braided uniform approached.

"I'm here about the mine job," I said to him, holding up the soaked medical journal and pointing at the picture of the man on the camel.

Rainwater dripped from the journal onto his shoes and he looked down, frowning.

I reached into my breast pocket and pulled out one of my cards.

"If you might find someone who I can talk to, I would appreciate it."

The doorman took the card with as much dignity as he could muster and, without saying a word, disappeared up the stairs.

I sat down on a bench to wait, the busily revolving door beating in time with my heart – *thump, thump, thump...*

On the opposite wall was a large, ornate 'EMC' all in gold lettering. Everywhere I looked in fact, gold paint decorated the place. The EMC reeked of serious money.

Maybe I wasn't acting completely irrationally – perhaps by working for these people I would be moving up in the world and not throwing my career away at all.

When I looked towards the stairs again, I could see a man following the doorman down to the vestibule. He walked slowly, like an old man, though as he got closer it became clear that he wasn't as old as his bearing suggested. Even so, an aura of 'greyness' hung about him; forty years old, but going on eighty.

He held up my card.

"You're Doctor Hunston?"

I stood up.

"That's right."

"I'm Sir Robert Egremont's private secretary. You're interested in the medical officer post in the Australian colony?"

"I am."

"Well, I'm afraid you've missed Sir Robert. He's already gone to the country for the weekend."

My shoulders sagged. I wanted to begin there and then. *I'll have bloody well changed my mind by Monday,* I thought.

". . . But I have taken the liberty of telephoning him," the secretary said in an unexpected turn, "and he's happy to see you down there this evening. He can interview you tonight, if that's acceptable."

"Capital."

I must have been out of my mind because I grasped the secretary's hand with both of mine in delight, an action surprising us both. He raised his eyebrows and glanced down at the hand knot, with an expression of mild disdain.

"Witworth Park, Surrey," he said, taking his hand back. "He's expecting you for dinner."

Witworth was only half an hour's train journey south of London.

On the way, the dreary suburbs ended and the majestic oaks and rolling patchwork fields of rural England came into view – the heart of the Empire.

It stopped raining.

At the village of Witworth, the stationmaster told me Egremont's place was only two miles away and, being in good humour and still excited about the job, I decided to walk.

My ebullient mood didn't last long. As I strode down a high banked lane, trodden and re-trodden by so many generations that it had sunk deep into the earth like a trench, I started worrying about the impending interview and the likelihood of my clamming up, just like I had done at the Blue Boar Club when people tried talking to me.

Until Bloemfontein and Freddie's death had derailed my thundering steam train of success, everything had come easily – be it social interaction, exams, interviews or jobs. I just needed to reassemble the pieces from the twisted wreckage of the once proud 'Hunston Express', and become the confident young doctor again, but it was a task which felt near impossible, hence my current concerns.

Would they see it? Would they see that zoo animal look of defeat in my eyes, and know I had given up on the world?

By the time I reached the sweeping entrance to Witworth Park, my legs were aching and I was breathing hard – the enduring after-effects of the typhoid. Slowly, I climbed the stone stairs up to the front door, knocked and waited there, bent double with my hands on my knees.

A butler in a white jacket drew open the door a fraction and peered out as if I were some ne'er-do-well.

"The tradesman's entrance is around the side," he said.

My God, I must have looked even worse than I felt. He was staring at me like I was dirt, an attitude I had met before in the staff of the well-to-do – they would see themselves as the Lord of the Manor, often more snobbish than their employer. But I wasn't going to be an arse about it and make a scene; once upon a time, perhaps, but not any more. The charade of status could go to hell. I was weary of it all. In South Africa I had seen the true human condition. We were all the same.

"No, you misunderstand, I'm a guest of Sir Robert. His secretary rang earlier from London. I'm Doctor John Hunston."

From his expression, he found this hard to accept.

"May I see your visiting card?"

For the second time that day I handed one over, finding myself in the slightly undignified position of waiting on the porch as he read it. They were quality cards, from a quality printer, and had cost me a small fortune.

He opened the door wider.

"Ahh, yes," he said, his manner a shade more respectful, "Dr Hunston. Sir Robert is still hunting with his guests; out by the Devil's

Punch Bowl, some three miles distant. I'm afraid it's too late to catch up with them now."

"Oh, I see…"

"But please do come in. He knows you're coming."

I entered a hall adorned with magnificent hunting trophies; bears, lions, tigers, eagles. Some of the stuffed predators were mauling stuffed prey; fish, gazelles, small furry animals and the like. It was like walking into a three dimensional killing spree, frozen in time.

"This is all very impressive," I said, not meaning it.

A few seconds passed in silence.

Even the deadpan butler seemed to have detected the sarcasm of my comment, a suspicious frown breaking out on his face.

"Yes, all very impressive," I said again, more animatedly this time.

His eyebrows raised a notch in acknowledgement at my effort.

This was an example of my new awkwardness in social situations, the same phenomenon which had frightened away the Blue Boars. If I acted like this at the interview there would be no chance. This was only the butler and I was losing it.

Through an open doorway nearby was a room containing book cases filled with leather-bound tomes.

"The library?"

"It is."

"May I take a look?"

"Very good, Doctor," he said, "but first allow me to show you to your room. You are a staying visitor, of course."

"Yes, *of course*."

He led the way up the sweeping staircase and along a wide corridor.

"The house has thirty two bedrooms," he said, "eleven bathrooms, two dining rooms, a palm court and a theatre. Sir Robert has also installed an observatory and a velodrome. Being a medical man, you'll be interested to know there's even a private hospital."

He counted out the facts on his fingers as if it was a list that he had memorised especially for visitors but he said it in a flat, tired tone which made me think he had told it so often the original aim to impress had long since gone.

He stopped at a door, seeming to pick it at random from the immense choice on offer.

"Seven o'clock on the terrace for aperitifs. Dinner with the other guests will follow. If that will be all…"

I checked my watch. Almost six thirty.

"Thank you."

He sloped off down the corridor.

He had said dinner with guests. I hadn't brought spare clothes; in fact I was still wearing the same get-up I had worn to work that morning. Quickly, I ran a personal inventory; the dark blue rowing blazer could pass for traditional dinner jacket and, being a 'Blues' blazer, it had the added bonus of being a useful talking point if things became stilted. Stuffed deep in my pockets were my white gloves. I was already wearing black trousers, a white shirt and black patent leather shoes. Excellent – a passable uniform. I just needed a black bow tie.

The butler had only gone twenty paces.

"I say… hello there."

He stopped and turned round.

"Yes, Doctor?"

"Can I cadge a bow tie?"

A look of such perplexity came over his countenance that you might have thought I'd asked him to solve Fermat's last theorem.

"For my neck," I said.

This seemed to bring him back.

"Yes… certainly, Doctor."

He returned a few minutes later with the item, 'New and Lingwood', no less, sixteen inch neck. I didn't like them too tight.

"You got the right size," I said.

He looked at me with a flicker of pride.

"If that will be all?"

This man wasn't easy to warm to.

"What's your name?" I said.

"Sir?"

"I just wondered…"

"It's Smith, sir."

"Well, thank you very much, Smith. You've made me feel very welcome… you're a very personable fellow."

This seemed to disorient him. He almost staggered backwards when I said it, then nodded uncertainly and left.

I tied the bow tie and went downstairs to wait in the library.

Two sides of the room held the book stacks and one side comprised a large bay window with a view out onto the garden terrace. The remaining wall was covered with more hunting trophies: a dozen stuffed stag heads. Stretched out on the floor was a huge bearskin rug. You got the impression Sir Robert Egremont was top of the food chain – the most dangerous predator of all.

Dominating the centre of the room was a large globe, set a foot off the floor within a grand wooden frame. I searched for Australia on the hidden underbelly, but Egremont's globe was hopelessly out of date, and where Australia should have been, there was only a partial piece of coastline tinted blue, a segment of the Cape York Peninsula south of Java. Beneath this was written: *'TERRA AUSTRALIS INCOGNITA'*. I might have been in the bottom Latin set at school, but I remembered enough to piece it together. It meant: 'the great unknown land of the south'.

Still tired from the walk, I sank into the chair at an enormous oak desk. A leather bound volume was lying there and I read the title:

'An Account of the Voyages Undertaken by the Order of his Present Majesty for Making Discoveries in the Southern hemisphere, and Successively Performed by Commodore Byron, Captain Wallis, Captain Carteret, and Captain Cook, in the Dolphin, the Swallow, and the Endeavour. Editor, John Hawkesworth 1773.'

The wordiness reminded me of a punishment Freddie had once been given at school – one thousand lines; *'I must not become intoxicated by the exuberance of my own verbosity.'* He had tied five pencils together and done it in less than an hour.

Next to the volume, a journal of some kind was open, its entries written in a distinctive longhand, the ink browned with age, along with the paper it had been written on.

A letter was poking out of the inside cover:

Sir Robert,

Please find attached Cook's holograph journal of the Endeavour voyage, as promised. My great uncle bought it some years back and I had the good fortune to inherit. In return for the remarkable hospitality you showed us this summer, I should like to loan it out to you, pending our next visit to Witworth this Christmas.

Yours, Henry Bolckow

P.S. You'll find plenty here that your precious Hawkesworth volumes edited out.

I carefully replaced the letter in the journal and started to read on from the open page:

'22 August 1770. After landing I went upon the highest hill... and in the Name of His Majesty King George the Third took possession of the whole Eastern Coast...'

I looked over at the globe, trying to imagine walking up a hill, hoisting the Union Jack and claiming a piece of land the size of Europe.

"Terra Australis Incognita," I said out loud.

An elegant telephone was on the desk with a wide base and a tapering central shaft. Out of sheer impulse I lifted the receiver off its hook and spoke into the mouthpiece: "Hello...Operator?"

A voice came down the line straight away.

"Which number, sir?"

"Oh..." I said, taken aback. I had only half expected an answer. "Errm... Redhill 9813 please."

"Please hold..."

In the pause that followed, I idly read some more of Cook's journal:

'23 August 1770. From what I have said of the Natives of New-Holland they may appear to some to be the most wretched people upon earth, but in reality they are far more happier than we Europeans; being wholly unacquainted not only with the superfluous but the necessary conveniences so much sought after in Europe, they are happy in not knowing the use of them… they covet not Magnificent Houses, Household stuff etc… In short they seem'd to set no value upon anything we gave them…'

"Connecting you now, sir… Please go ahead."

"Hello?"

"This is Mr Hunston," said the disembodied voice of my father.

I hadn't seen him since Freddie's funeral three weeks before.

"Hello, Father."

"John? Are you all right?"

A straight question – I decided to give a straight answer.

"Not really."

The line crackled with static.

My father was not one to talk about such matters. 'Not really' covered it for him. It told him all he needed to know.

"Where are you?"

"Nearby as it happens. Witworth Park. Sir Robert Egremont's place."

"Of the Egremont Mining Company?"

"Yes, the one and the same. I'm considering… well… I'm…"

Just say it, I thought.

"I'm thinking of going to work in Australia, as a doctor for the company."

There was a pause and I wondered if the connection had gone.

"Hello… Father?"

"I'm still here."

"They want to interview me tonight."

"That's good."

"You don't think I'm being crazy?"

There was another, shorter pause. "No."

He had already come to terms with the fact that I was going to be gone a long time.

Now I could feel tears brimming.

"I'll call again soon. We'll meet up before I leave, if I get the job."

"That would be good, John."

"All right… Goodbye then."

"Goodbye."

The line clicked off.

I replaced the receiver and rested my forehead on the green leather of the desktop, struggling to regain my composure.

I took out Freddie's tobacco tin and made myself a roll-up, a poor cousin to one of his masterpieces. Then I went and lay down on the bearskin, using the bear's great head as a pillow and my palm as a makeshift ash-tray.

As I smoked I stared up at the ceiling and replayed the telephone call in my head.

God, I had almost cried.

Appalling really – all they had ever taught us at school was that expressing one's emotions was 'bad form'. My father hadn't said much, but it was enough that he seemed to understand.

It was the same quiet tolerance he had shown when Freddie had gone away on his five year odyssey after quitting school. He was already a man accustomed to major pain and loss; his wife – our mother – having died soon after giving birth to us. When you took this into account, together with what had recently happened to Freddie, it was little wonder that he had been able to process my going to Australia in approximately three seconds.

Chapter Four

I jerked awake to the sound of laughter coming from outside.

Fumbling around for my pocket-watch, I saw with horror that it was a quarter past seven and I was late to the party.

Five people were drinking champagne on the terrace, gathered beyond a narrow oblong bathing pool. They were admiring an elephant, carved from stone, from whose outstretched trunk water was cascading and then running down a landscaped rivulet to a lake in the lower part of the grounds.

As I hastened towards them, the group turned to face me as one.

"Aha," said a large man, "it's the doctor... late for his evening round." A quip prompting a good natured murmur of laughter.

He held out his hand for me to shake. It was soft, plump and dry, with a giant signet ring squashed onto the little finger – a capitalist's hand.

"I'm Egremont," he said, booming out the words powerfully.

He reminded me of a walrus, albeit one wearing a pair of gold mounted pince-nez eyeglasses. Long whiskers sprouted from his cheeks, chin, nostrils and ears, in fact, from almost everywhere but his scalp; a sea mammal and not a future employer.

"John Hunston."

In comparison to his bluster I sounded like a dormouse, too harassed about my tardiness to match his confident jovial volume.

So far he didn't look impressed. I had arrived late and not laughed at his joke. His eyes seemed to be saying: *Come on, you're going to have to do better than that. Do you want this job or not?*

"Do forgive me, everyone," I said, turning up the volume and smiling broadly, "I was in the library exploring the globe... ended up in Australia and completely lost track of the time."

Now Egremont laughed, along with the others.

"No problem at all, Doctor," he said. "Glad you could come down at such short notice."

Relief washed over me − I had salvaged things for now.

He faced the group.

"Everyone, may I present Dr John Hunston?"

I bowed to each as they were introduced in turn: Egremont's glamorous wife, Anna, Sir James Southgate − 'personal physician to the Queen' − and then the handsome couple of William Grenfell, and his wife Ethel.

I knew the Grenfells to be much fêted in the society columns of the press. Their club, 'the Souls', boasted the likes of Arthur Balfour, Margaret Asquith and George Curzon, the Viceroy of India. Yeats, Chesterton and Kipling were all regulars.

Egremont turned his attention back to the elephant, patting its trunk.

"Big, isn't it?" he said to me. "I was just telling everyone it was carved from a single block of marble weighing eighty tonnes, right here on site. Had it specially imported into the country. The block got stuck under a bridge on the way here from Southampton docks − wouldn't budge at all."

Mrs Grenfell inclined her head. "What on earth did you do, Sir Robert?"

"Why, we lowered the road."

Haw, Haw, Haw!

During the ensuing group laughter, I realised he wasn't joking.

It was my place to escort Lady Egremont through to the dining room. Although she was a good dozen years younger than her husband and stunning to boot, my mind was on other things. Traditionally, the gentleman accompanying the lady of the house was supposed to offer to relieve her of the duties of hostess, or at least be prepared to help if asked. As soon as I saw the roast platter on the dining room table, my worst fears were confirmed.

Please no, my eyes begged her, but I already knew what was coming.

"Why, Doctor, could I prevail upon you to carve?"

My heart sank. In effect the interview had already started. With these people, to fumble such a task would be considered unpardonable.

"Certainly, Lady Egremont, it would be my greatest pleasure."

I tried to sound as relaxed as possible, hoping she would not detect my rising panic. I had never carved in my life. When I was a boy, my father had always watched for the first few seconds before grabbing the knife from my hand and going about the task himself; a surgeon's prerogative. And later, at Oxford, there had always been someone who did that kind of thing for you.

The roast was 'Witworth Venison' – the result of an earlier hunt – and I made a complete bloody botch of it. *Christ*, I thought, on catching Egremont's pained expression and his wife's barely suppressed giggles, *maybe I won't be going to Australia after all*.

"Why Doctor Hunston, you must surely be a surgeon," Mrs Grenfell said. I could have sworn she winked at me.

"A general practitioner, actually," I said, managing a smile. "My father was the surgeon."

Fortuitously I found myself placed next to her when seated. My new supporter – "Oh do just call me Ettie, darling" – sat to my right, and as protocol demanded I gave her fifteen minutes of conversation.

I had heard it said that Ettie Grenfell told enough white lies to ice a wedding cake, and the more I talked to her, the more I could see it was true, but she was also blessed with a particular skill; that of focusing all her attention on you, to such an extent that you really believed she thought you were the only interesting person in the room. It turned out we had something in common – she had once visited the Military Hospital in Southampton and met Professor Almroth Wright, the pathologist behind the typhoid inoculation. We touched upon the professor's work and of the calamity of Bloemfontein, but she was very diplomatic, not letting on what she thought of the army brass's decision to veto the inoculations. I didn't linger on the matter either, because I had heard that when you chatted to a member of the Souls you were supposed to stay away from politics; apparently it was their one and only rule.

I devoted the next fifteen minutes to William Grenfell, sat to my left. He seemed a decent enough chap, just as cordial as his wife, and I could tell by his bearing he had an athletic pedigree. This was confirmed as the meal progressed; three ascents of the Matterhorn, big game hunting in the Rockies, even swimming across the Niagara rapids. Like me, he had been to Oxford – a Balliol man, just over a wall from my alma mater as it happens. After University, he had worked as a war correspondent for *The Telegraph* out in the Sudan.

"Once stumbled across a group of hostiles," he said. "I was alone and armed only with my umbrella... good job I was wearing my tennis shoes."

I frowned at this odd detail.

"Oh? How so?"

"Because it meant I could outpace the blighters."

As everyone at the table erupted in laughter I bit down on a piece of shot, damn near breaking a tooth, and while I was dealing with this trauma, missed out on the next part of Grenfell's story. Surreptitiously, I slipped the shot onto a spoon, just like an olive stone, and conveyed it calmly to my plate, feeling around the tooth gingerly with my tongue to assess the damage. By the time I realised my tooth was going to be all right, Grenfell had moved onto his latest athletic passion – a form of all-out fighting called 'Bartitsu' – and how he was training out of a club in Soho.

"You should see it," he said. "Engaging in the combat makes me feel like a wild beast."

I noticed Egremont's eyes light up at the mention of big game.

"Show us some of your moves, dear boy," he said.

Obligingly, Grenfell got up from the table and to my horror, insisted on employing me as a foe, presumably because I was the youngest male present.

Reluctantly I got out of my chair.

"Darling…" Ettie said to her husband, attempting to intervene on my behalf.

He didn't appear to hear her.

"Try to hit me, Hunston," he said.

Half-heartedly, I swung in his direction and missed.

He cuffed my ear so hard that it stung.

"By Jove, Hunston, have a real go!"

I hesitated.

"Well come on, man!" he said.

I took a proper swing.

There was a sharp intake of breath from the two ladies present. Luckily I missed.

"Come on… try again. You can do better than that."

So I had another go, but trying to tag him was like trying to catch a shadow; he leant back on my second swing and ducked the third, then caught hold of my hand and twisted it backwards at the wrist until I had to concede. He didn't hold back either – had me yelping and tapping the table frantically, all to the loud guffawing of Sir James Southgate and Sir Robert Egremont.

Embarrassed, but smiling gamely, I retired to my seat and the sympathetic consolation of Ettie Grenfell, and a glass of red wine. I could see that across the table, the beautiful Anna Egremont was concerned for my welfare too. She caught my eye with a knowing expression, which I read as saying: "I would like to come over there right now and be with you, but I married this walrus and now I'm trapped. I'm sorry." Right there in that shared look, we conducted a three second affair, short-lived but very sweet nonetheless.

Egremont started bragging how his yacht – 'Sybarita' – had beaten Kaiser Wilhelm II's at Cowes the week before. After that he told us all how he had made and lost a fortune in the silver mines of Colorado and New Mexico several years before. "Gold is my venture now," he said, with the look of a cat that had got the cream.

Judging by what I had seen at Witworth Park and in Piccadilly, he was doing all right so far.

At the end of his story he sat back in a self-satisfied way and said: "Auri sacra fames," not seeing fit to translate for the benefit of the company.

"You seem to know your Virgil, Sir Robert," Ettie Grenfell said. "Perhaps you would be kind enough…"

"It means 'the cursed hunger for gold'," he said, interrupting her.

"…to pass the salt."

William Grenfell howled.

"I do beg your pardon, Ettie dear," Egremont said. "I completely mistook you."

"Non omnia possumus omnes," she said as she salted her food elegantly.

Egremont's face creased into a frown.

"Virgil again, Sir Robert – and it means: 'we can't all do everything'."

Egremont had been dropping clangers left right and centre, tearing up the rule book on etiquette all the way through the meal. He was too loud, too crude. Certainly, Grenfell had been forthright as well, but the subtle difference was that he *entertained* the company with his escapades. Even when sparring, the atmosphere in the room had been one of exhilaration, caught up as we were with his zeal for Bartitsu. You could not help but admire him. With Egremont though, there was a cruelty to his nature – the stuffed hunting trophies, the harsh laughter at my being on the receiving end of Grenfell's torture – and his bragging was too self-congratulatory, as if emanating out of some inferiority complex, which it probably was. What the hell had Anna Egremont been thinking? Money, I suppose.

Dinner over, the ladies having excused themselves, Egremont asked the gentlemen to go outside, but instead of smoking cigars on the terrace, he invited us to head down to the lake. The path ran past the marble elephant and alongside a walled kitchen garden, leading into a copse. There under the trees was an arched doorway set into what looked like a low concrete bunker. Egremont stepped inside – leading us all into a tunnel which spiralled gently downwards, lit at regular intervals by the most up-to-date electric lamps. The tunnel became a descending spiral staircase. At its foot was another tunnel – hundreds of feet long – which, if my bearings were correct, was taking us out under the lake.

I was right: the passage opened out into one of the most fantastic rooms I had ever seen. An underground – or to be more precise, an *underwater* billiards room with an extraordinary glass domed ceiling. Beyond the glass, the eerie yellow-green water of the lake could be seen, long tendrils of water weed gyrating in the murky depths and giant orange carp gaping at us as they swam past.

It was an engineering marvel; hundreds of panes set into wrought-iron struts, all curving gently up to the apex. The glass must have been at least three inches thick, but I could not help thinking it would only take one pane to give way for the bubble to implode and drown us all – an unsettling feeling and one which made my thoughts turn inward.

Earlier, on the train ride over, I had fantasised I was in the heart of the Empire. Standing here now I knew I was in the innermost chamber of the heart, among its rulers, the richest and most powerful people in the country. Grenfell probably owned great swathes of England and, through the Souls, had the ear of the great and the good. Southgate controlled Medicine and Science – the new religions. Egremont provided the financial clout, owning the biggest goldmines in Australia, and much else besides.

He was handing out expensive Cuban cigars now, clipping off the ends with a gold cutter.

I took a few puffs, but as the outsider, found myself standing slightly apart from the main group. An animated discussion began concerning

Egremont's new venture – an underground rail line in London called the 'Baker Street and Waterloo'. I was way out of my depth when it came to business, and frankly not that interested, so I disengaged myself and perambulated the underwater room alone with my cigar, peering through the windows at the fish in the water beyond. Glancing over at Egremont, I couldn't help but notice that when he puffed on his cigar, he looked just like the bulbous-headed carp in his lake. I revised my earlier theory of his being a walrus.

Sir James Southgate was drunk.

In fact he had been drunk by the end of the first course that evening. Egremont must have asked him to probe because he came over to where I was smoking and started rolling a billiard ball on the felt, bouncing it off a cushion, back and forth. He kept doing this for a minute or so before finally opening his mouth.

"Tell me about Hunston," he said, as if we were both analysing an inanimate object from afar. He was grinning inanely, obviously thinking himself quite the wit.

Play the game, just for tonight, play the bloody game in order to get out of the game.

Now was the time to metamorphose into the 'old John Hunston', realising that if I didn't then the Australian adventure would be over before it had even begun. I needed to redeem myself after the carving fiasco and the humiliation of the Bartitsu fight.

"Well... it's a short story, Sir James," I said, sounding cheery, "I gained my DM at Oxford in the summer of ninety nine and shortly thereafter took up work in Harley Street."

"Oh? Which practice?"

"The Manor, Sir James."

"The Manor, indeed."

Southgate sounded impressed. It wasn't surprising he had heard of it; the Manor's reputation and earning power was the envy of every other doctor in town.

"And how did they come to choose the young Hunston?"

I pondered the question privately for a moment.

I had just 'fitted the bill'; well-educated, said and did the right thing. Most importantly did it all with apparent *effortlessness*. Things had to be effortless in those kinds of circles; anything else was seen as crass. That's what the partners at the Manor had seen. Well, that and my club tie; it turned out one of them was a Blue Boar too.

I remembered the interview: "You're not Catholic are you, JH?" the senior partner had said, as if we were back in Elizabethan times.

"No. Why do you ask?"

"Well...We don't have *those* here."

"And what else can't one be?" I had said, not quite believing he was serious.

"Well, obviously not a woman... and no homosexuals, or bankrupts either..."

I didn't say any of this to Southgate; I gave him the benign version.

"I met the doctors from the Manor on a shoot, Sir James. And while the beaters were preparing the next wave of pheasants, the senior partner made me an unexpected offer. He was eating a beef and horseradish sandwich at the time as I recall: 'You seem like a decent chap, JH,' he said, 'and I like a man who can shoot straight. We want you to come and work with us. What do you say?'"

Southgate laughed and stared back at me with glazed eyes.

I had known he would laugh. I was playing the game you see. The interview was going well – it was almost *too* easy.

'DR JOHN HUNSTON DM' it said on the bronze wall plate of the Manor.

I had arrived.

The partners paid lip-service to the less well-off by working at the Charing Cross Voluntary Hospital one day a week, but avoided anything grimier than that – wouldn't have been caught dead in a Workhouse hospital, that was for sure. They supplemented their income by providing medical cover at the racecourses around the city – Kempton Park, Sandown, Royal Ascot. Though the racing was well paid, the real money was made at the Manor, with all the private practice. My God, it had poured in.

Then the Boer War had kicked off. With Freddie's regiment heading out there I felt a brotherly urge to protect him somehow, but if I am being honest that wasn't the only reason I joined the RAMC – the imperialistic fervour affecting many men of my generation had seized me too. 'Misplaced fervour' I called it now. Needless to say, my colleagues at the Manor had strongly encouraged it: "Good idea, JH… Off you go. We'll keep your seat warm." Being much older, they had firmly rejected the notion of going themselves: "Good God, JH… You young chaps deserve the chance of glory – we're past all that. Middle aged men going off to war – what a vulgar notion!"

"And then I did my stint at Bloemfontein," I said, hoping Southgate might change the subject.

"Ah yes, Bloemfontein. I heard Conan Doyle was down there."

"Yes, I believe so… worked in one of the private tent hospitals, the *Langman*. Pitched their tents on the town's cricket oval and used the pavilion as their main ward as I recall."

Southgate chuckled: "Yes… I heard he was in such a state that when a journalist from the *Illustrated London News* asked him which Sherlock Holmes story was his favourite, he could only reply: 'the one with the snake'. He meant *The Speckled Band…*"

Ha Ha Ha.

Southgate had a snorting laugh that sounded like a pig.

It didn't surprise me at all that Conan Doyle couldn't remember his own story. In those tent hospitals, there was simply no time for any thoughts other than treating the sick. You became an automaton. If someone had asked me my name, let alone anything else, I would have struggled. It was something Southgate would never understand.

"Know him, Sir James?"

"Conan Doyle? Yes, of course…" he said, with a smug grin.

I stared at him, hating him.

The pretence was going – I was starting to lose it now. His arrogance was really starting to get on my nerves.

This idiot gets to live and my brother gets to die?

Thoughts like this had been happening a lot since the funeral – an on-going and one sided rant I was having with a God I didn't even believe existed, but who nevertheless was proving a useful punch bag. My disposition would flip into one of anger at even the smallest provocation.

"No trouble with the typhoid himself, I hope?"

"Good God, no," Southgate said. "He had the inoculation – he was fine. Said the Army had made a big error by not making the inoculations compulsory – made his thoughts public…"

This was news. Earlier, in the Blue Boar, I had thought everyone had overlooked it - the inoculation question that is – but it seemed Conan Doyle hadn't.

They would do all they could to keep *that* out of any future inquiry, that's for sure.

Southgate's next comment seemed to confirm my suspicions.

"Ruffled a few feathers high up I'm afraid… I might have to put a quiet word in his ear. You know… tell him to step back from the politics and stick to the detective writing."

"Indeed," I said, not meaning it.

I drank some more wine and tried to think about something else, my mood simmering on a quiet boil. I didn't say much after that, just in case it became too obvious that I wanted to punch Southgate right in the middle of his smirking face.

Egremont led us all down another tunnel ending at a second staircase, which led up and out onto a small concrete island set into the middle of the lake.

A dozen yards away, the billiards room shone yellow beneath the surface of the water. I imagined summer parties with bathers swimming down through the weed curtain, tapping on the glass tiles and looking into the room like the fish.

Something made me start. A man was out there standing on the water.

Right in my ear, Egremont roared with laughter:

Haw, haw, haw: a different kind of laugh to Southgate's, but equally annoying.

"You look like you've seen a ghost, Hunston."

Squinting into the gloaming, I saw the figure was too still to be alive. It was a statue with its plinth perched on the top of the underwater dome, giving it the semblance of walking on the water.

I wondered how many guests Egremont had tricked in this way, just to see their reactions. Was it some kind of test? Was this part of the interview too?

I felt him watching me intently, weighing me up, wondering what the catch was. Why leave Harley Street? He could probably detect the disillusionment I gave off like a warning scent. Somehow, I was going to have to convince him I was the man for the job. Southgate had been too drunk to report back. At the moment all Egremont knew was that I was a shifty, nervous type who didn't laugh at his jokes and who couldn't carve meat.

Back in the underwater room I played Grenfell at billiards.

As the game wore on I found myself studying him, in particular the way he stood in between shots with the cue behind his back. There was a strange familiarity about it and I wondered if I might have met him before this evening, perhaps at some event before the war.

"I see you're wearing a Blues blazer, Hunston," he said, leaning over his cue to line up the next shot and not taking his eyes off the ball.

"Yes, that's right," I said, surprised he had known what it was.

If you rowed in the University Boat Race between Oxford and Cambridge, you won a 'Blue', an accolade which came in the form of a distinctive dark blue blazer if you were from Oxford, or a light blue one if you went to the other place.

I looked down at my jacket and brushed cigar ash off it self-consciously. Some of the silk ribbon trim was already beginning to look ragged, but even so, I still preferred it to my RAMC dress tunic which only came with bad memories.

Grenfell made his shot and straightened up.

"What years did you row?"

"'96, '97 and '98," I said.

He furrowed his brow.

"Close one in '96 I seem to remember… down at Hammersmith by three quarters of a length, weren't you?"

"That's right."

"Must've been tough."

"Yes, it was."

I was instantly thrown back into that race; a four mile slog, much of it into a headwind. It is a merciful thing that pain is impossible to describe from memory. We had crept back on Cambridge around the outside of the long Surrey bend and by Barnes Bridge were level, going on to win by a narrow margin – the closest race in years. For at least half an hour afterwards I was too tired to even open my bottle of champagne. At the time, I thought that nothing could be any tougher, but I knew more now; that 'nothing' was in fact typhoid fever.

"Two-fifths of a length, wasn't it?"

"That's right."

Grenfell certainly knew his stuff. He started swinging the cue around his body in what I presumed were Bartitsu moves, bringing it so close I could feel the breeze created. I tried not to flinch.

He spun round to face Egremont.

"Hunston's winning margin was the length of this billiard table Sir Robert."

It was just the three of us in the underwater room. Southgate must have stayed out on the concrete island; probably asleep in a drunken stupor.

"It was close that year, the next few were easier," I said, making light of it.

Grenfell had stopped swinging and was holding the cue behind his back again.

Then it came to me – the place I knew him from. He was the man in the Vanity Fair cartoon on the wall at the Blue Boar Club. Here he was, in the flesh, holding the billiards cue the same way he held the riding crop in the picture. A younger version in the cartoon, granted – the hair not so grey, but the subject unmistakeably one and the same.

"My race was even closer," he said in a quiet voice.

It took a moment for me to register what he had said: 'my race'.

Of course, Grenfell was an 'Old Blue'.

At that moment, the one thing I knew for sure was that, no matter what I had said or done wrong that evening, the job in Australia was mine. It had been mine ever since I had come out onto the terrace wearing my blazer. Grenfell had known all along. In his eyes I was an 'Old Blue' – and it meant *everything*. This was the old boy's network in action, where connections carried more clout than anything else.

By telling Egremont my winning margin, he was nominating me for the job.

There was only one race in history closer than mine and that had been in 1877. All boat race rowers knew that.

"You were in the dead heat?"

He brought the cue round and rested it ominously on my shoulder.

"It wasn't a dead heat, the umpire was drunk… we won that bloody race by six foot."

A victory denied more than twenty years previously made Grenfell's face contort now as if he were chewing on a lemon. It was the one time during the whole evening when I saw a chink in his armour. It always amazed me how the 'Old Blues' retained crystal clear memories of their rowing days; the winning margins, who had wronged them in some way, what a bystander had shouted in the crowd. Maybe I would turn out the same way.

"Got my revenge in '78," he said. "I was President in '79 but my doctors forbade me to row – said I had strained my heart on the running track. Bloody doctors, they think they know everything."

"Not this one," I said.

Grenfell laughed, realising his gaffe.

"Dear boy, do forgive me."

"Don't mention it."

Egremont stepped up and tapped at my chest with his pudgy index finger,

"Australia won't be what you're used to… Harley Street and all that."

"I know."

"When can you leave?"

The man in khaki from the advertisement was screaming at me again, telling me to grab this with both hands.

"Right now, if you want."

They had both laughed at that, thinking my answer a light-hearted acceptance. But I had meant it. I couldn't wait. I was that desperate. My old world in London was completely alien to me now. I was a pariah. That's what Freddie's death had done to me – turned me into a pariah – and I wanted to begin my self-imposed exile immediately.

Later, on the sea voyage, an uneasy feeling of doubt settled in my stomach, like dead leaves slowly sinking to the floor of a pond. Something had been wrong about Witworth – those stuffed predators, the huge marble elephant they had to lower the road for, the lake and the incredible underwater room. All that sheer opulence was too good to be true, and by 'true', I mean legitimate. Out on the lake, when I had sensed Egremont was judging me, it should have been the other way round; I should have been the one wondering what the catch was. The paranoia grew during the voyage – I was certain I had been the only person they had interviewed. No one else would have touched it with a bargepole.

When I told Rennie about my nagging worries, he laughed and quoted Proverbs - 'Pride goeth before destruction and a haughty spirit before the fall,' – something which didn't exactly made me feel any better.

Chapter Five

Twentieth century communications had definitely arrived in the town of Fremantle; forests of creosote-stinking telegraph poles dominated the streets, their wires looping low like jungle vines between the man-made trunks. Outrageously coloured birds smudged across my vision in a blur of green, red and blue. I already knew the laugh of the kookaburra, but there were other strange calls out there. Every so often the air was split by a deafening 'OOOOOOAAAAAGGGGHH', an otherworldly screech which only served to reinforce the fact that London was a very great distance away.

At the fish market on South Terrace, it seemed as though half the Pacific had been dredged up and put on ice; octopus, shrimps, oysters and a whole range of particularly ugly fish specimens were out on display. Here at least the stench overwhelmed that of the creosote. I leant over the great piles of pungent dead marine life and inhaled deeply to try and clear my head.

"That's a John Dory," Rennie said, pointing at a fish with spiked dorsal fins and a large dark spot on its flank. "A very good omen."

"Oh? Why is that?"

"It's a biblical fish. 'Go thou to the sea, and cast a hook, and take up the fish that first cometh up, and when thou hast opened his mouth, thou shalt find a piece of money.' Matthew: Chapter 17: verse 27." He pointed to one of the spots: "Look. Do you see St Peter's thumbprint?"

"It looks like an eye to me," I said. "Probably an evolutionary adaption to scare away prey, but it's still amazing… it still has a beauty when you think about it my way."

"Yes, you're quite right, John. But I prefer the Good Book's version."

After eight weeks together, I knew when to leave it, so I kept quiet.

The fishmonger was staring at us both, with a dark look on his face.

"Do you want to buy the bloody fish or not?"

By now Dudley had marched on ahead of us. He kept looking round to check we were behind him, and then he would shake his head and laugh to himself. While he stayed out in the glare, limping his way down the middle of the street, the heat had Rennie and me heading for the shade at every opportunity. Dudley seemed oblivious to the sun, his leathery tan and slouch hat providing all the protection he needed.

In the shadows of an arcade of shops, the merchants leant easily against their doorways, watching the world go by. One man, arms folded over an apron, held my stare briefly.

'Snowfoots', the sign on his shop window read: 'Hairdresser, tobacconist, cigar divan, newsagent, bookseller and stationer'.

"G'day, new chum," he said. "How about a haircut?"

The 'Esplanade' hotel on the seafront was of the colonial style, with long verandas matched by balconies above. Once in our room, I dropped my bags and watched, fascinated, as sweat dropped from my forehead onto the floorboards. The air was stifling. Rennie flopped onto one of the beds and lay still.

Dudley threw open the doors to the balcony.

I followed him outside and leant against the handrail, enjoying the breeze. Beyond a line of pine trees was the sparkling turquoise ocean.

"Enjoying 'the Doctor', Doc?"

He kept looking out to sea.

"What?"

"The onshore wind," he said. "It's called 'the Fremantle Doctor'. Blows in every afternoon."

"Why's it called that?"

"You feel better, don't you?"

I stared out to the horizon and closed my eyes.

"Yes," I said, "I suppose I do."

"Enjoy it now; it's not like this in the goldfields."

"Really? It's worse?"

It was hard to imagine a hotter day than this.

"Hot as bloody hell itself, Doc. You think you're sweating now. Out there you'll be sweating a like a whore in church."

Dudley turned to me, beaming a big grin.

Then he looked at Rennie, still flat out on the bed.

"Perhaps it's best you don't tell your mate I said that."

We went back inside and he poured out three glasses of water from the jug on the washstand. Rennie roused himself and came over to join us.

"Cheers," Dudley said, passing out the drinks. "It's safe to drink, but don't assume it will be everywhere."

I understood the implications; even here, on the coast, there was the risk that the water could be contaminated with one of the big three: typhoid, dysentery or cholera.

"This is the best place in town. They've even got a flushing 'dunny' down the corridor. That's the lavatory to you. By the way, food and drink are on the company here, but if you two new-chums want to try something different, I suggest Carlo's – back down on South Terrace. Good tucker."

He glanced at his watch. It was the new wristlet type – one of the Mappin's 'campaign' watches the commanding officers had worn in South Africa to help co-ordinate their attacks against the Boers. A luminous dial could show the time on the darkest of Veldt nights and the steel casing made it dust and damp proof. Seeing the timepiece told me Dudley must have been a CO in the war and my respect for him went up a notch.

"Anyway, I've got to be going," he said. "Meeting an old mate in town tonight, but I'll be here to pick you gents up at ten tomorrow."

He finished his drink quickly and slammed the glass back down on the table.

"Mañana" he said as he walked out.

After he had gone, Rennie looked at me and cocked an eyebrow.

"Man - yana?"

"It's Spanish for tomorrow," I said.

"Why would he say it in Spanish?"

"I don't know."

He shrugged and went out onto the balcony. A moment later he was back in the room and striding determinedly towards the door.

"Where are you off to?" I said.

"That beach… to swim."

"What, now?"

"Yes, now! Come on, John."

In Rennie's world there was no yesterday and no tomorrow; he only ever concerned himself with the present moment. It wasn't just this temporal quality which I found so appealing about my friend's manner, it was the fact that he was genuinely interested in what was right in front of him, be it a fish out on display in a market or a sandy beach in view from our hotel balcony. All I had done on the balcony was worry about the dreadful heat in an inland city I hadn't even visited yet.

"GERONIMO!"

Rennie had stripped off to his undershorts, and was running as fast as he could down the sand and into the water. Tearing off my heavy clothes, I did the same, bounding through the shallows and falling headlong into an oncoming wave. In a single second the plunge obliterated all the grime and sweat of the day as well as the accrued mustiness of the entire eight week voyage.

The water held surprises: first there was the warmth, and then there was the intense saltiness, which stung the eyes and made you stagger around half-blinded. It sluiced out the sinuses, returning them to the air pockets they were supposed to be, instead of the soot repositories they had become from London's coal dust.

Further out, waves crashed down in a great foaming mass and we challenged these white horses head on, letting them thump into us and toss us around. An even larger set came in and I found myself floating in a surprisingly peaceful watery cavern, holding my breath and allowing myself be spun underwater by the wave's power as it broke over me. Finally, just as I thought my lungs were about to burst, I was cast out onto the shore.

I limped back up the beach to our pile of clothes and lay flat on my back, exhausted and vaguely aware of my skin tightening under the strong sun. I felt like an old shirt which had been vigorously cleaned on a scrubbing board and left out to dry.

"Well, that's certainly blown out the cobwebs," Rennie said, emerging from his Australian baptism.

When Rennie was dry, he opened up his bible and started reading to himself, every now and then looking out to sea when mulling on a particular passage. He would then jot down a note in the margin of the page and move on.

Many an afternoon had passed like this on the ship; in a comfortable silence. Despite his one-liners, Rennie rarely shared his thoughts when he read scripture. For him, it was a sacred act, the one time when I could tell that underneath all his eccentricities and buffoonery, he was the real deal. He never seemed to mind me being there, sharing in his quiet reflection and it was another aspect of his character that I particularly admired; certainly he talked of religion, but he didn't ram it down your throat and that was no mean feat for a Wesleyan.

While he read, I watched the great red orb of the sun sinking slowly into the ocean. The last of it dipped away and a flash of green glowed briefly on the horizon, so transient that I soon doubted it had happened at all.

Strolling back into town we passed by 'Snowfoot's', the establishment I had seen earlier.

The man in the apron, presumably Snowfoot himself, was still standing outside touting for customers.

"How about a haircut?" he said again.

Rennie stopped in his tracks.

"Yes, why not? Anything to make this infernal heat more tolerable."

For several minutes Snowfoot clipped away, but in the end the only way to get rid of Rennie's self-inflicted divots was to get out a razor blade and shave his head.

That was when Rennie started to look worried.

"Is something the matter, Reverend?" Snowfoot said.

"'...If I be shaven, then my strength will go from me, and I shall become weak, and be like any other man' – Book of Judges."

"Ah... Samson and Delilah. Don't worry – I'm not a conniving Sheila, just a simple barber."

He laughed so much I thought he might accidentally scalp my poor friend with the razor.

After Snowfoot had finished and was showing Rennie the back of his head with a mirror, he said, "How about your mate?"

Rennie answered before I had even had the chance.

"He'd love one."

The barber turned his attention to me and grinned, like Count Dracula weighing up his next victim. I went over and sat down in the chair. I was willing enough. Rennie was right about the heat being infernal – it made me want to peel off as many layers as possible and my hair was a good start.

"I'll have the same as him," I said.

Ten minutes later we emerged onto the street, feeling the contours of our bony heads with a sense of fascination and disbelief. We looked like a couple of French Foreign Legionnaires with 'boule a zero' haircuts. In the legion, you threw away your past and started anew. Even your country of origin was irrelevant. That was us all right; shaven headed men from a far-away place, the location of which counted for nothing now. Out here we were starting again.

Carlo's, the eating house Dudley had recommended, was a one man show.

Carlo himself stood behind the counter at a grill, black hair plastered onto his forehead with a combination of brilliantine, cooking fat and sweat. Despite his heavy jowls and greying stubble, you could still see the thinner young man of ten years before, fresh-faced from Italy at the start of the gold-rush.

Burly dock workers were crowding the café. Earlier that day Dudley had called them 'lumpers'. They all had similar haircuts to ours, though at various stages of growing out. Carlo was speaking to the men in a remarkable language, halfway between Italian and English, and peppered with swearwords he must have picked up from his rough and ready clientele. He saw us and shouted across the room: "You two fuckin' mongrels take a bloody chair over there."

Then Carlo noticed Rennie's dog collar and made the sign of the cross on his chest.

"Shit. I'm sorry, Father. I didn't-a-bloody see you. Oh, Christ, I'm sorry… I start again…"

He valiantly tried to tone down his language, though the only way he could do so was by reverting fully to his native Italian, "Buon giorno, Padre… Si metta as sedere," he said, pointing out a spare table. A few minutes later, he served up two plates of unidentifiable meat the menu termed 'tinned dog', and a type of bread called 'damper'. The menu said that if you had the bread fried, then its name was upgraded to 'Jonny Cake'.

"Buon appetite, amici."

After the lumpers had left, Carlo brought out a bottle of Chianti from under the counter and filled three small glasses.

"Oro," he said, holding up his glass in a toast. "Capiche?"

He was toasting gold; the precious metal that meant business was good for him and the rest of the colony. I drank my wine fast. Carlo refilled the glass and I kept drinking. Soon, the combination of sun, food and wine hit me and my eyelids began to lower like french blinds – there was nothing I could do to stop them. I could still hear Rennie in animated discussion with the Italian, oblivious now to the multiple profanities which had crept back into Carlo's English. Then their words turned into a mass of sound, like the waves at the beach and finally the roar faded away into nothingness as I ducked under the surface of consciousness.

It is a testament to Rennie's great physical strength that he was able to haul my half-witted bulk all the way back to our digs. The only thing I recall from this journey is the vague jolt of my head making contact with the door frame as he carried me into our room.

Someone was banging hard on the door.

I sat up in a panic.

In the other bed, Rennie hadn't woken despite the racket. I could just make out his form in the darkness, his massive barrel chest rising and falling in time with each rasping snore. The whole room seemed to be shaking with the sound. After the boat journey, I was immune to his snoring – it was only the insistent knocking which had disturbed me.

BANG! BANG! BANG!

"All right, all right…" I said, wiping the dried saliva from the side of my mouth.

I rolled off the bed and then stubbed my toe on a bed post as I navigated my way to the door. When I opened it, still wincing with pain, Dudley was standing there.

"Christ Almighty," he said. "That's what I call a haircut, Doc."

Because I was still half asleep, his words seemed out of synchrony with the movement of his mouth and it took me a moment to process. 'Haircut' he had said. I rubbed my scalp where all my hair used to be, only now remembering the visit to the barber's.

He handed over a drinking can which looked to be army issue; made of tin with rope webbing wound around the rim.

"Here," he said, "take a drink."

I looked at him uncertainly, suspecting it was more of his rum ration.

"It's only water, Doc."

He was telling the truth. It was nicely chilled and woke me up fast.

"What's going on?"

Dudley got straight to the point.

"Need your help at the gaol – Egremont man's injured."

"At the gaol?"

"Yep, that's what I said. I've got a buggy waiting outside. We'll be there in five minutes."

I rubbed my head again and raced through the various scenarios the next few hours might bring. One thing was clear – my night's sleep was over.

"Give me a moment."

I was already dressed because Rennie had just thrown me onto my bed, only choosing to remove my shoes and socks. I couldn't find the socks in the dark, so I just slipped my bare feet into my boots. Grabbing my Gladstone, I followed Dudley out to a waiting hansom cab. At this time of night the temperature had dropped a few degrees and it was almost comfortable.

"What am I dealing with?" I said, as we rumbled through the still streets of Fremantle.

"Oh, just a few cuts and bruises, Doc, nothing to write home about."

"Why's he in gaol?"

Dudley snorted.

"He was in Quarry Street, not bloody Harley Street, Doc. Out 'ere, men tend to argue more with their fists than with their mouths, especially when liquor is involved."

"Is he a miner?"

"No."

"Is he a friend of yours?"

"Jesus… you're all questions tonight, Doc."

He reached into his pocket, pulling out his silver flask. He took a swig of the rum and held out the flask to me. "Maybe this'll shut you up."

I shook my head. "Better not, if I'm working."

"Bloody good on ya, Doc. I like a man with principles."

He looked out of the carriage window and screwed the top back onto his flask. "Aaah, here we are now."

We stopped at a stone gatehouse and climbed down from the buggy. Lanterns were burning on each side of the heavily fortified entrance. I half expected someone to raise a drawbridge. Instead, a guard came out.

"We're here to see Eugene Tickell," Dudley said. "This here's the doc."

The guard peered at me.

"You don't look much like a doc."

"I had my hair cut at Snowfoot's yesterday."

He nodded. That seemed to make sense to him.

"Black fella's in Moondyne Joe's cell," he said, waving us through. "Cut up pretty bad…"

We headed towards the main cell block, our footsteps echoing around the walls of the central courtyard. The prison building reminded me of the Military Hospital back in England, the way it had looked on those midnight runs out to the pier – forbidding and austere with the same pale stone – though here the windows were barred and the stars brighter, a great mass of them cutting a swathe through the blackness overhead.

"Who's Moondyne Joe?"

"He was a con who kept escaping," Dudley said. "So they made a specially reinforced cell to hold him. The Governor promised Joe a pardon if he ever managed to escape again. Then one day, during yard time, Joe broke a hole through the limestone wall with a hammer and escaped. Got caught again too. The Governor went back on his word and gave Joe another ten years. Luckily for him, a new bloke took over, made good the promise and let him go."

"That's it?"

"Pretty much – he stayed out of trouble after that… Got married. Last I heard they were in the goldfields somewhere.'

Another guard, holding a lantern, was standing at a door to the main cell block, waiting for us.

Without a word, he opened the door and we stepped inside and followed him along a long dark passageway, the only sounds our footsteps and his jangling set of keys.

Up ahead the guard stopped and rapped hard on a door with his truncheon.

Two taps.

"Doc's here to patch you up," he said, peering through the Judas hole. "No trouble now, ya hear me?"

He put down the lantern and used both hands to turn the key and push open the door. Then he stepped back and looked at me: "All yours."

By the flickering light, I could see the cell was very small – no more than eight by five feet and entirely lined with brick-red timber, studded with hundreds of iron rivets. The window at the end was covered by two layers of steel bars. I understood now why the former governor had been so confident Moondyne Joe would never escape.

A man was standing in the shadows at the back of the cell, stripped to the waist and barefoot, his hair splaying out over his shoulders. When he stepped forward into the light it was as if the shadows came with him – as black a human as I had ever laid eyes upon, blacker even than the Zulus of South Africa. He was an Aboriginal Australian and he was looking right at me with a penetrating gaze. In the dimness of the cell, with just the light from the guard's lantern, his stare was so powerful that it seemed his eyes were lit from within, as if there was another lantern inside his head.

Parts of his skin were shiny, and as my eyes adjusted I saw that the gloss was in fact blood. I swallowed my rising bile, hoping no one could see my expression; I had never got used to the warm, metallic smell of fresh blood, and this man was covered in it. Tentatively, I stepped inside the cell. *Don't faint now.* I wondered if he could detect my fear, whether he could see the all the panicky thoughts buzzing around my head like the bush flies down on the dock.

"I'm Doctor Hunston and I'm here to help you," I said, my words muffled within the wooden sarcophagus.

"Eugene Tickell," the Aboriginal said. "That's my white fella name. Sorry to get you up, Doc."

His voice had a distinct sing-song lilt, not at all concordant with his fearsome appearance, and that helped calm my fears and allow some of the old confidence to return. I turned to the guard. "I'll need two buckets of water and some towelling, please."

He was leaning against the doorway swinging his baton and it was only now I noticed he had a mean looking face – probably stuck that way from scowling at the inmates for so long.

"What do I look like? Florence bloody Nightingale? Just do the best you can. He's only a bloody Abo."

"Do it, mate," Dudley said to the guard, in a way that didn't sound matey at all. "Or the company will be asking the governor why our man wasn't fixed up properly."

The guard hesitated and then left, swearing under his breath.

"Thanks," I said.

"Doc, I've been surrounded by fifty angry Boers, so backing you up after you've asked for two buckets of water isn't as daunting a bloody prospect as it might seem."

He thumped the wall with the side of his fist.

"Swan River mahogany… Black fellas call it Jarrah. Isn't that right, Eugene?"

"Jarrah," Eugene said, smiling now.

Dudley thumped the wall again.

"This stuff built the colony. Bridges, wharves, railway sleepers, ships, telegraph poles – you name it. It doesn't bloody rot. Why you could build your bloody bath tub out of it if you wanted to."

When the towelling and buckets arrived, I sponged off the blood until I found the sources of the bleeding.

Eugene had three lacerations – obviously knife wounds. One ran through his left cheek, the others were on his forearms, sustained, I suspected, from parrying the attack. I didn't ask about the fight, I wasn't interested in the rights and wrongs of it; I just wanted to fix up the mess and get back to bed.

Using the thinnest catgut in my armoury I worked on the face wound first. Eugene refused local anaesthetic and didn't flinch once.

Thinking back to my practice in Harley Street and the patients with their winsome complaints, I almost laughed at the comparison. Despite the blood, I was actually enjoying this; some real doctoring for a change.

During the voyage I practised my suturing technique on pig's knuckles. The chef would give me leftover cuts and I would suture in the lounge each afternoon while Rennie read his bible in the next chair. I was glad for the training now because the wounds were closing well. Even the guard looked impressed.

Eugene had old scars crossing his chest horizontally; three stripes in linear formation, too neat to have been made with injurious intent. As I worked I pondered if these scarifications meant he was special in some way among his people; some kind of chieftain, perhaps? I didn't know anything about the Aboriginals. Maybe they didn't even have chieftains. In truth, he looked too young to be a leader, and too skinny to be a warrior. What I did sense was that he already knew me, that in his first glance he had completely worked me out.

When I was finished, I snipped the thread and put the needle into my makeshift sharps box – an 'Ogden's Guinea Gold' tobacco tin – and then washed my instruments in the bucket.

Dudley inspected the stitching with admiration.

"You all right there, Eugene?" he said.

"Better now, Tom. Thanks."

Eugene was also examining my handiwork.

"Don't thank me, mate," Dudley said. "Thank the Pommy doc. The bloody prison surgeon couldn't be bothered to get out of bed for a black fella."

Dudley turned to me and started explaining.

"Was supposed to be meeting Eugene in town for a beer, but he was a no show. So I went down to the police station. Seems a couple of ruffians decided to have a go and we all know why. Eugene here was the one who got locked up for his trouble – if you happen to be a black fella then getting in the way of a knife turns out to be a bloody crime."

The guard was sneering and shaking his head.

"I know what you're thinking, mate," Dudley said to him, "and you're entitled to your opinion. But I'm not afraid to say it – black fella or white fella; it's all the same to me. Doc, that man you've just sewn back together happens to be the best tracker in the entire colony. Helps mining parties survive out in the bush; saved my skin once or twice. Isn't that right, mate?"

"Right," Eugene said, joining Dudley in looking directly at me.

I applied iodine to the wounds and then washed my hands in the clean water of the second bucket.

"The stitches will dissolve in a week or so. Don't get them wet."

"Thanks, Doc," Eugene said.

"Glad to help."

He looked at Dudley.

"When will they let me out, Tom?"

"I saw the police report. A witness came forward. You'll be out by tomorrow morning, mate."

The guard handed me a clipboard with a prison injury form attached.

"This needs filling out... please," he said, mustering as much civility as possible.

The guard and Dudley moved out into the corridor to discuss the arrangements for Eugene's release the next morning and I started filling out the form. As I did, Eugene turned his attention to the cell wall, rubbing his hand up and down on the smooth wood.

"What do you see, Doc?"

I glanced up at the thick studded Jarrah for a moment, before going back to my form-filling.

"I see wood panels."

"No," he said. "They are Jarrah; they once lived and grew, each one had its own place on earth. Now they are flat."

He knelt down and tapped the form I was writing on, smudging it with blood.

"Same for this paper... was alive once too. White fellas took the trees away from the place where they lived and made this paper. It locks up white fellas in compartments of time, where they sit and tremble with fear. White fellas will stay in the dead world as long as they don't

72

know the difference between this," he said, tapping the page again, "which means fear, and a tree, which means life.'

The sky was lightening with the first flecks of dawn as we rode back into town. Dudley dropped me outside the hotel, but I knew I wouldn't be able to get back to sleep so I wandered down to the beach.

Without socks, my feet had chafed in my shoes, so I took them off and stood barefoot at the edge of the water. I bent down and scrubbed away the traces of Eugene's blood from my fingers. Helping the Aboriginal made me think about the part in Robinson Crusoe when Man Friday places his head under Crusoe's foot after being rescued by him, a gesture to show he owed Crusoe. On a beach like the one I was standing on now.

Eugene and his X-ray stare had been unnerving; he seemed to be half in this world and half in another. Despite all the night's trauma, he'd been profoundly calm inside the inescapable Jarrah-lined gaol cell. He may as well have been standing on the sea shore like I was now, looking back over his shoulder towards the coming sunrise. Then there had been all that strange talk about the trees and paper and fear. Eugene wasn't afraid, but I was. He had been right about that.

There was something about Dudley too. Not just the steel I had witnessed in front of the guard, but his whole demeanour. Here was a man with no time for social pretence, someone who actually said what they thought, with no finesse – you got the blunt truth whether you liked it or not. He was classless in the sense that he didn't fit into any category with which I was familiar – upper, middle or lower. I wondered if all Australians were like him – or at least the best ones.

And just like Eugene, he seemed to be afraid of nothing. Fearlessness was one possible outcome if you had survived a war I supposed; it just hadn't been the outcome for me.

Chapter Six

Nine Months Earlier

The RAMC had been unprepared and undermanned for the Boer War.

As a consequence, when disease struck, which it did with overwhelming viciousness, the medical services became a complete shambles.

Ignorance and a condescending attitude from the top probably hadn't helped matters to begin with – the commander-in-chief of the Army, Lord Wolseley, had advised in his 'Soldier's Pocket-book' that generals leave their sanitary officers at the base, referring to sanitation as a 'modern fad'.

It was only once the conflict was underway that the War Office realised the enemy were both tougher and more strategic than expected; in December 1899, the British had experienced the so-called 'black week' with defeats at Stormberg, Magersfontein and Colenso resulting in many thousands killed or wounded.

With more medics urgently needed, it had been easy enough to join as a volunteer. I put my name forward in the new year of 1900, and after passing a basic medical, was attested into the RAMC on a year's short service commission. By late February, I was boarding the *SS Sunda* at the Royal Albert docks, along with a large group of doctors from St Mary's Hospital.

Nearing the Canary Islands, a call was put out for anyone wanting typhoid inoculations to report to the Senior MO.

I had never given typhoid fever too much thought. To me it was a sideshow to the real excitement of war – I was still in the mind-set that Boers, not bugs, were the enemy. I kept well back, in part from thinking it an irrelevance but also because I was dubious about its effects. I had heard it made you sick for a week.

The rumours were right: twenty five officers were inoculated into the flank with 1cc of the anti-typhoid serum and within a few hours all twenty five were having rigors, fevers and vomiting. The next day, the lymph glands in their groins and armpits stood out like quail's eggs and they all remained bed-bound with fever. A large area of skin around the injection site became acutely inflamed with red streaks running down the lymphatics to the glands. It took three days for the fever to pass and another three before any of the men were seen out on deck again. After this, we were offered a half dose, and a lot chose to take it, but there was no way I was going to go through that ordeal on a voluntary basis.

One of the other MOs had a go at trying to persuade me.

"Listen, Hunston, I was part of the medical team involved in the Maidstone outbreak of '97. Inoculations were given to eighty-four of the staff working in the psychiatric hospital there. Know how many of them caught typhoid?"

I shook my head.

"None," he said.

"How many weren't inoculated?"

"One hundred and twenty."

"And of those, how many caught typhoid?"

"Four."

I smiled at him benignly. The numbers could easily have been chance findings.

"I think I'll risk not having it. Besides if the War Office hasn't made it compulsory, they must doubt its efficacy too."

I remember thinking how very clever and logical I sounded when I said this.

"No, Hunston, they don't know anything, they're just men in offices debating everything by committee; and in committees what gets decided is always a compromise. If you catch typhoid fever you have a one in five chance of dying, slightly worse odds than playing Russian roulette. Believe me, the inoculation is the lesser of two evils."

When I still declined, he looked at me seriously and shook his head, the same way Crosbie used to look whenever he had seen the superior speed of a rival rowing team – as though he felt sorry for me.

I knew better than to believe the anecdotal evidence. I was an Oxford man, for God's sake.

Journeying further south, I soon forgot all about the inoculation issue.

There was a holiday atmosphere aboard the ship: after drills in the morning we even played cricket and ran egg and spoon races out on the deck. My fellow officers and I were certain nothing could harm us – our youthful hearts touched with the spirit of the age: 'Progress'. We were modern men, rational and logical, but we still thought that we were immortal.

In the evenings we discussed the implications of Darwin's theories over the finest claret, served in crystal cut glasses by servants in starched white uniforms, but this was nothing new; I had come to expect only the best in my privileged world.

Darwin was our hero, and we bastardised his theory nicely to suit our purposes. "If it's all about survival of the fittest," one of my colleagues said, "then surely as officers of the greatest empire the world has ever seen, *we* – sitting at this table – are the fittest. It is the mark of a highly evolved society when its fighters are made virtually indestructible by a cadre of healing men."

Such were our delusions.

We arrived in Cape Town on 1st April, stayed a day, then moved on to Port Elizabeth where we finally disembarked and headed inland to Bloemfontein by train. The British had captured the town on 13th March, the Boers having just packed up and left.

I walked right into the middle of a typhoid epidemic – around a thousand were filling the hospitals by the time I showed up.

It was only then, when it was too late, that I wished I had listened to my colleague on the SS Sunda.

Water rationing had proved intolerable to the British soldiers in the South African heat; the daily allowance of half a bottle, in conditions where a man needed a quart and a half per hour, meant they drank straight from the typhoid-laced Modder River, deliberately polluted by Cronje's men further upstream. The soldiers also ignored orders to boil the water before drinking it, presumably having the same opinion as Lord Wolseley when it came to basic sanitation. With Bloemfontein now a garrison town, its population had swelled from 4,000 to 40,000, and the disease had come to town with them.

On 1st April, the same day I had first laid eyes on Table Mountain, the Boers had cut off Bloemfontein's water supply twenty miles away at Sanna's Post. With no clean water, the epidemic worsened. The military cemetery to the south of the town soon became lined with hundreds of rocky dirt mounds, fresh ones surrounded by groups of men in pith helmets with rolled up sleeves, standing there with shovels.

I was immediately seconded to the field hospital of the 12th Brigade, two miles west of town, as they were short of doctors. It was fairly basic – essentially a hodgepodge of bell tents and marquees on sloping stony ground at the base of a mountain called the Spitz Kop.

My new colleagues had been inoculated against typhoid on their voyage out.

Instead of risking it with the water, I started squeezing the oranges to drink, picking them off the trees in a nearby orchard.

For those few days at the Spitz Kop, I lived in the midst of death.

The facilities were truly appalling, as big an insult to the comfort and dignity of the dying soldiers as the disease itself. Burdett-Coutts's subsequent newspaper article had said it all, although I could sum up the whole miserable situation in one word: complacency.

In their arrogance at an easy victory, the War Office had not provisioned for adequate medical care. To under-estimate the opposition was to break the cardinal rule of any competitive activity, be it in war or in sports. As an oarsman I knew it well. When I saw how the War Office had made this schoolboy error, I smouldered with anger as I rushed from tent to tent, tending to the men.

Complacency was actually too nice a word for it, because this implied a 'head in the clouds' ignorance – perhaps the word should have been negligence because that implied a wilful, considered attitude by people who should really have known better.

At medical school I had seen death of course – but it had been in ones or twos, and usually the old. Seeing young men die in such numbers was truly shocking.

I became numbed to it quickly, but I never got used to those bloody flies everywhere, landing on faces and crawling up orifices, the typhoid germs coating their legs and probosci. They were distributors and disseminators – evil little bastards. The scenes belonged more to the pit of hell than a sunny African plain, that's for sure.

With only one bed pan per tent, those still able to walk staggered outside to relieve themselves and, before long, the whole hillside around the Spitz Kop was contaminated – a veritable mountain of shit. We renamed it the 'Kak Kop'.

When I asked my colleague why no nurses from Bloemfontein were being brought in to help, he said that the PMO, Surgeon General Wilson, *'wasn't very responsive or sympathetic to the idea of lady nurses'*. The few soldiers we had acting as orderlies were going down with the typhoid fever themselves, making the workload even more unbearable. Wilson hadn't even put in a call for more doctors yet, let alone nurses.

Another PMO, Exham – a stickler for rules and regulations – was apparently keeping basic supplies, such as brandy, from the sick and instead stockpiling them for use by journalists, civilians and senior officers. I might not have believed the rumours had I not seen it for myself.

In my desperation to try and secure some supplies I visited the quartermaster's shed in Bloemfontein one morning; a hut filled with hundreds of tins stacked in neat pyramids – quail in foie gras, truffles in crystallised ginger – you name it, they had it. The place was like the food hall at Fortnum and Mason.

In contrast to this fare, the Boers – from their foot soldiers to their generals – ate a dried salted meat called biltong, so tough that it shook your teeth to their very foundations. Along with a rusk biscuit, a piece of biltong formed the bulk of the Boer standard ration pack and with this their mounted Kommando units were able to operate out in the veldt without supply lines for weeks at a time.

Knowing what the Boers lived on and comparing it with the foie gras in the quartermaster's shed, I began to see why a country of backwoodsmen, whose entire population was no more than an average British town, were making such a stand against the British Empire.

The quartermaster was a portly man with his cap set at a jaunty angle, and he was reading a newspaper on the other side of the counter when I walked in.

"I need some condensed milk, blankets, mattresses and bedpans," I said.

Without looking up, he pushed a set of papers over the counter.

"Fill out these forms in triplicate."

"I don't have time for this. I need them now. Men are dying."

He looked up for a moment before going back to his article.

"Fill out the forms," he said again, tapping his index finger on the papers. "We need to have the paperwork."

Shaking my head, I grabbed a pencil and scrawled as fast as I could before shoving them back towards him.

"Put them in the in-tray," he said from behind the newspaper.

He cocked his head towards an empty box with the words MONTEBELLO CHAMPAGNE stamped on the side.

I slapped the papers down in the box.

"Done," I said, my voice tense with frustration. "Now can you help me?"

"I'll deal with them later. They'll have to be counter-signed by the Surgeon General."

Up until that point I had stayed relatively calm, but after days of stumbling through the blood and faeces of delirious men, something inside me snapped. I was so angry that my lower eyelids had started to sizzle. Without thinking, I reached across the counter and yanked him over it by his collar, breaking off two of his buttons in the process. I heard them bounce onto the counter and then to the floor. Then, to his further shock, and mine, I reached around behind his back, grabbed hold of the waist of his underwear, and yanked roughly several times until the white shit-stained garment was more out of his trousers than in. This novel form of torture had been inflicted on me once at school by some wild prefect called Prosser, after I had given him cheek in the tuckshop. He had pulled me over the counter so that I was sprawled over the chocolate bars, and had practically torn my arse in half. The incident had lain dormant all these years, but it was still there just near the surface, because I acted out the punishment automatically in this moment of mad rage, albeit now as perpetrator.

At last I had his full attention.

"Get me the fucking equipment. NOW!"

"I can't. There's nothing left… The trucks are supposed to arrive any day now. I'm sorry. I'll get you what you need then, I'll make sure of it."

In disgust I pushed him back over the counter, sending him sprawling into a pyramid of stacked tins which collapsed with a tremendous clatter.

"And some bloody pyjamas for the men too," I said, kicking the door to the shed open and storming out.

Nobody ever came to question me about the assault that day and I could only assume the quartermaster never told. To give him his due, he was right; medical supplies did arrive; sixty-two truckloads on 17th April. I later heard that the PMOs even put in an SOS request for three hundred orderlies and thirty doctors in late April, but I never got to see any of it, because by then I had typhoid fever myself. I had only been in South Africa for ten days. With an incubation period of a week or so, I suppose I must have contracted it as soon as I had arrived in Bloemfontein.

Trembling and sweat soaked, with a rash covering my chest, I was taken back to the 5th Stationary Hospital on a cart. The hospital was housed in the 'Raadzaal' – what had once been the Boer's parliament building. The large chamber was filled with dozens of beds and medical equipment now, yet in spite of the British Army ripping out the richly patterned carpet to lay down linoleum, the Raadzaal retained a certain style. It was easy to picture the Boers sitting there in session the year before, thumping the heavy desks with their fists in defiance and shouting: "Bloedige Engels."

For a week my fever spiked daily, making my temperature chart look like a child's drawing of a mountain range. My memory of that time is vague and disjointed. Delirious, I became convinced the nurses from the Princess Christians Army Nursing Reserve, dressed in their red capes and starched aprons, were actually angels in disguise. Even after I had passed my crisis, I still half believed it and I would watch them surreptitiously, trying to catch a glimpse of the wings folded away under their capes.

Spending all those hours with my brow burning at temperatures of 105 degrees changed me. It was as if the neurons in my brain unravelled and then rewired themselves into a different pattern. Though I didn't know it yet, I was not quite the same person I had been.

A few days later, I was transferred to Cape Town on the 'Number 3' ambulance train, packed with ninety-six bunks in six carriages – one of which was allocated for officers. Another carriage contained a pharmacy and the kitchen, and the last had the private quarters and dining room of the two on-board surgeons and two nurses.

Kipling was on our train, set up in the private dining room and writing a piece about the 'state-of-the-art' hospital facilities at the front. We all thought that was a good one. At one point he came through our carriage and stopped to chat.

"Where have you been?" he said to me.

"Bloemfontein… with typhoid, Mr Kipling."

Everyone in the carriage gave him the same answer.

"*Bloeming typhoidtein*," he said, shaking his head as he left.

At Cape Town I was put onto a hospital ship heading back to England – a white one with a big red cross on the hull – and that was where I encountered Freddie.

"John?" I heard a voice say from within the isolation ward. "What are you doing here?"

When I looked over, I hardly recognised him. Only the voice was familiar.

In my shock, I took in the scene all in one go as it was laid out before me, my mind making no judgment.

Freddie's pith helmet was perched on the apex of a distinctive five-strutted stand, bolted to the footboard of his cot. All the cots on the ward had these strange-looking contraptions, some holding helmets like Freddie's, others with clothing. At first glance – before you realised there were too many struts and no cameras – they resembled tripods, as if the room had been set up for a photographer to capture men contemplating their own mortality.

The man in this bed didn't look much like the brother I had seen the year before, though he still sounded the same. All the other men in the ward stared up at me from their mattress lairs, watching the reunion play out.

"Freddie?" I finally managed to say to the gaunt man in the cot. "Christ… Is that really you?"

His dark hair was a mess of sweat and his eyes had sunk deep into their sockets. Typhoid did that; it sucked out all the moisture and turned men as dry as Farley's rusks.

"Who the bloody hell else do you think it is?" he said, which was the moment I definitely knew it was him.

When the nurses found out we were brothers, they re-jigged the placings and put me in the cot next to his.

He had already boarded in Durban, along with some others from his unit who had been injured. Because he was covered in blankets, I didn't even realise his right leg had been amputated below the knee until he told me later.

It was on that journey home that I saw just how much Freddie had changed since our school days; how he had become an 'everyman'. On one occasion, we were making our way slowly along the deck together when we came across a private, sitting with his head in his hands reliving some horror or other. Freddie bent down, took the cigarette he was smoking from his own mouth and wordlessly gave it to the man. Another time, I spotted him drinking with a group of senior officers in the communal area of the ward. Freddie was in the middle of telling a story or a joke, and though I couldn't hear much of what was being said, I could see him waving his arms in the air as he spoke. At the end he raised his voice and said: "How the hell do you think this got started?" which I presumed was a punchline because there was an instant almighty roar of laughter, and for a minute afterwards the men were slapping at their knees in hysterics and reaching over to pat Freddie's shoulder in acknowledgement.

All ranks liked him. You felt better for having been in his company.

The amalgamated experiences from his years of vagrancy and the year in the army had percolated down through his character in a most agreeable way, leaving him with a quiet solidity and wisdom which drew people in, like orbiting moons around a planet.

I found myself observing him from a distance, admiring him – my own brother – even wanting to be like him. I remember watching him leaning against the ship's rail as we were approaching Madeira to take on water – a wide smile, eyes closed and his chin raised – a sheer enjoyment of life itself. Minus a leg and weakened by typhoid, but it seemed an irrelevance to him.

What had changed? What was going on in that head of his?

I did a lot of thinking on that boat trip home and recalled the pivotal moment at school when he had left. Something very simple and powerful had happened in that chemistry lesson, and for years I had not properly understood it. His actions hadn't just been a fleeting rebellion; they represented something much more positive – a seismic shift in his world view from fear to fearlessness, a kind of faith if you like – a belief that all was well with the world and everything in it.

At school he had day-dreamt for years, reading adventure yarns and the *Boy's Own*, poring over books on other cultures and countries –

always the dreams. Then in a single moment during that chemistry lesson, he was finally set free. I had witnessed the very moment of transition; when Sadist had wanted to hurt him and Freddie had refused and held fast.

I think it is entirely possible that, had the benzene question not come up, Freddie might have drifted into a University course somewhere and then followed the usual route we all did, but instead he had been jolted out of that path. Most people read books and magazines and think to themselves: 'I *would love* to do that.' In a moment of clarity, as the class laughed and the master belittled him, Freddie had finally decided: 'Enough. *I'm going* to do that.'

The difference between the two outlooks is night and day. It is death and life.

Chapter Seven

Fremantle
September, 1900

I woke up on the beach at seven, my dreams of South Africa evaporating away in the morning sun, which had risen inland and was climbing into another clear blue sky.

Not wanting to go back to the hotel and disturb Rennie, I headed to Carlo's for some breakfast.

Despite my fatigue I felt buoyant; the same bleary eyed euphoria you get after nights on call – a feeling of having faced the unknown alone, and made it through. The sense of freedom always brought the simple pleasures of life sharply into focus; today it was the feel of the ocean swirling around my bare feet on the beach and the smell of Carlo's scalding coffee, the sounds of the world going about its new day. Most of all, there was the anticipation of a good rest, because once the excitement of the night had faded I knew that the sleep would be blowing in like a sea fog.

Just then, Rennie pushed his face up against the front window of the café, hands shading his eyes to cut out the glare.

He spotted me, waved and pushed open the door.

From his galley kitchen, Carlo held out my plate of breakfast: "Your bacon an' eggs, Dottore."

Hearing this, Rennie grabbed the plate and brought it over. He sat opposite me in the booth, picked up a fork and started eating.

"Be my guest," I said.

In Rennie's world everything was for sharing.

"What happened to you?" he said, talking with his mouth full. "I've been looking everywhere."

He reached over and took a gulp of my coffee before I could warn him. It was still too hot and he started panting and thumping his chest.

As I recounted my nocturnal exploits, he listened with his head cocked to one side. Whenever he got excited – for instance, when I told him how Dudley had chastised the guard – he would rub his hands together rapidly as if warming himself from the cold, and go slightly cross eyed at the same time. In neurological terminology you would call it an involuntary tic. Combined with the 'boule a zero' haircut, a casual observer might have been forgiven for thinking I was sitting opposite a madman.

At the end of my tale, I started feeling weary. Leaning forward slowly, I rested my head on the rim of the coffee mug and fell silent.

"Don't you want any of this?" I heard him say to me.

"I'm not hungry any more. You have it."

I listened to the scraping on the plate as he finished it and I stayed there in that position – head on cup – enjoying the heat on my forehead. Through the sound of hissing bacon on the grill came the distant laugh of a kookaburra.

I raised my head and looked over to my right.

A strange man with no hair was staring back at me from the next booth. It was only when I noticed the red ring on his forehead and the bloodshot eyes that I realised the wall was mirrored and the stranger was me.

At ten, Dudley picked us up and we boarded a steam locomotive travelling north to Perth. Crossing the Swan River Railway Bridge afforded us a grandstand view of the whole port – there was our steam ship, still berthed, her bright orange funnel distinct against the blue backdrop of the Indian Ocean. Beyond the harbour mouth, two immense concrete breakwaters reached out to sea like a giant claw.

Dudley pointed out of the train window.

"Two years ago all the shipping coming to the colony arrived at Albany in the south. Then they blasted out a limestone bar blocking the entrance to the Swan River and this became the main port… annoyed the black fellas no end."

"Why?"

"Well, traditionally, the northern side of the river was for men's business and the southern side was for women's business. And sometimes the men would cross the reef to go and see the women… for ceremonies and the like. Anyway, the black fellas warned the engineer not to break up the reef. Bloke called O'Connor, an engineering genius… he ignored them and went ahead and blasted it anyway."

Some miles off shore lay a strip of dark green on the horizon. I hadn't noticed it from aboard the ship, though we must have passed right by.

"Is that an island out there?"

"Yeah… Rottnest," Dudley said. "Ages ago, when the sea level was lower, the black fellas say the limestone bar was part of an old land bridge out to Rottnest. They say their ancestors could walk out to the island, and that ancient burial sites are out there. Perhaps O'Connor should have listened, because not long after he dynamited the bar, the local clans put a curse on him."

"Come come, Mister Dudley," Rennie said. "A curse? That's just mumbo jumbo… superstition and nonsense."

Dudley didn't look so sure. He paused and frowned, as if what he was about to say might be hard for us to understand.

"I heard they *sung* him… I wouldn't want that hanging over my head."

"Sung?" I said.

"The clans got together and chanted a song to send him bad energy. One bloke took an emu bone and pointed it at O'Connor's house as they did it. Just to make sure O'Connor got the message, they left the bone on his porch. When he found it the next morning, he knew he'd been sung."

"Did it work?"

Dudley shrugged.

"Dunno. He's alive, but he's certainly had some bad luck recently… Been accused of corruption by the papers and he's having a hell of a time with the water pipe. They say when you've been sung you get crook, turn morose and start to waste away. People who've been sung and had the bone pointed tend to die sooner rather than later…"

Rennie snorted with derision.

"You're telling me you believe in spells, Mr Dudley."

Dudley nodded slowly and thoughtfully.

"A few years ago I would've laughed along with you, Rev… but now, I'm not so sure. I've seen some of what the black fellas can do. Nothing about them surprises me anymore."

We got off the train at Perth Central Station and walked the short distance to the Manse on Hay Street; a decent sized brick building with an ornate trellised balcony, next door to the Wesleyan Church. Half a dozen children dressed in white aprons and long black socks were sitting on the steps outside and they all stopped talking when we approached.

Though they had never actually met in person, Rennie was greeted like an old friend by a moustachioed Minister at the front door – a tall blond man with clear blue piercing eyes, evidently certain of his destiny.

This then was the esteemed Reverend Rowe of whom I had heard so much. For nearly a decade he had been recruiting ministers for the goldfields; men who could build makeshift chapels in the bush with their own hands and who could cycle for miles in the heat to pursue their calling. Driven, single-minded individuals, as tough as the prospectors – they had even been known to hold their own in fist fights with the more aggressive elements of their congregations.

All this appealed to Rennie. "Behold, I send you forth as sheep in the midst of wolves," he had said on the voyage, rubbing his hands and going cross-eyed in anticipation of the task ahead.

As well as recruiting ministers, Rowe had also formed a nursing order called the 'Sisters of the People' – qualified nurses who felt called upon by God to help tackle the typhoid problem in the colony. The Wesleyans were caring for the whole human package, body and soul.

Dudley clapped Rowe's forearm in a firm double handshake, stirring up clouds of chalk dust.

The reason for the chalk was because the Manse doubled up as a school – the children outside were pupils having their break and Rowe was their teacher. He must have been one of those types who rubbed everything out with his sleeve. In the front room were several small hinged desks with holes for the inkwells and a blackboard covered with simple sums. One poor lad was still there, trying to work out the answers.

For several minutes Rennie and Rowe chatted bombastically, religious zeal radiating from every pore and filling the air around them as thickly as the chalk dust. Their sense of purpose was palpable – the same energy that 'men of the Empire' exuded, men like Grenfell and Egremont – all so sure of themselves.

To their evident delight, Rowe gave his class the afternoon off.

We left our bags at the Manse and strolled over to Perth Park – an expanse of grass and gum trees on a piece of high ground called 'Mount Eliza'. The grass was coarse and wiry, making English lawns seem prissy in comparison, and the trees were different too – sinuous gums which appeared to be shedding their skin. Large sections of bark hung down in great ragged sheets, exposing the raw salmon-pink surface underneath.

Dudley pointed out one tree with a large elliptical scar on its trunk.

"See that?" he said. "The bark's been deliberately cut. The blacks use the bark to make bowls – a coolamon they call it. Mix herbs in it. Stir it all around and sometimes make medicine…"

A familiar smell made me search for its source and soon I found it; a large brick brewery with a narrow chimney down on the foreshore. The smell of the hops took me back to the London Tideway and the brewery at Mortlake and the thought of English beer; a waft of nostalgia for home. Back in England, the nights would be drawing in by now – I could be drinking a pint of ale in the Blue Boar Club after work and warming my feet next to a roaring fire.

Later, we sat in the shade of an avenue of trees – 'Fraser Avenue' Rowe called it.

Couples and families were parading up and down the concourse, their parasols and straw boaters keeping off the sun. Superficially, they looked like the crowds at the Henley Royal Regatta but on closer scrutiny, the men were harder and the women more robust – not the 'society set' at all, but the flotsam and jetsam of colonial immigrants who had washed up on the shores of this isolated, sunbaked, continent.

A canon went off.

"That's the one pm time signal," Rowe said. "They fire it every day up at the observatory."

He pointed up the hill at a building.

"They're mapping the heavens in there, or cataloguing the stars, if you prefer," he said, addressing me specifically, as if he had already worked out my scientific leanings.

This started Rennie off: "'Canst thou bind the sweet influences of Pleiades, or loose the bands of Orion?'"

He was about to continue, when Rowe cut in, "'Knowest thou the ordinances of heaven? Canst thou set the dominion thereof in the earth?' Job: Chapter 38. Why my dear fellow," he said, patting Rennie on the shoulder, "in all our correspondence, I never would have guessed what an expert you are in the scriptures."

Rennie reddened, though whether it was with pride or humiliation I couldn't tell.

To see my friend meet his biblical match was quite something. I caught Dudley's eye and together we shared the silent joke.

But Rennie wasn't giving up and the two Wesleyans were soon embroiled in another discussion, this time concerning one of the red flowers lying on the ground.

"Sicut lilium," Rennie said, peering at it closely.

"Like a lily of the field," Rowe said, translating the Latin. "From the Sermon on the Mount… and by the way, Rennie, it isn't a lily at all, it's from a red flowering gum tree, a completely different taxonomical category – I see your botany needs some work."

"If you don't mind, gents," I said, "I'm going to go and take a closer look at the observatory."

Rowe waved me away.

"Not at all, Doctor. I'll keep Rennie here — teach him something about the Australian flora and fauna."

"Hold on there, Doc," Dudley said, jumping up. "I'm joining you."

From the top of the observatory tower, we were rewarded with a magnificent view of the coastal plain to the east. Dudley pointed out the features to me: the meandering Swan River, the surrounding city and the distant ridge of high ground.

"Want to thank you for what you did last night, Doc," he said. "Not many people would have got out of their bed like that."

"It was no problem helping your friend; like I said at the time, I was glad to do it."

"You're pretty mean with a piece of catgut, that's for sure."

"Plenty of practice… In Harley Street I was so bored I even sewed new elbow patches onto my tweed jacket."

Dudley slapped the hand rail and laughed. "Good one, Doc."

I managed a smile. It was the truth.

"He was lucky to survive a knife attack," I said.

"Oh, don't worry about Eugene. He can take care of himself."

"You said he had saved your skin in the past — what did he do?"

Dudley was leaning on the handrail now with his eyes on the horizon.

"A few months back we were stuck out in the bush on a mine inspection trip… just me and him. Got lost in a dust storm and ran out of water. I thought we were gonners. Not Eugene. He found water in the rocks as easily as turning on a tap."

"You respect him," I said, stating the obvious.

"Sure do. Got to know him as we waited out the storm. We got talking. He's as religious as those Wesleyans you know, just in a different way. With the black fellas, it's the land — it means everything to them. Most of what you see is special for them… See the Darling ranges over there? They say a giant snake died there way back in the mists of time and turned into the hills."

"A giant snake?" I said, as if my repeating it would confirm the sheer lunacy of the statement.

I wondered whose viewpoint was the craziest – men thinking that a giant snake had created a ridge of hills, or men who thought the entire planet and its contents had been created in seven days.

"He'll want to pay you back you know," Dudley said. "It's the Aboriginal way – every gift is repaid in kind."

My musings on Crusoe and Man Friday came back to me.

"You're talking about reciprocity," I said.

"That's a long word, Doc. I tend to see it more as: if you scratch my back, I'll scratch yours."

"That's a lot of words, Dudley, when one would do."

He turned his head to look at me, surprised I was competing with him in the banter. He started smiling and nodding in agreement.

"Yeah, you know what, you're right…I suppose reciprocity about sums it up."

Back at the Manse, we all rolled up our sleeves to prepare dinner. Dudley chopped the vegetables and I scrubbed potatoes. Rowe had a secret Irish recipe for gravy and took care of that. Rennie kept an eye on the pork which was pot-roasting over the kitchen fire. It was a fine evening and we sat out on the veranda to dine.

"Shall we say grace?" Rowe said, clasping his hands in prayer.

It wasn't really a question; you couldn't have said, 'no, let's not'.

Everyone automatically bowed their heads and closed their eyes.

"For these and all thy blessings, Lord, we thank thee. Amen."

I kept one eye open, scanning the penitent – an old habit dating back to my childhood.

Whenever my grandfather had said grace, my father would cock an eye open. I only knew this because Freddie and I would be peeking too. And when he saw us, my father would give us a mischievous grin, the way a devil might in the middle of a prayer. Remembering it now made me feel close to my father. He wasn't a devil of course, and in a way, had his own belief system. He would have called these men 'Godbotherers'. 'I don't need to do any of that Church stuff with all those Godbotherers on a Sunday,' he used to say. 'Because all I ever do is help others – all week… And if there's a God, he knows it.'

"Amen," the gathering said in unison.

Rennie tucked in with characteristic gusto: "What a blessing!"

"Better than tinned dog," I said.

My comment drew a roar of laughter and the meal passed in good spirits.

Before long the talk had turned from the excellent food to the subject of the gold rush.

Rowe delivered his opinion on the motives of the men who had flocked to the colony in the last decade: "Mammon," he said. "They seek gold. It's a fever as violent as that of the typhoid. They jettison their existences, leave their families and they flock here, all hoping to find their fortune."

He looked at me.

"Hoping to find something out here, Doctor? I suspect not gold – well, not the sort you can dig out of the ground, anyway. Perhaps you are running from something? Seeking something?"

I smiled at his insight. I had done just that – run away.

"A good question, Reverend…"

"And?"

I wasn't going to be able to evade this.

"I suppose that I am seeking something… some kind of, well… peace, I suppose."

Everyone at the table was quiet now.

"I lost my brother," I said, and didn't offer any more explanation.

Hopefully, that would shut him up.

Rowe stared at me, like he was reading me – peeling away the few feeble layers of protection I had, and seeing my pain raw. When he spoke, his words were tender and heartfelt.

"Blessed are they that mourn," he said, "for they shall be comforted."

Rennie reached across and put his hand on my shoulder.

"Amen to that," he said.

My mind was drifting. I thought of the astonishment at the Manor when I had told my colleagues I was off to Australia. "What on earth has got into you, JH?" It was a shock for them to see someone spurn all they held dear – and on a whim. They hadn't concerned themselves about it for too long though; within a week they had already recruited the next non-catholic, non-homosexual, non-bankrupt doctor.

For most of my life the grim realities of existence had been hidden from me. Then I had seen the worst at the Spitz Kop and lost Freddie. My old life in London had felt as much a mountain of shit as the Kak Kop had been, and that's why I had been impelled to get out.

At least out here I was surrounded by men who had done the same thing, kindred spirits to whom I need give no explanation or apology.

I heard my name mentioned.

Rowe was talking again: "Keeping busy certainly helps… and I'm sure Doctor Hunston will be a busy chap in the colony. I hear you've already found something for him to do, Tom…"

"That's right," Dudley said, finding his voice for the first time in the meal. "His first patient was a black fella; the doc here stitched him up in no time."

Rowe pushed away his empty plate.

"An interesting people," he said. "The Aboriginals, I mean… much misunderstood and maligned. Do you know they have no words for the concept of possession, as in ownership – one of the issues that most torments modern man? And they also have a very acute notion of what we might call symmetry or evenness. I once witnessed an anthropological test in which an Aboriginal tribal man was shown nine evenly spaced matches. One match was removed from each end of the row, so seven were left and the Aboriginal was asked to comment – he said there was no difference. This was repeated again and again until there were only three matches left. Each time, he said the same thing

– that there was no difference. Then the nine matches were re-laid and one taken away from the right hand side only. This time he said: 'Everything is different, the balance is gone.'"

Rennie was frowning now, like Rowe's pupil puzzling over the sum on the blackboard.

Dudley pulled out a box of matches and put five matches into two separate groups in front of me on the table.

"I know about those experiments too," he was saying as he lined up the matches. "What do you see, Doc?"

I studied the arrangement, wondering if there was a catch to the question.

"I see a group of three and a group of two."

Rennie and Rowe were leaning over to see and they both nodded, agreeing with my simple observation.

"Yeah, that's what the black fella said too."

Then Dudley moved one of the matches over.

"Now what do you see?"

"Now I see group of two and a group of three."

Dudley laughed.

"That's exactly what I thought… You know what the black fella said?"

"No idea."

"Get your head round this. He said there were two groups of two, two groups of three and a three-making match." Dudley held up the one he had moved like a tiny magic wand. "A three making match," he said again.

Slowly I began to see it, like a photograph appearing in the developing room. The Aboriginal had taken the past into account – had viewed the matches as unbounded by time. He had seen the before and the after and merged them into one picture. Not only that, he had allotted a potential to the moved match – as if it had a special power. The way he saw things made my interpretation seem static and one dimensional.

"A three-making match," Rennie said, laughing and going cross-eyed. "Oh, I like that… I like that very much indeed."

That night I couldn't sleep. I lay awake and thought about O'Connor, the Engineer who had been 'sung', and how he must have felt on finding the bone on his porch, knowing he'd been cursed.

I felt cursed too.

Not by the Aboriginals, but by my involvement in the Boer War. Everything since Bloemfontein had been bad for me. It was as if the Boers had 'sung' me and pointed the bleached bones of their fallen comrades in my direction. I had experienced the misery of typhoid, lost all my enthusiasm and thrown away my burgeoning career. Worst of all, I had lost my beloved brother.

Chapter Eight

The Royal Victoria Military Hospital, Netley, Southampton
May, 1900

The hospital ship arrived back from South Africa on 15th May 1900 and an ambulance train took us the short journey from the docks to the hospital at Netley.

Built in the late 1850s, the hospital was the biggest in the world, its central corridor running for a quarter of a mile and our ward just one of one hundred and thirty-eight others.

The architect must have had the British class structure in his mind when designing it because the building was divided into 'us' and 'them'. The centre section, C Block, was for the officers and was the most ornately built. All the other ranks were restricted to the wings – A and B blocks – housing the medical and surgical wards respectively, each block essentially its own separate hospital with separate kitchens, dining rooms and offices.

There was an asylum too – D block – hidden away from the main building in the woods. People didn't mention it much and if they did, the talk was muted because the patients in there were the ones who had lost their minds. The doctors called it 'disordered action of the heart' or 'rheumatism', but they were basically men who had seen too much, and everyone knew it.

Officially, the complex was called the Royal Victoria Military Hospital. To the locals it was known as 'Netley' because of the nearest village, but to the patients it was known simply as 'Spike Island'. The nickname perplexed me; it wasn't an island and no one seemed to know exactly where the name 'Spike' had come from either. It may have been named after the thorny gorse that grew thereabouts, or possibly the spike-shaped piece of land the hospital was built upon, sandwiched as it was between the Itchen and Hamble Rivers. But I liked Freddie's explanation the best – he told me that before the hospital was built, convicts awaiting transportation to Australia were kept here, shackled to a big spike in the ground.

Our arrival coincided with an intense flurry of activity because the Empress, Queen Victoria herself, was due to visit the very next day. Freddie and I spent the afternoon sitting on wicker chairs in the spacious corridor outside our ward, watching as a small army of florists and their assistants filled the hospital with ferns and aspidistras.

She came by locomotive on the same branch line we had used the day before. Dressed in black crêpe de Chine and attended by her turbaned Indian secretary, the diminutive and elderly Empress was wheeled from patient to patient in her bath chair.

Some of the lads from the Royal Lancasters were there in bath chairs too, amputated limbs tastefully covered by rough woollen blankets, their eyes on a level with their ruler as she pinned on their medals. What could not be discretely hidden away were their thousand-yard stares, and looks of permanent astonishment, as if they were surprised to be alive at all.

They were being awarded Queen's South Africa Medals, the central orange stripe on the ribbon standing out vividly against the faded blue cotton of their hospital undress.

In January, they had all been at the battle of Spion Kop.

Freddie's Regiment – the Second Middlesex, or 'Die Hards' – had been there too and he had told me snippets during the journey back to England.

In the early hours of January 24th, the Lancasters had climbed the Kop, hoping to get the high ground, but when the morning mist lifted it became clear they had made a disastrous error – the Boers were occupying a higher ridge, looking straight down onto their position. All day long the British were shelled by the Boers' Maxim-Nordenfeld gun, a terrible weapon. With characteristic dry wit the British called it the 'pom pom', an allusion to the noise it made.

In the early afternoon, Freddie's regiment had been sent up as reinforcements. He and his men had managed to repel some advancing Boers before the shelling had forced them to take cover. "It was a patch of scrub no bigger than a parade ground," Freddie said. "And all you could do was curl up in the main trench like a child, the way we used to when playing hide-and-seek. Jesus Christ, it's hell of a thing, shellfire… Every few seconds another one would come down and explode, the noise and the dirt and debris violent enough to make you want to shit yourself. There were those senior officers who still thought they were immortal, working under some gentleman's code which forbade their taking cover under fire. They didn't stand a chance. I saw a man staggering for two or three steps, without his head, decapitated by a shell fragment… Another one killed four men crouched in the trench together. Their clothes were smouldering afterwards… bloody smouldering, like the end of a bonfire. We lost forty-two men from our regiment that day."

We had all been made to line up for the Queen and Freddie had insisted on standing, despite his amputation. As instructed we avoided eye contact, focusing instead on an imaginary spot on the floor.

When she reached Freddie, she spoke sharply to her assistant:

"The medal, Munshi."

The turbaned man handed her a medal and Freddie bowed uncomfortably low so she could pin the decoration onto his breast.

"Well done, young man," I heard her say.

It was a Queen's South Africa Medal like the others.

A military man read aloud from a piece of paper, speaking in low and respectful tones:

"Second Lieutenant Hunston from the 2nd Middlesex Regiment was involved in a fixed bayonet charge at Spion Kop, Your Majesty, helping to recover a lost trench."

The Queen looked at Freddie.

"How did you encourage your men?"

"I yelled out: 'COME ON DIE HARDS', Your Majesty. It's our regiment's nickname…"

"Yes, the Battle of Albuera in 1811, I believe… during the Napoleonic Wars. One of your predecessors was surrounded and he told his men to hold their position by saying: 'Die hard, 57th, die hard!'."

"Why that's right, Your Majesty. You certainly know your history."

"Yes, indeed. Well, I'm impressed you thought to use a similar call to inspire your men."

"Thank you, Your Majesty… although I only did so because my captain was yelling it at me… and the yelling was simply making its way down the ranks. It's how things get done in the Army…"

For the briefest moment there was a flicker of a smile.

"Quite so…quite so…" she said.

After the Queen's procession had moved on and the invalids had slowly shuffled or wheeled themselves back to their wards, I found a newspaper clipping on the floor. It was an article from *The Morning Post*, an eyewitness account by a journalist who had been at Spion Kop:

'…*corpses lay here and there. Many of the wounds were of a horrible nature. The splinters and fragments of the shell had torn and mutilated in the most ghastly manner. I passed about two hundred while I was climbing up. There was, moreover, a steady leakage of unwounded men of all corps. Some of these cursed and swore. Others were utterly exhausted and fell on the hillside in stupor. Others again seemed drunk, though they had had no liquor. Scores were sleeping heavily. Fighting was still proceeding, and stray bullets struck all over the ground, while the Maxim shell guns scourged the flanks of the hill and the sheltering infantry at regular intervals of a minute.*'

I tore up the piece of paper and sprinkled the pieces onto the soil underneath one of the aspidistras. Perhaps one of the lads from the Royal Lancasters had dropped it. Men with missing legs and blank stares didn't need reminding of such things. And I expect Freddie didn't either.

War forced people to extremes; in South Africa, soldiers had swallowed half penny coins to get out of the firing line. At the Spitz Kop I had assisted a military surgeon during an operation, using an instrument called the 'coin catcher', a long metal probe with a hook on the end. He had plunged it down the soldier's throat and swept it from side to side in search of the coin. After watching him rummage around fruitlessly for several minutes and then accidentally perforate the soldier's stomach, I decided I would prefer a quick end courtesy of a Boer bullet rather than risk a meeting with that deadly instrument.

When Freddie had told me about Spion Kop, I asked if any of it had got to him, and what he came out with was one of Crosbie's Latin sayings: "Memento mori," which meant: *remember you will die*.

I began to understand.

In the war and after it, Freddie had death in his mind at all times, acutely conscious of life's precariousness. Not frightened of death, just aware of it. I saw that trait whenever he talked to anyone now, how he went to the nub of things, however brief the exchange. He wanted to know the truth. Life could be short, so there was no point in wasting time – every conversation was entered into as if it might be his last, with total commitment. This was part of the reason people were drawn to him – they detected this aura and saw he wasn't hiding anything beneath some veneer. Freddie's fearlessness gave them strength.

I had seen hints of this even when we were much younger. At school he had dared climb the outside of the library, a building made with blocks of stone allowing hand and footholds for fifty feet. The so-called 'bookstack' was an unofficial school tradition dating back hundreds of years. Spectating, I had become unnerved the higher he had gone: "Come down Freddie," I had said, "...come down now." But he had continued all the way up, as relaxed as if he were only a few feet above ground. That was when I realised we were different – he was tougher, braver, more dangerous, and while we both knew of the 'what ifs', I was afraid, whereas he was not.

On the afternoon of the Queen's visit, Freddie and I decamped to the deserted chapel where the exhortation: *'be ye doers of the word, not hearers only'* was carved into the wooden pulpit.

In the filtered light from the stained glass windows, I studied the medal and the two clasps pinned to the ribbon:

RELIEF OF LADYSMITH
NATAL

"How come there's not a clasp saying 'Spion Kop'?"

"Because we lost," Freddie said. "Anyway, it's included in the Relief of Ladysmith, which was a win."

He flipped open his tobacco tin

"You can't smoke in here," I said.

"Why not?"

"It's a bloody chapel."

He sighed and shut the tin again.

"If it still contained chocolate you wouldn't be allowed to eat it in here either," I said.

There was I, still fearful of petty rules, and there was Freddie, ready to bend them.

"I wish I had some of that chocolate left," he said, "but I gave it to an Indian from the volunteer ambulance corps."

"You gave away your chocolate?"

To get chocolate out of my brother was practically a miracle.

"He deserved some. Those Indians... they were tough."

Freddie lay down on the pew, stretching himself out with his hands behind his head and staring straight up at the high chapel ceiling.

"It was the morning after the battle," he said, "Thursday 25th... My men had left me by the Tugela River under the shade of a Mimosa tree and another group of stretcher bearers came and took over. Indian carriers. They had a much better stretcher than the one I'd come down the hill on, with a canvas hood to keep the sun off. Anyway, while we were resting at a dressing station, I saw one of them sit down to eat an Army regulation biscuit. Those bloody things taste like compacted dirt…"

"Didn't he have any of his own chocolate?"

"No. Indian volunteers weren't eligible for chocolate. Amazing isn't it? Medals – yes, chocolate – no. I'd been saving it up until then, but I gave my bar to him right there and then… Felt he'd more than earned it… He said he'd been in the firing line for a day, helping carry the wounded over the river on the pontoon bridge to the Field Hospital at Spearman's Farm."

"He spoke English then?"

"Spoke it well. He was a lawyer who had been living in Natal for several years. He said something that stayed with me. Watching the injured men shuffling down the track, he shook his head and said, 'You know my friend, *non-violence* would be a much better way to sort out differences.' I think he had a fair point."

I gave Freddie his medal back.

"I always wondered what made you join up," I said.

He sighed and thought about this for a few seconds.

"Self respect, I suppose… And some money. That girl I told you about in New Zealand – I wanted to prove myself to her." He tapped his stump against the edge of the pew. "And now look…some bloody man."

"If she's the right girl, that won't make any difference," I said.

"I hope so, John… I hope so."

I was about to ask him more – whether he might go back out there to her – when he made a sudden snort of harsh, sour sounding laughter.

He was looking at his medal and rubbing the outer edge with his thumb, the part where 'Victoria Regina et Imperiatrix' was engraved.

"What's funny?"

"That a bullet finally got me, and not a shell."

"What's funny about that?"

"Nothing very much, I suppose."

I looked over at Freddie, bathed in the ethereal light of the chapel. He was still lying on his back on the pew. It was the first time he had ever spoken about being shot.

"Spion bloody Kop," he said. "Fuck… I can't forget the sound that bullet made – Shhhhiiiieeeeuuww! Like a sudden bicycle tyre puncture. Didn't feel any pain at first, just crawled away and lay wedged under a rock barely feeling anything. There was no exit wound, so I guessed the shot had been fired from long range… Maybe a thousand yards, made by a sharpshooter – no closer, or else the bullet would have gone straight through."

My ballistics knowledge was poor.

"Really? They go right through at that distance?"

"A bullet from a Mauser fired from 5 yards away travels five feet into a log of pine wood, so I imagine one coming from the Boers fifty yards away wouldn't have hung around… The only thing I wanted to do was be somewhere on my own and stay out of the way, like a wounded animal. I lay there for an hour or so, the shells still dropping around me. It was only a shot to my calf but the wound started giving me gyp and the bleeding wouldn't stop. I made a tourniquet out of my puttee but the blood still kept dripping onto the ground…clotting there like claret jelly."

"Jesus Freddie…you might have bled out."

"Might have," he said, "but I didn't. Felt a thirst like I'd never felt before though. I had to go crawling around, checking dead men's water bottles. Eventually, two of my unit carried me down the Kop on a stretcher they had made from two rifles and some slings. By then the British had been given the order to retreat and everyone was going back down – the Kop was lost. An X-ray in the field hospital confirmed the bullet was still there. The surgeon used these tweezers to reach it. Whenever they touched the bullet a bell would ring. Or least I assume that's what he did, I don't really know, I was completely knocked out with chloroform."

"If you were anaesthetised, how do you know?"

"Because I saw what he did to the man before me. The operation tent had its flaps wide open you see, and us injured waiting our turn on the ground outside could see what was going on. Six hundred admissions that day... A fraught session for the surgeon. It was basic stuff – a table at the centre of the tent between the two poles, some water buckets, some instruments and dressings laid out on field panniers, but not much else. I remember the grass floor being covered in blood, and the sweating surgeon working in shirt sleeves and riding breeches probing away with his strange bell-ringing tweezers and pulling out bullets."

I knew this piece of apparatus.

Freddie was describing 'Longmore's bullet retractors', part of the standard army box of surgical instruments. Green and purple electrical flex connections ran from the handles of the forceps to an amp meter and when the tips made contact with any metallic object, the connection completed the circuit, swinging the needle on the dial. Just to make sure the surgeon knew he had it, a bell would sound too.

"Anyway, before I was put to sleep the surgeon held up my X-ray and said the reason the bullet hadn't passed through cleanly was because it had ricocheted off my shin bone – shattering it – his exact words were: 'a severe comminuted fracture of the upper tibia'. The bone fragments, together with the bullet, had nicked an artery and that was why I had bled so much. He was a decent enough fellow – introduced himself even: Mister Treves. I appreciated the fact that he took the trouble to explain what he was going to have to do. He said some of the tissue in my foot had already died from the disruption to the blood supply...and not wanting to risk the chance of gangrene, he was going to amputate straight away..."

Freddie's voice was steady and without emotion.

"Not the best news to have," I said.

"No... though it could've been worse, I suppose. There was one poor chap whose face had been half shot away and who was having to write everything down in a notebook to communicate. He even wrote 'did we win?', and no-one had the heart to tell him we hadn't."

Freddie sat up again on the pew.

"So that was the end of the leg," he said. "When I woke up they had my bullet in a metal tray and asked if I wanted to keep it."

"Did you?"

"No. I didn't need reminding, but seeing it did prove one thing – that it had been a clean Mauser round, and not a dum dum or one tipped with poison. Rumours had been going round about that kind of thing, you see, and I was relieved to know it had been a 'fair' shot, so to speak, that losing the leg was just the result of an unfortunate bullet trajectory."

"God, Freddie," I said, "I suppose that's one way of looking at it."

"They wanted to keep me in the same place to give the stump time to heal, to get my strength back from the blood loss. Luckily there was no infection and things went well. In early February, the hospital was moved back to the railhead at Chievely. Then, just when I seemed to be doing all right, I came down with the fever. To keep me isolated they put me in an abandoned farmhouse near the hospital that had once been under Boer control. Right behind my bed, scrawled all over the wall, were the words: 'Enjoy Mauser country Boys'."

"That must've rankled…"

"Showed a good sense of humour I thought – so I wrote a reply underneath in capital letters: 'NO FEAR, BOERS, NO FEAR'."

I laughed at his small act of defiance.

That was Freddie all right, a leg lost and fever ravaged – but still the same person who had climbed the bookstack back at school.

"I managed to get through it, but it was a close run thing as I'm sure you can empathise. Eventually they put me on the hospital train to Durban. Well…you know the rest…"

The days passed slowly at Spike Island.

Throughout May, more sick and injured soldiers arrived. That month the typhoid incidence peaked in Bloemfontein, higher even than in April. I felt sorry for the poor MOs still out there.

Freddie and I would sit out on the pier, filling our lungs with ozone, feeding the seagulls and playing cards with the other patients. Time out on the pier meant time away from the oppressive hospital building.

A lot of the men just sat in silence, staring out at the water. It wasn't possible to tell if they were compulsively replaying battle scenes in their heads, or succeeding in keeping the images at bay. And though we were from different army units, had different ranks and came from different parts of the country, I felt there was one connection we all shared – we were all trying to work out why we weren't the same men we had been before the war.

When the hospital had been built, the original intention was for returning injured soldiers to disembark at the pier, but for some reason it was too short for transport ships, which could not berth in the shallows. So instead, ships passed us by, moving slowly up river towards the Southampton docks, and each arrival would prompt some of our card-playing group to guess at how many soldiers were aboard, and what proportion of those had caught typhoid fever. We made bets and found out the correct answers from the ships' rosters later.

They said the same engineer who had built our pier had also designed the West Pier in Brighton.

I could not think of a greater contrast between the two structures – one pier full of people squealing loudly with the excitement of the funfair and the other populated by men screaming silently in their heads.

It never occurred to us to swim, not even on sunny days; the waters were always cold and the currents too dangerous. Early one morning during our stay, a soldier had jumped in and not resurfaced. They wrote: 'ACCIDENTALLY DROWNED IN SOUTHAMPTON WATER' on his gravestone, though no-one really believed it.

On the morning ward round of 31st May they cleared Freddie for discharge.

Sitting out on the pier that day, he was a little despondent, studying his medal and wondering what to do next. He liked to wear it all the time, pinned to his hospital undress. Of course I wasn't going to say it, but I sometimes wondered if he thought it had all been worth it for the paltry reward of a small medal.

I remember him coughing too – a deep seated, persistent cough which had started up before that morning's ward round, though the medical team had been happy to sign him off.

For an hour he had been moping around like this, when from out of nowhere, his whole demeanour changed and he said to himself out loud:

"I can't believe I'd forgotten…"

"What is it now?"

"I've just remembered when our Regiment arrived in South Africa."

"And?"

"Before we got to Durban, we stopped in at Cape Town. It was Christmas day and they allowed us off the ship for a few hours. I met some Australian soldiers on the docks. They had already been there a week or so…"

"So?"

"Well, we fraternised… you know… shared a few drinks, and their senior officer went on and on about the gold there was to be had out in the Western Australia Colony… said he had come from there… and that with a bit of graft and luck, you could make a bloody fortune. I remember making a mental note to get out there after the war was over, and in all the chaos that happened after, I completely forgot."

I held my breath. I could feel the plan locking itself into Freddie's brain with typical spontaneity – one of his life choices being made in a matter of seconds. This didn't mean the decision was any less certain than if he had ruminated on it for a month, if anything it was probably the other way round – they were set instantly and irreversibly, like quick drying concrete. It was a dangerous, trigger-happy way of going about things, but attractive at the same time. Frantically I was trying to think of something to say to change his mind.

"Freddie…"

The resolve in his features told me I was already too late.

"Yes!" he said, clapping his hands together in delight, "that's what we'll do."

"We?"

"As a team we'll be formidable. It'll be the old double scull team again... Kekule... the Snake rings!"

"What about my job in Harley Street?"

"What about it? You can always come back... They'll understand. They let you go to war, didn't they?"

"I don't know, Freddie."

"I need you, John. I need your help. Don't let me down."

He tapped his prosthesis to make his point.

"You don't know what it's like losing a leg," he said. "I feel like half a bloody man. I need you, brother. If I can go back to New Zealand for that girl a rich man, I'll be set."

He was laying it on pretty thick.

"I'll think about it," I said.

Nothing on earth was going to drag me out to another typhoid-ridden hell-hole in the name of gold.

Chapter Nine

I was sitting on Rowe's balcony smoking Freddie's tobacco when a voice interrupted my daydreaming.

"Good morning, Doctor."

Rowe was standing there holding two cups of coffee.

My memories of Spike Island drifted away into the blue sky, along with the wisps of smoke from my cigarette.

"Morning, Reverend."

He handed me one of the coffees and sat down.

"Sleep well?"

"Yes, very well, thank you."

Perhaps Rowe could see the lie in my haggard features, because he smiled knowingly into his cup.

"So," he said, "I suppose you'll begin work as soon as you get to Kalgoorlie?"

"Yes, I expect so."

"Do you know which hospital you'll be working at?"

I recalled what Egremont's secretary had told me back in London. "The St John of God."

"Ah… the Catholic hospital," he said, "built a few years ago by Bishop Gibney – my opposite number, so to speak. He established a group of nursing nuns called the 'Sisters of St. John of God', much like my 'Sisters of the People'."

Sisters of St John of God – it was quite a mouthful. I pictured the looks on my old colleagues' faces if one of the 'Sisters' had applied for a job at the Manor: *Catholic and a woman? Good God, JH!*

Perth Central station was heaving with people and, judging by the languages and accents on display, representatives from every nation in Europe had been lured out here by the prospect of wealth. And in amongst the mix were Orientals in black cotton smocks and men in turbans whose languages were entirely unfamiliar.

A large sign hung from the station ceiling: *'YILGARN LINE'*.

"Do you see it, John?" I heard Rennie saying.

"See what, Sean?" I looked around. "See what?" I said again.

"The look in their eyes. They're all hoping to make their fortune. It's like Rowe was saying last night – about mammon…"

A station guard's shrill whistle rang out and cut him off.

"'No man can serve two masters… Ye cannot serve God and mammon.' Matthew: Chapter six."

It wasn't quite how I would have put it, but Rennie had a point; there was indeed a generic look of expectancy on the faces in the crowd, an insane and irrational optimism which made me feel jaded.

"Everyone's heading for the goldfields," Dudley said, having to almost shout to be heard.

At last we boarded the train and found an empty cabin, a cocoon from the din outside.

"First Class, gents," Dudley said. "All on the company."

Rennie looked uncomfortable. "I don't want the Egremont Company to feel they have to pamper me" he said. "I'm not even part of the company… You've been far too generous already. I'll be fine in second class."

Dudley rolled his eyes.

"Let me guess… you're about to tell me how the meek shall inherit the earth."

"And blessed are they," Rennie said.

Without another word, he opened the door leading to second class and stepped through. Before he shut the door behind him, I glimpsed the loud, smoke-filled carriage full of the rowdy chatter of a hundred miners.

Dudley rubbed at the neuralgia in his temple and fixed his eye on me.

"How about you, Engels? Want to rough it with comrade Marx?"

"No, first is fine."

Soon we were out of the city and trundling over the coastal plain. Dudley played a game of patience on the pull-down table and whistled a ballad to himself as he did so.

I closed my eyes and focused on the sound of the locomotive on the tracks, a voice in my head whispering in time with the rhythm – 'wait and hope, wait and hope, wait and hope'.

****

Spike Island
1st June, 1900

I lay there listening to the sounds of the hospital as it came to life – the creaks of the heating pipes for the morning baths, the rattle of a distant trolley being pushed down the corridor, the gossip of the nursing staff around the ward station.

"Hey, wake up," I said.

Freddie didn't stir.

I threw my pillow at him. "*Hey*... didn't you hear?"

Something wasn't right – he was too still.

I sprung out of bed.

His skin was cold to the touch and, in that second, before everything went to shit, one lucid thought entered my head.

It was this: one possible future had been eradicated and replaced by another. I felt I had been in a train carriage trundling along a mainline and then the points had been switched; now I was hurtling down a branch line into the unknown. Nothing would ever be the same again.

The sensation was one of severe disappointment, acute in nature, but when boiled down, just that – disappointment. Disappointment at his non-existent future and disappointment at my future without him in it. Sitting there on the edge of Freddie's bed, staring at him, I felt as though my soul was sinking, down through to the ground floor, then down through the foundations of the hospital, all the way down into the deepest pit in the bowels of the earth, where the very worst disappointments lived.

That was the first second. After that, the actual grief started.

A short while later they took him away, stripping the sheets and the pillowcases and leaving a bare mattress and pillows.

I could not stop staring at the emptiness that had been Freddie's space.

Pale with shock, and red-eyed, I finally summoned up the courage to approach the nursing station. They were quiet and subdued.

When I spoke to them, my voice came out strange and cracked.

"Didn't the nurse checking on him last night notice any deterioration? She must have noticed something."

They looked at one another in confusion.

"Doctor Hunston, you must be mistaken," the ward sister said. "No nurses were on duty last night, only a male assistant ward officer."

"But I saw a nurse…" I pointed to the foot of Freddie's bed. "And she was standing *right there*."

I was beginning to sound hysterical.

The nurse had been there in the night, I wasn't going mad.

It was the cold that had woken me in the small hours. I was shivering and could see my own breath. My clothes were still damp from having been out in the rain on our nocturnal pier trip, but it wasn't just that making me cold, the temperature in the ward had dropped too. And there was this peculiar flowery smell which I could not place. That was when I had seen her. I was drawing up my blanket when I noticed a woman's figure standing very still and monochrome in the dark. She was looking down at Freddie, her expression blank and sad. With the smidgeon of moonlight in the room I could just make out her features and the outline of her nurse's uniform. I had even whispered, "How is he, Sister?" but she had not responded. Instead, she turned away soundlessly and left. I assumed she had not heard and I soon drifted back to sleep, reassured that at least the staff were monitoring Freddie closely.

Everyone was avoiding my eye. The ward sister stood up, put her hand on my shoulder and led me over to a table in the centre of the ward where she sat me down.

"It's normal for you to be upset... You must have dreamt it or mistaken the nurse for the male ward officer."

I shook my head.

"No... I saw a woman."

"I'll make you a cup of tea," she said.

She disappeared off into the small kitchenette and I buried my head in my hands and waited. Yes, how British; a cup of tea would sort it out.

"Did you see her uniform?" a voice said.

I looked up to see one of the older nurses standing there.

"What?"

"Her uniform... what did it look like?"

I had the briefest image of the nurse leaving the ward in the night.

"It was a lot longer than yours... the hem went right down to the ankles, almost to the floor."

The nurse nodded to herself, her expression grim.

"Do you remember anything else?"

"Well, just that the ward was cold... colder than usual, and that she was looking at my brother."

I pointed over to his stripped and empty bed.

"She was standing right there. And there was this strange..."

"What? What else?"

"Well... a strange smell..."

"Lavender?"

"Yes, exactly right... lavender. That's what it was. Do you know the name of the nurse? I would like to speak to her..."

"You won't be able to."

"Why not?"

"She's dead."

"What? Has there been some sort of accident today?"

The nurse shook her head.

"You don't understand… not today. Forty years ago."

I wasn't getting it.

"What on earth are you saying?"

"You saw the hospital ghost… the Grey Lady."

"Oh come on," I said, angry now. "The last thing I need to hear is your superstitious claptrap."

The nurse ignored my insult.

"It's true I tell you… I've seen her too. You didn't imagine it. She was a nurse in the early days of the hospital. She jumped off the roof after accidentally killing a patient with an overdose."

"You're saying that last night I saw someone who died years ago?"

She kept her eyes on mine, her expression deadly serious.

I shook my head. "No," I said.

"I'm very sorry, Doctor… I didn't want to upset you. I just wanted you to know that you weren't hallucinating. Believe what you want, but I've worked here for twenty years and I've seen her a dozen times. I've smelt her lavender perfume. She turns the room cold and the patient she checks on dies the next day. They *always* die the next day, without fail."

The sister came back out of the kitchen with my tea and the nurse who had been talking to me scurried off.

I sipped the hot drink, going through the night's events again in my head. As I relived the scene, my skin turned to goose bumps, and despite everything, despite the fact that I was a man of science, I started believing what the old nurse had said.

I spent some of that day in 'Skull Alley', to escape the well-meant enquiries and looks of pity from the other patients on my ward.

Skull Alley was in the grand entrance to C block and consisted of glass cabinets containing dozens of human skulls, the descriptions of their origins neatly written on yellowing cards. Aboriginals from Australia, Maori warriors from New Zealand, Tribesmen from South Africa; it was a grim collection, serving as a warning to the rest of the world.

As I sat there, a professor from the Army Medical School arrived with his class and started to lecture them right there in front of the display: "We are here today to study the skull shapes of the 'inferior races'," he said, sounding as if he was giving a sermon in church.

His cohort of students stood in rapt attention, wide-eyed and adoring. I had been like them once, believing the rubbish they had spouted at medical school in the classes on race.

Then the professor unlocked one of the cabinets with a key and lifted out one of the specimens, holding it like a modern day Hamlet.

"Eminent scientists have confirmed that greater cranial capacity equals greater intelligence, and I'm afraid to say that our young Aboriginal friend here does not score very highly on that scale. In fact, the Australian black is the most lowly of all living races. Note how the facial bones have an almost ape-like appearance..."

There was a titter amongst the group.

"Excuse me, Professor," someone said, "but I've read that some of the Neanderthal skull finds have shown they had a greater cranial capacity than ours, does that mean they were more intelligent than us?"

The class laughed along with the witty student, while the professor launched into a long winded and unconvincing answer as to why this was an exception to the rule.

As he spoke I had a moment of revelation; that he didn't know anything, nothing about anything that really mattered anyway.

Science was full of deficiencies and everyone was scrabbling around in the dark trying to guess at what was going on.

The story of the old nurse that morning had convinced me I had been in the presence of the unknown. And in my new world, all the ghosts of the skulls of Skull Alley were standing there among the students, glowering at the professor and his self-important opinions.

That night I ran out to the end of the pier and shouted at God.

When I woke the next morning, for a split second I thought it had all been a nightmare. Then I saw Freddie's empty bed and felt again the dreadful lurch of my sinking soul.

The world was not an ordered or controllable place, it was chaos. There was an invisible wrecking ball called 'chance', swinging in a great destructive parabola and once in a while it swung in your direction and if you didn't get out of the way in time it would smash you.

After that, I spent every night out on the pier, afraid that if I slept on the ward the Grey Lady would come for me too. I worked out that something else had woken me the night Freddie had died, not just the Grey Lady. Death itself had been in the room, dark and cold and waiting in the shadows. I had sensed it before, in the tents of the Spitz Kop hospital, the waiting void ready to claim the next dying soldier. Death was an entity and the phantom nurse was just a facet of that − a sad ghost heralding the approaching black wave.

I had no doubt she was doing her rounds each night, drifting down the flights of stairs and along the cavernous corridors. Perhaps she even stopped on occasion to gaze out of a window at the lone figure sitting way out at the end of the pier. I wondered if it was her who had been watching me cross the lawns on the night of Freddie's death, that presence I had sensed.

Huddled under a blanket, I tried to put her out of my mind, instead dreaming of the ghost ships of Viking raiders sailing up the inlet to plunder Southampton. In my troubled dreams, when the wind blew and shook the pine trees and ruffled my hair, it became the raging breath of those long dead warriors.

My father came down for the funeral and didn't speak − not at all, not for the entire day − just a silent force of sorrow with the same thousand yard stare as the Royal Lancasters. It made me feel guilty to be the one who had lived. Freddie's coffin was on trestles in the chapel of rest and looked far too small to contain him. I found it very hard, knowing this was the last time I was ever going to see my brother. It is true what they say; he just looked like he was sleeping. The skin was hard now, hard and pale like alabaster. Only his hair felt real. Someone had carefully dressed him in his uniform, with the Queen's South Africa medal pinned to his tunic. My father took the medal off and put it in his pocket.

The military cemetery was in the woods behind D Block. The Army could be efficient when it chose to be because a gravestone was already in place:

ALFRED HUNSTON
MIDDLESEX REGIMENT
DIED JUNE 1, 1900
FROM FEVER CONTRACTED IN SOUTH AFRICA,
AGE 25.
'MEMENTO MORI'

'Memento mori' had been put on at my insistence, and the Army had listened.

The pallbearers were other convalescing soldiers, some of whom I recognised from the hospital ship, some from our ward, all people he had befriended in his inimitable way. They lowered the coffin to the bottom of the grave and we stared down into it and said our silent farewells.

On a flat board nearby was an ominous-looking mound of soil from his freshly dug grave. A gravedigger was standing there, shovel at the ready. I knew that as soon as the service was over and we were gone, he would be filling in the grave and burying my brother for good. He noticed me staring and gave a nod, as if to say, 'Yes, you're right – that's exactly what I'm going to be doing'.

I was finding it difficult to come to terms with Freddie being down there in that box. While the prayers were being read I kept glancing towards the forest at the edge of the cemetery, my imagination and the tricks of the light telling me that Freddie was not in the coffin at all, but watching us from the tree-line.

Towards the end of the service a strange thing happened – my mind went completely blank and I 'came to' on a bench nearby. It must have been a little while later because only my father was left at Freddie's graveside. The gravedigger was still waiting, leaning on the handle of his shovel like a spectator on the football terraces.

A patient who had attended the funeral was standing in front of me and holding out my RAMC cap.

"You threw this onto the ground," he said. "Then you rubbed your head a bit and walked off to this bench."

I took my cap back.

"Sorry… I don't remember."

"You looked gone, pal." There was a slight pause and then he said, "I met your brother at Spion Kop."

"You were in his regiment?"

"No, I was with the Second Dorsets. Your brother was in the Second Middlesex. Together we formed the tenth brigade under General Coke."

I looked at him blankly, not taking any of it in. Military jargon was another language.

"Anyway… I'm sorry, pal."

He sat down next to me and together we shared a few quiet moments staring over to the grave and my broken father.

The gravedigger had lit himself a cigarette now and was looking at his pocket watch.

"I don't know what happened," I said.

The soldier looked down at his feet and when he spoke it was hushed, as though the information he was imparting was top secret.

"I've seen it in battles. I've seen men break, and when they do, they take off their headgear and run their hands through their hair. Don't ask me why, but that's what they always do."

****

Western Australia Colony
September, 1900

I woke with a start and realised the train had stopped.

There was no station in sight, just a landscape of red dirt, wiry bushes and stands of gum trees.

Dudley had his head in a book: *The War of the Worlds*. His playing cards lay on the table next to his open hip flask. When he saw I was awake he put his book down.

"You've slept for seven hours, Doc," he said. "Comatose through every stop. I tried to rouse you back at Southern Cross, but you were dead to the bloody world."

I rubbed my eyes.

"Have we broken down?"

"No. We're at Bullabulling."

"Is that supposed to mean something?"

"They're unloading some Mephan pipes. It's going to be a little while."

"Mephan pipes?"

"For the pipeline," he said.

Dudley took a quick swig from his flask, then stood up and rolled his head on his shoulders so that the bones in his neck cracked.

"Come on, Doc. Let's go and take a closer look and I'll explain."

As soon as I stepped down from the carriage, flies swarmed around my head and I flicked at them vainly with my hand – the 'Aussie salute'.

Rennie was already outside, near the back of the train where sections of white piping were being unloaded by a gang of toughs. I went and joined him and the small audience of other passengers. The pipes were wide enough for a man to fit into, and about thirty feet long at a guess.

Dudley squatted down with his elbows on his knees like the wicket keeper in a cricket match. He scooped up a handful of the red dirt and rubbed his hands gently with it.

"Where's the water going to come from?" I said, looking around at the dry scrub.

"They dammed up a river in the ranges three hundred miles away."

He stood up straight and pointed a red finger towards the gang lifting a pipe from the closest wagon.

"See those men? Sometime in the next few months when they have enough ready, they'll join the pipes together with molten lead. No rivets. Means the pipe won't leak. Need 66,000 of the things before they can start though. That's a lot of trainloads yet…"

"With lead?" Rennie said, looking surprised. "Don't they know what happened to the Roman Empire?'

While Dudley went into the finer details of pipeline construction for Rennie's benefit, I wandered away a few yards to watch the unloading.

The men were all yelling at one another and sweating profusely. As they carried a section of pipe past me, their hostile stares reminded me of the Thames watermen back in London; a look which said: 'New Chum, you have no fucking idea how hard our lives are.'

Dudley came over.

"Two and a half million pounds this is all going to cost. Residents of Perth don't like it, that's for sure… all that funding for the inland goldfields, in other words, not for them. They think it'll leak and that there won't even be enough water for people to to dilute their bloody whisky with. They're wrong though. O'Connor has designed it, the same bloke who made the port at Fremantle and annoyed the black fellas. He'll have five million gallons of water a day reaching the goldfields in the next year or so. Believe me."

A small shack stood next to the pipeline, the words 'ROCK HOTEL' daubed in whitewash on the wall. Inside, the proprietor served up some bitter coffee with such a bitter sneer that the stares of the pipe men seemed friendly in comparison. There was no civility out here. As far as I could tell, the men in the bar could have been Neanderthals dressed in modern clothing – they all had brow ridges and huge hairy forearms and communicated mainly with grunts. A skinny man was sitting in the corner playing the fiddle but no-one seemed to be listening. They were all concentrating on the top of their beers and frowning, perhaps wondering why they hadn't made their fortunes yet and whose fault it was.

A scuffle broke out and the barman quickly moved in to break it up, threatening the drinkers with a black truncheon. I drank up quickly and left.

Not far from the shack was a rocky outcrop, rising up some fifty feet from the surrounding plain. I walked up its gentle slope to the top and was afforded the spectacle of the sun setting to the west, clipping the distant tree line. It was a landlocked island in the middle of an unending sea of red dirt and gum trees. The flies had thinned out, preferring to marshal their forces down amongst the ugly, sweating men. Up here the crowds were out of earshot too. No sounds, just the view and the warmth of the ochre coloured rock.

The stillness at Bullabulling rock was absolute. I had never known such a feeling of isolation, of remoteness from civilisation. In South Africa there had always been cities or towns nearby. This place felt like another planet. I remembered Dudley's book about the Martians and fantasised that, instead of us travelling towards the goldfields while I had been asleep, we had somehow flown to Mars instead.

For a few moments I felt alone and free… Tantalising really, because I knew it wouldn't last. Sure enough, a long whistle from the train signalled the unloading was over and I had to hurry back down before I was left behind.

"It won't be a moment too soon they get that bloody pipe finished," Dudley said, as we took our seats again.

I looked at him. "Because of the typhoid?"

"Spot on. It's taken out more Egremont men this year than the Boers did from my unit. Doc, we're heading to the typhoid capital of the world."

A list of statistics I had seen months earlier came to mind, from those last painful days at the Military Hospital.

Chapter Ten

Spike Island
June, 1900

On my penultimate day, I decided to pay a visit to Professor Almroth Wright in his laboratory on the third floor of C-block. I did it to try and set the record straight, thinking it might provide me with some kind of resolution after typhoid's part in Freddie's death.

For the occasion I even wore my RAMC dress uniform; blue with dull cherry and old gold trim. I had once been proud of the smart uniform, but now my favourite part was the 'V' on the shoulder, signifying 'volunteer'. My short commission was ending early because I was no good to them now.

I could not wait to be out of the Army.

I knocked on the glass panelled door of the lab.

"Come," said a voice.

A man was bent low over the eyepiece of a microscope.

"Sorry to disturb you, Professor…"

He straightened up and I saw him properly for the first time. Fairly tall, perhaps six foot, a serious countenance, bushy moustache and half-moon spectacles – a combination of attributes which reminded me of my father.

"I'm Dr Hunston."

"Wright," he said, making no move to shake my hand. "I don't know you."

"I'm actually a patient here, recovering from typhoid fever as it happens…"

"Hmmm… And you are here because…?"

Not a man to mess about with pleasantries then. I had hoped for some kind of sympathy by mentioning my illness, but so far the man had shown no emotion whatsoever.

I decided to skip the small talk.

"Well, I'm sorry to have to admit this, Professor, but I declined to have your inoculation on the way to South Africa, much to my regret. After seeing the side-effects I thought I would take my chances and avoid it, but after being on the receiving end of the enteric these last few months, I know better now. I wanted to personally apologise."

I felt that Wright was observing me closely as I spoke, using his diagnostic skills to gauge the remnants of the *Salmonella typhi* in my body, assessing how the bacterium had ravaged me. My cheekbones were prominent and my skin still colourless, despite the afternoons passed in the sunshine on the pier. Nearly two stone in weight had dropped away and my tunic hung loose over my emaciated body.

He didn't seem bothered about my humble admission. Instead, he gestured to one wall of the lab, where some wooden crates were stacked haphazardly, dried watermarks clearly visible on the pale pine.

"The coastguard fished them out and returned them to me last week," he said. "The consignment was thrown overboard into Southampton Water, before the ship had even left for South Africa. I'm amazed the men on your vessel even had the chance to get inoculated. They were lucky, even if there was the odd idiot who refused to have it. The War Office will be stopping all vaccinations within months, I fear, even for volunteers…"

He grunted at his own comment and put his head back down to the eyepiece of the microscope. I tried to ignore the fact he had just called me an idiot, and despite having lost his attention, I continued:

"Yes, well… I'm afraid there was a lot of mistrust among the ward staff out there. I overheard one ward sergeant point to a ward full of sick soldiers and say to his colleague: 'If they hadn't been inoculated they wouldn't have caught the disease in the first place'."

Professor Wright pulled away from the microscope, sat up straight and then shook his head, smiling wryly.

"Such is the confusion generated when you inject typhoid bacteria into healthy humans, albeit dead typhoid bacteria."

"Why do you think the War Office didn't take you seriously?" I realised I had said this out loud and not just thought it. "I'm sorry, Professor,' I said. "That came out badly."

He waved his hand in the air, dismissing my words.

"No, you're right, and I suppose that in a way I should be flattered; after all, the real pioneers have always been derided. They thought Copernicus was mad when he said the earth orbited the sun, and that Darwin was a laughing stock for suggesting we were related to monkeys..."

He wasn't really answering the question, about why no-one had taken him seriously.

I leant back against the labtop and stared at the gas outlets for Bunsen burners, running my hands along the grains of the table like a blind man reading braille. I let a silence linger a few moments.

"Schoolyard politics," he said, finally getting to the point. "That's why they don't listen. The most influential man on the board of the Medical Advisory Office, Bruce, still holds a grudge about my being made Professor of Pathology here over him. I was a civilian you see, and he was a serving officer. They made him Assistant Professor. We don't get on. So you can imagine how it's all going to play out – the Medical Advisory Office will meet with the War Office; there'll be a quiet word in someone's ear and my inoculation will be black listed. It's not what you know, it's who you know."

Wright picked up a journal lying on his desk and handed it to me.

"Read this," he said. It was a dog eared copy of the *BMJ*, folded open at an article in which a sentence had been circled heavily in red ink:

'...initial results appear to justify the conclusion that inoculations lead to at least a two-fold reduction in the incidence of the disease...'

"You're preaching to the converted," I said, giving it back.

"It more than halves the mortality rate and that's a fact. Then *Pearson* goes and rubbishes it with his correlations, selection bias and bloody statistics."

Wright imbued the word 'Pearson' with such contempt that I was reminded of the way we had said 'the filth' back at University, when referring to our rowing rivals at Cambridge.

"Here's a statistic for you," he said, picking up another journal, *The Lancet* this time, and waving it in the air. "I tested the inoculation on nearly 3000 soldiers going to India, where typhoid fever is rife... Do you know how many of those men went on to catch it?"

I looked at the journal for a clue, but it was still scrunched up in his fist and it didn't look as though he wanted to give it to me.

"Errm... No."

"Five."

He slammed the journal down on the lab bench so hard that all the glass vials rattled in their wooden stands, the violence of the action making me jump. There had been masters like this at school – and not just Sadist – who would act with this same sudden anger, like throwing a piece of chalk at a miscreant pupil, or even the blackboard rubber if they were really annoyed. Sometimes, they got so worked up, you would feel sorry for them, especially if they were decent enough the rest of the time. You would start to worry more about their suffering a paroxysm of the brain for instance, rather than the imminent pain of their projectiles making contact with your head.

"Five out of three thousand, and Pearson had to gall to tell me I needed to improve the serum and the dosing. He even suggested I call for volunteers and inoculate every second one, to see for sure if the damn thing works or not. Can you imagine telling every second soldier he'll be unprotected so that the statistics can be improved?"

"I wouldn't like to be the one to have to do that," I said.

I thought of Freddie and me standing in line – one being selected to live and the other being selected to die.

"The War Office will believe him and Bruce – and they will ban my inoculation. Disraeli was right you know, about there being three kinds of lies: Lies, Damned lies and Statistics – I *know* the inoculation works – I tested the bloody thing on myself for Christ's sake!"

Wright's face was nearly beetroot red with anger now.

I had heard a rumour that his rival scientists – the ones trying to persuade the War Office to ban the inoculation – called him 'Almost Right' behind his back.

"It doesn't help that all those *activist* groups oppose mandatory inoculations… whining that it smacks of government interference with individual liberty. The War Office are lapping it up. How many soldiers have died needlessly? You've seen it yourself, man."

He snatched the *BMJ* out of my hand and tossed it back onto the desk.

"Yes, I certainly have, Professor."

There were a few moments of silence and his angry mood subsided.

"Hunston, you say?"

"Yes."

He picked up a sheet of paper, which appeared to contain a list and checked it.

"Yes, I thought I had seen that name somewhere… let me see… ahhh… here we are…Hunston, Alfred. No relation I hope?"

"My brother, I'm afraid."

"Oh dear… They report any typhoid related deaths to me." He put the page back on his desk and then looked down at the floor. "I'm sorry."

"Thank you, Professor."

He raised his head and stared at me.

"I won't give up, you know; I'll go somewhere else to finish what I've started if needs must. I'll have it ready for the next war. They'll be begging me for it by then."

Looking around, it was clear he meant it – every spare inch of the worktops was covered with boxes of syringes and jars of inoculation serum. The lab was Wright's own inoculation factory.

"And you, Doctor?" he said, trying to lighten the tone. "What will you do when they let you out of here?"

"Me? Well, I do have a general practice in Harley Street waiting for me."

"Indeed."

He said it with raised eyebrows, seeming to lose interest in me as soon as I said it. He put another slide on his microscope, looked back down the eyepiece and started twisting the side dial to get the focus.

I felt I had been struggling to hold his attention from the moment I had walked in here. All he seemed to want to do was get on with his research.

Without any real forethought, I found myself talking about Freddie's plan. His dream had sown a seed, you see – fallen on barren ground at first, but since his death, it had started taking hold, insidiously and against all the odds, and begun to grow.

"I've been toying with the idea of working out in the Australian goldfields."

He glanced up from the eyepiece. "Really?"

"Well, nothing's finalised yet," I said, lying easily.

"Western Australia?"

"Yes."

He sat back to appraise me, sensing my defensiveness.

"There's no decent water supply out there," he said. "You'll be a busy man if you go."

"Yes, I expect I will."

"And you don't mind that?"

"Well, the one bonus of having had typhoid and survived is that I've got some immunity for a while. So I don't have to worry about myself at least."

Wright nodded his head at that.

"Yes," he said, "I suppose you're right."

He rifled through a stack of papers on his desk until he found the one he wanted.

"Here," he said, passing me a piece of paper. "Take a look."

TYPHOID FEVER DEATHS IN WESTERN AUSTRALIA
FOR YEARS 1891-1899.

POPULATION	YEAR	DEATHS
53,279	1891	19
58,658	1892	55
65,037	1893	28
82,014	1894	73
101,143	1895	325
137,796	1896	400
161,694	1897	407
167,810	1898	296
170,651	1899	148

I scanned the numbers quickly.

"I've seen worse."

"I agree," he said. "It's certainly not on the scale of Bloemfontein, but it is sustained – years as opposed to months; a slow burn, so to speak."

I held out the sheet to give back but he returned to his microscope.

"Keep it," he said, without looking up.

"Thank you, Professor."

He raised his hand in a farewell gesture and I left him to his world of bacteria.

Despite my show of bravado in Wright's lab, I still wasn't sure about Australia – though I could not deny there was a part of me acceding to Freddie's last wish: *'Promise me you'll think about it…'* I was supposed to be heading back to my old Harley Street job; a fortnight before it had been a certainty, but now that plan was beginning to falter, like a man racing in the hurdles and getting his stride lengths all messed up.

I spent the rest of the day in my usual place on the pier, torturing myself by thinking how it might have all turned out if Freddie and I had been inoculated.

I would miss the pier – my last good memories of Freddie were of him out here, dancing around on the boards as a pirate and holding up an invisible nugget of gold.

Daydreams came and went. I pictured the pier eventually being taken down, the gargantuan hospital being levelled and the whole place returned to nature. It was easy to see in my mind's eye – despite the solid reality of all my surroundings.

For me, no matter what became of this place in the future, even if the Grey Lady found her own peace, it would still be a sad place, haunted by the ghosts of those young men who had fought so bravely abroad, but succumbed on this shore to, *'fever contracted in South Africa'*, as recorded by their gravestones.

I crumpled up the list of death statistics and threw it over the rail, watching it drift out to sea on the tide.

Chapter Eleven

Western Australia Colony
September, 1900

The train still hadn't moved. Watching the labourers set up camp for the night, it occurred to me that if I got off the train right now and offered to help them laying out the pipeline, it would be a lot more effective at tackling the disease than my doing any actual doctoring on the wards. Prevention was the best medicine.

"What do people use for water at the moment?"

"They condense salt water from the shallow lake-pans," Dudley said. "Or condense brackish and heavily mineralised water from the bores and mine-shafts. The Egremont condenser is the biggest of 'em all. You need water for gold mining you see, Doc. Our plant also provides drinking water for the miners – four gallons a day for married men, two gallons for single men, like you and me."

"That must cost."

"Sure does… The wood to heat the boilers costs fifteen shillings a ton. The man on the street pays ten to twelve shillings for a hundred gallons."

"Of course," he said, with a grin. "That's after a bit of a mark-up made by the owners of the condensing plants. People pay it though, because if you don't, you die."

He went back to reading his book and I went back to staring out of the train window.

In the last light of the day, the endless acres of dust were turning terracotta – just like the Martian landscape I had been thinking about, or at least how I would imagine one to look. My daydreaming up on the rock wasn't completely mad; this place was other-worldly.

And in *The War of Worlds,* the invaders had all died of bacterial infections to which they had no immunity. There was a fine line between fact and fiction.

It was dark when the train slowed into the township of Coolgardie. Dudley tapped the window with his fingernail.

"This is where it all started, Doc… where Bayley and Ford struck it rich in 1892. Then a year later a man called Hannan got lucky twenty miles further east in Kalgoorlie."

The train lurched to a standstill and a few scruffy passengers got off. Otherwise the platform was empty.

"Before the miners came ten years ago, this place was just desert and bush… It was nowhere."

"It seems like nowhere now."

"Yeah well, the gold rush came to Coolgardie first, and then the circus moved on to Kalgoorlie."

A whistle blew.

The train built up a head of steam and started to move.

Beyond the station and the rooftops, the gum trees and the red earth took over again. Civilisation was just a thin covering here – only scratching the surface. Compared to the vast area of scrubland surrounding us, mankind's impact seemed laughably insignificant.

We pulled into Kalgoorlie less than an hour later – city lights in the desert night. Hundreds of passengers spilled off the train and into the streets.

After all the miles of silent emptiness, the sudden metropolis was bewildering; as busy and bright as Piccadilly Circus.

All day on the train it felt as if I had been slowly baking, like a potato in the oven for a Sunday roast. And now, despite it being evening, the temperature was still hot enough to cause significant discomfort.

Once we had found Rennie, we negotiated our way through the milling crowds to the Manse on Dugan Street, a small shack next to the Wesleyan Church, itself no more than a slightly larger shack. Earlier that day, Rennie had been given the keys to both buildings by Rowe. The previous minister had died of typhoid three months before and they had been locked ever since.

By the doorway of the church was a box of candles and I lit one with a match from Freddie's tobacco tin, which I had inherited. The light from the candle was weak – probably a good thing, because the interior wasn't much to look at. A large crucifix hung on the wall at the far end, and several wooden packing cases made up the pews. That was about it.

Rennie walked up to the crucifix, before slowly coming back down the centre of the room to stand at the entrance. He stared down at his shoes, caked in red dirt and stomped up and down a few times.

"So this is what the sharp end of Christianity looks like," he said, in a way that sounded more despondent than excited.

Dudley put his hand on Rennie's shoulder.

"If you get hungry or thirsty, Rev, you go to the Palace Hotel. It's at the main crossroads."

Rennie gave a distracted nod, but otherwise didn't reply.

For once, my friend looked like he had bitten off more than he could chew. No biblical quotes, the usual fervour absent. I thought of something to say to lift his spirits.

"I'll come to one of your services when you've fixed the place up, Sean."

He smiled sadly.

"Yes, John, I would like that."

A loud grunt made us all turn around.

It had come from a camel.

There was an enclosure opposite the church and three of the creatures were eyeing us, their necks poking over the fence. A turbaned man wearing a pair of baggy paisley-patterned pantaloons was busy doing odd jobs around the yard.

"An Afghan," Dudley said. "That's what we call Mussulmen wearing turbans. They've cornered the market in the carrying business... using camels that is." He swept his arms in a great arc. "That's why the streets are so wide... so the camel trains can turn around without stopping."

We left Rennie there, in the street with the camels and the Afghan cameleer. My friend would be fine on his own. He had his God. It was me I was worried about – how without his constant companionship I might start to retreat into myself again, take to sitting in the corner of some bar and spend all my time staring at the walls.

The Palace Hotel was a decent sized two storey building straddling the corner of Hannan and Maritana Streets. Wrought iron verandas ran along both street frontages, the ironwork festooned with electric lights. A downtrodden version of the Ritz; the flies, dust and oppressive heat, added features. *Why on earth had I come to Australia?*

Dudley helped to check me in at the front desk.

"Are you all right from here on in?" he said, seeming to sense my uncertainty.

I could see my doubting face reflecting back at me in a large gilt framed mirror in the reception area. Whenever I fretted about something, one eye would open wider than the other and make me look a bit lop-sided.

"I think so, Mr Dudley."

"For Christ's sake, mate, call me Tom."

"All right, Tom."

Before I had the chance to make the same offer, he was talking again.

"This place has its own condenser – fresh water piped to all the bathrooms. Food and board is courtesy of the Egremont Company... Best bloody tucker in town too. Rest of your salary is gold, paid in kind by the miners. Bet they didn't tell ya that part..."

"No, they didn't."

At that moment, the image of Freddie on the pier holding his imaginary nugget came back to me: *'You know how the doctors get paid out there?'* He hadn't been lying.

"I'll be getting along then," Dudley said. "My gaff's just up the road at the British Arms. Any problems, you just let me know."

"Thank you, Tom."

It felt strange to say his name. The only other people I had ever called by their Christian names had been Freddie and Sean Rennie.

"Mañana."

He pushed open the doors, stepped into the street and was immediately swallowed up by the throng of people, who seemed to sweep him away like a fast current in a river.

A porter led me up a wide sweeping staircase to a first floor room.

Beside the bed was a small table with an electric lamp. An open doorway led through to a large adjoining bathroom. Shouts and the jaunty chords of a piano from the bar downstairs filtered up through the floorboards and a fan on the ceiling circled lazily, making next to no impact on the sweltering heat of the room.

I opened the door onto the balcony hoping for a cooling breeze, but Dudley had been right – there was no 'Doctor' out here.

The view was of Maritana Street, and directly opposite was the Exchange Hotel. I saw a miner ejected from the establishment horizontally through a swing door, landing in a swearing heap in the dust.

To my left was the crossroads with Hannan Street and, on the far side, another hotel called The Australian. Hannan Street, the main artery of the town, was pulsating with prospectors and prostitutes. The hordes of young men – some suited and some in workman's garb – moved from hotel bar to hotel bar. The women of the night wore virtually nothing on their top halves. Everyone was drunk and shouting loudly. There didn't appear to be a single respectable-looking body in the whole motley crowd.

Not for the first time, I wished I had thrown that bloody *BMJ* into the wastepaper bin back at the Blue Boar Club.

Behind me, I heard the sound of someone clearing their throat.

The porter was still holding my valise and Gladstone. I had forgotten all about him.

"We've got ninety-three hotels, eight breweries and a population of thirty thousand," he said, looking past me out onto the street.

"Is that right?" I said, my voice tired.

He put down my cases and scratched his head, searching his mind for something else interesting to say.

"Kalgoorlie's 'Abo' for silky pear bush."

I gave him half a shilling to get it over with.

"Much obliged, Doctor," he said, touching his forehead.

After he had gone, I ran a shallow tepid bath and soaked in it for an hour until the skin on my hands crinkled up like a prune.

The next morning I woke early, missing Rennie's rendition of *Rule Britannia*. I went out and walked the quiet streets of Kalgoorlie, because there was nothing else to do and no-one to talk to.

Rising early was a routine I had adopted after leaving Spike Island. I would pound the pavements of London while the rest of the town slumbered – an hour's circuit, marching as fast as my weakened body would allow. At least that way I could fall asleep exhausted at night.

At this time of the day, the air was still cool, though the portent of heat was there, like the tension on an exam day. I could smell the desert air, clear and unpolluted, the dust as yet undisturbed by vehicles, horses and people. It wouldn't last long. Once the big hard sun appeared it would bring out the sweating, grimy masses in search of their stupid fortunes.

Kalgoorlie wasn't a big city and I soon located the two main hospitals: the Government Hospital was down Maritana, out beyond the train track, whereas the 'St. John of God' was closer to town, on the corner of Maritana and Dugan Streets. In fact, just two blocks down from the Palace.

A small bronze plaque was on the wall at the main entrance:

ST JOHN OF GOD HOSPITAL
FORMALLY OPENED ON 21/3/97 BY DR GIBNEY DD

It wasn't much to look at – just a one-storey building set into the ubiquitous red dirt of a fenced reserve, fronted by a few spindly gum trees. Not quite the elegant Georgian frontage of 'the Manor' in Harley Street, that was for sure.

Dudley was in the Palace bar when I got back, drinking coffee and reading a newspaper called the *Kalgoorlie Miner*. His tawny hair had been swept to one side with a wet comb and he was wearing moleskin trousers and an olive green shirt made of thick linen. The eye patch and the sober clothing made him look like a pirate trying to go straight after a lifetime of plundering.

I took the seat next to him and looked around.

The arched windows of the bar were made of stained glass, each dominated by an ornate letter 'P', standing for 'Palace', I guessed. The lavatory door in the corner was labelled '*MINERS*' rather than '*GENTLEMEN*'.

A barmaid came over and poured me a fresh coffee. She was a glamorous older woman with curly auburn hair piled high on her head and a dress belonging more on the stage than behind a saloon bar.

"There you go, darling."

"Thank you very much."

"Good on ya, Violet," Dudley said as she poured. "The young English doc here is just finding his feet in this beautiful city of ours."

She laughed loudly. "A young doctor from England… Just say the word, handsome, and I'll run off with you."

She winked and moved on to another customer.

"Morning, Doc," Dudley said.

"Tom," I said, still blushing at the barmaid's words.

"Came to see how you were doing on your first day. Been out?"

"I felt like… er… walking."

"Fair go" he said, snapping his paper out and folded it in two and then four, before shoving it into his back trouser pocket.

"When do you start?"

I looked down at my pocket watch.

"Not sure – I suppose I should wander over there soon and show myself."

He drained the rest of his coffee and yawned.

"Got a busy day myself – Egremont wants a full report on the current state of his mine – how much gold is left – which is not a lot by the way, though I suspect he doesn't want to hear that."

Just then the door swung open and a smartly dressed gentleman of about fifty entered the Palace bar. He was short and portly, and walked with his hands clasped behind his back like Napoleon.

He came straight up to me.

"Doctor Hunston?"

I stood up.

"Yes?"

"I'm Doctor Cutfield, PMO for the St. John of God."

As we shook hands I recalled the name. A few days after the interview at Witworth Park I had gone back to the Egremont offices in Piccadilly to thrash out the details with the grey secretary. He had given me a ticket for the ship's passage and said who I would be working with in Kalgoorlie – a Dr Cutfield.

I hoped Cutfield hadn't noticed the frantic rifling through my memory banks.

"Yes. Sir Robert's team mentioned you."

He puffed out a little when he heard this.

Dudley got up and stood next to Cutfield, towering over him.

"Cutfield," he said.

Cutfield looked straight at Dudley's chest and avoided eye contact. "Dudley."

No Christian names here, I noticed.

"I'll be getting along gents – got a mine to run."

Just before Dudley limped out of the bar, he said two words to me under his breath: "Good luck."

Cutfield motioned towards the exit.

"Shall we, Doctor?"

"Yes, certainly," I said, pushing my stool back towards bar.

He led the way, walking quickly, his short legs having such a disproportionately long stride that I had to jog along a little to keep up with him. The last time I had felt like this was at school when being marched over to the headmaster's study for a caning.

Cutfield's office in the hospital administration block looked out onto the junction of Maritana and Dugan Streets, Dugan being Rennie's street. I could even see the Manse a few hundred yards away.

As I was looking out at the view, Cutfield pulled down the blinds half way, turning the room sepia yellow.

On the wall behind his desk was a painting of a bushman in a gum forest clearing; a fellow lost in thought, one hand propping up his head with elbow on knee, the other hand poking at a campfire with a stick.

The only other pieces of furniture were a threadbare chaise longue against the back wall and a bookshelf filled with medical tomes. It felt like I was in a waiting room at the very edge of the known world.

Cutfield opened his desk drawer and pulled out a bottle of whisky and two glasses. Nine o'clock in the morning – this was a town of bad habits.

He poured a dram into each, handed one to me and then sat on his desk, rolling the liquid around his glass. Already, I sensed he was a strange one. On the walk over he hadn't talked at all.

Awkwardly, I drank the whisky in one go.

"So," he said, "how was the voyage?"

"Long."

He smiled briefly.

"And the train journey?"

"Very comfortable, thank you. Dudley treated me to first class."

"Oh… he did, did he?"

It was immediately obvious Cutfield didn't like Dudley and, from what I had seen back at the Palace, the feeling was mutual.

Cutfield held up a telegram and gave another forced smile.

"I received this yesterday. From the prison surgeon at Fremantle… he wanted to know why one of his prisoners was seen by another doctor in the middle of the night without his permission."

"Oh, that," I said, somewhat taken aback at his serious tone.

He waved the paper in the air with a questioning look. "Yes, that."

"Well," I said, "apparently he declined to see the patient himself, so Dudley roped me in."

He placed the telegram back down on the desk and turned to me.

"I must say, I have to agree with the prison surgeon on this point. Strictly speaking, Doctor Hunston, you shouldn't have attended to the prisoner."

Cutfield wasn't smiling any more.

I waited a few seconds to see if this was a joke but his expression remained stern.

"From what I understand, the man I attended was an Egremont man, so as I see it, he came under my umbrella too."

"Your umbrella..." Cutfield said, rolling the answer around his mouth like a cow chewing the cud.

He stood up from the desk, walked around behind it and sat down in his swivel chair.

"Your umbrella," he said again. "That may well be the case, Doctor, but the man you treated was a criminal... a criminal who could have waited for the prison doctor the next day. Not only that, but I also understand he was a native."

"As I said, he was an Egremont man, innocent by all accounts... Attacked in an unprovoked assault."

"Oh, I very much doubt that – it's always their fault."

"Their fault?' I said, my mood darkening. "You have something against the Aboriginals?"

Cutfield laughed with derision. "Not just Aboriginals. All savages."

I was actually angry about his having taken the prison surgeon's side against mine, but this Aboriginal issue had become the tool I was using to retaliate.

"I didn't realise the Hippocratic Oath made the distinction," I said.

He straightened up in his chair and smiled again.

Why do people do that? I thought. *Why do they smile when what they really want to do is tear your head off?*

"Why, Doctor Hunston, surely you are aware this is commonly accepted Darwinian doctrine? We have a moral duty to colonise such peoples, and not to gallivant around pandering to them in the middle of the night."

I shook my head and closed my eyes. This was like a bad dream. The whisky was already taking the sharp edges off my thoughts and, before I could think of a suitable response, Cutfield was pressing on with his worldview: "I must say, your ignorance astounds me, Doctor Hunston. I would have expected more from an Oxford man. You're obviously not familiar with Henry Morris's *History of Colonization*, published just this year."

He reached over to his shelf and lifted off one of the volumes.

I glared back at him, feeling the blood throbbing in my neck and flushing my face.

"No, I'm not familiar with it."

Cufield licked a finger and leafed through to a page in the introduction.

"Ah... here it is," he said, proceeding to read: "*'Under the Union Jack the American Indian, the negro of Africa, Australia and the West Indies, the heterogeneous and numerous peoples of East India, the Malays, the Hottentots, the Polynesians, the Chinese, and several other races inferior in the scale of humanity, live, labour and die.'*"

Triumphantly, he slammed the book shut.

"If I remember correctly, Morris says colonisation is the only expression of civilisation," he said as an addendum.

Cutfield would have loved Skull Alley; he would have drooled all over the bleached crania of the Empire's racial types. Hearing him quoting his backward pseudoscience had pushed me close to the edge. I wasn't going to back down now. A pre-war John Hunston would have done, but not this one.

I set my glass down on his desk.

"I seem to remember the Martians thinking the same thing about us in *The War of the Worlds*."

"Fiction, Doctor Hunston? You mean to tell me that you are resorting to cheap fiction to argue against decent science?"

"At least it's honest fiction, as opposed to the fiction you've just quoted, which masquerades as fact."

Cutfield stood up quickly and leant forward over his desk, his fingers turning white as the weight of his body squeezed the blood out of them. I had laid a punch at last. His arrogant sneer had gone now.

Come on then, I was thinking. *Come on, you bastard.*

A long silence ensued as he stared at me.

"You don't believe in the Empire?" he said, making the comment sound like an accusation of treason.

"I'm sorry to have to disappoint you, Doctor Cutfield, but I'm not the imperialist I once was. South Africa turned me off it. As a matter of fact, I've come to find the whole idea quite delusional."

Cutfield's eyes turned coal black.

Maybe I had gone a little too far, but in this remote outpost it felt like the old rules of civility and pretence no longer applied.

In the stand-off, my thoughts drifted off down surreal avenues.

His pudgy fingers reminded me of sausages on display in the covered market back in Oxford. Butchers there displayed all kinds of meats; rabbits and pheasants, sides of ham, carcasses of deer and pigs as well as prime cuts and piles of offal. An array of dead meat – strung up and slowly rotting, as yet unnoticeable from the outside.

Abruptly I was dragged back to the present.

Cutfield was talking again, his indignation seemingly vanished. His voice had become monotone, distant and emotionless.

"...I'm taking some annual leave at the end of this week. Mrs Cutfield and I shall be away for two months. We like to escape the heat and dust of the early summer by retiring to the coast."

He made it sound as if he was royalty – my God – the Queen at Spike Island had sounded more humble.

"Two months..."

"Oh, I'm sure you'll manage, Doctor Hunston. After all, you are a Harley Street physician."

Two bloody months, I thought to myself. *You lazy bloody bastard.*

Our earlier spat was completely irrelevant. Even if I had been the deferential and obsequious new arrival he was hoping for, siding with him against the 'inferior races', it would not have mattered a jot. Cutfield had been biding his time, waiting for the new man to arrive so he could get out.

"Let me show you around the house," he said.

We had got off to such a bad start, I thought it best not to say anything else, so I just nodded my assent. I was missing my colleagues at the Manor very much indeed.

It had been a while since I had heard a hospital called the 'house'; not since my houseman years in fact. As a junior doctor, you spent so much time there, you got to know the place intimately – its corridors, the short-cuts to the wards, where to find the quiet places. In that way, it was like a home. The hospital chapel was always the best refuge; not for any particular religious reason, but because nobody else ever seemed to go there.

Cutfield led the way out into the hall.

"In addition to my office, this block houses the mess, the kitchens and the nurses' quarters."

He was sounding very open now, all traces of the earlier argument gone, so much so, I wondered if it had actually happened.

Soon, we came to a covered passageway at the rear of the building, open to the elements on both sides and linking the admin block to the hospital proper.

"See the verandas running along the outside of the wards," he said, halfway along the passage. "It's a very innovative design."

I scowled. 'Innovative' was a word people used because they thought it made them sound clever.

"It's so the patients can convalesce in the fresh air, should they so wish."

If you can call one hundred degree heat 'fresh', I thought.

He barged open the swing doors to the hospital block with his shoulder and I followed in his wake. Straightaway I smelt carbolic. The distant sound of a bed pan clattering onto a ward floor filtered through into the main hall.

143

Each ward had a sign above the doorway leading to it – to the left was a room marked *'CASUALTY'*, straight ahead was the *'PRIVATE WARD'*, to the right, a much larger *'GENERAL WARD'*. From where we were standing, we could see into each one.

"The patients from the Egremont mine are in there," he said, pointing into the private ward, which was almost empty.

"You cover the general ward as well as the private ward," Cutfield said.

From what I could see, every bed in the general ward was taken.

It was a crucial piece of information – that I was not just looking after the private Egremont patients – but he dropped it into his guided tour like another insignificant detail. He probably wanted me to take umbrage, so I didn't. I wasn't all that surprised at work being dumped on me... back at the Manor, as the junior partner, I was given all the 'heart sink' cases to see, the ones no-one else wanted to deal with because they came with so many complex insoluble problems. Even so, the senior partners were forever telling me how much harder things had been in their day: 'Why JH, when I started I even had to fill up the coal scuttle every morning!'

What Cutfield didn't realise was that I wanted to be busy – when I was busy, the hurt went away.

I poked my head around the doorway of 'Casualty'; an admission room where patients were assessed and clerked. There were three beds along the wall – each surrounded by curtains hanging loosely from rails, there to be pulled around for privacy if required. On the opposite wall, glass fronted cupboards housed the usual equipment; bandages, boric lint, rubber tourniquets, kidney dishes, assorted forceps, wooden splints, jars containing cotton wool balls, you name it.

In the far bay, a doctor in a white coat was leaning over a patient and peering into his ear with an auroscope.

"Hmm... looks like your eardrum is infected," he was saying in an American accent.

"I'll introduce you to the new man at rounds, Dr Poyntz," Cutfield said.

The stooped figure didn't deviate from his examination.

"Yep... there in a minute..."

"Dr Poyntz officially looks after all patients who are not Egremont employees – a much larger proportion. You'll be dividing the work between you though... or have I already said that?"

"Yes, you already did."

There was enough disrespect in my reply to make Poyntz look up.

Cutfield took me through to the general ward – a typical layout, with a wooden floor. Jarrah wood possibly. If it hadn't been for the heat, I could have been back in London doing my one day a week at the Charing Cross voluntary hospital.

Dominating the centre was a table with a large potted native palm, similar to the ones I had seen back at Mount Eliza Park in Perth. The ward plants were strikingly different to England's and the longer I stood there, the more differences I started to notice. This seemed more flimsy in comparison to Charing Cross, more temporary – as if it had been built in a hurry, like the rest of the town. A dado rail, made of the same fluted iron as the roof, ran around the walls at about head height. The rest of the walls were varnished matchboard. Ten beds lined each side of the ward – female patients occupied the four beds at the end and the area was half curtained off to separate them from the men. At the back of the ward was a door labelled: *'BATHS'*.

A nurse in a black uniform was attending to one of the patients. As she turned towards us I saw she was wearing a long white apron over the black, pulled tight at the waist by a blue belt. A white headdress completely hid her hair. She must have been one of the nursing nuns Rowe had told me about – one of the Catholic 'Sisters of St John of God'.

As she approached, a pair of scissors and a thermometer rattled in a chatelaine hanging from her belt.

Cutfield made the introductions.

"Sister Bernadette, this is the new doctor."

"Doctor John Hunston," I said.

Close up, despite being pale from what I suspected had been a long shift, she was very pretty. No, on a second analysis, I decided she was *extremely* pretty.

"Doctor," she said, leaving out my surname altogether.

Her accent was continental – at a guess, French.

All the male patients in the ward were under her spell – their eyes swivelling round and following her every action. She possessed the kind of beauty that would encourage men to get better fast, just to please her. There had been a few nurses like that in the Raadzaal, the ones I had thought were angels, but none quite as stunning as this.

"I look forward to working with you," she said, making a slight bow.

"As shall I, Sister Bernadette."

She laughed and narrowed her eyes as if we were co-conspirators.

"Call me Sister B."

Her immediate familiarity was beguiling. If I wasn't careful I was about to become a blushing, bumbling idiot.

Just then, Poyntz, the American doctor, ambled through from the receiving room.

Now that he wasn't leaning over a patient, I could see he was a tall beanpole of a man, his white coat hanging off his wiry shoulders like an outsize garment from a bargain shop. Close up, his face bore the scarred traces of a bout of adolescent acne, but he was handsome in spite of it. Poyntz was rubbing his short, straw-coloured hair with both hands, as if he was trying to make static electricity.

"Ah, Poyntz, this is Doctor Hunston – the Egremont replacement."

I looked at Cutfield. No one had said anything about replacing anybody.

"Hey," Poyntz said, shaking my hand loosely.

His voice had a strong nasal tone as if he were suffering from a case of chronic rhinitis. I smiled at this odd American. There was something about the way he walked and talked which made him instantly likeable; the type of person who made you feel better about life, and I certainly needed some of that.

"Right let's get on with the round," Cutfield said.

Poyntz knew the patients well. All twenty were suffering from typhoid fever – at various stages. Sister B held out the observation charts for Cutfield to check and, while he casually browsed these, Poyntz presented a history on each patient for my benefit, followed by a brief update for Cutfield.

As the round wore on I grew to like Poyntz's natural bedside manner. He was careful to include the patient in his little speech, sometimes touching their shoulders when emphasising a certain detail – the humanity they didn't teach you at medical school, and which I had only begun to discover in Bloemfontein.

Whenever Cutfield gave an order, Poyntz wrote it down on his list of jobs and said, "Yep."

In contrast to Poyntz, Cutfield stood sideways on to the patients, and made little or no eye contact with them, much the same way he had avoided Dudley's eye earlier that morning.

Cutfield would slot the chart roughly back into its metal holder at the end of the bed and stride on to the next case, giving me the strong impression that he wanted to be somewhere else. With one of the patients, he even started leafing through their newspaper while Poyntz gave the history.

Finally, we came to the small private ward: there were only two patients here, both Egremont mine engineers injured in an explosion near the rock-face. They were educated men, and it transpired one hailed from the same University as Cutfield. Well, Cutfield became a different person, talking animatedly with the man like a long lost friend: "Oh, you must know so-and-so. And tell me – is the so-and-so café still there? Oh, it is? Jolly glad to hear it."

In the middle of all this I caught Poyntz rolling his eyes at Sister B, the most hopeful thing I had seen since arriving in Kalgoorlie – I might actually enjoy working with these two.

The round over, we wandered back out into the hall.

Cutfield was checking his pocket watch.

"How many bodies?" he said, glancing up at Poyntz.

Poyntz didn't say anything, he just held up three fingers.

"Have the funeral directors come and collect them sharpish," Cutfield said. "We'll need more room later, I'm sure."

"Yep."

Then Cutfield turned to me. "We do the round at nine each morning. The doctor who's been on the night shift has the day off after the round. You alternate with Poyntz here – a one in two on-call. I think that's all you need to know, right Poyntz? Let me know if I've forgotten anything."

Cutfield didn't look at Poyntz as he spoke. He checked the time on his watch again instead.

Poyntz's face remained deadpan and again he didn't bother acknowledging Cutfield.

It was a big relief to see Poyntz wasn't playing the game. Most doctors turned into sycophants when the boss was around, laughing at their jokes and asking questions to which they already knew the answers. Not Poyntz. He seemed to feel the same way about Cutfield as I did.

"Well, Hunston, that's about it. I'll leave the team to show you the rest. I must begin to pack; my wife is keen that we're ready to head off by the weekend."

He made to go but leaned backwards slightly as if pulled by an invisible string.

"Oh, and by the way, if patients pay in gold, put it in my office. There's a good chap."

This time, like Poyntz, I didn't bother replying.

"Good, good," he said on his way out.

Sister B murmured something under her breath; it was in French but you didn't have to be a linguist to know it wasn't complimentary. Poyntz smiled before breaking out into a laugh and clapping me on the back.

"We're sure glad to have you here, pal. Thanks to you, our beloved leader is going on furlough for two months. Thank God. Another week with that guy at the helm and I swear I'd be in one of the beds myself."

I laughed at his frankness.

"I'll leave you boys to it," Sister B said. In a way only the French can, she managed to pretend to be annoyed with our male fraternising in a supremely attractive way.

We watched her walk back to the ward.

"Hey," Poyntz said, "waddya think?"

"About what?"

He tilted his head in the direction of the retreating figure of Sister B. "Her."

"She's lovely."

"She sure is… she sure is," he said.

Poyntz fixed me with a mock wary look.

"Hey… that's all I need, some hot-shot British doc to steal her heart. But I guess you're only human."

"I meant it as an objective fact, not a declaration of love."

Poyntz laughed again.

"I get the feeling I don't have to worry about you."

I frowned, remembering her religious nursing order.

"Isn't she a nun?"

"Nope… She's a postulant. There's still time for me to change her mind."

"Oh, I see… good luck with that."

My spirits dropped as it became clear I wouldn't be able to muscle in on Poyntz's girl. Not unless I wanted to spoil everything.

"How about I take you on the unofficial tour," he said, smiling at me again now.

"Are you sure? You've been up all night."

"No, come on. I grabbed four hours sleep on Cutfield's chaise longue. I feel fine."

He took me down a corridor to a small operating theatre where a steel 'Maquet' operating table, complete with a sawdust box underneath for collecting blood, took up a central position. There had been one like it at my university teaching hospital, surrounded by viewing terraces for students and junior doctors to spectate from, like a miniature football stadium. Once a week we all trooped in to watch one of the esteemed surgeons delving around in a patient's gut. Some of them thought themselves 'God-like' – you could tell by the way they grandstanded in front of the crowd. Others just shut up and got on with the job and you always sensed these were the better ones.

Next to the operating table was a steel trolley with sets of silver instruments laid out on top. On the lower rack of the trolley sat a large glass vat of carbolic acid, labelled with skull and crossbones, and a bottle of chloroform.

Poyntz sat on the Maquet table.

"I can do a few basic operations," he said. "Appendectomy, hernia repairs, caesarean sections if need be. Cutfield claims he used to be a surgeon, but I've never seen him do anything more complicated than an appendix and he made a dog's dinner of that. I think he only got the job because he went to school with Egremont. But that's how you guys do things in England, isn't it? The old school network?"

"Basically."

Poyntz laughed at my honesty and hopped off the table, making it rumble like thunder.

"There's more to see. Come on."

Next to the theatre was a room with a large drum on its side, raised on brick housing with iron doors underneath. '*THRESH CURRENT STEAM DISINFECTOR*' read the engraving on the drum.

"Since this was installed six months ago, the post-op infection rate has fallen to next to nothing. We even use it to clean the sheets."

"I've got some sharps from the other day. Can I use it later?"

"Knock yourself out," Poyntz said. "I heard about Fremantle. You should've seen Cutfield – went crazy. Didn't like the fact you fixed up a native. Or that Dudley had been there with you. He hates him almost as much as he hates the blacks."

"I didn't want to make any trouble for Dudley."

"Oh, don't worry about that. He can take care of himself. But watch out for Cutfield – he'll go behind your back the whole time. I've figured it's best to ignore him. He soon gets bored if you don't rise to his bait."

"Where's he going on leave?"

"Some big shot has loaned him his Perth residence. He's more into social climbing than clinical medicine."

"I noticed."

"The guy doesn't care two hoots for patients, unless there's the possibility of profit involved. By which I mean gold."

"Hmmm... Can I ask what happened to the doctor before me?"

Poyntz furrowed his brow, as if trying to remember.

"Let's talk in the mess," he said. "It's more comfortable there."

Hands in pockets, we walked back to the admin block along the covered passageway.

In the doctor's mess was a brass primus stove with a small black kettle perched on top. Poyntz made coffee and set the tin mugs down on the table.

The coffee was good; hot and fresh, and the aroma cheered me up.

"So?" I said, "...my predecessor?"

Poyntz took a seat on the bench opposite.

"So... you've seen Cutfield. People generally want to get as far away from him as possible. The doc before you went back to England after three months. The one I replaced died of typhoid."

"You've stayed, though."

"Yep, that's true... a whole year."

"So what's the story there?"

"Three reasons," he said, listing them off on his fingers. "Number one – Sister B; number two – I've had typhoid already, so I'm kinda immune; and number three, apart from Cutfield – I kinda like this place... Australia I mean."

"Where are you from, Poyntz?"

"Washington DC, East coast, trained in Baltimore – Johns Hopkins Medical School."

He didn't volunteer any more information and I left it there. Like Rowe had said back in Perth, everyone had their reasons for leaving their former lives. Apart from the gold diggers and crazy ministers, no man came to this sort of place unless they were running away from something. Poyntz could explain things in his own time.

Sister B walked in, pulled off her cap and ran her hands back through a swathe of blonde hair. *In another life,* I found myself thinking.

Poyntz stood up straightaway and poured her a coffee. When he sat back down, she perched next to him and leant her head gently against his shoulder.

"So, you two have it all under control, yes?" she said. "Yes, Doctor John?"

"Yes," I said, smiling shyly.

She was the one who had it all under control.

Holding her gaze rattled me, and I found myself switching my attention between her face and the table, like a lovestruck teenager.

We sat there together and did the handover. I would be looking after things for the rest of the day.

Poyntz was starting to look tired now.

"Where are your digs, Poyntz?"

"I've got a place on the outskirts of town – the Catholics don't have the same money for their doctor that Egremont has to throw around for his, so no fancy room at the Palace for me… Probably a good thing though, with the racket in the bar there, I don't think I would ever sleep."

"How about you, Sister B?" I said. "Are you going to grab some rest?"

"Don't worry about me, Doctor John. I have more jobs and will be up a while yet. My quarters are in this block. I grab sleep when it's quiet."

"Right, you two," Poyntz said, standing up, "I'll be back at five to see how you're doing."

He stretched out his arms and yawned. Poyntz had quite an arm span – like the albatross Rennie and I had seen riding the warm air over the funnel of our mail ship during the voyage over.

"And I'll do tonight as you're new," he said.

"Are you sure?"

"Just say thanks."

"Thanks, Poyntz."

"Hey," he said, "it'll be your turn soon enough, right?"

He left the mess, his white coat billowing out behind him like a ship's sail.

Chapter Twelve

Poyntz had the neat flowing Spenserian script favoured by educated Americans, the style which made everything look like the Declaration of Independence. Still, his examination findings were written in the same cryptic medical shorthand all doctors used:

0300
O/E: rash, T104, p 120, BP 90/60, CR >3s, Abdo – soft, tender RIF

I had gone back to the general ward to review the notes of one of the more serious cases – a Swedish Miner called Carlsson who had come in overnight. There were so many foreign miners that the 'place of birth' column in the hospital admissions book read more like the index of an atlas.

I deciphered Poyntz's jottings at a glance: Carlsson had presented to the hospital in the early hours – 3am to be precise. On examination Poyntz had seen the characteristic rash of typhoid fever – red spots on the chest. Carlsson's temperature had been 104 degrees, the pulse 120 and the blood pressure 90/60. Not good. He had been dehydrated too, with a capillary refill time of over three seconds. To assess this, Poyntz would have pinched the miner's finger and counted how long it took for the colour to return. Carlsson's abdomen was still soft when palpated but Poyntz had noted it was tender in the right iliac fossa – the right lower quadrant – a sure sign the large bowel was affected.

From my time at the Spitz Kop tent hospital, I knew how it would play out. With typhoid, large ulcers formed in the lower alimentary canal and, if this led to the bowel being breached, it was all over. The abdomen would become firm and the patient would die of peritonitis. That was why the morgue was stacking up.

I spent the rest of the morning finding out where things were kept. Sister B showed me how to work the steriliser and I cleaned the suturing needle and scissors I had used on Eugene. It felt novel to have to do it myself; back in Oxford and Harley Street, there had always been a man who did that kind of thing for you.

Working together, Sister B and I were able to discharge four patients. Two of them, the mining engineers, had received free treatment under their Egremont contracts, but the others on the general ward were diggers from another company and had to pay up. They each handed me a number of small misshapen gold shards, so thin that they were more like flakes than nuggets. Collectively I guessed they weighed no more than half an ounce. Cutfield's desk was starting to look like a small geology display.

I went back to the Palace for lunch.

Dudley was perched on the exact same barstool he had been on earlier that morning. I took the one next to him.

"Get the doc a pie and a beer, there's a girl, Violet."

"Coming up, Sweetie," she said, winking at me. I smiled back.

Dudley chuckled to himself.

"Watch out, Doc, she'll break your heart."

"Don't get jealous now, Tom, just because he's better looking than you."

She disappeared down a ladder into the cellar to change the beer keg.

"Violet Cook," Dudley said. "The boss's wife, but for Christ's sake don't ever call her that. Violet runs this place like her own little kingdom. She's as close as you get to royalty out here in Kalgoorlie.

Used to be a singer and an actress, the world was her oyster. Then she married my ugly friend."

"I heard that!" said a voice from below the floor.

"One of my oldest mates, he is too," Dudley said back to her. "Just thought I'd be the lucky one... why'd you go for a gargoyle like him, Violet?"

She climbed back up the ladder.

"He listens," she said.

Dudley erupted into a raucous laugh and was still going when she brought out the pies.

After all the joshing, we ate in silence, pausing only to swig from our schooners of beer.

I noticed Dudley was digging his fingers into his right temple again, clearly in some pain. He had finished his beer in double-time and was now taking a long slug from his flask.

"Where were you injured?" I said. He looked at me warily. "If you don't mind me asking. I was out there too... with the Medical Corps in Bloemfontein."

I think he took that as an acceptable qualification for me to hear his story. He stared straight ahead for a few seconds, and started to recount his tale as if he were looking at an internal cinematograph.

"Near Slingersfontein... 16th of January. I was leading a routine patrol of twenty-one men – fourteen from the New South Wales Lancers and seven from my unit, the 1st Australian Horse. We'd almost made it back to camp when we came under fire from about fifty of them, five hundred yards away, riding towards us at full gallop. Jonny Boer had been lying in wait for us, using a concealed fold in what looked like open veldt. Some of our patrol managed to escape, the rest of us headed to some high ground nearby. I managed to dismount and open fire, with the idea of making a stand until help arrived. But we soon became heavily engaged on all sides. More Boers were hidden on the hill we had occupied. They shot our horses out from under us within minutes. We fought until we were out of ammo and then the buggers rushed us...'

I gave Dudley's account a few moments of respectful silence.

"Where are the 1st Australian Horse from?"

"New South Wales. I'm from a small town called Muswellbrook in the Hunter Valley. Ridden horses all my life and was ready to fight for the Empire. So I left the goldfields last year and went back home to join up. Our squadron was attached to the Royal Scots Greys under General French – nice bunch – bit of history… Waterloo, Balaclava… but we still could teach them a thing or two. Showed them how to scout, take cover, ride and shoot – in short, to play that particular game as it should be played. No offence to the Greys, but the Veldt could've been the Australian bush. We adapted quickly to conditions out there."

Once more, he dug his fingers into his right temple. I imagined it was like a buzzer sounding off in his head, the same noise the Longmore's bullet retractor made when it touched metal. Except that in Dudley's case it was his damaged nerves firing erratically.

"When we got to South Africa, we moved north towards the Orange River to link up with the Kimberley relief force under Lord Methuen. We were in the Colesberg district when I was injured."

"What happened after the ambush?"

"Some made it out. Fourteen of us were taken prisoner. My sergeant-major, George Griffin, was killed outright – shot in the head – I knew him from way back, before I even came out to the goldfields. He was an accountant in a gold mine when he joined up. Another mate was mortally wounded, Corporal Kilpatrick – schoolmaster from Sydney. To tell you the truth, I don't remember much; but a reporter mate of mine was on the scene the next day."

He opened out his wallet and handed me a newspaper clipping. The author's name was Paterson:

'…They saw a man making efforts to lift his leg to attract attention. It was Kilpatrick. He was a terrible sight; all the lower part of his face shot away. He could not speak. He had been there all night and had written 'cold' on the ground with his fingers. His wounds had been bandaged roughly with field dressing, evidently by the Boers, but strange to say they hadn't taken his bandolier, which contained a few cartridges.

Nothing was in his pockets. The rocks were all spattered with blood and pieces of field dressing. Then the searchers came across the body of Sergeant Griffin, First Australian Horse...'

I gave the clipping back to Dudley and he stared at it.

"They buried Griffin where he lay," he said. "Kilpatrick died later that day."

"What happened to you?"

"I'm not sure quite why, but the Boers seemed to want to save me. I ended up in the Bloemfontein Free State Hospital as a POW. When the British took the town I was a free man. Couldn't serve anymore though; not with all the holes in me. I was invalided back and came out here to start again."

I must have missed Dudley in Bloemfontein by a matter of days.

"At least they didn't shoot you with dum dums," I said without thinking.

Dudley snorted.

"I never thought about it like that," he said, "but you're bloody right, Doc."

He held up his thumbless hand. "It could have been the whole bloody arm. I might've even lost my entire head!"

Ha, Ha, Ha!

At least I had cheered him up again.

"Listen, Doc, I hope I didn't get you into any trouble by seeing Eugene," he said. "With Cutfield, I mean."

"No trouble I can't deal with."

Dudley laughed.

"Not sure what the story is with him exactly," he said. "He wasn't here before I left for the war, but he was when I got back. Some old school chum of Egremont's, I think."

"That's what Poyntz said."

"Yeah well, I've heard about those Pommy schools – they were probably bloody in love once. All I know is Egremont must have given the Catholics one hell of a financial inducement to let Cutfield run the place. From what I can make out, he's more administrator than physician. For him, the hospital is there to make money – and a nice little profit he has going on with payment too – exchanges the gold at the bank for cash and pockets the lion's share. Poyntz doesn't see much of it and neither will you, Doc. Christ, I've seen gold fever in my time, but that Cutfield is the worst case I've ever witnessed and he's not even a bloody miner."

"I was told to keep out of his way."

Dudley smiled wryly. "Poyntz said that too, did he?"

"How well do you know him?"

"Who? You mean Poyntz?"

"Yes."

"Oh, only a little bit. He saw me a couple of times when I got back from the war – about the pain in my face and my leg – not that he could do much. Says it like it is. His exact words were, 'I can't do jack to help you'. Well, that cheered me up more than any medicine and we got chatting. Told me he came over here from Alaska and that Cutfield's been working him like a slave for the last year. You don't have to be a mind reader to see why he puts up with all the shit though. It's because he's got a thing for that French nurse."

"Ah yes, Sister B… What do you know about her?" I said, as casually as possible.

Dudley seemed to know more than I did about my own feelings. "Jesus H. Christ," he said to Violet, "the doc here's in love, on his first day… with a bloody nun!"

She smiled knowingly from behind the bar and continued to polish a glass. I turned red and picked at the crumbs on my empty plate.

"She's not a nun," I said. "She's a postulant… and I'm not in love."

Dudley pushed back his chair and grabbed his bush hat from the bar top, shaking his head and grinning.

"Whatever you say, Romeo. Right, I'm off to go and work out what to do with this bloody mine. Drink later, Doc?"

"I'll be here."

"Good man."

He clapped me on the back and walked out into the dust of Kalgoorlie.

As the door swung back and forth on its hinges, the sounds of the street came into the room intermittently, like waves crashing onto the beach. Here I was, living in a furnace of a town, inhabited by chancers, doing a job where I had to answer to a man like Cutfield. And being paid next to nothing.

The chatter in the room stopped and I glanced round at the other drinkers who were all looking towards the door. Sister B had walked in and was heading over towards me. The eyes of a dozen men followed her, just like the patients in the ward.

"Doctor John… Carlsson is worse."

As we left the bar, the chatter resumed even more loudly than before. I was pleased to be the object of Sister B's attention and on the walk over to the hospital tried desperately to think of something interesting to say to her, but all I could come out with were a few professional enquiries about the patient's condition.

The big Swedish miner had vacant, glassy eyes. He was dehydrated now and shivering with a rigor.

Sister B held up the chart. The fever had spiked. Most of the temperature charts from the morning's round had looked like mountain ranges and Carlsson's mountain range was the highest of all. It was the Himalayas.

"Let's try some phenacetin and sponge him down," I said.

Sister B went off to get the medicine.

I jotted my notes onto the yellow hospital paper, drawing a hexagon to represent the abdomen and cross-hatching the tender areas. At the end of the entry, I wrote a simple plan: *strict bed rest, regular fluids, half hourly obs*. The essential treatment was keeping the patient as rested as possible in order to reduce the chance of bowel perforation. If they made it to a week, the chances were they would be all right.

The basics for typhoid care were: careful sanitation, careful nursing and a careful diet. In South Africa we had used water and condensed milk for the dehydration – the problem then as now, was that clean water had been hard to come by. There, the river had been polluted. Here, there was no river.

"What fluids do we use?"

"Poyntz uses... American fluids."

"What's that supposed to mean?"

She shrugged: "They come from America."

"I'll get them," I said, in a blatant attempt to try and impress her.

"He keeps them in the morgue."

"The morgue?"

"Yes... to keep them cold."

The morgue was the first cool place I had encountered in Australia and I stopped sweating as soon as I shut the door behind me. On the earlier tour, Poyntz said it was cooled by a machine imported from the farming area further east, previously used for a meat locker. You could just hear the faint hum of the engines beyond the walls. Had this been any other room, the atmosphere could have been described as pleasant, but it was a storage room for the dead, tiled from floor to ceiling in white. I had a flashback to the makeshift morgue at the Spitz Kop – a white bell tent pitched on the African scrub, full of stinking bodies stacked unceremoniously in the heat. The flies had liked that tent the most.

Here, there were just three cadavers in a steel rack, loosely covered in white sheets. I could see the toe tags hanging down: small brown labels with name, date of birth and date of death written on them.

The crates of drink were in the far corner of the room, as far from the body rack as possible.

To me, the three silent forms on the rack represented a void – one into which Freddie had plunged. The floor of the morgue became like a great chasm. I was standing on the precipice and looking down. I found myself edging slowly around the sides of the room, talking out loud to myself: "Just a few more feet... come on... almost there."

I picked out a bottle from the crate and made a dash for the door, my pulse racing.

Sister B prised off the lid using a bottle opener hanging from a piece of string on the wall and gave the concoction to Carlsson in a glass tumbler.

An hour later, his skin turgor had improved and he even managed to smile back at me. Though an encouraging sign, I knew from bitter experience it was early days.

I studied the 'American fluids' by the bed. Such had been my haste to get out of the morgue I had barely glanced at it before. The liquid was dark and came in a square sided bottle. The label was written in that same Spencerian script that Poyntz used: *'Coca-Cola – bottled in Chattanooga'*. From what I could make out, it was a tonic consisting of carbonated sugar water and a cocoa leaf extract. I took a sip. Not bad, though I couldn't see it catching on.

Poyntz wandered in at five o'clock and I filled him in on the day's events. He was particularly pleased I had used his favoured rehydration treatment.

When he saw the pieces of gold on the desk he laughed out loud, bending forward and examining the payments with his hands behind his back.

"What's all this?"

"Today's patient fees," I said, leaning over his shoulder to get another look at the gold. "I didn't know where else to put them."

He straightened up.

"My fault, I guess."

He walked over to the oil painting of the despondent bushman and lifted it up to reveal a small recessed wall safe.

"This is where you put that stuff. Once a week Cutfield goes to the bank and cashes it in. Code's 21397, the date they opened this hospital."

"I'm surprised he trusts us."

Poyntz shrugged.

"What the hell are we going to do with it? Run off into the sunset?"

"I suppose not."

"Cutfield knows we're not interested in gold. Anyone who comes out to this place who isn't a miner isn't interested in making a fortune."

"Except for him."

Poyntz looked at me.

"Dudley filled me in at lunchtime," I said.

He frowned.

"If you're lucky you might see some of the money, depending on what mood he's in. More often than not, there's no payment at all. He pays me a token amount, but it nowhere near corresponds to the amount of work I've done. Because he's thick with Egremont, no-one dares challenge him. And the St John of God let it go because they need the Egremont business to keep this place functional. He's got us bent over a barrel."

I remembered Poyntz's three reasons for wanting to stay: Sister B, his immunity to typhoid and the fact that he liked the place. The first two reasons applied to me too, but after only one day, I was seriously doubting the third.

Poyntz looked at the collection on the desk.

"Anyway, leave it there for now – he'll be in soon – he usually checks in at the end of the day to collect the gold."

Right on cue we heard Cutfield talking with Sister B in the corridor.

"Good evening, gentlemen," he said, striding into the room. His mood seemed a little better than it had been that morning.

"Doctor Cutfield," I said.

Poyntz lifted his hand and just said, "Doc," in his deep nasal voice. With his accent, it sounded like, 'duck'.

Cutfield examined the gold flakes.

"All well?" he said, without taking his eyes off the gold. It was as if he was addressing the precious metal and not his house staff.

He looked up from his booty and was met by a set of blank, tired looks. Nobody seemed to have the energy to respond.

"Good, good," he said.

It was Poyntz who finally spoke. "Funeral directors are coming first thing tomorrow. It's the earliest they could make it. They've been busy."

I looked at him with silent thanks. I had forgotten all about that.

"Good, good," Cutfield said again.

I watched in silent irritation as he gathered up the gold into a starched white handkerchief, folded it carefully in on itself and then slipped it into his breast pocket.

"Right, I'm out to the theatre tonight with friends. See you all at rounds tomorrow morning."

He was out the door before I even had a chance to reply.

Nobody else made any attempt to bid him farewell and there was a depressed silence after his departure.

"Don't be so worried, Doctor John," Sister B said. "Didn't Socrates say a bad man can do a good man no harm?"

"A nurse philosopher," I said, my mouth engaging before brain. Luckily, she laughed.

Poyntz ruffled my hair. "She thinks you're a good man. Cheer up, buddy."

With the collective mood lifted a fraction, we all headed back to the ward.

Carlsson had deteriorated again. It had been his chart that Sister was trying to discuss with Cutfield in the corridor, though he had shown little interest.

The Swede's face was slate grey and his skin sheened with sweat. Every few moments he would shudder and grip his abdomen, muttering in his mother tongue. Poor Carlsson was in his crisis and being in a hospital made little difference; his fate was in the lap of the gods now.

I shook my head in resignation.

"Don't let him see you do that," Poyntz said to me in a low voice. "Don't take away his hope."

"I'm sorry. You're right, Poyntz."

He put his hand on my shoulder.

"One of my professors at Johns Hopkins once told me that and I never forgot it."

The misery and hopelessness of the situation in South Africa had skewed my views of typhoid fever. But Poyntz was right. We weren't in the squalor of the Spitz Kop tent hospital now. For a start there was a nurse. Carlsson was in a bed with clean sheets. We had Coca-Cola.

We injected Carlsson with morphia and watched his agonised expression ease as the opiate took effect.

"A Priest…" Carlsson said.

Physically spent, it seemed he had accepted his fate.

Poyntz looked at Sister B, nodded at her and said "Go", and she left the ward. Ten minutes later she was back, with a man in black.

"I'm Father Long," the man said, shaking our hands.

His accent was Irish.

Looking down at Carlsson, he sized up the situation quickly.

Father Long sat on the edge of the bed, placed his hand on Carlsson's shoulder and started reciting the Lord's Prayer in a low voice. Carlsson whispered the words in time with the priest, while Poyntz, Sister B and I watched on.

When they had concluded with the 'Amen', Carlsson smiled and closed his eyes. The priest stood up, made the sign of the cross and looked at us with a nod.

Sister B stayed to watch over Carlsson while Poyntz and I took Father Long to Cutfield's office – the only smart room in the building. After filing into the room, I let Poyntz do the talking.

"Appreciate what you did for that man, Father."

"No problem, Doctor, no problem at all."

"Some coffee?"

"That would be grand."

Poyntz went to brew some coffee in the mess, leaving me alone with the priest. He wandered over to the painting of the bushman covering the safe.

"A McCubbin," he said, not taking his eyes off it. "A copy, but a good one. You know what this painting is called, Doctor?"

"No, Father."

"*Down on his luck*. You know what it's about?"

"No."

He pointed at the bushman.

"An unsuccessful gold prospector."

I joined him in staring at the painting. Miserable and forlorn, the prospector could have been me in my corner chair at the Blue Boar Club.

"I've always thought that he looked like a man in need of salvation," Father Long said. For some reason it felt as if he was directing his comments at me specifically. "Know that feeling, Doctor?"

Christ, he was trying to convert me in the time it was taking for Poyntz to make the coffee.

"Not really, Father."

He smiled.

"I do," he said.

Come back soon, Poyntz, I thought.

I didn't probe into Father Long's cryptic comment; I just let it hang there in Cutfield's office like the dust particles in the evening sunlight.

Fortunately, my wish was granted and, a few moments later, Poyntz pushed the door open with his back, trying not to spill the three coffees he was holding precariously.

I stood there listening to Poyntz talk to the priest and drank as fast as I could without burning my mouth. The priest made me feel uncomfortable – he had essentially told me that he was the one in need of salvation, not me. That didn't make any sense – how could a man of God feel the need for that? Surely that part came automatically with the job and it was other people he needed to be concerned about. He had an air of distraction about his person though, a sad weariness about the world that I found familiar. It took one to know one.

Perhaps it was just because he was doing a hard job in a hard town, like the rest of us.

After the coffee, we returned to the ward to check on Carlsson.

While Poyntz and Father Long continued to whisper at the doorway, I stood to one side and watched Sister B tend to her patient. He looked ready for Valhalla, his skin almost a luminous white now. The sun was going down and the ward was suffused with a strange light, not quite daylight and not quite shadow. I looked around for the Grey Lady and shivered despite the heat.

I remembered what Poyntz had said about not taking away hope so I leant in close to the Swede and said, "Hold on... keep fighting... you'll get through it."

"It is not as hard as cross country skiing," he said, grinning at me through gritted teeth.

I understood what he meant. When I was sick I too had tried to trick myself that I had been in more painful situations in the past. Laid up in the Raadzaal I had remembered my rowing days and the times in training when I had rowed myself into near oblivion, turning my legs blotchy and my windpipe raw. It had helped, up to a point.

Soon after, Poyntz told me to go home, making good on his earlier promise that he would cover the first night.

Dudley and Rennie were in the Palace bar. Compared to the evening before, when I had left Rennie standing alone outside his new church, he looked back to his old usual self. He was telling Dudley some story about Jesus on the shores of Lake Galilee and his wooing of the fisherman apostles.

"Ah, Doc, join me and the good Reverend," Dudley said, seeing me come in.

I squeezed onto a bar stool next to them.

It was good to see Rennie again. I had missed him. After spending nearly twenty four hours a day in each other's company for two months, it was strange to have been separated for so much time.

Dudley held his hand out towards the barman.

"Gentlemen, allow me to introduce Mister Cook, proprietor of the Palace and an old friend. Everyone calls him Cookie, so you'd better do the same, if you want him to answer you. He used to be a bloody bank manager if you can believe that. Then he married Violet – that bombshell you met earlier today, Doc – and he's never looked back. A schooner for the good doctor if you please, Cookie."

Cookie reached across the bar to shake my hand before going back to the business of pulling the drink with the long jarrah handle.

"This place," Dudley said, sweeping one hand through the air and drinking with the other, "it's the best in town. And this beer's probably the safest thing to drink – been boiled and sterilised over at the brewery… even managed to persuade your mate here to partake when I told him that."

That was when I noticed Rennie's glass on the bar top, a few sips gone.

I accepted my beer from Cookie and raised my glass to Dudley and Rennie in acknowledgment.

Dudley drank half his beer in two large gulps, his Adam's apple moving up and down like a piston. He wiped his face with the back of his hand and then belched loudly, saying "Arch Bishop," forcefully as he belched out the word 'Arch'.

Something told me this wasn't his first drink of the evening.

He emptied out his pockets and started lining up samples of yellowy grey rocks on the copper bar top.

"Why are you putting rubble on the bar?" Rennie said.

"An easy mistake to make, Rev… to call this rubble, I mean. That's what the first prospectors thought it was back in '93, when they were digging holes all around here looking for shiny yellow gold. They used this stuff for potholes and ruts in the roads. They even used it in the bricks and mortar for the town's buildings."

Dudley held up one of the rocks so that it was inches away from Rennie's face.

"Gold bonds to an element called tellurium to form gold telluride – which we miners call telly. Its other name is calaverite. But for three years everyone dismissed it as *bagoshite*. They were literally paving the streets with gold. Anyway, when the drongos finally cottoned on; they dug up half the town's roads to get the rubble back. Buildings were dismantled and old refuse heaps were picked over. That's what caused the second rush of '96. See the black areas there… that indicates high gold content. This stuff yields around 500 ounces of gold per ton of rock. The few acres beneath our feet contain the richest gold bearing seams in the world, and that's a fact."

"Doesn't anyone just pan for gold out here?" Rennie said, "you know, like the Americans."

Dudley laughed. "Need a river or a stream to pan, Rev. No, all the stuff you could pick up has long gone. It's mostly in the telly now, deep underground."

Poor Freddie, I was thinking. His venture would have been a non-starter – everything had been industrialised. He would have been at least five years too late.

"Know the Aztecs, Doc?"

"I've heard of them."

"Their word for gold was 'teo - cuit - latl'," he said, breaking the word down. "Nicely put, it means excrement of the gods."

I could see that Rennie liked that. It fitted with his and Rowe's view that mammon and the Almighty did not mix. He smiled and did his usual: rubbing his hands together in excitement and going slightly cross-eyed at the same time.

"And then there are the words of the one true God, Tom," he said, "quoted in the book of Proverbs: '…my fruit is better than gold, yea, than *fine* gold'…"

Sister B burst into the bar, out of breath but smiling and I stood up off my stool so fast I almost fell over.

"Sister B?"

"Poyntz sent me to tell you, Doctor John… the miner has stabilised."

"Really?"

I was stunned Carlsson had pulled through. His dreaming of Scandinavian snows had worked. I would have given him less than a 1 in 5 chance of survival an hour ago. Poyntz had been right to keep hoping.

By now, Dudley and Rennie had stood up too.

"Ah, where are my manners? Sister Bernadette. This is Tom Dudley…'

She evidently knew him.

"Yes, I remember when you came to see Doctor Poyntz about your injuries. It's very nice to see you."

Dudley touched his forehead in greeting.

"And this is my good friend, Sean Rennie" I said, "…the new Wesleyan Minister in town."

Rennie took her hand and shook it ever so gently, as if his normal grip might cause her some harm.

"I prefer Sister B, Reverend" she said with a smile, correcting my earlier introduction.

Rennie looked as lovestruck as I must have been earlier in the day, a big doe-eyed grin appearing on his face.

"A great pleasure… What a blessing to meet you."

She waved her hand in the smoky atmosphere of the bar.

"Do you mind if we get some air?"

"Certainly," Dudley said, clearing away the rock specimens and putting them back in his pocket. "Follow me."

We all moved out onto the ground floor veranda and leant against the balustrade, taking in the bustling vista of the street. Off duty miners were moving around like predators; their hardened eyes the same as those of the Bullabulling men who had lifted the pipes. Filtering through the din of the crowd was a rhythmic pounding, like the heartbeat of a giant somewhere out in the desert. It was the stamping batteries, Dudley told us, crushing rock to get at the gold, never stopping in their relentless quest for more production. The more I watched the scene, the more it seemed to me that the miners were walking in time to the beat.

Dudley's attention had switched to Sister B now, since she was a lot nicer to look at than Rennie or me.

He raised his glass to the crowds:

"Out there, Sister, you have all that humanity has to offer… and they're all here because of the telly under the Golden Mile."

"Yes," she said, "I see them all, Mr Dudley, when they get sick. And when they have typhoid they are all the same, they all are afraid and all want to hold my hand."

That shut Dudley up.

A drunken miner staggered down the street; so far gone he couldn't walk straight. He would stand stock still and then lean so preposterously that it looked as if he might topple over, only to right himself again at the last possible moment. It was as if he was on the deck of a ship in rough seas.

"Looks like you when you got off that ship in Fremantle, Doc."

The sight made everyone laugh and, before I knew it, I was laughing along with them.

I couldn't remember the last time I had laughed properly.

Chapter Thirteen

Next morning I walked up Hannan Street and then east towards the Egremont head frame, an iron girder structure half a mile away in the town of Boulder. Close up it looked like a diminutive Eiffel tower, perhaps a hundred feet high. Men were entering a cage at its base, carrying sandwich boxes in one hand and pick axes in the other. I wanted to see what it was that made this town tick; Dudley's realm of telly and rock, the reason we were here at all.

The wheels at the top of the frame started to turn, and the mine cage disappeared off into the belly of the earth. When it did, my heart lurched in sympathy as I remembered the feeling I had experienced when Freddie had died, of being carried down to a place of darkness. Here in Kalgoorlie, people were doing it as a job; with Egremont's great girdered machine providing their means of transportation to the underworld.

On the way back to the Palace I found The British Arms, Dudley's gaff, so small and insignificant a building that I had walked right past it on my way out to see the head frame.

"Welcome to the skinniest pub in Australia," the publican said as I pushed open the door.

The bar-room wasn't much bigger than my room at the Palace. The wood was dark and the atmosphere more 'dingy basement' than 'ground floor saloon'.

He noticed me looking around.

"Only built last year," he said. "I know it's small. I think they ran out of bricks that day. Hell of a lot better than living in a hessian tent though."

Immediately friendly, he introduced himself as Jim McKay. While his wife Edith brewed the coffee, he asked me why I was in town and when I said I knew Tom Dudley, he said, "Put your money away, mate, the coffee is on the house."

"Likes my coffee, does Tom," Edith said, as she poured me a mug. "He'll be down as soon as he gets a whiff."

"Unless he's put his bloody patch on the wrong eye again," Jim McKay said, laughing.

They busied themselves around the bar area, cleaning up from the night before, so I took my mug and looked at the framed pictures on the walls.

One was a large map of the Western Australian Colony, with another boundary within the state, shaded yellow.

McKay came over.

"A few years ago, we wanted to make this area into a separate state," he said, tracing his finger over the yellow lines, "to include the goldfields, the port of Esperance and the desert right up to the edge of the border with South Australia."

"Some state," I said. "That's about three times the size of England."

"Yeah… would've been big. Everything to the east of the 119th meridian and to the south of the 24th parallel."

"Why did you want a new state?"

McKay blinked as if it should have been obvious to me.

"Ten years ago, this whole area was considered desert and worthless, but by our energy it became the largest producing goldfield in Australasia. Tom Dudley and I are originally from the east. In fact, most of Kal are from the eastern states, those who aren't from abroad,

173

that is. The older inhabitants of the colony – the 'sandgropers' – view us all with suspicion. You know what they call us?"

"T'othersiders," I heard Dudley say, answering McKay's question. He was standing at the doorway leading to the back stairs.

"Morning, Edith, and thank you my dear," he said, taking the steaming cup of coffee she had ready for him. He joined us at the map.

"Auralia," McKay said.

Dudley sipped his coffee and repeated the word slowly: "Auralia."

The way these two were going on made it seem as if they were talking about an old sweetheart.

"Auralia would have become part of the new Australia, joining up with the other states. The rest of Western Australia – basically the coastal portion – wanted to remain independent you see. They thought they didn't need the rest of Australia to prosper. Out here though, we realised that if we weren't in a government-controlled federation, things would go downhill – law and order included, like the Wild West. Tom and I were part of the 'separatist movement' for the state of Auralia to be cleaved from Western Australia. We even prepared a case to be presented to the queen."

He tapped another frame, housing a printed document, yellowing at the edges:

Separation for Federation
MANIFESTO
of the Reform League of Eastern Goldfields of Western Australia.

Underneath was one of those long waffling sentences of officialdom:

We, the delegates from all public bodies representing the people resident on the Eastern Goldfields of Western Australia, in conference assembled, have decided by a majority of 60 to 1 to initiate a movement to take advantages of the clauses existing in the Constitution Act of Western Australia which allows the division of that colony into separate colonies…

174

I moved on to the last picture on the wall; a photograph of twelve men sitting at a large table. In spidery writing in the bottom right hand corner of the photograph, someone had scratched: *'Executive Council, Goldfields Reform League'*. The general demeanour was one of firm resolve. Papers lay scattered over the conference table. In the background, the windows were wide open and it was dark outside. Nobody in the picture was smiling. It gave me the impression of a meeting that had gone on too long. Dudley, McKay and Cookie were among the group.

"We got a petition with the signatures of thousands," McKay said. "The piece of paper stretched for a mile."

He stretched out his arms expansively to illustrate his point, inadvertently revealing large sweat stains in the armpits of his shirt.

"We spent weeks putting our case together – the petition, the map, our declaration…"

McKay jabbed his thumb in the direction of the frames on the wall. "But the bloody governor of Western Australia never even presented it to the queen."

His face wrinkled with the memory. He wasn't a good looking man anyway and when he did this he looked like a bulldog.

"Bastard left us high and dry," Dudley said.

I was confused.

"But I thought Western Australia *is* joining up."

"You're right. It is now," McKay said. "The British piled on the pressure for the whole colony to join up – Perth included. They made it clear that 'imperial assistance' wouldn't be forthcoming if Western Australia didn't federate. They had those politicians in Perth by the balls. Premier Forrest came to his senses and fought hard to federate. So in the end we joined forces."

McKay went back behind the bar and leant on it, opposite Dudley, as if he was about to start an arm wrestle.

He caught my eye.

"A few months back, the Western Australians went to the polls and voted by more than two to one to federate with the five other colonies."

"When will it happen?"

"New Year's day," Dudley said. "In two months, a new country is going to be declared, Doc – the Commonwealth of Australia."

Cutfield was punctual and kept quiet on the round, nodding curtly as Poyntz and I presented the patients. Afterwards we all trooped over to the mess and Cutfield joined us, although he declined a drink.

"Tonight there's a welcome dinner for you," he said to me.

"Oh?"

"At the Egremont Stope – underground – Dudley will show you where. Evening dress. Of course your friend Reverend Rennie is invited."

"I'll look forward to it," I said, not really understanding. I assumed that when he said underground, he meant a basement room.

"Poyntz and Sister Bernadette can cover your shift."

I couldn't help but notice the looks Poyntz and Sister B gave to one another. 'Side-lined again,' they seemed to be saying.

I realised it also meant a third night in a row of on-call for Poyntz.

"Can't we get some cover so they can come?"

Everyone stared back at me

"That would be slightly… irregular," Cutfield said.

"I would really appreciate it if you can find a way for the team to be invited, Doctor Cutfield. I'm sure we can get a nurse for the night and one of the doctors at the Government Hospital to be on standby."

"Umm, aaah… well…"

For several seconds he blinked and stammered, before finding the reply I was waiting for.

"Well, Poyntz, if you can get the cover, I suppose I don't see why not – perhaps you can talk to the Matron over at the Government Hospital."

"Yep," Poyntz said, looking straight at me.

"Good, good. I'll see you all this evening then… eight o'clock sharp."

It was hard to work out whether I had won a victory or not, such was the lack of expression on Cutfield's face. He strode back down the hall to his office and slammed the door shut behind him.

"I left London because of rubbish like that," I said, breaking the silence. "I hope you two don't mind… it would be good to have you there."

"You actually made him relent," Sister B said in amazement.

"Yes, I suppose I did."

Poyntz downed the rest of his coffee and got up to go.

"You didn't have to do that, but I appreciate it. The look on his face was priceless. You're a strange one all right. Fancy a walk, B? Suppose we'd better take a stroll over to the Government Hospital and find someone to cover our shifts."

After they had gone, I lay down on the bench and waited for my heart rate to return to normal. It was going like the clappers, partly because of Edith McKay's strong coffee, and from having locked horns with Cutfield again, and yes, I admit, part of it was because I had impressed Sister B.

It wasn't just my schoolboy crush that had made me stand up to Cutfield. I could overlook the fact he was a stuck up prig, but what really got on my nerves was that he didn't pull his weight. If he had been in a rowing team, the coach would have kicked him out straight away.

I began to calm down, taking deep slow breaths and trying not to think about anything much.

The rising sun came into the room through a slatted blind, decorating the floor with bright stripes. For a long while I stayed on the bench, watching the light move slowly across the room as the sun climbed higher and just enjoying the feeling of lying there in utter silence.

The rest of the morning passed unremarkably, just minor ward jobs and a few routine admissions. Carlsson continued to improve. A dusty hearse belonging to the funeral directors drew up at the back of the morgue and took away the dead.

At lunch in the Palace, I told Dudley about the underground dinner and what I had said to Cutfield. Cookie was there, watching from behind the counter and trying not to smile.

Dudley almost choked on his mouthful.

"Hear that, Cookie?" he said. "This Pom's got some nerve. Not a week in and he's telling his boss what to do. Jesus, Doc, you've got balls the size of Cape oranges!"

Back on the ward I went to check on Carlsson and take his blood pressure.

As I lifted his pyjama sleeve I noticed a tattoo on his arm – the word *'BURGERWACHT'*. It was Afrikaans for 'militia'.

"You fought in the war?" I said. "For the Boers?"

He looked at me, perhaps detecting the slight panic in my voice.

"I joined the Boers because I thought they were the weaker side, and I did my best for them."

I took a step backwards – we were still at war – I half expected he might lunge for me. For all I knew he might have been the one who had shot my brother on the Kop. The horror must have shown on my face.

Carlsson laughed. "Don't worry, Doctor. I'm not a soldier anymore."

I approached his bed again, not quite knowing what to think. Automatically, I took his pulse. It was ninety – better than the day before.

"I heard you rubbed poison on the tips of your bullets," I said, remembering what Freddie had told me.

"No. We used a green wax coating to keep our rifles clean – it lubricated the chamber and the rifle barrel. It wasn't poison."

I looked closely at him, trying to judge if he was lying or not.

"What about dum dums?"

His looked turned grim.

"Yes," he said, "some of the men I fought with used them. I saw them rubbing away at the nickel apex, but not me. My country, Sweden, signed up to the Hague convention in 1899. Anyway, you should also know that the bullet that hit me was a dum dum. Both sides were using them."

He lifted the sheets and showed me a large ugly scar on his thigh as proof.

Ignoring the leg, I palpated his belly.

"Does it hurt here?"

"No…"

"Here?"

Carlsson shook his head.

"The nurse told me you were the Egremont doctor," he said.

"That's right."

"Know a fellow called Dudley?"

"I do."

Carlsson raised himself onto his elbow, becoming more alive.

"Toughest man I ever saw," he said.

"How's that?"

"I was in the Kommando the day we cut down his squadron. A real tiger cat he was."

"He's only told me that he stopped a few − bullets, I mean…"

The Swede's booming laugh rang around the ward like a peal of thunder.

"Stopped a few? Is that what he said? He's being too modest. Let me tell you this − if all the soldiers were like Dudley, the Boers would have run out of bullets in a fortnight."

Sister B came over.

"Shhhh! You two are disturbing the other patients."

Carlsson gazed up at her and spoke to her in French.

"Oh la la… Ma belle femme, si j'etais le docteur Americain…"

She blushed, which only served to confirm her feelings for Poyntz.

"Mon dieux… ils sont comme les petit enfants," she said to herself as she smoothed out Carlsson's pillows.

"Tell me about Dudley," I said, once she had gone.

Carlsson lay back on his pillow, his expression becoming deadly serious

"We'd waited overnight for them," he said. "We knew the enemy were carrying out reconnaissance in the area and that if we waited long enough they would pass by. Sure enough, mid-morning, a troop of

Australian Horse came into view, with Dudley riding out in front. We had been hoping for a bigger force to ambush, but this would have to do. We fired at them and Dudley's horse went down, and him with it. He was up on his feet immediately, shouting to his men to make good their escape. We charged them, and as we closed in, your friend started firing at us…"

As he spoke, Carlsson transformed in front of my eyes. No longer a frail patient – he was a huge, well-built warrior who made the puny hospital bed look small. The ends of his straw coloured moustache almost reached down to his chest and, if he had been wearing a horned helmet, he could easily have passed for a Viking. It was easy to see him charging out on the Veldt with his Burgerwacht towards Dudley's small troop, but rather than a Mauser rifle, I saw Carlsson carrying a giant hammer, like Thor.

"One of us shot him at close range and hit him in the eye. But that didn't stop him – and he was only down for a moment before he was taking aim again. That's when I took a shot. I aimed for his arm so that he would drop the rifle, but the bullet hit his right hand instead and took away the thumb. My shot had its desired effect because he let go of the rifle. He was completely surrounded. So you can imagine our astonishment when he pulled out a revolver with his left hand, and started firing at us again. He was fearsome; his face covered in blood, his lame right hand hanging useless, but still trying to fight. So we shot him in the legs to take him down once and for all. Even then he wouldn't surrender, crawling for his revolver to try and continue. We were all standing there watching him, edging his way over the rocky ground to get his weapon. He was never going to give up. It wasn't until my friend Jan Viljoens knocked him out with his rifle butt that Dudley was finally stopped. We knew that if we left him until the British ambulance people found him, he would have bled to death amongst the rocks, and he was too brave an adversary to be allowed to die like that. So we gave him to our medical team. We couldn't quite believe the courage we had all witnessed. Not just that – his almost suicidal fearlessness. If he had simply surrendered after the first injury, we would have probably left him to the aasvogels."

"Aasvogels?"

"Vultures," he said, seeing my frown of incomprehension.

Now I could see that Dudley's extreme actions had paradoxically determined a more favourable outcome. Some kind of warrior's honour code had saved him.

"What are you doing out here, Carlsson?"

"Your friend Dudley, as it happens. When I got injured I ended up in the same hospital in Bloemfontein, and then became a prisoner of war when the British took the town. We got to know each other a little. Dudley said there were opportunities out here, and that once we stopped fighting each other over gold, we should dig it out of the ground together instead. I thought about what he said and decided he was right. By then I had done my bit for the Boers."

"What mining company are you with?"

"None. I just came out on my own and did some fossicking in the bush. Somewhere along the way I drank the wrong water. And I found no gold. When I'm better I'm going back home. I've had enough of this heat. I can't sleep properly and I miss the snows and the forests of Sweden. But it's not just the heat… There are no gods out here… no gods that I'm familiar with anyway."

"I have a Wesleyan friend who would beg to differ."

Carlsson shook his shaggy blonde head.

"No. There are no gods, I tell you. Not for the whites anyway. Perhaps the blacks have their religion, but for me this place is just a great emptiness. I feel nothing here."

"I find it strange that a soldier like you would believe in a god anyway."

He smiled.

"If that's all there is – blood and gore and death – then I would have given up long ago. Withered away and died in a hole somewhere. But I didn't. There's something else…something good amongst the bad."

It was my turn to shake my head.

"Then tell me why I still care?" Carlsson said. "Tell me why I still believe in beauty? That French nurse, for example, she makes me feel good about the world."

"That's just hormones, Carlsson."

"No. I love her. Not like a lover and not like a sister. I know she's with the American doctor. I love her with no strings attached. It's something pure… something else in the background. Don't you ever feel there might be something special underneath all the mess?"

I shook my head again.

"No… I don't."

Carlsson's face clouded over.

"Well, that makes me sad." Then he looked up and smiled broadly again. "But you must come to visit me in Sweden one day, Doctor. I'm from a town called Kiruna in the Arctic Circle. I swear that once you've seen the Northern Lights, you'll believe there's a god."

At six o'clock, a locum nurse and a doctor arrived and I left the ward shortly after, my thoughts preoccupied with the matter of hanging out my evening dress and putting some fresh creases in my trousers.

Outside the admin block I was bending down to tie a shoelace when a dark shape appeared in front of me, as if from nowhere. The street had been empty seconds before – it seemed impossible that anyone could have approached so noiselessly.

It was Eugene, the Aboriginal tracker I had tended to in Fremantle.

"Great God," I said to him, "you made me jump."

"Came to thank you proper for what you did, Doc."

His mass of springy hair was pulled back tightly by a woven headband and I noticed for the first time he had a wispy beard protruding out from his chin at a forty five degree angle. In the daylight his brow cast a heavy shadow over his eyes. Curiously, his front hairline had been plucked clean right back to the top of his scalp. The combination of the strong brow and the high forehead shining in the sun made him look like a polished statue carved from a block of jet. He was barefoot, but otherwise wearing standard European dress for these parts; some old moleskin trousers and a hemp shirt. I was pleased to see the face wound was healing well.

Smiling, Eugene held out his right hand, unfurling his fingers as he did so. There in his palm was a gold nugget the size of a plum, strikingly bright against the contrast of his dark skin. Not telluride, but pure glistening gold.

I took the gold out of Eugene's hand, weighing it in mine in wonderment.

Christ Almighty, I thought, *where on earth did he get this?*

His hands were now outstretched, one palm up and the other down and he was raising and lowering them still in parallel – perhaps a gesture of the reciprocity which Dudley had spoken about.

A payment for services rendered. In theory it was the hospital's to divvy up amongst us all – I was the Egremont doctor and I worked for the St. John of God. Me, Poyntz, Sister B and even Cutfield all had a right to a share. Then I thought about what would happen when I deposited the gold in Cutfield's safe.

"Keep it," I said, giving it back.

His look turned grave.

"I mean no offence. Listen Eugene, it was my pleasure helping you that night. It's my job. You owe me nothing."

"Take the yellow rock, Doc."

But all I could think about was Cutfield emptying the safe, cashing it in and keeping all the money, so I shook my head.

"I can't... This place is corrupt. It will end up in the wrong hands."

I pointed at the windows of Cutfield's office.

When I did that, Eugene put the nugget back in his pocket, seeming to understand.

"Bad fellas love the yellow rock," he said. "I'll pay you back another time, Doc."

We made our way down Maritana Street, and didn't talk again until reaching the crossroads by the Palace. People were staring – a 'black fella' and a 'white fella' together in broad daylight.

"Tell me, what happened that night on Quarry Street, Eugene?"

"Argued with some lumpers about Wajemup – the Island – the one the white fellas call Rottnest."

"I saw it from the railway bridge. What about it?"

"Before white fellas came it was a healing place, where black fellas learn to heal; become medicine men – just like you, Doc. Now they just lock up black fellas there, even young ones. These two blokes asked me why I wasn't locked up there."

"What did you say to them?"

"Told them to get stuffed. They didn't like that, so they had a go at me."

Eugene laughed at the memory, as if they had drawn toothpicks and not knives.

"Dudley told me the man who built the harbour in Fremantle was cursed."

"Yeah. He was sung by the Fremantle mob."

"Can something like that be stopped?"

I was thinking about reversing my imagined curse by the Boers.

"Very difficult," he said. "Thoughts are like dust storms. Once set on their course, it takes a lot to stop them."

He held up his scarred forearms which had parried the blades.

"Like my arms stopped that knife, the death thoughts have to be made to change direction and go somewhere else. New thought must be powerful to do this... bloody hard to do."

I pictured 'death' thoughts travelling through the ether, set on destruction.

"Where are you heading, Eugene?"

With a slow and graceful motion, he extended his long thin arm and pointed east: "Aboriginal camp on the Kanowna road, two miles out from Kal."

Before I could shake his hand he was already striding off.

"I hope your wounds heal well," I said.

"I hope yours do too, Doc."

I stood there watching him go for a full minute, his silent footfall making it seem as though he was floating and not walking away from me.

Chapter Fourteen

Back at the hotel, I didn't bother hanging out my clothes. The heat would smooth out any creases; everything hung limp in this oppressive desert air anyway – flags, the ears of the camels and horses, even the telegraph wires seemed to droop down lower here than in Fremantle.

Dudley was in the billiards room with a man who reminded me of Poyntz, though a good deal shorter and stockier. The resemblance was in the way he held himself; an air of unconventionality combined with self-reliant confidence – not English, anyway.

"Ah, Doc," Dudley said. "May I introduce Mister Herbert Hoover, geologist and partner at Bewick Moreing and Company – one of our rivals. This Yank has already made his first million.'

"Doc – how's my friend Poyntz been treating ya?" Hoover said, shaking my hand.

American, of course – they were a different breed, unshackled by the invisible chains of class that bound all Englishmen. I envied them their freedom.

"I've not had to work a night yet, so he's treating me well, I would say."

Hoover laughed and missed his next shot.

Dudley took over, leaning over the cue in a way that reminded me of William Grenfell in the underwater room. I couldn't imagine Grenfell having his thumb shot away and then chatting amicably to the man who had done it later in a hospital. No grudges, I liked that.

The billiards room was filled with the strong aroma of cigars. I didn't mind – it was just good to be away from the hospital and the sickly sweet smell of illness and carbolic.

Hoover and I watched Dudley go on to win the game.

"Gee whiz, Dudley, you sure you're a mine manager and not a hustler? I'm glad we're not betting – woulda lost all my dough…"

"A misspent youth, Mr Hoover," Dudley said, smiling modestly.

The three of us retired to the upstairs saloon and drank schooners of the local beer – 'Hannans' – named after the prospector who had put Kal on the map. Less than a week in and I was already getting a taste for the stuff.

At six thirty, Rennie arrived dressed in his usual attire and was introduced to Hoover.

"They said the dinner is in a Stope, Mr Hoover," Rennie said. "What on earth does that mean?"

"It's an underground cave – the leftover space once the ore has been removed."

Rennie slapped his hand down on his knee.

"A cave, you say."

"You'll be impressed, Reverend, I promise."

Rennie could not hide his sarcasm: "Oh… an *impressive* cave."

"You'll see," Hoover said. "It'll be like having dinner at the Ritz; you'll think you've never left London."

Poyntz arrived with Sister B. The chatelaine belt and white apron had gone and she was all in black. A small silver crucifix hung around her neck. Seeing the cross made me wonder if Poyntz really stood any chance in his quest to win her over.

Hoover kept looking at the young barmaid serving the drinks with what seemed to be more than just passing glances. When we were alone at the bar, I asked Dudley about it. "What's the story with Hoover and that barmaid? Or am I imagining it?"

"You're not," Dudley said. "A few years ago when he first came out here to work as a young bachelor, he fell for her, hook, line and bloody sinker. Cookie watched it all unfold. No-one quite knows what happened next, but suddenly it was all off. Rumour was she broke his heart."

Later, Hoover's wife came into the saloon and accepted a drink from the same barmaid. "Why thank you, my dear," she said, seemingly oblivious to the history.

Lou Hoover was elegance personified, an American version of Ettie Grenfell in a way; attractive, highly educated, and blessed with the same sparkling sense of humour. After five minutes of conversing with her I decided Hoover had come up trumps in the end.

She laughed as she recalled how he had proposed to her – by cable from Kalgoorlie.

Rennie was having trouble assimilating this.

"Let me get this right… You were in United States of America?"

"Indeed I was, Reverend."

"And he sent you a telegram asking for your hand?"

"Indeed he did, Reverend."

"So… what did you do?"

"Why, Reverend… I accepted by return wire."

At the Egremont head frame, red carpet had been laid up to the base and at first I assumed Dudley had brought us out there to play a prank. But then he ushered us into the metal cage, slammed shut the grill doors and nodded to the winch man. After a jolt, we started to descend, picking up speed so quickly that my stomach climbed up into my chest. It wasn't a joke – it was the way to the party.

The smooth rock wall flashed past us, illuminated by the electric lights in the lift, and I tried to appear nonchalant in front of Dudley and Hoover, as if this was the kind of thing I did all the time.

Finally, God knows how far down, the contraption shuddered to a halt and we stepped out.

A waiter in a starched apron stood at the lift exit, offering everyone glasses of champagne from a silver tray. I took one, speechless.

It *was* a giant cave – but Hoover hadn't been exaggerating, it could have been the Ritz. Makeshift chandeliers hung from the stone roof, lighting up a long table which had been laid with a white linen cloth and full dinner service.

Sister B started to laugh giddily, holding onto Poyntz's arm unselfconsciously. On the way over, Hoover had told her about the venue and she had been as incredulous as Rennie.

Along the table were several platters of oysters, piled high on mounds of ice.

"They're fresh in from the coast, sir," the waiter said.

In that moment I fully appreciated the immense riches being made on these goldfields. Eating oysters and drinking champagne in an underground mine made Kalgoorlie feel even more opulent than Egremont's underwater room.

The walls were streaked grey blue with telluride.

Dudley rubbed his hand on the rock.

"Tomorrow morning, all trace of this dinner will be gone and a miner will be hacking away at this with a pickaxe."

The sound of laughter disturbed us. Cutfield was at the far end of the stope with a group of older gentlemen and they were all chortling heartily together.

"Bunch of bloody Champagne Charlies," Dudley said under his breath.

At that moment, Cutfield started banging a knife on his glass and then made a welcome speech in my honour. It was an odd one though, in which he waxed lyrical about the previous doctor and what a hole there was to fill now he had gone.

Rennie frowned and caught my eye, instantly knowing that Cutfield and I wouldn't be getting on.

In reply, I stumbled through a few sentences about the great honour of seeing to the health of the Egremont mine workers and their families. Then I raised my glass to the telluride in the underground cave, a sentiment greeted with a ripple of polite applause.

Cutfield introduced me to his wife as 'Hunston from Harley Street' and did it with a friendly wink, like we were the best of friends. Mrs

Cutfield was good-looking woman, dressed in an outfit which hugged her body tightly. Striking. Her eyes lit up at the mention of Harley Street and I spent a protracted ten minutes fielding her questions about possible mutual friends and acquaintances. She was one of those society lady types who talked fast, without a break, as if no-one had ever told her about punctuation. I just let it flow over me, nodding occasionally, speculating as to why she had the urge to fill the air with meaningless blather.

After it had transpired I knew absolutely none of her old London set, she finally ran out of things to say.

"And now you are here," she said in conclusion.

All I could think of saying in reply was to repeat her words back to her. "Yes, now I am here."

She cut me adrift then, turning on her elegantly clad heel and leaving me standing there alone. It hadn't taken her long to work out I was not quite right. Everything she held dear in the world – the status, the class and the money – was a pile of rubble in my mind and she had sensed it.

I watched her go and introduce herself to Rennie who was with Sister B, examining the strata in the rock. She blanked Sister B completely, facing Rennie with her pretty shoulder angled towards the beautiful nurse. I was glad when Rennie deliberately moved sideways to make sure Sister B was included. He was retelling the story of the calaverite that Dudley had told us in the bar. Mrs Cutfield listened, bored, but her tight smile afforded the respect a man of the cloth deserved. Poor Rennie didn't realise that someone like her thrived only on gossip, not geology lectures.

That was what the class system did; it divided people up into small cliques, and there they stayed, comfortable in their little domains. You went to the right places, wore the right clothes, and said the right things.

Soon after returning to London from Spike Island, I visited the Zoological gardens and watched the wolves pacing up and down their enclosure for most of an afternoon.

Freddie had been right way back in school – what was the bloody point of it all? You spent a few years in the wild and then the next forty in captivity. I knew exactly how the wolves felt.

In the first week of July, I went to the Royal Regatta at Henley, as was my custom. Rowing was the pastime I had loved since childhood, so surely a day at the races would set me straight again. But something was way out of kilter. Dressed in my Blues rowing blazer and parading around the immaculate lawns of the stewards' enclosure, I felt none of my usual excitement. For most of the afternoon I had sat in a deckchair, trying to numb myself with glasses of Pimm's, but all I got was sunburn and a nasty headache.

A week later, I returned to Oxford and went out in a single scull, to try and re-connect with Freddie through our shared bond of rowing. By being physical, with dripping sweat the proof of my efforts, I hoped it might have at least provided some kind of salve. I stayed out on the river until my hands were a mass of new blisters and my thigh muscles ached, but I had been unable to find my brother again...

"John?"

Rennie was waving his hand in front of my eyes. He and Sister B were looking at me with concern.

"Thought we'd lost you there," he said.

"Was it Mrs Cutfield's manner?" Sister B said, her eyes knowing. She had correctly read my thoughts, and her tone told me that she empathised with my plight. Poyntz was a lucky man. Just having this small sign of support made me feel a lot better.

I smiled and toasted them both.

"Friends," I said.

We chinked our glasses and drank the champagne. I noticed that Rennie was partaking again – clearly opting for the safer goldfields fluids.

"Come on," Sister B said, linking her arms with ours, "since we're in a cave, let's go and eat like cavemen."

Rennie and I both beamed with pride as she escorted us over to the table; amazing how her most seemingly insignificant actions, a consoling word and the touch of an arm, had raised my flagging spirits. I tried to just enjoy this the way Carlsson had said, without expecting more.

Shortly after sitting down to dinner, the night became a blur, due to our glasses being continually topped up and my choosing to drink it freely.

The main course was roasted fillet of beef, so tender it seemed to melt in the mouth.

"This steak's so rare, a vet could bring it back to life," Dudley said.

Hoover was some talker and, after a few drinks, had started sounding off about England.

"As far as I can make there are two types of people in your culture," he said, "the haves and the have-nots."

No-one could argue with that.

"I would say your ruling elite make up about twenty per cent of your population; the rest being the masses. Between these groups there may as well be a wide bottomless chasm."

He looked at me specifically.

"Professionals like you, Doctor," he said, "and city men are, for the most part, classed as gentlemen and inhabit the hallowed realm. The other eighty percent are simply the dregs. Why, I daresay most of the white Australian population belongs to this latter category too. Isn't that why you sent them over here in the first place? And you know what I find funny? You English elite really do think you are superior, not only over your lower classes and the inhabitants of your colonies, but over us Americans too… not to mention every kind of native spread throughout the world."

I laughed at his analysis. He might as well have been reading from the rule-book of the Blue Boar. Though I didn't consider myself part of the elite any longer, Hoover's observations were right on the mark, but he was just getting warmed up.

"And it's better in your country?" I said.

"Well, we have a better starting point. Our Declaration of Independence holds it as a self-evident truth that all men are created equal…"

I wanted to ask him about America's black citizens and the Red Indians and where they fitted into all that, when Hoover turned to Dudley.

"I've witnessed their ridiculous conventions, Tom: the weekends in the country and the snobby London clubs. I've seen how the elite traipse around from event to event in the social season – Royal Ascot, Henley and Cowes Week – before retiring to their country homes in August to hunt foxes and shoot pheasant… and they do it with scant regard for eighty percent of their citizens. I can tell you, it all convinces me that this group is not worth preserving."

I laughed again but not quite as freely. He was getting too close to the bone now, with the mention of the Clubs and Henley.

Dudley lifted his glass.

"That's about bloody right."

Hoover kept on: "And this elite has one dominating obsession – 'the Empire' – it is amazing how a small island can justify its rule over one quarter of the world's population. While you value fair play in your sports – when it comes to the Empire, these principles are thrown to the winds. You British have a habit of placing any business deal for your precious Empire right on the summit of the moral high ground. Just look at the Boer war… They said it was about political ideologies, but it was really about gold, plain and simple."

Mention of the Boer War had put me back into a dark frame of mind and I wasn't laughing now. I was about to say something I might later regret: such as 'and what exactly do you know about that?' when Rennie, perhaps sensing this, interrupted Hoover instead, with just enough humour to lighten the mood.

"How many other deficiencies do we have, Mr Hoover… surely there are others?"

"Well, let me see now…"

His wife was attempting to restrain him, gently placing her hand on his and saying: "Now, Herbert, you've said enough…"

He didn't hear her, or seemed not to have heard, and Lou Hoover looked at Rennie apologetically. "I majored in geology in college," she said, "but as you can see, I have majored in Herbert Hoover ever since."

"Your urban poor…" Hoover was saying, regaining his flow. "By God, I thought America was bad, until I saw the British slums. While thousands of the poor sleep rough in London parks, the upper classes across the street live in the lap of luxury."

"You paint a bleak picture," Rennie said. "Is there any hope for us?" Hoover looked thoughtful.

"Yes, there is. One thing springs to mind: your integrity and sense of honour – admirable traits. I speak of personal experience in my business dealings. You can trust an Englishman's word. I would rather have a verbal agreement with an Englishman than the most elaborately drafted contract with any other civilised man."

Over coffee, I happened to mention Father Long helping out the evening before and Hoover's ears pricked up immediately.

"Aaaah… Father Long you say? Let me tell you a story about that fellow…"

Once more, he had the diners at our end of the table hanging on his every word.

"Two years ago, talk swept the goldfields of a huge nugget of gold weighing one thousand ounces. It had been seen in Kanowna one night by a newly arrived priest from Ireland – none other than the aforementioned Father Long. What he didn't realise was that around here a big nugget doesn't stay secret for long, and pretty soon the story had found its way into the papers. But Father Long wouldn't say any more about it, or give the names of the prospectors who'd found it, because he had them given his word on that. A week went by, and then another, and yet no nugget was lodged in any of the local banks, nor any Reward Claim made. Now if the reputed size of the nugget was anything to go by, the location of the find was potentially a fabulously rich surface reef and if unclaimed, then still fair game. Recognising the increasingly tense atmosphere in the town, the authorities managed to persuade Father Long to at least reveal *where* the prospectors had said they had found it."

Hoover turned to me:

"Picture the scene, Doc, the balcony of the Criterion Hotel in Kanowna, Father Long standing there in front of about *six thousand* people. First he made the crowd promise, by raising their hands in agreement, that once he'd said the location they would never ask him about the gold again. All six thousand put up their hands and then fell completely silent as he spoke: 'Very well, the gold was found a quarter of a mile on this side of the nearest lake on the Kurnalpi Road'. No sooner had he had finished his sentence than there was a stampede out to the area – only four miles distant. Now here's the strange part – no gold was ever found there, not a single damn ounce. There should have been other specimens, *something*. There were plenty of disappointed and angry people, but few if any, felt any resentment towards the priest, since his honesty was beyond doubt. It was obvious he'd been hoaxed, but the question was, why? Anyway, because of Father Long's involvement the affair became known as 'the legend of the sacred nugget'. Why you must know all about this, Dudley. Wasn't it when you were in charge of the 'Alluvial mine'?"

"Yeah" Dudley said, "I was among the six thousand."

I could tell his neuralgia was playing up, because he had started massaging his temple.

"Did anyone ever find out what happened?" I said to Hoover.

"No, but I think there's more to it than we know. The last time I saw him was some months afterwards. We talked about Irish history and politics and the nugget was never mentioned. It was only as he was saying goodbye that he turned to me and said, 'Thank you for never questioning me about the nugget. I hope someday that I will be able to tell you more about it than I have ever told anyone else, but I cannot do it now.'"

Later that night, I dreamt fitfully of gold nuggets scattered around the field hospital at the Spitz Kop, of fly-covered bodies and soldiers dying in pain. Then I dreamt of the Grey Lady standing over Freddie and woke up in a sweat. My head was pounding from the alcohol and I went to the bathroom and drank a dozen handfuls of water from the tap.

It was still dark outside.

I lay in bed and went through the events of the evening. Something Cutfield had said to me before leaving the stope dinner was bothering me. He had said, "You look haunted," and it seemed like an aside, in amongst vague pleasantries, so that I almost doubted he had said it at the time. But now, in my sober analysis, I suspected he had said it with the intention of undermining what little confidence and well-being I had left. I had no doubt he was the type of person who knew exactly how to take a person down with a carefully chosen comment. I hated Cutfield for his arrogance and laziness, but I also hated him because he wasn't stupid. I *was* haunted.

It made me think of the last time I had seen my father, just before leaving for Australia. We had met at a riverside inn near Hammersmith Bridge, and after ten minutes, had said everything there was to say, which wasn't a great amount because all the swirling emotions ran deeper than words could express. Drinking our beers in silence, we had looked out at the sweep of the Hammersmith bend and the mercurial waters of the tideway. I had once trained for the Boat Race there and knew that stretch of water intimately − where it flowed fastest, what it looked like at the different tides, even its smell. The river had once been a friend − a liquefied chameleon, changing colour with the weather, sometimes bright green, sometimes a muddy brown. But there was no solace to be found there… All I could think about was the Grey Lady standing over Freddie's bed.

"Are you all right John?" my father had said. "You look like you've seen a ghost."

Cutfield left for the coast the next day. I wondered if his wife would talk all the way to Perth or whether she clammed up when they were alone. The former was my guess. I could imagine her peppering him with salacious gossip and it all blending into a harmless noise in his big arrogant head.

Unsurprisingly his leaving made no difference to the workload. "One less damn problem," was how Poytnz put it.

That Sunday I made good my promise and attended Rennie's first service.

He had been busy all week – building new pews out of the shipping crates to cater for his new congregation. Exhortations of a non-biblical nature filled the room: *'THIS SIDE UP WITH CARE'*, *'STOW AWAY FROM THE BOILERS'*, and *'KEEP IN A COOL PLACE'* – all a far cry from the *'be ye doers of the word, not hearers only'* the chapel pulpit at Spike Island had boasted.

I sat at the front next to a miner, his wife and two grubby children. Every time anyone moved, the pew wobbled and I pondered whether Rennie was as good a carpenter as his hero. I sat stock still in the sultry heat and hoped the nails would hold.

On one side, a blackboard was leaning up against the wall with broken bits of chalk scattered on the floor underneath. Just like the Manse in Perth, the room doubled up as a school and Rennie held classes each morning. Sunday was his big day for evangelising though, and instead of chalk dust he was caked in red dust, having already given four other services that morning in other parts of the city.

As Rennie cleared his throat, it occurred to me that I had never heard him deliver a sermon, or at least one meant for a crowd.

"It is well we are here, my friends. This is the sort of place where Jesus would have been at home, for many of the people in this city are poor, with simple shacks or tents as dwellings. It should cheer you to know that Jesus preferred the company of the lowly and the poor – he thought they were close to the Kingdom of Heaven. He was, in fact, homeless – often relying on the goodwill of others to put him up for the night. So be comforted that the Lord would recognise and feel your plight. You all know that this is a city with untold riches beneath its foundations, but also one which on the surface is rife with poverty and disease…"

Someone in the congregation went into a fit of coughing, as if the mention of the word 'disease' was their cue to start hacking up their lungs. It was probably silicosis. I had diagnosed a few cases of it already; caused by scarring of the lung tissue from inhaling the silica and other fine dust particles in the underground mines. The chest X-ray showed white streaks of disease which stood out like cirrus clouds. Dynamiting had made things worse and the incidence was increasing.

Rennie raised his voice over the coughing: "In a way, Jesus is like a miner in a city built on gold and He is the only one who knows how to get at it."

The coughing stopped, and then started up again.

Pausing for a moment, Rennie continued on, even more loudly: "When He was on the earth, He spent His time trying to get the people to believe there was gold inside their heart. Yes, he certainly would have been at home here... CAN SOMEONE PLEASE THUMP THAT GENTLEMAN ON THE BACK..."

Enthusiastically, judging by the sound of the thuds, the request was carried out and the coughing finally stopped.

Rennie took a moment to scan the congregation, picking out a few select individuals for special eye contact. I thought I would be next, and made a concerted effort to study the floor, wishing I had not come. I looked over my shoulder to plan my escape, but the room was packed: a hundred sets of eyes were staring back at me. There was no way out.

When Rennie was sure he had everyone's attention, he started again. "What I am trying to say, my friends, is that Jesus wasn't a social climber. He didn't care about that. He deliberately mixed with the forsaken. Tax collectors, fishermen, prostitutes and lepers. The Son of Man wore no fancy clothes and he shunned wealth; he could spot a proud man a mile off, and he told the rich men to give away all they had..."

He was on a roll now, and had started windmilling his arms to make his points.

"He said we would be judged one day: 'I was sick, and ye visited me; I was in prison and ye came unto me'; 'Inasmuch as ye have done it unto the least of my brethren, ye have done it unto me'."

The passage made me think of Eugene in the Fremantle gaol cell.

Who was Eugene? Someone with serious knife wounds who, when treated, seemed not to have a care in the world, someone who could produce a fist sized nugget of gold as easily as a balled up piece of paper. I remembered what he had said in the street – about my wounds healing. He had meant to say it. He had seen right into my soul and seen the hurt.

Rennie's voice filtered through again.

"Jesus wanted people to clean out their hearts. Not outer cleansing, but INNER cleansing. I preach a religion of the heart, my friends."

From the back, one of the miners yelled out: "What about baptism, Reverend? That's an outer cleansing…"

The congregation laughed and so did Rennie.

"Yes, you're right; but baptism is just an *indicator* of someone wanting to be clean on the inside. That's why it's so important… to show everyone, and God, that you want to change."

"But you need water for that," said another voice, "and there isn't any."

Again, laughter filled the church and Rennie had to hold up his hands to quieten them.

"And the water will come one day, my friends. One day it will arrive. I've seen the pipe being prepared east of here at Bullabulling… for whoever drinks the water I give him will never be thirsty again. For my gift will become a spring in the man himself, welling into eternal life."

That received a round of spontaneous applause. I was proud of my friend – a quote for any occasion. It had gone well for him.

Rennie wound up with the Lord's Prayer. As he and the congregation chanted the words, 'Our Father, who art in heaven, hallowed be thy name,' I looked at the crucifix on the wall and my mind prickled with resentment.

Instead of saying the prayer along with everyone else, I thought back to the night when I had screamed up at the sky and berated God for allowing Freddie to die. Where the hell had He been then? Without a sound, I started berating Him again: WHERE WERE YOU? WHY DID YOU LET IT HAPPEN? YOU COULD HAVE STOPPED IT.

"John? Are you all right?"

Rennie was standing in front of me.

The chapel was empty.

My face was covered in sweat, my hands were trembling and there were pins and needles in my fingertips. I had missed the last minutes of the service, caught up in a maelstrom of painful memories, anger and fear.

"It wasn't that bad, was it?"

I stood up slowly and tried to smile.

"No, it was very thought provoking," I said, at least not lying.

Dudley was in the Palace saloon when we got back, dressed in his Sunday best.

"Good service," he said to Rennie.

"Why thank you, Tom."

Dudley turned to me.

"I was at the back... saw you moping about at the front. Didn't know you were Church."

He said it as an adjective, not a noun.

I gave a non-committal shrug of the shoulders and was aware of Rennie watching me closely. Had I just denied his God? I half expected the cock to crow.

We took our drinks out onto the veranda – three schooners of beer – and before long Rennie and Dudley were embroiled in a religious discussion. I sipped my drink and fought hard to keep the bitter feelings from resurfacing, like dead fish in a river. I envied my friends their solace. Funny, I hadn't pegged Dudley as a churchgoer – I assumed he would have believed in nothing.

Life in Kalgoorlie took on a familiar pattern; in the mornings I walked the streets early, never tiring of that fresh smell in the air, suffused with the rawness of the desert. I would have a coffee in the British Arms with Dudley and then go to rounds at the St. John of God and do a morning's stint before a beer and a pie with Dudley at the

Palace for lunch. Each evening, Rennie would join us at the Palace in the private bar for dinner.

Sometimes I saw groups of Aboriginals. They would all be sitting under a tree at the top of Hannan street, silent and unfathomable, perhaps twenty or so of them – the old and the young – and they would all stare at me as I walked past.

Their stares chilled me – no recognition, no smiles, no common bond. Save for my two encounters with Eugene, I felt no connection with them, nothing whatsoever, and whenever I thought of O'Connor's curse, I shivered.

Then again, if strangers came in great numbers and turned my home into a wasteland of ore dumps I would probably stare at them in the same way they were staring at me.

To the Europeans, the Aboriginals were virtually invisible. I remembered the journal in the library at Witworth Park. "No dwellings and not one inch of cultivated ground," Cook had said when raising the Union Jack and claiming the entire Eastern Seaboard for King George the third.

One night I dreamt of a boatload of Aboriginals arriving on the shores of England and planting their flag on the white cliffs of Dover, claiming England. "We wish no harm to England's native people. We are here to teach you how to live without possessions and to think of the three-making match."

Their only public ally in Kalgoorlie seemed to be Rennie. He gave them food parcels, clothing and treats, and they loved him for it. All they had to do in return was sit and listen to his street preaching. They would watch Rennie with what looked like sincere interest and I liked to think the interest was down to the fact that he was virtually the only person in town passionate about something other than gold.

One morning before rounds, I got to work early and found Poyntz in Cutfield's office, staring out of the window. He heard me come in because he lifted a hand in acknowledgment, but he didn't turn around and I joined him at the window to see what was holding his attention.

A camel train was down in Maritana Street. One particularly bedraggled specimen had decided to kneel down in the street and hold everything up. A driver was pulling hard on the nose line and remonstrating with the recalcitrant beast: "Yula! Yula!" But the camel wasn't budging. The driver threw his hands up into the air, said the word, "Inshallah," and then sat on the ground next to the camel to wait it out.

He noticed us watching on from the window.

"If God wills it," he said in a loud voice.

Presently, in a series of graceful movements the camel lifted its hindquarters and then its front legs. A bell tied around its ankle rattled as it moved off. The Afghan waved at us as he led the camel away.

"Inshallah!" he said again, laughing.

"You know why I'm in this place, Jack?"

Poyntz had taken to calling me Jack; his way of Americanising me.

"No."

He took a deep breath as he steeled himself for the story.

"I finished med school in the summer of eighty seven. Worked on the east coast for a while, but I was hungry for adventure. You know what that's like, right?"

"I do."

"One day my father came to me with some news. My uncle William, a Jesuit priest from Baltimore, was stationed some place way the hell out of the way and needed some help. He was in Dawson City."

"Where's that?"

"On the Klondike River, in the Yukon Territory of Canada. A Gold town – it sprung up at about the same time that Kalgoorlie was taking off here." He clicked his fingers. "That fast!"

I had heard of the Klondike gold rush. Freddie had been there on his travels before the war. He had sent me a letter about riding a husky dog sled into the wilderness.

"Just getting there was dangerous; you had to cross a mountain pass in the Rockies called the 'Chilkoot trail'. The day I crossed, I'd just got to the top when the whole damn mountain slipped away behind me; an avalanche killing sixty people. Thirty seconds earlier and I would have been the sixty first. After that, I made a raft trip five hundred miles down the Yukon River. Manned by some crazy kid river pilot called Jack… like you. Said my Uncle Will had helped cure his scurvy in Dawson, so he let me ride for free. There were so many rafts being made, the forests at the river head were stripped bare. Dozens capsized and drowned."

Poyntz stared out of the window at the retreating camel train with haunted eyes, reliving his treacherous journey.

"Eventually I made it to Dawson and worked in the hospital alongside my uncle. I've never met a man more selfless…we're talking real devotion. I was already a Catholic, but being around him made me feel like I had just been playing at it all my life. He just wanted to help his fellow man; no Cutfield, that's for damn sure. I tried to match him in intensity and together we worked non-stop. We had one hundred and thirty five admissions on one day in the summer typhoid outbreak of '98. Caught it myself not long after. Anyway… as you can see I survived. My uncle didn't though. Wore himself down to the nub and caught double pneumonia in the January of '99… died within a few days."

"My God, Poyntz, I'm sorry."

It was easy for me to sound empathetic. As far as calamities went, Poyntz had lived a parallel life with mine – typhoid and pneumonia changing everything.

Poyntz fidgeted with the flaking window frame, picking out splinters and dropping them on Cutfield's floor.

"I hung around," he said. "The nuns and I kept going for a while. They were the 'Sisters of Saint Ann' over there. Then in April, a fire levelled the entire town. By then, everyone was leaving for the Nome gold rush anyway, so I went west and joined them. In Nome you could literally pick up the gold from the sand on the beach. I stayed in a place called the 'Dexter Saloon' run by Wyatt Earp and his wife Josephine. But Nome was too quiet for a doctor. There was hardly any disease and I wasn't really needed. The only drama was when I beat Earp in a chess game and, for a joke, he pulled out his Smith and Wesson…"

I smiled. "So how did you end up here?"

"Same as you, I guess… Read in the paper about a new Catholic Hospital in Kalgoorlie needing a doctor. As you know, my predecessor died of typhoid. I was immune. Arrived a year before you did."

He turned away from the window to look at me.

His eyes had reddened. No tears, but enough to show me how much he was hurting inside. In that moment I decided I would always be friends with him.

He rubbed his face with both hands, as if to wipe away the past.

"Let's do the round" he said, turning to go.

The ward was still full of typhoid cases.

"They just keep coming," Poyntz said. "Two more admissions yesterday, and another dead."

Most of the cases lived in the same part of the city, where the water was shared in communal bath houses; it always came down to basic sanitation.

I ran my hands through my hair, which by now had grown out more than an inch since Snowfoot's cut. All this death; I was surrounded by it. What a place.

Chapter Fifteen

Late November, 1900

I had just sat down at the bar in the British Arms and not even taken my first sip of coffee.

"You'd better take a look at this, Doc," Dudley said, pushing across his copy of the *Kalgoorlie Miner*. His look was grim and there was none of the usual humour in his bearing. I read the paragraph:

NEW MAN FOR THE EGREMONT

Tom Dudley, who had the Alluvial and now the Egremont, is to be relieved of his duties, at his own request, in December. He claims to be finished with pleasing John Bull and his crowd in London. Cowdray, the new man, has lately arrived wearing high-collar and patent leather boots on his tour of the mine workings...

From behind the bar, McKay was looking worried.

"Are you sure about this, Tom?"

"I'm no stooge, mate, and no London gofer either. This is our country. It doesn't belong to those bowler hatted bastards."

"What the hell's been going on?" I said.

McKay and Dudley looked at each other and then Dudley turned his head and fixed me with his one eye.

"Bulls and bears. We're talking basic economics, Doc. A bull market is optimistic – which means increasing investor confidence. That's what the London boys thrive on, people like Egremont. A bear market is the reverse – fear and pessimism – death to the London investors."

None of this was making any sense.

"Tell me from the start," I said.

Dudley took a breath and let out a sigh.

"Before I went to South Africa I was the manager at 'the Alluvial', one of the other mines. I didn't know it at the time, but the London financier in charge of that outfit was a crook – bloke by the name of Sir Horatio Casher. While I was on the Veldt getting my eye shot out for the bloody Empire he was playing fast and loose with the stock market. The mine manager who took my place, in cahoots with Casher, took some assays and deliberately exaggerated the amount left in the mine. Not only that, he stockpiled the rich ore to give spectacular monthly returns when they were needed. That's insider trading, Doc. Casher got filthy rich buying and selling 'Alluvial' shares. When I got back and found out what had been going on, I went to work for Egremont instead. Thought they couldn't all be crooks. Should've known better though… it turns out Casher wasn't the biggest kid in the playground. Egremont and another financier attacked Casher's hold on 'Alluvial' gold – a 'bear' attack, and ended up taking him to bankruptcy court. A chum of Egremont's took over the 'Alluvial'. A crook for a crook…"

He was rubbing his temple now.

"Egremont's the worst wildcat of 'em all. Ever since I started, he's been putting the pressure on me to manipulate production to make money off the stock market. He's been puffing the shares…"

"Puffing?"

"Exaggerating their value, Doc; been falsifying the financial statements of the Egremont Company. Did it last year and he's doing it again now… cooking the books. Fact is, he's a million quid out of pocket."

"You're telling me the EMC is on the way out?"

"Yeah, Doc, that's exactly what I'm telling ya. When I started earlier this year I cabled Egremont to tell him we'd discovered a new seam of telly that would yield 30,000 ounces a month. Didn't know how big it was though. Rather than wait to find out he began a bull movement in his own shares, the greedy bastard."

"And?"

Dudley grinned.

"Turns out it was only a small seam, but didn't tell him that. I told him that there was at least a decade's worth of rich ore left and watched him commit all his resources to the rise in shares. Fact is, there's bugger all left. Cut out last week. Monthly production is about to crash. He's going to lose everything."

"But this is your reputation too Tom."

"Bugger reputation. He's going down."

I pointed to the name in the newspaper article.

"What about this Cowdray?"

Dudley shrugged.

"Just another Champagne Charlie – knows no more of mining than a mangy camel does of the differential calculus. He has no idea what's about to happen."

"One of the 'yes men' Egremont has in his pocket," McKay said. "Another bloody Pom – no offence, Doc. Came in here one night this week for a drink; thought he was as flash as a rat with a gold tooth."

McKay flexed his tattooed forearms and balled his hands into fists.

His right forearm was decorated with the Federation flag. You couldn't miss it at the British Arms – it decorated the wall next to the framed history of the Separatist movement, a simple design; blue cross on a white background with a Union Jack in the top left corner. Each limb and the centre of the cross contained a white star, representing the dominant constellation in the Southern hemisphere – the Southern Cross. Underneath the tattooed flag on McKay's arm were the words: 'One people – One destiny – One flag'.

On his other forearm the word 'Auralia' was tattooed in the same blue colour the ancient Britons had once used. I could see McKay's red-headed Pictish ancestors of several hundred years before, covered in blue woad and taunting the Romans from the forests north of Hadrian's Wall, clenching their fists in the same way he was doing right now.

"Crooks," Dudley said, "all lying and skimming off the top."

He swilled the dregs of his coffee around the bottom of his mug with a snarl, his look one of triumphant rage.

I took out the Queen Victoria tin and rolled a cigarette. I didn't smoke often, but when I did, it was because I needed to calm down. It was Freddie's tobacco and there was still some left, a testament to how long I had made it last. In my mind, eking it out somehow kept me connected to him.

"It was the same thing in Harley Street," I said. "You look after number one first. It's a law of human nature."

"Survival of the fittest?" Dudley said. "Your man Darwin's law?"

"That's right."

I could hear the defensiveness in my own voice, but chose to be devil's advocate anyway. Dudley sneered.

"Well, explain why you turned your back on it all, if it's a law of human bloody nature."

I said nothing.

"I'll tell you why, mate… You saw through the shit. It might not seem so now, but you did the right thing."

I didn't believe him. I thought my desertion of England complete madness now. Here I was in a town full of greed, crooks and death, bathed in the perspiration of anxiety.

I took a deep drag of the cigarette and tried to stay calm.

"Is Egremont really that bad?" I said. "I ate dinner with him not three months ago. He seemed all right. A bit pompous maybe, but surely he's legitimate."

Dudley shook his head with certainty.

"He's as crooked as a snake with the colic."

I thought of the other snake, Cutfield – and his safe full of gold – most of it destined for his own bank account, his empire of small scale corruption set within Egremont's empire of large scale corruption.

As I left the bar to get to nine o'clock rounds I looked at the Egremont head frame in the distance and thought back to the vast estate in Surrey.

All built on lies; non-existent profits, fabricated out of thin air. Out on the lake, Egremont's statue was walking on water, standing atop the cupola of the cavernous underwater room. Everything had been a sham. Here, the mine frame straddled Egremont's empty mine – purged of all its telluride, gutted of its wealth.

"You look dog tired, Poyntz."

He was standing at the end of a patient's bed in the subdued light of the ward.

"Tough night," he said, his eyes weary and without their usual sparkle.

We didn't even do the round. He went straight home to bed and I took care of the day shift alone. Work was a welcome distraction – standing over the patients, noting their fever spikes and working out how best to proceed. It felt better to concentrate on something I understood: pulses, temperatures and blood pressures, instead of shares, dividends and stock market manipulation.

I didn't have time to worry or reflect because the typhoid fever was all pervading.

The undertakers came for a pick up.

In the afternoon I told Sister B to go and get some sleep, but she refused and stayed to help me.

Towards the end of the day, we had time to talk alone in the mess. She told me about her previous life, just as Poyntz had done a few days before.

Sister B was from a tiny French hamlet in the middle of the Dordogne forest where the wild boar crashed around at dusk. Like Poyntz's, her family was devoutly Catholic. Along with a brother, she had spent her teenage years assisting their doctor father in running a clinic from home, but eventually chose to answer a calling towards a life set apart in the service of the church. At the age of eighteen she joined the 'Bon Secour' order of nuns in Paris and was soon assigned the goldfields post by her Mother Superior because of her nursing skills. In her first month in Australia, Sister B caught typhoid, but pulled through. The other Bon Secour 'Sister' who had made the voyage out with her died, just like Poyntz's predecessor. So far, no replacement had been forthcoming – hence Sister B's backbreaking shifts with little or no respite.

When I asked her what she missed most about France, she replied, "Le vert." I could empathise with that sentiment; in this place of red dust and straggly gums it was the greenery of our European homelands we missed the most.

God, she was looking damn pretty.

I found myself staring at her face as she talked and made a mental photograph of her to preserve in my formalin jar of a brain. I loved her, it was true, but I think it was innocent enough – in Carlsson's pure way – that is, 'not as a lover and not as a sister'.

I hoped Poyntz would take her away from all this one day, before she became worn out by the fifteen hour shifts, her measly two pint daily water ration and the fierce climate.

The hours would take their toll in the end. Even now, in my mid twenties, getting up in the middle of the night was a trial. Gone was the stamina of my houseman days when I could work a straight seventy two hour shift without sleep. Though I was still young, this job made me feel like an old man.

"Docteur Jean, reveille toi…REVEILLE TOI."

I was on Cutfield's chaise longue, sleeping the dreamless sleep of an on-call, and Sister B was calling to me from the doorway, in such a state that she had reverted to speaking French.

I rolled off onto the floor with a heavy bump.

"What the… What? What's wrong?" I said, blinking and trying to work out where I was.

"There's a man with typhoid, and he's very sick."

Bent double in a chair in the admission room was a pallid young man in black cleric's garb, wet with perspiration and clutching his stomach. To my shock, I recognised him as Father Long.

I held onto his shoulders to stop him falling off the chair.

"Father, let us help you into a bed."

He tried to stand on his own, but he wasn't able to and it took both of us to transfer him.

I could tell how sick he was just from looking at him. My initial examination served only to confirm that; pulse rapid and thready – well over one hundred – and a burning fever. His abdomen was rock hard when palpated – peritonitis – his bowel had already perforated. He didn't have long left. God only knew why he had presented at this late stage.

I injected him with some morphia and tried my best to hide what I was really thinking, which was that I was looking at a dead man.

Sister B and I retreated to the calm of the hallway outside the room.

"How did he get here?"

"He was on horseback," she said. "His horse is out the front."

I walked out into the warm night air.

In the lantern light of the hospital entrance stood a grey horse, almost white in the moonlight. Its legs were covered in red dust and neck flecked with foam from the exertions of a long ride.

"He had nothing else with him?" I said, stroking the horse's mane.

"Only that," she said, pointing to a leather water bag on the steps of the hospital porch.

There was a little left inside, probably contaminated with typhoid. I emptied it out onto the ground and then ran the two blocks to the Manse to fetch Rennie.

Back in the admission room, the morphia was taking effect and Father Long had become calmer.

Even though no other patients were in the admissions bays, Sister B had drawn the curtains around the bed, perhaps in an attempt to comfort him further.

Father Long saw me and spoke.

"Doctor…"

"Yes, Father?"

I sat on the edge of the bed and leant in closer. He was taking rapid shallow breaths.

"I have to tell you something."

My instinct was to tell him to rest, to try and save his breath, but who was I to refuse a dying man's wish? Besides, it wasn't going to make a difference to the final outcome.

"What is it, Father?"

"The sacred nugget," he said, straining to make himself heard. "I know where it's buried."

"What are you talking about?"

He was delirious.

"The sacred nugget…," he said again. "The sacred nugget of Kanowna…"

I had been focusing on his medical symptoms so much I had completely forgotten Hoover's story from the stope dinner. Now I remembered how Long had told the crowd where to find it, but to no avail.

"Yes, Father. I've heard the story."

"Not the whole story… I lied to the crowd. I told them the wrong place."

He was cut short by a spasm of pain, which appeared to engulf his entire body.

"Let me get you some more morphia."

He grabbed my arm with both hands.

"No!"

I tried to pull away, but his grip was firm.

"I… I need to tell someone why I lied. I need to be forgiven."

Rennie, who had been standing back, now leant forward so that he was in Father Long's line of sight.

"Tell me, Father," he said. "Tell me why you need forgiveness."

I had the feeling that we were about to be saddled with more than we could handle.

Father Long spoke rapidly, as if to throw off his burden as fast as he could.

"It's in a cairn grave at the 'Wealth of Nations'. I was sick of their greed. I lied because I wanted them to run like the Gadarene Swine."

Rennie nodded at this, appearing to understand.

"I had to protect the men who had told me…because I had given them my word, but I had no right to judge the crowd, Reverend. It is for God to judge, not I."

Tears were streaming down his cheeks.

His breathing quickened further, he was sinking fast.

"Then I won't judge you either," Rennie said, gripping the priest's hands. "In God's name, I forgive you your sins."

Father Long smiled and tried to say something more: "Fools… fools…"

His mouth opened to form another word, but he had breathed his last and the word never came.

I felt for a carotid pulse… nothing.

"He's gone," I said.

Rennie made the sign of the cross and bowed his head in silent prayer.

We moved the dead priest onto a wheeled trolley and then to the rack inside the morgue. Though I was used to death, as was Rennie – all he seemed to do in his spare time was conduct funerals – there was something poignant about this poor Irish priest, who had been so beset with his personal demons only minutes before. I covered him in a white sheet and for a few more moments we stood there in a respectful silence, our heads bowed.

I went to Cutfield's office and filled out the death certificate, writing the same thing I had written so many times before:

Causes of death:
(a) Peritonitis
(b) Typhoid fever

This was the clinical part of a death, with the humanity and empathy removed. Father Long would become a statistic now – another number on a table of typhoid fever deaths for 1900 – to be used by epidemiologists comparing the numbers to other years to try and gauge the severity of the epidemic.

When I had arrived the book of death certificates had been new and now it was almost all stubs, with the certificates filled out and issued to the next of kin.

In the mess I boiled some water on the primus. The only light in the room was the blue flame which cast an eerie glow and projected our large flickering shadows onto the walls like a ghoulish pantomime.

I brought over the coffees and sat next to Sister B and opposite Rennie. Though the primus flame was out now, there was just enough moonlight coming in through the windows to be able to see their features. No-one had thought to light the kerosene lamp and we sat there in the dark.

I was first to break the silence:

"I'm not imaging it, am I? He said where the gold was hidden."

Sister B put her hand on my arm as if trying to protect me, to stop me going any further down this road.

"You heard him," I said. "He was very specific; buried in a cairn grave at The Wealth of Nations."

"Isn't that a book on economics?" Rennie said.

"Yes, but he can't have meant that."

"Maybe he was hallucinating," Sister B said.

"No, it must be a place."

Rennie looked at me:

"Are you suggesting we go on some kind of a treasure hunt, John?"

"What have we got to lose?"

Sister B spoke in a low voice: "You two don't know anything about gold. You don't know the desert. You don't even know where he meant."

"That's true, John," Rennie said. "If we're going to do this, we need someone we can trust and who knows what they're doing."

Chapter Sixteen

Dudley was in his usual seat at the British Arms early the next morning.

He and Edith McKay were guffawing with laughter when I walked in. I was twitchy, my hands trembling from lack of sleep and the drama of the night.

The saloon fell silent.

Sensing the tension, Edith walked to the far end of the bar and started washing up glasses from the night before.

"Remember that story about the sacred nugget?" I said, sitting down next to Dudley. "You know, the one Hoover told us all?"

Dudley stared ahead at the bottles of spirits on a shelf on the other side of the bar, and I saw the crow's feet around his good eye crease up in a flash of recognition.

"Father Long came in last night," I said, "and died of typhoid fever… but not before saying where we could find the gold."

The creases disappeared as his eye opened wide in surprise and he swung round to look at me, the colour draining from his face.

"Where?" he said. "No… wait. First of all, why are you telling me?"

"You're the only one we can trust, Tom."

"We?"

"Rennie, Sister B and me. We were all there last night… Long said the nugget was buried in a cairn grave at the Wealth of Nations. Do you know what that means?"

Dudley frowned. "The Wealth of Nations?"

"That's what he said."

He turned to me.

"You're sure that's what he said?"

"I'm positive… Well?"

"It's an old lease north of Coolgardie. It was mined out years ago. There's no gold out there."

"We need your help to show us the place… to help us to find what we're supposed to be looking for. Rennie and I wouldn't know a piece of quartz from a sacred nugget."

Dudley laughed momentarily and didn't reply.

Edith McKay was polishing the glasses now, and watching us.

"What's got you two whispering away like a couple of naughty schoolboys?"

"Gold," Dudley said.

"That doesn't narrow it down much, Tom."

She went back to her job, whistling as she did so to give us some privacy.

Dudley was staring straight ahead again, lost in thought.

"Tom?" I said.

"I hear you. I'm thinking."

Eventually, he looked at his watch.

"Get Rennie and meet me here in an hour."

During the morning handover round, I told Poyntz about Father Long's admission and quick death. He just listened like it was any other patient. He didn't ask for details and so I didn't say anything about Long's last words. I guessed B would tell him later.

The grey horse was still tied up outside the hospital.

I walked it round to the Catholic Church and gave it to one of the young priests. He must have already heard about the death because his eyes were red rimmed and sunken. I pulled out the death certificate from my coat pocket, handed it to him and left him there, holding the reins with one hand and the sad document with the other.

Rennie was in his chapel painting the pews white, covering over the stencilled lettering of the boxes. I watched him from the doorway for a minute before going inside. His handiwork was not much better than his carpentry. He had missed bits and as much paint was on the floor as on the boxes themselves.

"Sean."

"Good morning, John."

He stood up to greet me.

"Why are you doing that?"

He looked down at what he had done, seemingly as bemused with his job as I was.

"I think it is distracting the churchgoers. All that loose chatter during my sermons. I thought my whitening the place would help them focus their attention on what I had to say. Make them feel as if they were in a holy place and not some junkyard chapel."

"That makes sense."

"Hmmm," he said, looking doubtful. "Well, we'll see. I've actually started wondering just how much good I can actually do out here. All anyone really cares about is the gold."

He was dead right of course. And now I was one of them.

"Come on," I said, trying not to sound too desperate, "Dudley's taking us to find the nugget."

He put the lid back on the paint tub without saying anything. It was if he had been expecting me to come in and say those exact words all morning.

Dudley was at the British Arms with three bicycles all leant up against the side of the building; old Raleighs with wide handlebars and worn leather seats. He had also brought a large leather water bladder which sloshed and gurgled when he moved it, like a patient's bowel sounds under the stethoscope.

"Gentlemen… thought you were never going to come."

Rennie walked over to the nearest bicycle and peered at it.

"What's all this then?"

"They're called bicycles, Rev."

"I know that, Tom. But why are they here?"

"It's the easiest way of getting where we need to go."

"What? Riding?"

"Trust me, Rev; compared to riding a camel, it's like floating on a magic carpet."

We pulled into Coolgardie by lunchtime and ate meat pies in a pub called Faahan's.

"My God," Dudley said under his breath as he ate, looking around and shaking his head.

I followed his line of sight. Apart from a couple of hardened drinkers propped up against the bar, it was quiet.

"What's wrong?"

"It's dead in here," he said. "It's as quiet as a woman the first day and a half after she's married."

I checked his expression, trying to work out if this was just another of his similes or whether he was speaking from personal experience. He had never mentioned a wife before and didn't wear a wedding ring. I dared myself to find out.

"Ever been married, Tom?"

He drank from his beer before answering.

"Once," he said, not meeting my eye. I knew that look. It was how I felt now if anyone asked me if I had any brothers or sisters.

I instinctively knew what had happened, but Rennie seemingly hadn't picked up on it.

"She left you, Tom?"

"You could say that, Rev… Went off with a bloke called Vibrio Cholerae…"

Rennie frowned. "An Italian?"

"'Fraid not, Rev." Poor Rennie was none the wiser. "Cholera, Rev… She died of the cholera." My friend turned bright crimson and Dudley smiled. "Don't worry, Rev…It was a long time ago. We had just come out to the goldfields. Poor girl was there one day and gone the next. The damnedest thing…" His words drifted off.

"I'm sorry, Tom," I said.

"Me too," Rennie said. "I didn't realise, Tom."

"This place brings back a few memories," Dudley said. "We used to come here when we were first married. Had some good times… It used to be so crowded that old Faahan would just throw the money into a large tin tub under the bar." He glanced over to the barman. "That's Bill Faahan there. Look at him, poor bugger."

Faahan was running his hand through his dark curly mop with a stunned expression on his face, as if he couldn't believe how far his establishment had fallen either. Even pulling the beer handle seemed like a terrific effort.

Dudley raised his glass and called over, "To the old camp, Bill."

Faahan poured himself a small drink and looked at an oil painting on the wall: 'Bayley's luck', showing the first gold strike at Coolgardie eight years before, when Bayley had picked up a half ounce nugget at a place called 'Fly Flat.'

"The old camp," he said, holding up the glass and then draining it. "Five years ago, this was the third biggest town in the state – after Perth and Fremantle. Now look, Tom…"

It wasn't just Faahan's; the whole place was dead. Outside, the street was lined with hotels which all stood silent.

Faahan retreated back to his world of apathy and disappointment and Dudley forgot about him and switched his attention back to the living.

"Eat up, gents… Got a long ride ahead. You'll need the energy. Plus we'll be staying out in the bush tonight. Won't be eating again until tomorrow."

This was news.

"We're not going to make it back to Kalgoorlie later?"

"No way, Doc. We'll have to camp at the find… Still got a way to go.'

It meant I would miss rounds the next day and Poyntz would be on his own after a night on-call.

Flustered, I went to the telegraph office and wired a message to him, addressed to the hospital.

POYNTZ. WILL MISS MORNING HANDOVER. BACK TOMORROW PM. SORRY. J

I knew he would manage; he and B had coped well enough before I had arrived, but I still felt bad about it.

A track led off to the north from the main street: *'WEALTH OF NATIONS 28 MILES'* a weathered sign read. 'A way to go' Dudley had said. That had just become a number.

Dudley caught my grim expression.

"No bloody Sunday school picnic is it, Doc?"

I shook my head briefly, trying not to rise to the bait, and pedalled onwards. I was a 'Blue', for God's sake, easily fit enough for this jaunt.

We crossed the train line at a small cluster of buildings at Bonnie Vale.

Dotted along the track were lonely graves, which made me think Father Long had been telling the truth. *Men on their death beds don't lie,* I said to myself.

Dudley recited a chant as we pedalled past each grave:

'Out on the wastes of the Never Never –
That's where the dead men lie!
There where the heat waves dance forever,
That's where the dead men lie!'

Flies swarmed in their thousands.

The only sounds were our laboured breathing and the hum of the tyres on the track, the dirt compacted by old camel trails and then baked hard by the sun. Where sections were too soft and sandy for cycling, we made short detours through the sparse bush bordering the track.

Dudley was wearing his slouch hat, and Rennie had knotted his handkerchief securely onto his head. I took off my shirt and tied it around my head with my belt so that I looked like one of the Afghan cameleers.

The red dust found its way everywhere – it filled our nostrils, mouths, hair and permeated our clothes. Combined with our sweat it formed a thin red paste on any exposed skin, so that after a few miles we looked like three demons out for a ride.

Every half hour we stopped to drink. On one stop, Dudley took off his hat and shirt and poured some water from his leather container over his head and down the back of his neck. The Federation flag was tattooed on one forearm and the word 'Auralia' in blue ink on the other, just like his friend McKay's. On his upper back, across the shoulders was the legend: '1st Australian Horse'.

There were only two geographical features on the ride to distract us from the monotony of the dirt, gum trees and flies. The first was a rise called 'Mount Burges', about twenty miles out, like a giant beached whale in the surrounding sands and not much higher. Whoever had named it had the same raw sense of humour as Dudley, because it was only a dozen yards in elevation, no bigger than the rock outcrop I had climbed at Bullabulling.

The other feature appeared not long after the 'Mount' – a circular dip in the ground near the track, perhaps fifty yards in diameter.

"What is that? A sinkhole from an old mine?"

Dudley shook his head.

"Meteorite crater."

"A meteor landed there?"

"Sure did. Plenty of them out in the bush."

Out of instinct, I looked up at blue sky, half expecting to see a vapour trail still lacing the heavens.

He was looking up too.

"Imagine that, Doc? A boulder from space slamming into the ground faster than the speed of a bullet… You're sitting here, minding your own business and then... KABOOOM! Why, it'd bloody ruin your day."

At five o'clock we finally arrived at an area of old mine workings. The site certainly looked abandoned; just a dozen rusting windlasses with fraying metal wires quivering like guitar strings in the desert wind.

"This is it," Dudley said, dismounting. "This is the Wealth of Nations."

There was no sign to tell us so. It didn't look like much. I had been expecting more.

Everything on the ride had been on trust; there were no signs telling us the outcrop was called 'Mount Burges' or that the dip in the ground had been a meteor crater. It was all Dudley telling us so. He could be saying whatever he wanted and Rennie and I would have been none the wiser.

"You're sure?"

"At one time this place was staggeringly rich on the surface," he said. "Twenty thousand ounces were taken from its quartz reefs in a few weeks – but it was doomed to fail at depth because the reef was only a shallow one. They abandoned it in 1894."

"Strange for it to have been missed..." I said, frowning.

"How do you mean?"

"Remember Hoover's story? The whole episode only happened two years ago, so four years after you're saying it was shut down. That's odd. Surely it would have been found during the Wealth of Nations' heyday?"

Dudley was thinking about this with his index finger on his forehead when Rennie's voice cut into the silence: "Over there!"

Dudley and I looked to see where he was pointing.

Thirty yards away was a solitary cairn, surrounded by a few scrawny saltbushes. Only the top half was visible. It was perhaps four feet high, and looked just like one of the makeshift graves we had seen earlier by the side of the track. Some of the rocks were the same colour red as the bush floor, dusty and caked, whereas the rocks at the top were whiter in colour. There was no cross or sign or plaque to indicate if anybody was buried there.

We set our bicycles down and approached slowly.

Dozens of fresh footprints were impressed in the red dirt around the cairn, not just shoes but hoof prints too. I recalled how Father Long's trousers and the legs of his horse had both been covered with the stuff. They had been here less than twenty four hours before.

"These footprints are recent" I said. "Very recent. He was here for some reason…"

Rennie came over to inspect the prints.

"Why would he do that?"

"I don't know. But from the state of his clothes he was probably here yesterday at some stage. He must have ridden straight on to the hospital."

Rennie took a swig from Dudley's water bag and didn't say anything. He was being uncharacteristically quiet. I assumed he was thinking the same as me – what we would do if the gold was there. What would the ramifications be?

"Are you all right about this, Sean?" I said to him, "… about disturbing a grave, I mean?"

He wiped the water from his lips and jammed the cork into the nozzle.

"I don't know, John."

"I'll do it then," I said.

Without further discussion I started to lift away the rocks one by one, placing them to the side so that they started to form another separate pile. Within a few minutes I had reached the red dusted layer a foot above the ground.

"I don't think it's there," Rennie was saying. "Come on, John. Put them back and let's get out of here."

The grave had really given him the fear.

Dudley hadn't even bothered to help; he was just standing there spectating, like the gravedigger at Freddie's funeral. Except he wasn't smoking, he was swigging from his silver rum flask.

I didn't mind no-one helping. I wanted to make the discovery all on my own.

It was late afternoon now and the sun was low in the sky, turning everything golden, except in the place where I needed it to be.

"Come on, Doc," Dudley said, "Rennie's right. There's nothing here. The priest has hoaxed us all again."

I stood up and glared at them both angrily.

"He wasn't lying. I saw it in his eyes. He said it was here. It must be bloody well here."

I went back to the task as they both sat on the ground, looking on and shaking their heads as if they felt sorry for me.

Then, as I lifted another rock away, a glow shone out from among the base layer of rock. Quickly I lifted away two more rocks and it came into full view. A huge nugget – as big in diameter as one of the medicine balls I had trained with back in my rowing days.

"Look at this!"

I felt a surge of excitement suffuse through me.

Rennie got up to take a look.

"Good God!"

"Here," I said, putting my hands underneath it, "help me get it out."

We could only just manage. It weighed as much as a man. Together we hauled out the nugget, set it down on the dirt and sat there watching it glowing in the gentle light.

So the legend was true – the solid reality of it lay not two feet away. I stroked it like I would a cat, marvelling at the contrast between my dirt reddened sweaty skin and the glittering golden surface of the nugget.

I can see why mankind prizes it so highly, I was thinking, *it is truly beautiful.*

For a minute, Dudley stood rooted to the spot, staring and shaking his head. Then he came over to examine its surface carefully. Squatting down, he traced its contours with his fingers, before rolling it over on the ground to look at the underside.

He shook his head again and looked up at me.

"Jesus H. Christ."

"Just gold, Tom," Rennie said. "It's just gold." Though the way he said it made him sound even more spellbound than Dudley.

The site howled with a sudden gust of wind – as though Father Long's ghost had arrived amongst us, and was trying to say something too.

Dudley stood up, put his hands on his hips and met my eye.

"Listen," he said, "we bring this thing back into town and there'll be bloody chaos. There'll be all sorts of probing. Everyone knows this place has been a duffer for years and they'll want to know how it ended up here. We'll be hounded night and day. Remember there were six thousand people in the crowd when Father Long said this thing was somewhere else altogether. If they find out he lied, his reputation will be ruined."

Dudley had a point. It would be impossible to keep this thing under wraps.

"We would need a horse to carry it back anyway," he said. "It's too big. I suggest we leave it here for now until we work out what to do."

I think I was still in shock at the find and couldn't think of anything else to say. It all felt such an anti-climax now. I looked to Rennie for some support.

"I agree with Tom," he said, with a shrug. "What else can we do?"

With no other practical choice on offer, we reburied the gold under the cairn and then cycled back a few miles to set up camp in the meteor crater. Everyone seemed subdued; gone was the energy of the ride out here.

Dudley made a simple tripod of long sticks held fast at the apex by an upside-down tin can and put it over the fire. He had threaded a wire through a small hole in the can and tied the end around a hooked stick. From the hook he hung his billycan and boiled the water.

His tripod reminded me of those contraptions in the hospital ship, the ones the soldiers had perched their Pith helmets on at the ends of their beds.

"Billy tea," he said, pouring us each a mug when it was ready.

Considering all the effort he had gone to, he didn't drink much. Instead he kept swigging from his rum flask.

I sat there, sulking about the fact that I didn't have the nugget next to me, knowing it was two miles down the track waiting to be found by the next passer-by.

The story of the sacred nugget started going round and round my head.

I was finding it hard to fathom why the priest had lied that day. To honour his promise, yes, but there was something darker, an element of taunting the crowd: 'I wanted the crowd to run like the Gadarene swine.'

"What are the Gadarene swine?" I said to Rennie.

"They're from Mark's gospel… One night, Jesus met a man possessed by demons in the country of Gadarenes. He sent the demons into a nearby herd of swine on the hillside and then they stampeded into the Sea of Galilee where they all drowned."

Eugene had said the only way to avoid a curse was to divert the bad energy. Jesus had steered the demons into the pigs. Perhaps Rennie's and Eugene's beliefs were not so far apart.

"You think he wanted the crowd to run like crazed pigs to teach them a lesson?"

There was a pause before my friend replied.

"Yes, and there's something very interesting here. When Jesus asked the demon its name, the reply was: 'My name is Legion, for we are many.' Mark, Chapter 5, verse 9. Now where have you heard that word before?"

"It was a Roman Army unit wasn't it?"

"That's right John. And how many soldiers do you think there were in a Roman legion?"

I shook my head.

"Sorry Sean, my history is shaky."

"Six thousand" he said.

"So the same number as the crowd outside the hotel that day? That's quite some coincidence."

Rennie took a sip of his tea, before continuing.

"I believe that there are no coincidences, John. I believe there's a plan."

I looked over at Dudley, who was 'Church' too, to see his reaction to that statement, but he remained deadpan – just kept staring into the fire with his rum flask hanging from his fingers.

Plan or no plan, what Father Long had done that day suddenly crystallised in my mind: "So he was trying to get a legion of people to realise they were chasing the wrong goal in life…by sending them nowhere, he thought that somehow their gold demons would be metaphorically drowned."

"Yes" Rennie said. "At the time I think that's what he had in mind. Later though, he realised he had just been cruel. It wasn't for him to teach them a lesson. They were people, not swine, human beings whose hopes he was dashing. I've heard some were trampled in the rush and that friends deserted each other to get there first. Father Long must have felt a terrible guilt to have been the author of all that. You saw how he begged for forgiveness on his death bed. How broken a man, he was."

"But why come all the way out here yesterday?" I said. "Just to see it? He was sick with typhoid and the ride probably killed him. It doesn't make sense. Priests don't ride for fifty miles into the desert on a whim, just to look at a piece of gold."

"It does seem strange on the face of it," Rennie said.

"And how in hell was it even found here in the first place – if the Wealth of Nations had been mined out years before?"

Rennie shrugged.

"I don't know" he said. "But it exists…We saw it today."

I turned to Dudley, appealing to his goldfields experience: "Is that possible, Tom? Could something that big really have been missed?"

He looked at me, eyes glazed from the rum.

"No way."

"So the prospectors must have lied to Father Long," I said, seeing it all clearly. "The gold must have come from somewhere else."

"Why?" Rennie said.

I looked at him. "People lie all the time, Sean."

He seemed to accept this and did not reply.

"What followed is full of irony" I said, "With all the hullaballoo, the prospectors decided to come and bury it out here for safe-keeping, probably waiting for the fuss to die down. What better a spot to hide it, than in the very place they had told the priest? No-one was going to come here looking for gold, and after Father Long lied to the crowd, they knew he was never going to tell."

Dudley didn't look impressed. "I suppose you could call it a theory, Doc... But you're putting assumptions onto assumptions."

"But why would it still be here after all this time?" Rennie said. "It's been two years. Surely they would have retrieved it by now."

"That's true" I said.

I was beginning to worry now, thinking we might yet lose the nugget to others, that there were men out there somewhere who were coming back for it.

I could feel my greed growing. It was *ours* and I didn't want anyone else to take it away. Then the answer came to me.

"There's only one explanation," I said. "They must have died from typhoid. If they haven't come for it by now, they won't be coming at all. We probably rode past their graves today. Perhaps that's why Father Long rode out... to see if it was still here. He wanted someone to know the secret – it didn't matter who. It just happened to be us."

I felt a surge of relief at my logic.

It was still ours.

I looked across at my friends to see if they were as excited about it as I was, but they were both just staring blankly into the fire, seemingly unmoved.

To Rennie it was just mammon. As for Dudley, he still appeared to be in a state of mild shock and that was unlike him. He hadn't said a great deal since making camp, but just sat there swigging from his rum flask.

Minutes went by.

"What happened at the end of the Gospel story?" I said to Rennie.

"Well, the wild man was cured, but the townspeople told Jesus to leave."

"Why? Weren't they pleased he was back to normal?"

"No."

"Why not?"

"That's a big question."

"Well, what do you think?"

Rennie was poking the fire with a stick and lifting it out and watching the end glow in the dark.

He looked at me.

"I think that people don't like having their status quo disturbed. People don't want to know anything new, because then they might have to go through the mental sweat of rethinking things and coming to new conclusions."

Dudley got drunk on the rum. I hadn't seen him this far gone before and that was saying something. When he finished it, he threw his flask on the ground, picked up his sleeping mat – still rolled up – and started to sing and dance with it around the fire. It was the same tune he had whistled on the train out to Kalgoorlie.

"Oh there once was a swagman camped in the billabong,
under the shade of a Coolibah tree,
And he sang as he looked at the old billy boiling,
'Who'll come a waltzing Matilda with me?'"

After a while he collapsed in a heap on the fireside dirt and lay there, breathing hard and looking up at the night sky.

"Mate of mine wrote the words to that," he slurred. "He's a journalist. The one who wrote about my dead mates in the newspaper."

"I remember," I said. "Paterson, wasn't it?"

"Yeah, that's it, Doc…We go back years me and old Banjo. Used to row a double scull with the bugger out of Sydney Rowing Club. We weren't much… real slowcoaches, nothing like you Oxford boys, but we had fun. We once sculled alongside Harry Searle – the greatest of them all. Admittedly there were two of us and one of him, and we only just kept up…"

Searle was a rowing legend, a childhood hero of mine and Freddie's.

"The Clarence Comet," I said.

"I'm impressed, Doc. He rowed a boat on the Clarence River, taking orders and doing meat deliveries for a local butcher. Blonde-haired giant. Seeing him walking through town was like seeing a gladiator amongst degenerate Romans. You know the other scullers believed he had one more rib than any other man, because his chest was so big. I'll never forget seeing how he made the Canadian Champion Hanlan look like a little boy in practice."

"I remember when he came to England… I was still at school."

"1889," Dudley said. "Defeated the American champion O'Connor on the Thames, and then contracted the enteric on the way back to Australia. Died not long afterwards in Melbourne… only twenty three years old. After they brought back the body to Sydney, more than 100,000 lined the streets, some even said 200,000. I was one of them. It's a bastard of a disease…"

Dudley was quiet after that, motionless in his drunken stupor.

It cheered me up to hear he had been an oarsman. I had a lot in common this Australian, more than I would have ever thought possible when we had first met.

"Something happened to me on the day I was shot in South Africa," Dudley said out of the blue. "Something I didn't tell you before."

I looked across – he was studying his thumbless right hand.

"What Tom?"

"This is going to sound strange… I don't know how, but those Boers blasted me out of my body."

"What?"

"Don't know how else to say it. I was shot three times anyway and some big bugger clouted me over the head with his rifle."

I remembered the name Carlsson had told me: Jan Viljoens.

"That was when it happened," Dudley said. "My body left me so quickly I wasn't even aware of its falling down. I went on without it, stepping through the Boers and screaming, but none of them noticed me anymore. I never felt more alive than that moment. Then I looked behind and saw the bloke that was me, down on the floor, a dozen yards away. I was lying dead down there. I realised I would have to go back."

On the other side of the fire, Rennie was nodding to himself.

"This body," Dudley said, "it's not really me... just a cloak I wear. You and the Rev must think I'm crazy."

"Not at all, Tom," Rennie said.

I kept quiet.

"Tell you this, though... I'm not scared of bloody dying anymore, because I've seen what happens."

"You've seen what happens when you die?" I said, thinking that by repeating it, Dudley might realise how crazy he was sounding. But I had done this to him before, when he had talked about the giant snake forming mountains, and it had gone over his head.

"That's right, Doc. This bit rots," he said, smacking his leg. Then he tapped his temple. "But this bit survives... in here somewhere. It's as much of a fact as the force of gravity. Black fellas know all about it. Anyway, once you know, it changes the way you live. Material possessions mean bugger all. Gold means bugger all. You can choose to live without fear. Also, I know I'll get to see my girl again one day. God bless her soul."

"Amen to that," Rennie said.

I found myself envying these two men, both sure in their own ways that there was life after death.

My dreams that night were crystal clear, tinted with the bright light that had beaten down on us all day. I thought she might leave me alone for once, far removed as I was from civilisation, but I was wrong. The Wealth of Nations became the Spitz Kop. I was back in the tent hospital and the Grey Lady was there, wandering from tent to tent. I was chasing her, but never getting close. Soldiers were dying around me and I was burying them in shallow graves, placing rock upon rock over their uniforms until they disappeared from sight. As far as I could see, the plain was covered in cairn graves. Then I was in the ward at Spike Island, watching her staring at my sleeping brother and knowing that he was for the next world. She turned her head and looked straight at me.

I woke up in a cold sweat and stayed awake until the horizon glowed with the promise of the new day. The coming dawn lifted my spirits and the bad dream receded. Rennie and Dudley slept on soundly – not a single worry or fear in their God-fearing heads.

For an hour or so, I stared up at the sky as its colours slowly changed from dark to light. The hassles of Kalgoorlie life and drama of the previous days remained in the background. I watched as the sun came up, and remembered it wasn't the sun moving at all, but the earth I was lying on – a massive orb travelling around an even more massive orb at many thousands of miles per hour, both within an almost infinite vacuum.

Maybe this was how all mornings should begin – with an unobstructed view of the heavens – to help remind you there are bigger and more important events happening out there than in your life. Lying in the meteorite crater near my two still sleeping friends and having these thoughts brought me a kind of peace I had not known since… well, since long before the war.

Chapter Seventeen

By the time we arrived back in Kalgoorlie, it was early afternoon. The world was going about its business, indifferent to our adventure, ignorant to the fact that we had become millionaires overnight.

We split up at the crossroads – Rennie back to his manse, Dudley back to the British Arms, while I cleaned up at the Palace and then went straight over to the hospital.

Poyntz was sitting in the mess, leaning against the wall with his hands behind his head and his feet up on the table, singing quietly to himself. It was to the same tune he sometimes whistled as he moved between patients on rounds:

'... Look away,
look away,
look away Dixie land.
Well I wish I was in Dixie, Hooray! Hooray...'

When he saw me, he stopped singing and swung his feet off the table, holding out his hand to indicate I should sit with him. He looked pleased to see me back again.

"I thought you were from the North," I said. "Dixie was the anthem of the South, wasn't it?"

"I am from the North, but the Confederates had better songs."

"You got the telegram then?"

"Yep."

"Sorry to let you down."

"We coped."

I walked over to the primus and poured myself some lukewarm coffee from the pot.

"Where'd you get to anyway?"

"Out by the old camp where the dead men lie," I said.

He laughed.

"Sounds a bit cloak and dagger... B told me about the priest and the gold nugget. Said you boys were going off on a treasure hunt."

I opened my mouth to speak, but he held up his hand to stop me.

"I don't want to know, Jack. It's your business."

He just smiled and went back to singing Dixie.

We wandered down to the ward and Poyntz brought me up to date on the patients before leaving.

Two more empty beds; one recovery and one death.

The log book was full of cases he had seen in my absence; some minor operations – lacerations, a child with a pulled elbow, a miner with a dislocated shoulder. I turned back to the previous page – Father Long's name was there, listed in deaths for that day. Twenty seven years of age.

I felt the long ride in my legs now that the excitement had gone. Luckily for me the ward was quiet that afternoon and, after doing a final check at eight o'clock, I went back to the admin block and flopped onto the chaise longue in Cutfield's office.

It felt as if I had just closed my eyes, but when Sister B woke me, it was three in the morning.

"Doctor John... DOCTOR JOHN"

I snapped awake.

"Yes?"

"Someone needs you…"

She sounded and looked slightly strange, almost a look of amusement coupled with mild disapproval.

I struggled to my feet, threw on my white coat and walked disjointedly down the corridor, gathering my wits along the way. I vowed to find a job one day where I could sleep the night through – once I cashed in the sacred nugget, nights on-call were going to be someone else's bloody problem.

Waiting for me in the main hall was a striking looking woman in a velvet dress, her hair a deep russet red spilling down over her shoulders in a cascade of ringlets.

In Kalgoorlie, women either worked as nurses, barmaids or prostitutes and it was easy to work out which category this one fell into.

"Are you all right, madam?"

"Not really… some bastard's attacked my friend with a knife, and she's bleeding all over the place." I was trying to avoid staring at the ample cleavage on display and focused on her rouged cheeks instead. Now I knew why Sister B had given me a funny look.

"I'll get my Gladstone," I said.

A few minutes later, she and I were heading towards the red light area of town, Sister B having stayed to look after the hospital.

"What's your name?" I said.

"I'm known as 'The Russian Princess', sweetheart. We all have exotic names to attract the customers. My friend – the one who's been hurt – she's called 'The Hula Hula Girl'."

Despite being 'off duty', she oozed sexuality – the way she moved, the way she spoke, the way she looked at me. My heart was beating fast, far faster than it should have been from just walking down a street.

The brothels were at the lower end of Brookman Street – a good few hundred yards from the hospital. Some were in buildings, but some were just makeshift hessian tents, with red lanterns hanging from poles outside. It was to one of these that the Russian Princess led me, and I followed her inside.

As my eyes became accustomed to the poor light, the drab details of my new surroundings became clear; a carpet of hessian bags sewn together on the dirt floor – what the locals called a 'wogga', a rickety wooden stand with a washbowl and a plain iron bedstead holding a sagging dirty mattress.

A young woman was sitting on the edge of the bed, nursing her face with a large blood-soaked towel. She was naked, save for a rough woollen blanket half covering her body. Draped over the end of the bed were some stockings and a plum coloured velvet dress. A pair of long, un-laced leather boots lay on the floor – in her trade, these were what drew the miners in, those and the long thighs above them. Though she was a sorry sight, for some reason it was her discarded boots on the floor which depressed me most of all.

Above the bed was a framed doctor's certificate:

'I hereby certify that I have examined Bronwyn Jones, the woman also known as 'The Hula Hula Girl', and find that she is free of any venereal disease.'

I didn't recognise the signature, though I supposed it must have been my predecessor.

The Russian Princess unhooked a kerosene lamp hanging in the centre of the tent and brought it up close to her friend's face so I could carry out a closer examination.

What I saw made me inwardly wince; blood was oozing from a two inch laceration on her left cheek. Someone had tried to destroy not only her livelihood but her beauty, for it was apparent that in more normal circumstances the Hula Hula Girl was very attractive. Now though, tears and mascara had run down her face in black rivulets, mixing with the blood around the wound.

The one saving grace was that the laceration followed the Langer line on the cheek and jawline perfectly. Skin healed more effectively if surgeons used these natural lines as a guide when making incisions. This cut had been made by a very fine blade and was a smooth curve. By a miracle no artery had been damaged.

I used cocaine solution to anaesthetise the wound, and with the thinnest chromic catgut, made a running stitch. Her skin came together neatly, leaving only a thin red line.

"Done," I said.

She checked her face in the mirror and managed the faintest smile.

"It'll fade with time. I've used a fine suture, so only soup for the next week and complete rest. Probably best if you don't… er… work in that time… especially with your mouth…"

She nodded obediently. The Russian Princess helped her friend put some clothes on while I packed away my instruments and washed my hands. There was a pile of metal medallions on the dresser and I picked one up; it had an outline of a female figure on one side and, on the reverse, *'The Hula Hula Girl, 120 Brookman Street'*. All the medallions were the same.

"What do you do with these?"

"We give 'em to satisfied customers to pass on," the Hula Hula Girl said, when she saw what I was holding.

I put it down and turned to her.

"Are you going to go to the police about this?"

She shook her head. "He'd kill me," she said with utter certainty. "I've never seen him before. He paid for a 'short time' but was so drunk he couldn't manage it. I told him it didn't matter and that he could have his money back…" Her voice was trembling with a mixture of fear and rage now. "But he cut me with his Bowie knife anyway… the bastard…"

"Was there anything identifiable about the knife?"

"It had a white handle," she said. "Bone or ivory, I think."

"Surely the police would be able catch him if you reported it."

She shook her head again.

"I don't trust the police to keep him locked up. He said he would kill me if I told, and I believe him. The police don't care. We're on the edge of society here as it is.'

She pointed to some mended areas in the hessian tent behind the bed.

"See those patches? That's where we've repaired spy holes they've cut. They want proof we're having sex for money, but I think they just like to watch…"

There was no point in going on.

"All right," I said. "Just don't move your face too much. If you have any problems, come straight round to the hospital and see me."

I pushed through the door flap and stepped out into the sultry night.

The Russian Princess followed me. "Doctor, wait. We haven't paid you."

I stopped and turned to face her. Under the red light, she looked even more striking – red hair, red lips, red dress… red everything.

"Forget it," I said, waving my hand. "She's missing a week of business; she'll need all her savings."

All I wanted to do was to get back to Cutfield's chaise longue and go back to sleep.

The Russian Princess reached into her pocket and put a coin into my hand anyway. Then before I knew what was happening she had hooked her arm around the back of my neck and was drawing me down onto her lips. There was tenderness in her kiss that belied all the cold-heartedness I assumed she would need for a job like hers and I'll admit I lingered there for longer than was decent. After several seconds, she drew away and smiled at me. "It would be on the house," she said into my ear.

After she had slipped back into the tent I looked down at the coin in my hand. It wasn't money, it was one of those medallions: *'The Russian Princess, 130 Brookman Street'* it said.

As I walked back to the hospital, I thought of Dudley, Cookie and McKay and how much gyp they would give me if they found out.

The following day, after rounds and handover, I went back to my room at the Palace and slept for four straight hours. I woke at lunchtime and sat out on the veranda. A Cobb & Co coach rattled by, full to bursting with prospectors and miners. I waved at them. The kiss had really lifted my spirits. I was half considering a visit to the Russian Princess.

Then Rennie came through from the bar, carrying two plates loaded with pies and peas, the knives and forks tucked under his chin.

For once I did all the talking, rambling on about the Hula Hula Girl and the Russian Princess. I told Rennie about the kiss and showed him the medallion, as proud of it as Freddie had been when showing me his South Africa medal.

I asked him if it would be wrong to visit her.

Instead of lecturing me about sinning, the way I had expected he might, there was a long silence and I instantly regretted having even mentioned it. He put his plate down on the table and rested his head in his hands. I could tell he was ashamed of me, disappointed by my lustful thoughts.

"I was only joking." This wasn't completely true.

He rubbed his eyes with his fingertips and then moved them slowly down his face.

"It's all right, John. I'm just tired."

I noticed he had only picked at his food.

"Are you all right, Sean?"

"I think that ride has worn me out a little." He pushed his plate over to me. "You have mine. I'm going to get some rest."

Without another word he stood up stiffly and patted my shoulder, and then stepped out into the dusty thoroughfare. I watched him walk slowly up Maritana Street, hands shoved deep in his pockets and shoulders hunched, as though he was trudging through a cold English wind, rather than the stifling heat of a Kalgoorlie afternoon. I think I had really offended him with my talk of prostitutes. He was probably going back to his chapel to pray for my soul.

It turned out not to be that at all. Rennie had caught typhoid fever. I kicked myself for not having taken a jar of inoculation serum from Almroth Wright's lab, where dozens had just been lying around. If I had done that, I could have jabbed Rennie on the boat journey out to Australia and he would have been protected. Anyway, it was too late for 'what ifs' now.

The bad water could have been from anywhere really, perhaps from a drink on a visit to one of his congregation in the worst part of town a few weeks earlier. However he had caught it, the typhoid cut down my friend to a dehydrated, skeletal facsimile of his former self.

For a fortnight, we took it in turns to sit by Rennie's hospital bed in a round-the-clock vigil. Despite phenacetin, his temperature chart was alarming.

Empty Coca-Cola bottles filled his bedside table, but the big man kept slipping.

"Please don't die." I said it over and over, even when I wasn't at his bedside. I even visited the chapel and said it in there.

I lived on Cutfield's chaise longue.

In snatched bouts of sleep, I dreamt the Grey Lady was standing at the end of Rennie's bed and I would wake in terror and rush over to the ward.

One morning, his fever finally broke.

The sun was piercing though the windows of the ward and lighting the place up, as if God himself was visiting.

Poyntz was sitting in a chair by the bed, taking Rennie's temperature. His expression reminded me of the doctor in an oil painting I had once seen at the Tate. In the painting, the patient had been a young child, but the doctor's look of concern was the same. I stood at the end of the bed, waiting for Poyntz's findings. After reading the thermometer he took Rennie's pulse. Then his intense look of concentration relaxed and he grinned up at me.

"He's gonna make it, Jack."

At that moment Rennie opened his eyes, saw what Poyntz was doing and said, with a weak voice, "'And when Jesus was come into Peter's house, he saw his wife's mother laid, and sick of a fever. And he touched her hand, and the fever left her...' Matthew, Chapter eight."

Rennie pulling through was one of the best things that had happened during my time in Kalgoorlie, much better than finding the sacred nugget or even the kiss from the Russian Princess.

I walked in and out of the ward, continually taking obs and generally fussing over him like a mother hen.

A few days later, a telegram arrived from Perth. Reverend Rowe had decided that as soon as Rennie was stable enough, he was to go to the coast and recuperate there.

I went over to the manse and packed his things.

He didn't have much; just a few tatty clothes.

His bible was on his pillow.

I picked it up and leafed through its thin, almost transparent, pages. The margins were covered with his jottings, so densely written that they looked like the hieroglyphs on the Rosetta stone.

On the inside cover was a more legible piece of handwriting:

To Sean,
With an earnest prayer that he may prove a successful reflector of these eternal truths, from his affectionate father.
T.W. Rennie, 1895.

He left the next day. Dudley used his clout to procure a first class carriage so that Rennie could lie down comfortably on his long journey to Perth.

He was so weak he didn't even put up a fight.

Chapter Eighteen

December, 1900

They set aside the private dining room at the Palace for the replacement mine manager's welcome do.

I already knew the new man Cowdray was no Dudley, but even so, I was surprised at the strength of my reaction when I went over to introduce myself. The moment I saw him I knew he was trouble; just sensed it the way you sense food is off after the first bite.

He was wearing a Queen's South Africa medal on his lapel, which I recognised immediately. An elegant moustache and golden curling locks suggested he took considerable pride in his appearance. In fact, his hair was so long I found it hard to believe he could ever have served in the British Army. Close up, I saw that he had blue eyes with pinpoint pupils.

"I'm Doctor Hunston... the Egremont Company doctor."

He was only half concentrating on me; the other half of his attention was taken up by the rest of the room.

He raised his glass.

"Captain Cowdray."

That was the full extent of our conversation. He turned back to his friends and asked for his glass to be re-filled from a bottle one of them was holding. They closed their circle and continued their banter, making me feel like an invisible man.

So this was the new mine manager. We certainly wouldn't be putting the world to rights over morning coffee at the British Arms any time soon.

'Bloody Champagne Charlies' Dudley would have called them if he had been there.

Disillusioned and flat, I picked up a half-finished bottle of Mount Leonora whisky and found a quiet corner in the saloon bar, with the intention of getting well and truly plastered. I was missing Rennie and had seen a lot less of Dudley since he had left the company. He had holed up in the British Arms and was staying away from the Palace, presumably because the company was no longer footing the bill.

"Hello, Doctor…"

A man was looming over me.

I was relieved and a little surprised to see it was Carlsson. Smiling up at him, I gestured to the seat opposite mine.

"Care for some whisky?"

"Yes… Why not?"

He sat down and swigged straight from the bottle.

"I thought you were going back to Sweden," I said. "To the land of the Northern Lights where there's a god."

He wiped his mouth with his sleeve.

"Leaving tomorrow… but I wanted to see you first, to thank you for what you did for me."

"I was just doing my job."

"Yes, well, I was in a bad way and you made me believe I could pull through."

"Thank you, Carlsson. It means a lot."

"It wasn't all you… that pretty nurse helped too," he said, chuckling.

Just then the door from the dining room burst open and Cowdray and his cronies swaggered their way across to the bar.

"Four Cubans," Cowdray said to Violet Cook, in the same manner you might use if addressing a household dog.

She handed over the cigars without her usual smile. He grabbed them and continued talking with his friends, throwing a note down on the counter.

"Do you want the change?" Violet said.

"Keep it, my dear. Buy yourself a new dress, the one you're wearing has seen better days, or is that the fashion in this town?"

His friends laughed and Cowdray smiled as if he was a great wit.

Poor Violet... he had really got to her. She was looking down at her dress now, worried and insecure.

"Dudley's bloody replacement," I said, my eyes following the group as they headed back through the doors to the dining room. "He gives me a bad feeling, if I'm being honest."

Carlsson had become ashen faced.

He stood up.

"Carlsson?"

"I have to leave," he said, turning on his heels and striding out of the bar.

Grabbing the bottle of whisky I followed him out into the crowded street. "Carlsson? What the hell is the matter with you?"

"Not here," he said, looking past me to the Palace.

"What?"

"We can't talk here."

I was shocked by how agitated he had become.

"All right," I said, still confused, "follow me."

We walked the few blocks over to the hospital and sat on the front steps, near to the place where I had emptied Father Long's contaminated water bag that night. Carlsson was still distracted, looking about as if he was a hunted man. I gave him time to gather his thoughts.

"That man," he said, finally, "... the blond one... I recognised him from South Africa."

He said it as if he was referring to the bogeyman.

"You mean Cowdray?"

"Yes. He was a British captain out on the Transvaal – but before the war he'd fought in Matabeleland with Plumer's scouts. He was a lieutenant then – and a bloody ruthless one I heard."

"War is a ruthless game, Carlsson."

"No. You don't understand, he was different. He executed prisoners. Cowdray was the worst of them. He had a real taste for it…"

Carlsson took another drink of the whisky, his features full of dread.

"Now he's here… I can't believe it," he said. "Bulala is here."

"Bulala?"

"It means, 'he who kills or slays' in the Ndebele language. That's what the natives called him. The Boers knew all about his past – the stories made the rounds at night as we sat around camp fires. By God, we feared him – feared being taken prisoner I mean, because as far as Cowdray saw it the word 'prisoner' didn't exist. The usual rules didn't apply. In response, some of the Boers sent word to Cowdray that if he was ever captured, they would give him four days to die, meaning they would torture him for his previous crimes. For the Boers to have said that speaks volumes on what Cowdray had done, because usually they treated prisoners well."

This all seemed a bit melodramatic to me. I couldn't grasp why Carlsson was still so spooked.

"Listen, Carlsson, the war is over for Cowdray now, just like it is for you and me. You don't have to worry about him. What damage can he do out here?"

Carlsson shook his head as if I hadn't understood and got up to leave.

"Plenty," he said. "He's a sadist and a killer. You don't think that just retreats into the background do you?"

"Men can change."

"No," he said. "I don't think so. Not when you've crossed a line like he has – there's no going back."

I shrugged and stood up. The conversation was plainly over. I hadn't done much to make him feel any easier. I wanted to at least part on a positive note.

"If you want to say hello to Dudley, he'll be in the British Arms pub – opposite the station."

Carlsson took this in as he shook my hand.

"I may do that," he said. "Thank you again, Doctor, for all you've done."

The way he strode off, looking from side to side in fear, made me think that he was going to get out of town that very night, just to get far away.

After he had gone I paced the streets aimlessly, swigging the whisky.

I soon forgot about Carlsson's woes, because the alcohol had made my gold fever start to burn again.

When was Dudley going to give the go ahead to get the nugget?

Perhaps I should go round to the British Arms right now and force him to make a decision... I couldn't believe how reticent he had been. Why was he dragging his feet? All the answers to my problems lay under that cairn.

I came to the town swimming pool.

Kalgoorlie was preparing itself for the water-pipe's arrival and the pool had already been dug and tiled in anticipation. All it needed now was water. Everything else was ready – they had even made a large sign outside.

NO ASIATICS, CHINESE, OR ABORIGINALS, MALE OR FEMALE, PERMITTED TO BATHE.

I jumped down into the empty pool and followed the slope to the deep end.

Sitting with my back against the side, I let my drunken imagination wander. The sharp edges and echoes, combined with the red dirt which had blown in and settled on the white tiles, made me think of a Martian hangar from *The War of the Worlds*. The invasion force of fighting machines had left me behind following the turbulence of their departure and now I was all alone, the only person left on the planet.

I brought the bottle back to my lips, drained the last of the whisky and then spun it on the hard tiles.

As the sound ricocheted around the walls of the pool, I thought back to my last term at University. I had been studying for medical finals in the college library, surrounded by stacks of textbooks. That was where Freddie found me.

****

Tap-tap-tap… knocking on the window.

When I glanced up to see my brother's face pressed up against the glass, I was so surprised that I knocked over my inkpot, spilling the dark liquid all over the ancient desk. The ink sank into the old graffiti so that the scrawls of a hundred years ago stood out like new tattoos. I blotted it up as best I could with my handkerchief and then hurried out of the library.

I hadn't seen Freddie for five years, not since the Chemistry lesson of '93. Because of his letters, I felt I had been with him on all his adventures, but that still didn't make the shock of seeing him now any less overwhelming.

I hugged him briefly and then stepped back, my hands resting on his shoulders. He was in dress uniform of some kind; dark trousers with red piping and a red jacket.

"What's all this then?" I said, swallowing my emotion and trying to appear casual. "A fancy dress party?"

"I've joined up, John… wanted you to be the first to know."

"Joined what?"

"The Duke of Cambridge's own."

"Is that some kind of drinking club?"

"Middlesex Regiment, they're nicknamed The Die Hards."

My hands fell from his shoulders.

"You've joined the bloody army?"

He nodded. "That's right. I've been at the barracks in Hounslow for the last three months. I might even get to fight… They say there's going to be a war in South Africa next year."

"The army," I said again.

I had seen pictures of the Boers in the newspapers – tough unshaven farmers, standing proud with their rifles and staring hard at the camera lens.

"Here... look at my revolver," Freddie said, holding it out.

It was heavy. *WEBLEY MARK IV* was carved into the handle.

"Why would you want to fight the Boers, Freddie? They're half a world away."

He frowned and looked as if it was something he hadn't thought about.

"Dad will kill you," I said.

"I've got nothing, John; you've got it all. I want to make you both proud of me."

"We are, for God's sake!"

"Well I want to be proud of me... I don't have two shillings to my name."

"This is crazy talk; you know the old man and I live vicariously through your adventures."

Freddie shook his head. "You'd be surprised how people treat you when you've got nothing. I'm tired of being treated like a nobody."

"Freddie..."

"I met a girl in New Zealand..."

"Oh? And she thought you were a nobody?"

"No, but I have my pride. I wanted to look after her properly, but didn't have enough money to even begin to think about doing that."

Tears had welled up in his eyes. God, we had only seen each other for two minutes and already things were deep. No time for superficial pleasantries and idle chit-chat, we had gone straight to the bottom of the pond. I tried to bring us back up to the surface.

"Listen, Freddie..."

"It's all I can do," he said. "I'm not cut out to wear a suit and push numbers around on bits of paper. And I haven't got your brain, John."

I put my hands back on his shoulders.

"That's not true."

"Yes, it is. Soldiering is the one thing I'll be able to do well. I'm strong, it's an outdoor life and you get paid for it."

"You get shot at," I said.

"Back me up on this one. I need you to."

My bicycle was leaning against the wall of the library, right where we were standing. I had walked it into the college because it was a new one and I didn't want to have it stolen by leaving it out on the street. While I tried to decide what to say next, I squeezed the brake absent-mindedly.

"Is that yours?" he said.

"Yes."

Without saying anything else, he got on it and started to cycle away, ignoring me when I called out to him.

The library formed one side of a magnificent quadrangle, colonnaded on two sides and with an outer path surrounding an immaculate lawn. Freddie rode around the perimeter, and when he had done a lap, passed me and proceeded to do another. Up in the ornate east façade of the quadrangle was a black statue of King Charles I. For hundreds of years he had been gazing down upon the comings and goings of students within his domain, but I imagined he'd never yet seen this – a bicyclist doing laps.

I watched Freddie keenly, worried one of the college policemen – the bulldogs in their black bowler hats – might see what he was up to. But nobody came. It was that quiet time in the early evening and he and I were the only people around. I stopped worrying and started to admire him. In five years nothing had changed. My brother was still a rule breaker.

There was a loose paving slab on the path and every time he rode over it a dull stony thud rang out as it rocked in its foundations. The faster he cycled, the less time elapsed between thuds: it was like listening to the heartbeat of a giant slowly coming to life. Freddie kept riding, round and round, the shadows stretching ever longer over the lawn. The sounds of the loose slab ricocheted all around the quadrangle, and as I observed the scene it became emblazoned into my mind, powerful and unforgettable.

I had always thought him untameable, and that he would wander the globe for the rest of his life. Although his decision to become a soldier was the last thing I had expected, I could understand his reasoning. It would give him stability, camaraderie, some money – maybe enough to go and start a life with that girl of his. But the Boers wouldn't care he was a good man with a family and a life of good memories. They wouldn't care about the fact that he was someone's brother or that he had a nice girl waiting for him in New Zealand. They would shoot to kill.

Already I knew I was going to have to find a way to look after him.

****

Kalgoorlie
December, 1900

"You look like shit, Doc," Cookie said.

I had woken up in the deep end of the pool and stumbled my way back to the Palace, still drunk. Cookie was at the reception desk reading the *Kalgoorlie Miner*. It was two in the morning.

I held up the empty bottle with a broad smile.

"Jesus Christ," he said, "you must be drunk if you think that stuff tastes good. Get out onto the veranda – I'll bring you a cup of strong coffee."

I was chuckling as I walked outside, trying to picture the waiter in the Blue Boar Club speaking to me like that. Not in a million years. 'Sir, I hope you don't mind me saying so, but you seem to be a trifle inebriated, may I suggest, sir, a cup of finest roasted coffee to facilitate your recovery. And sir, I should remind you that blazers have to be worn in the member's dining room.'

Settling into my favourite chair, I looked out into the street. There were still a few people around. Every time I shut my eyes, my head began to spin and I had to grip the arms of the chair until the feeling passed. I slapped my face a few times to try and sober up.

Cookie brought out the coffee, handed it to me, and turned to go back inside.

"Hold on," I said. "Where are your tattoos, Cookie? Come on… where's the Federation flag? I know your other chums have them. You must too."

He rolled up his sleeve to show me the flag on his arm. I saw two, and then blinked and realised there was only one.

Cookie rolled up the other sleeve to show off his blue Auralia tattoo, in exactly the same place as McKay's and Dudley's.

"Sweet Auralia," I said, laughing and singing out of tune, "she was the one that got away… how I miss her so…"

"Take it easy, Doc," he said. "The other guests are sleeping."

"Sweet girl… beautiful…" I said, slurring and rolling my head around.

Cookie shook his head and went back inside.

I drank the coffee down in one, but it didn't make much of an impact and I soon felt my eyelids lowering again.

Instead of more vertigo, I sank into a whisky-induced stupor, going back once more to the night when Freddie had ridden my bicycle around the quad.

****

Oxford
May, 1898

My college room was up in the battlements and looked out over the wall at a towering stone memorial to long dead Catholic martyrs burnt at the stake for their beliefs. There was a lot of this kind of thing in Oxford – statues of dead kings and dead martyrs and the like. Practically every college had one. Half the time you felt there was more history going on than there was actual life happening in the present moment.

"This place is so stuck in the past" Freddie was saying.

It wasn't because of the old statues; he was saying it because I had decided to take him to 'Formal Hall' as a farewell dinner before he started his life with The Diehards. Whereas he could get away with wearing his smart uniform, I needed to get dressed up in tails.

"Why do you need to wear all that to eat?"

"Christ, I don't know," I said. "You *just do*."

As I was fumbling around with my bow tie, he saw the map on the wall with the pins marking the all the places he had visited.

"You did all this?" he said, peering closely at it.

"Yes. Every time a letter arrived."

Freddie moved his finger from pin to pin.

"I shot a bear there," he said. "Oh... in this place, I climbed a mountain...The woman I was telling you about lived there... Her name's Katherine."

I glanced over, to see where he was pointing, before going back to my bow tie.

"You've packed it all in, Freddie, I can't deny that."

He picked up the skull on my desk, the one I used to study anatomy.

The skull had been sawn in half so that the top could be lifted away. Two small hooks hung around nails and attached the two sections. He swung open the hooks and removed the skull cap, revealing a Lilliputian mountain range of bone within.

"John?"

"Hmmm?"

"What's the name of this part?"

I looked across.

"The Petrous bone... I think."

"Do all the bits have names?"

I laughed.

"Yes, and all of them in Latin... your favourite subject. Come on, let's go and eat."

The great hall was hung with dark oil paintings of old college presidents with serious looks on their faces, condemned for all time to endure the tables of laughing, drunken students below.

A thin scholar with a long black gown said Grace and we all bowed our heads in prayer: 'Benedicto Benedicatur per Jesu Christum dominum nostrum. Amen.'

It was the same prayer we had said throughout our school days – every time we had eaten – and it was hardwired into our heads.

As soon as the Grace was over, the room rang out with the sounds of scraping benches and chatter. Waiters scurried back and forth with bottles of wine and you didn't have to be a connoisseur to realise this was the good stuff. The cellars ran for hundreds of yards under the street in front of the college and were lined with thousands of bottles of the finest clarets, wall to wall.

When the high table left at the end of the dinner, it got rowdy.

A student climbed up on the table and started drinking wine from one of his brogues.

His friends urged him on.

"SHOE, SHOE, SHOE…" they chanted.

Wine ran down his face and soaked his white shirt. It was the initiation into one of the college's secret societies.

The club was honouring King Charles I, under whose statue Freddie had been cycling earlier that evening. I had once stumbled into one of their meetings by mistake. They made me sign their visitor's book and gave me a glass of sherry. I had sat around for a few minutes, waiting to see what all the fuss was about; half expecting them to produce the King's decapitated head from an old sack. But when nothing happened and they just continued sipping their sherry, I made my excuses and left them to it. It must be a fundamental human trait, to want to lord it over others. Thousands of years ago there were probably a group of Neanderthals with a special cave and a secret password, making the rest of the tribe wonder what on earth was going on inside.

As we extricated ourselves out from the bench to leave, Freddie's boot knocked against one of the drunken group.

"Hey… watch it there, sonny," the student said.

"Oh. Sorry."

"You'd better be," said another of the group, a bigger one than the others. He was a well known rugby player, his cheeks ruddy from the wine.

I stood up.

"He said he was sorry, gents."

Freddie leant over the table towards the big one.

"But not that bloody sorry..."

The big student stood up and shoved Freddie backwards.

That was the moment I let fly and clocked him flush on the jaw.

Then half of the table was up and we were all windmilling away, connecting with faces, teeth, noses and air. After ten seconds, it all stopped and all that could be heard was the voice of the wine steward trying to get us to see reason. For the briefest moment we all stayed where we were, hands clenching shirts, fists raised − frozen like a medieval fresco − then a curse came from one of the group and the fight started again, a total free for all. This time, the Bulldogs came in to break it up and somehow Freddie and I managed to escape the melee.

Later, we sat outside the college leaning against the white walls of the Lamb and Flag pub, dabbing at our bloody noses with handkerchiefs.

"Does that count as backing you up?" I said.

Freddie spat out a glob of blood.

"Yes" he said, "Come on... I'll buy you a beer."

We sat together in a cramped booth in the pub for the rest of the evening. I can recall Maple Leaf Rag being played by someone on the piano, but not a lot else except for pint glasses and loud conversation.

Sometime after midnight, when the number we had fought had risen from three to ten, we climbed back over the college wall and Freddie fell asleep in one of the large bathtubs in the basement of my staircase. Our last drunken promise before leaving the pub was that we would row together early the next morning, a reunion of the old double scull.

****

Kalgoorlie
December, 1900

When I came to, it was still dark and I was still out on the veranda. Cookie had covered me in a woollen blanket.

I checked my pocket watch – three o'clock.

What had I been teasing Cookie about? Ah yes, sweet Auralia – the secret love of all the separatists – like it was some kind of girlfriend. Thinking about girlfriends made me want to visit the Russian Princess.

She would probably be alone in her hessian tent at this time of night. I fished out the medallion from my pocket. 130 Brookman Street. Should I go? What a woman. All that red hair and those warm lips. Heads or tails – I tossed her medallion up into the air and caught it again. It landed with the female figurine uppermost. Was that tails? I threw again and it landed the other way.

Best of three...

It landed figurine up again and I got to my feet. My blood was up and Brookman Street wasn't far. With purpose, I stumbled out into the crossroads and zig-zagged my way across town. Her address was all the way down at the bottom of Brookman, further west, and not too far from Rennie's old digs. If he had been around I could have gone to him to receive absolution or something similar for what I was about to do. I smiled at that thought and walked on.

The city's buildings watched me pass, but they felt unfriendly tonight, as if there was some new malevolence to the place.

"Fuck you," I said out loud. "Fuck all of you."

A couple of passing miners rounding the corner heard my swearing.

"Language," one of them said, which made me laugh crazily. Damn miners telling *me* I was being too uncouth.

"Fuck you too," I said, growling the words. Maybe it was my dreaming about the fight back in Oxford, but I was filled with a desire to inflict suffering on anyone who even dared to challenge me.

254

They stopped for a moment, but I must have looked as wild and unpredictable as I felt, because they seemed to think better of it and went on their way.

Number 130 was a small shack – more a lean-to against the side of a larger building. A red lantern hung out front, just like at the Hula Hula Girl's place.

There was no need to knock because the Russian Princess was sitting on her doorstep, smoking and wearing only a loose satin slip. The way she was sitting there, knees together, bare feet slightly apart with her elbows on her knees, was all incredibly natural and relaxed. Never in my life had I seen a woman look so at ease with herself. Her shoulders were bare and the low cut of the slip didn't leave much to the imagination.

"Well, hello there" she said, in mild surprise.

I felt I was swaying in front of her, and so I knelt down to help steady myself.

Suggestively, she tilted her head to one side. "You look like you're about to propose."

I held out the medallion and put it down on the step next to her.

"Not quite," I said.

She smiled. "I never thought you'd actually take me up on the offer."

"It just occurred to me," I said, my voice slightly slurred.

"You've been drinking?"

"A bit, yes."

Still smiling and shaking her head as if this was a common occurrence, she ground out her cigarette into the dirt by her feet, stood up and held out her hand.

"Come on then."

I allowed her to haul me up and she led me inside, kicking the door shut behind her as she did.

It was just the one room with a bed. A lamp was burning on a cabinet, casting a low light in the small space.

I took off my jacket; it was my Blues blazer in fact, which I had worn for Cowdray's reception party all those hours ago.

"Where shall I put this?" I said, seeing there was no coat stand.

Coming near she took the jacket from me and threw it onto the bed, and then she started to undo my shirt, one button at a time, until it was open all the way. She removed the shirt and put it on top of the jacket.

"Well… I'm glad you decided to come over, Doctor, even if you did need some Dutch courage."

And then she was pulling her slip up over her head and letting it float to the floor. Completely naked, she stood there appraising me with her hands on her hips, no more self-conscious than if she was a model in an artist's studio waiting to be painted. I was so used to looking after human bodies that I had almost forgotten to admire them.

"Blimey," I said.

The Russian Princess laughed at that, and put her arms around my back, prompting me to reciprocate, so that we were both locked together. She gazed up at me, her eyes half closed and her mouth open and we kissed, picking up from we had left off previously. It was pretty damn good I must say – as good as I remembered it had been – and the warmth of her body seemed to be bringing me alive again. I felt like a man who had been out on a mountain for several hundred years, frozen in the ice, and that this woman was finally thawing me out.

I closed my eyes but it was a mistake because the whole world started to spin. I had to pull away and sit on the edge of the bed.

"God, I'm sorry" I said, "I've had a lot more than I thought."

Amused, she held my hand, waiting.

"What were you drinking?"

"Mount Leonora whisky."

"God help us" she said, laughing again, a light and easy laugh, not in the least hard or world-weary.

"It's going now," I said. "That's better… sorry…"

"No need to apologise."

She climbed up onto my lap and straddled me, her arms loose around my neck. She was so near I could smell the skin on her breasts, a little like vanilla. She arched her back so that it all came closer.

"Do you like what you see?"

Her voice was confident and soft and came from above so that I had to lift up my head to see her face.

"Very much," I said. "You're lovely, and very kind too."

"You look like you could do with some loving… could see it when I came to fetch you in the hospital that night."

We kissed again, this time with even more desire than before, but then everything went wrong in my head and I had to stop again. It wasn't the room spinning this time, it was something else. It was precisely *because* I was having an exquisite experience with this intoxicating woman that I had stopped.

"I can't."

I thought I had said it to myself, but I must have spoken out loud, because suddenly she was looking serious, the passion gone.

"What's that?"

I shook my head and she climbed off, sitting on the bed right next to me.

"Why can't you?" she said, her tone gentle.

She deserved to hear the truth. A stark naked woman wanting to know why a perfectly healthy young man had just rejected her – the decent thing was to explain.

"I lost my brother earlier this year," I said, shaken to hear myself admit it out loud. "And I've been in a lot of pain…"

I let out my breath.

Here I was, in the middle of the night, alone in her room and speaking from the heart. Some of it was the Mount Leonora Whisky, but not all. The sober part of me desperately needed to talk to someone.

She leaned against my shoulder.

"Oh dear…you poor thing."

"And just then," I said, "with you, I was escaping the pain. For a moment I felt happy. And as soon as I did, my conscience started pulling me down, telling me that he's the one who should be having times like these, not me."

I had remembered when Freddie came to Oxford and told me about the girl he had met on his travels, how he was going to become worthy of her in some way by joining up. That dream was gone forever now – all his hopes obliterated.

"You feel guilty to have been the one who lived."

"Yes, that's the truth of it."

I turned to look at her. The Russian Princess was as empathetic as anyone I had ever known, and as smart too. But she was sad now, as sad as me.

"God, I'm sorry," I said, "I've really gone and spoilt the mood, haven't I?"

"There's nothing to be sorry about… nothing at all."

I reached over and pulled out Freddie's tobacco tin from my jacket pocket.

"Do you mind if we smoke?"

"No, I don't mind" she said, rubbing my arm gently.

I rolled a cigarette, lit it and took a quick drag, then offered it to her.

For a minute or two we shared it in silence, passing it back and forth. I liked watching the way she smoked – so straightforwardly – it went very well with her nakedness. The smoke haze filled the room and in the half-light it seemed as though we were both locked in some holy and mysterious place from antiquity, far away from this age and the seedy red light district of Kalgoorlie. Sitting there on the bed made me feel very close to the Russian Princess and I opened up, telling her what had happened. While she asked the occasional question, she mainly let me speak freely; when I talked about the funeral, and of throwing my cap down, she reached over and stroked the hair on the back of my head, mimicking my very actions from that day.

After a while, the dawn came, and the light dismantled the magical feeling in the room in subtle phases, slowly bringing back the reality of life and my looming ward round. I had to be shaved and clean, and I would need to get some more coffee into my system to sober up.

Sighing, I got to my feet and started doing up my shirt.

"I'm going to have to go… I've got work in an hour."

She stood up and hugged me from behind. Perhaps of everything we had done, that hug was the most intimate action of all.

"Christ," I said, turning around to look at her, "… after all this time, you've still got nothing on and I don't even know your real name."

"It's Emma," she said, straight out.

"I'm John."

I started to reach out to shake her hand before realising the lunacy of such an action. "I suppose we're a little beyond shaking hands, aren't we?"

She laughed out loud again.

"Well," she said, "since we've been playing the truth game, then before you go, maybe it's best you see the real me too."

In one smooth movement, she put her hands to her hair and removed it. A wig!

It had never occurred to me that it was fake. With the damn thing sitting on its own now on the bed like a large piece of candy floss, it was very obvious. Far too dramatic and extravagant to be genuine. But to see her take it off still took me by surprise. Her real hair was much lovelier, pale brown and very short. She swept her hands through it, making it tufty and smiling at me shyly.

"I don't do that for anyone," she said, standing up on her tiptoes and giving me one last kiss on the lips, "which makes *you* special."

I stared at the new woman in front of me, her proportions better without all that red hair distorting things. I really didn't want to to leave – she looked just as good in the early daylight as she had done in the dark. Right then I could have lived in that shack with her forever.

"You're really beautiful, Emma" I said, "and just as beautiful for listening. I will never forget this night. I'm only sorry we didn't… well, you know…"

"Oh God… don't worry about that. This is the nicest thing I've done in a long time. You treated me like a human being."

On the way out I picked up the medallion from her front step. "Do you want this back?"

"No. You hold onto it," she said, "as a memory. I don't want you to come back here, John. I just want you to think of me as I was tonight. Will you do that?"

I gave her a single nod. Though I would have loved to return, I could understand what she meant. It would spoil everything, the innocence of this time. It wouldn't be the same at all.

"Goodbye then, Emma."

I had only gone a few yards when I heard her call out: "Hey, you've forgotten this." She was holding out my blazer.

I went back to her doorway. "He would want you to be happy, you know," she said, handing it over.

I managed a brave face and kissed her on the cheek before leaving, but once I was back on Hannan Street and on my own, my mood darkened, the way it had been on the way out when I had sworn at the buildings. Her words weighed heavy on my mind. Though her sentiment had been well meaning, heartfelt and true, in my remnant whisky-fuelled paranoia it became this: 'I really feel sorry for you... I've got this body and look as good as I do, and I really like you too, and *not even I* can bring you back from wherever you've gone. That's sad.'

Jesus, no wonder she didn't want to see me again.

I was dead inside, just cold ice. Nothing could thaw me out, not even the Russian Princess.

Chapter Nineteen

To help ease the boredom, Poyntz and I started playing chess every day.

We scratched out squares straight onto the mess table with scalpels, dying the dark squares with iodine. Using pieces of sandalwood, we whittled some rough chessmen, again using iodine for the dark set. You had to use your imagination to interpret which piece was which, but after a while we got used to it.

Long tracts of time would go by with us huddled over 'the board', trying to work out three or four moves in advance. Poyntz was always saying how Morphy was the greatest chess genius of them all, but he would say that because Morphy was an American. I argued the case for the German Lasker, the current world champion, and in our games we became Morphy and Lasker.

Sometimes Sister B would come in, see us deep in the middle of a game and walk out again.

"M'enfin! Ils sont comme les enfants," she would say.

Then one day Cutfield was there for the morning round, back from his 'eight week' leave, although it turned out to have been nearer to ten. He looked tanned and rested, a little fatter perhaps, and he was wearing a new smart suit, which made him look like a corpulent London executive rather than a doctor. He was a figure of ridicule to me now, just as he had always been to Poyntz. Compared to Cutfield's self-satisfied portliness and healthy glow, Poyntz and I were skinny and gaunt, worn out by the continuous stress and sleepless nights. Our tans only seemed darker than Cutfield's because of the contrast with the white coats we wore.

Since he didn't come to the Palace anymore, I had to go to the British Arms for Dudley's company.

McKay would join us from the other side of the bar and we would chat about this and that – monosyllabic man talk.

There were times when I wanted to press Dudley about retrieving the gold, but there had been the weeks of Rennie's illness which had put it all on hold, and whenever I saw him now, McKay was within earshot. I often wondered if McKay knew about the sacred nugget, but if he did, he never let on.

The more time that went by, the more the whole adventure out to the Wealth of Nations seemed like it hadn't actually happened. For now my gold fever had abated. Instead, the big issue became the imminent collapse of the EMC which we were both anticipating would happen at any time.

"Just remember," Dudley said, "Cowdray must be falsifying the weekly output to keep the shares strong in London. He and Egremont are treading a very fine line. If it should get out that the mine has run dry… say an anonymous letter… then the shares will plummet and the whole corrupt edifice will crumble. Do you understand what I'm saying?"

The further into December we went, the more unbearable the heat became – I even burnt my hand on the steel rail of the veranda at the Palace.

A huge dust storm – a 'Willy-willy' – swept over the town for three days, choking the population and colouring everything red. At night, lamps glowed faintly in the murky atmosphere. It was as if the city was suffering under some kind of biblical curse.

The dirt even found its way into buildings. Each morning I would watch the hospital cleaner, sweeping it from the floor of the covered walkway leading to the wards and from the entrance hall, and a few hours later, the dust would be back. You couldn't escape from it; the red dust would find its way into all the cracks and gaps. You couldn't board up your life from the storm outside. It would find you.

Christmas came.

Poyntz dressed up as Santa and gave all the patients small presents from his sack. Sister B and I followed him around the ward as he bellowed, "Ho Ho Ho."

Three days after Christmas, on the Friday morning, I left Kalgoorlie to visit Rennie, who was at a convalescent home on Cottesloe Beach, run by the Wesleyans. Poyntz agreed to cover me for the weekend, so I borrowed Dudley's bicycle and jumped on the train, pulling into Perth Station in the late afternoon. I rode straight out to the suburb of Cottesloe a few miles south.

Rennie was in a rocking chair on the veranda looking out to sea, his bible on his lap.

"John," he said, jumping up so fast that the bible fell to the floor.

He had lost weight, most of his muscle bulk gone, but it was good to see he had some of his old energy back.

"Hello Lazarus," I said, clapping his back and pulling up a chair. I hoped he would be impressed with my biblical reference.

His smile turned into a frown.

"You look terrible."

I didn't doubt it — a place like Kalgoorlie took years off your life. Not only that, but my failed encounter with the Russian Princess had thrown me into a real slump.

"Don't worry," I said. "It's not typhoid."

One of the orderlies brought out some tea and we drank it slowly, gazing out at the view.

Straight in front of our building was a line of pine trees containing thousands of red and blue birds, all screeching in unison at the setting sun.

"Are those parrots?"

"Lorikeets," Rennie said. "My noisy companions each evening."

The sun set lower into the Indian Ocean, bit by bit, until the last speck of orange dipped away, and as it disappeared I saw the green flash again, the same phenomenon I had seen the evening we arrived; less than a second in duration, but definitely there.

Rennie was holding something back, I could tell; we had been watching the sunset for the last ten minutes in silence.

Finally, he came out with it.

"I've got some news," he said, looking down at his feet. "I'm to be transferred."

"Oh... another town on the goldfields you mean? Coolgardie, or somewhere nearer the coast?"

"No, New Zealand."

"New..." My voice trailed off.

"There's a gold town on the North Island," he said, "... growing even faster than Kalgoorlie. The mission wants me transferred straightaway, more souls who need saving."

Selfishly, my first thought was of being stuck here on my own and not about his new opportunity. I pulled out a hip flask of rum and took a swig. I had copied Dudley and bought one. Dudley was right – it numbed things nicely.

"Well then... to New Zealand," I said, hoping I didn't sound as desolate as I felt.

Rennie heaved a sigh of relief and raised his cup of tea.

As I listened to him talk, I kept sipping the rum and tried to come to terms with Rennie's news. He said they had a new man already lined up for the Kalgoorlie post, someone with a few years' experience in the colony already.

"I met him a week ago," Rennie said. "They call him 'the Rev W.R.'; big man, moustache like a broom, late twenties... engaged to a nice local girl. Rowe thinks he'll find the Kalgoorlie circuit a new challenge. He certainly looks like he can handle himself. Carries the biggest Bible I've ever seen – this thick...' Rennie held his fingers five inches apart. "Makes my bible look puny... makes *me* feel a bit puny when I think about it. I get the feeling I'm being moved somewhere safer."

I wondered if old Crosbie would have been able to tear a Bible that thick in half.

In the Wesleyan world, the ministers moved on fast. I supposed that in theory it should only take a few weeks for someone to be converted, and that if they hadn't been by then, maybe a new voice was needed.

What with the typhoid fever and the replacement, it was becoming clear that poor old Rennie had lost some of his bombast. I tried to think of something to cheer him up.

"Sounds like mixing with Maori warriors isn't exactly a safe option," I said.

His eyes lit up.

"Perhaps you're right, John. Yes... perhaps this move will test me further."

I laughed.

"Anyway, what about you?" he said. "What's been happening with the nugget?"

"Nothing. Everything got pushed to one side when you were sick, and I never seem to be able to catch Dudley on his own."

"Maybe it's best that way."

"No. We'll go for it soon. I'll send you your share – we'll split it three ways."

"Don't worry about me. I don't want any of it."

That made me feel guilty – knowing that Rennie was on his moral high ground, spurning the riches that the sacred nugget would provide.

"You could build more churches with it; it could be good," I said.

He shook his head.

"No. It's tainted with that priest's shame and death. Sorry, John, I'm not interested."

I wasn't like Rennie. I wanted it badly. I couldn't obey those rules about rich men having to discard all they owned to get into the Kingdom of Heaven.

Now the sun had gone down, the Lorikeets quietened.

"Tell me something, Sean. These tests… this 'greater power'… what makes you believe it all?"

The rum had gone to my head and loosened my tongue.

Rennie put his feet up onto the handrail of the veranda and thought for a moment.

"You scientific types… you always need cast-iron proof."

"So?"

"You can't prove the most important things."

"Oh, come on, Sean."

"You loved your brother, didn't you?"

"Yes."

"Is there some equation you can give me to prove that? Is it in some textbook somewhere?"

I flushed and stalled. I thought about showing Rennie the tobacco tin with Freddie's tobacco still inside it, but realised that it was just a tin and wouldn't mean anything to him.

"So?"

"I just know it to be so."

"You *know it to be so*…" Rennie said, repeating my words. "Oh well… if you know it to be so, I'll just have to believe you."

I wished I hadn't started this. It was the bloody rum.

I could feel my eyes welling up with tears.

"I'm not trying to upset you, John," he said. "I'm just trying to point out that there are unknown quantities that we shouldn't expect to be able to define."

He was sounding like Carlsson now, when the Swede had said, 'Don't you think there might be something special underneath all this mess?'

"So, to answer your original question about believing in God," Rennie said, "I just know it to be so."

I stayed silent and rolled a cigarette.

I went through the solemn ceremony with the chocolate tin, following each action Freddie had made on the pier. I thought of smoking with the beautiful Russian Princess and of her sympathy.

When I spoke my voice was unsteady, like a man losing his balance on a tightrope.

"I thought I could escape the pain, but it followed me. It followed me to the other side of the world."

"His spirit lives," Rennie said. "I sincerely believe that... Your spirit, however, is ailing. Do you know what I say at the funerals I conduct?" I shook my head. "In the midst of life we are in death."

That's right, I was the Ice-man, on my mountain and separate from the world, preserved in a kind of frozen stasis.

"That's supposed to help me, is it Sean?"

"Yes. Well, try to focus on the fact that you are in the midst of life. Forget about the other part."

The advice was sound, I didn't doubt it, and he was essentially telling me the same thing as the Russian Princess had done. Well meant words. But I still felt as if I was disappearing, an inch at a time, deeper into that ice. The world was going about its business and I was slowly sinking, unnoticed and out of sight. One day it would be over my head and by then it would be too late to do anything.

At that moment Rennie turned and grasped my head between his two hands like a vice, with a grip so strong I felt my eyeballs would pop out of their sockets.

"What the hell are you doing?"

"Shut up! I don't care if you believe or not. Just listen."

It was as if all the hours we had spent together had been building to this, and now he was finally going to vent.

He didn't start shouting though, he started praying.

"Father, it is written that if two or more are gathered in your name you will listen. My friend and I want you to hear this. Lead him back from his wilderness. Help him find a way to experience your kingdom so that he can see the world as it is in your light. Help him find peace. Amen."

When Rennie let go, I thought I might float away, such had been the violence of the hold.

"Amen," I said, embarrassed at what had happened.

Rennie stood up and stretched.

"I'm going to get some sleep. See you tomorrow."

After he had gone, I stayed out on the veranda, imagining the prayer beaming out into the heavens, like a celestial telegraph message.

I tried with all my might to believe something might hear the prayer. I sat there all night until the sky began to lighten, hoping God would listen.

The next day we found a photographer and stood in the garden of the convalescent home posing for a shot. The man huddled underneath his black camera cloth and kept telling us to stop fidgeting, but in the end he was satisfied and promised to return later with two copies.

Afterwards, we walked slowly along the beach with our shoes off and our trousers rolled up to the knees, cooling our feet in the shallows.

Rennie said it had been his daily routine since arriving here.

We spent the afternoon sitting on the beach together, Rennie reading his Bible, me snoozing on the sand or watching the water.

"'Like as the waves make towards the shore, so do our minutes hasten to their end'," Rennie said.

"Which gospel is that from?"

Rennie laughed.

"I thought you were an educated Oxford man… It's the Bard."

"Sounds a bit final," I said. "Aren't you supposed to believe in everlasting life?"

"Energy cannot be created nor destroyed, only changed into another form… Isaac Newton… Correct? Everyone dies and their energy moves on. I happen to think that energy is a soul and that it goes into paradise."

I stayed silent. I didn't want to offend Rennie by saying anything stupid.

"You don't have to believe that if you don't want to," he said.

"I'm thinking about it."

I wasn't lying.

His spiritual talk of waves had reawakened memories of another school lesson; not Chemistry this time, but Physics.

****

The blackboard was covered with complex equations detailing Maxwell's theory on electromagnetism. All through the lesson, the Physics master had been telling us how revolutionary the theory was, how Maxwell was right up there with Isaac Newton. Freddie and I had never seen him this excited about anything before. He was usually dropping off to sleep at his front desk while we transcribed equations from the board into our notebooks.

Freddie had stayed behind to ask a question; to save the embarrassment of the class laughing at him. During the lesson, while everyone else had been diligently writing everything down that the master had said, he had just listened and not written anything at all.

Now I was hovering a few yards away, waiting for my brother, wondering what kind of trouble he was going to get himself into this time.

"Sir?"

"Yes, Minor?"

"I'm sorry to have to ask, but why exactly is this so important? I'm having trouble seeing it."

The Physics master was rubbing out all the equations with his back to Freddie, but when he heard this, he stopped what he was doing and turned round. I had thought he was about to chastise Freddie; give him lines or a silly punishment like cutting the grass on the school field with a pair of scissors. But he wasn't angry, he was smiling.

"Well, Minor... it's a fair point, and anyone who thinks they understand straight off probably doesn't."

"Revolutionary, sir? That was the word you used."

The master crossed his arms and thought for a minute, his brow deeply furrowed. Then he held his palm out.

"Hit it," he said.

"Sir?"

"Hit it."

Freddie balled up his fist, threw a light punch and knocked the Master's hand back a little.

"Scientists before Maxwell thought the world worked that way – like a machine with particles bumping into each other."

"And what did Maxwell think?"

"He said we live in an invisible particle-less energy field… that surrounding any electric charge is an electromagnetic force field… and these force fields are capable of affecting any other electric charge within their reach via an electromagnetic impulse. Understand?"

"Sort of, sir."

Freddie caught my eye as if to say, 'he's gone mad'.

"I realise this is hard to picture," the Master said, frowning and folding his arms again. "You row don't you?"

"Yes, sir. My brother and I both do."

"Well think of it it as dipping your oar onto the surface of the river. Think of the river as being the force field and the ripple created by the oar as being a disturbance in the force – an electromagnetic impulse. That's what those equations show…" he said, pointing at the blackboard. "In your river, those waves will eventually bounce off the river bank. In Maxwell's atomic world, those small waves will carry on forever unless something absorbs them; even out into the vacuum of space…"

Freddie still looked perplexed.

"But that must be happening all the time, sir… with any electric charge – that basically means anything…"

"Exactly," the Master said. "Now you're beginning to see… *everything* affects the field… the switching on of a light, a bolt of lightning, probably even the thoughts in our heads."

"You're saying that everything is connected, sir."

"Yes," the Master said, his face lighting up. "That's a good way of saying it, Minor. Everything is connected…"

Freddie had gone to the school library afterwards and thought about this for an entire afternoon. Later I found him there, sitting in the Science section, feet up on the desk and dreamily staring up at the rafters.

"Are you okay?"

"That force field…"

"You're not still thinking about that, are you?"

"I was interested in what he said about thoughts – how they might make an impact on the field. I didn't believe it at first, but then I did some research. Look."

I lifted up the volume Freddie had out on the desk. It was a textbook on the brain and the page he was on had the heading: 'The Electric Currents of the Brain'. The description centred on some experiments that had been carried out on rabbit and monkey brains seventeen years previously:

'…In every brain hitherto examined the galvanometer has indicated the existence of electric currents. Feeble currents of varying direction pass through the multiplier when the electrodes are placed on two points of the external surface, or one electrode on the grey matter, and one on the surface of the skull…'

I put the volume back down on the desk and laughed.

"You're saying my brain's full of electricity?"

"I am."

"So?"

"Remember the ripples in the water? If Maxwell is right, it means we create our own world by thought. The world is whatever we think it is. Whatever we wish it to be…"

"I suppose."

"Maybe prayers do work," Freddie said.

****

Cottesloe Beach
December, 1900

I slept out in the dunes on the Saturday night, and for once I slept well.

The next day I left early, but Rennie insisted on cycling with me all the way to the Central station. Before leaving the concourse, he passed me an envelope and shook my hand warmly.

Later, as the train carriage rumbled through the wheat belt towards the goldfields, I opened the letter. Inside was a photograph of two people with a note folded around it. At first I didn't recognise who the people were. Then I realised it was us. Rennie was thin and pale, I looked wild, my dark hair long and greasy now, the boule a zero haircut a distant memory. My face was deeply tanned and my eyes were sunken. My clothes looked almost ragged. Christ, if I had turned up at the Blue Boar looking like that I would have been given a penny to move on.

I unfolded the note.

> *John,*   *30 Dec 1900*
>
> *It is with much sadness that I leave you.*
>
> *You've been a good friend to me these last months – the best of friends. You have taught me so much; more than I can detail in this short letter.*
>
> *You once said to me the world is chaos. We make our plans and plot out our lives as if we are the ones in control, but – as you had discovered in the months before we met – this is in fact NOT the case. I agree with you John. We are not in control. But that doesn't mean someone else isn't. By that I mean God.*
>
> *Have hope, John. Like the Count of Monte Cristo says – wait and hope.*

It is not for me to tell you what to believe in, but if you remember anything from our time together, perhaps look at it this way – it might not be chaos at all; there might actually be a PLAN.

Sean

Chapter Twenty

After the ward round the following day, Cutfield called me into his office.

To my surprise, Cowdray was there, stretched out on the chaise longue with his feet up, his face partly obscured by long white smoke trails emanating from a cigarette. He didn't smile when he saw me.

I was annoyed he was lying there, on what was the unofficial on-call bed which Poyntz and I saw as our property.

"Doctor Hunston," Cutfield said to me, indicating Cowdray, "I believe you two have met."

"Mr Cowdray," I said.

He gave a vague wave of his right hand – the one that held the cigarette, making the smoke gyrate from side to side.

"Captain, actually," he said.

I remembered Carlsson's story and a chill ran through me, despite the heat.

"John, I've been checking the records from the time I was away," Cutfield said. "You were busy…"

He sounded impressed, had even called me 'John', though I sincerely doubted he had called me in just to commend me on my hard work.

"Yes, we were."

"I was particularly interested in one case," he said. "The priest who died. Could you tell me something about that?"

So this was where it was leading. In my peripheral vision I saw that Cowdray was studying me intently. I felt the colour drain from my face.

"Certainly. I remember him coming in some weeks back… terminal stages of typhoid. By the time he presented, it was too late to save him."

Cutfield looked at me and there was a momentary pause.

"Do you know the story of the sacred nugget?"

"Yes – I remember the American chap Hoover talking about it at my welcome dinner. Why do you ask?"

"Well," Cutfield said, scratching his nose and choosing carefully what to say next. "It may have slipped your mind, but that priest who died during your on-call, he was the priest from that story."

"Really?"

"Hmmm… My question is, did he say anything to you before he died?"

"No."

Damn, I thought. *That came out too fast*.

"Nothing at all?"

My pulse quickened. "All he did was ramble – it was nonsense."

"Tell us about this nonsense," Cowdray said, joining in.

I turned to him. He was busy stubbing out his cigarette against the sole of his boot. He latched his stare onto mine, still holding the stub.

"Just as I said, Captain – nonsense. He was talking about biblical scenes – hallucinating. I can't recall exactly what he said."

He smiled a great leering grin that might as well have been a scowl. "Is that so?"

Cutfield took up the reins again. "Doctor Hunston, I understand you took a day's leave soon afterwards. That in fact you left Kalgoorlie the very next morning. I have a telegram here, addressed to the hospital – to your colleague Poyntz – informing him you would not be back for another day. The sending office is the telegraph station in Coolgardie."

The telegram – Poyntz must have innocently filed it in the ledger.

Cutfield held up a little piece of paper with 'Reuters' printed across the top.

"Er… yes… that's right. I went to see the preparations for the water pipe between Bullabulling and Coolgardie. I wanted to see how things were progressing as I believe the typhoid incidence will fall once clean water arrives."

"How very public-minded, Doctor," Cutfield said. "Were you alone?"

"Yes, it was just me."

"Is that so? Would your Reverend friend say the same thing?"

"What are you trying to say? That I'm lying?"

He smiled at me.

"Are you?"

"Why don't you go and ask him, if you don't believe me?"

"I might just do that."

"He's on a ship in the Pacific somewhere…"

"How convenient," Cowdray said.

Cutfield stepped up the pressure. "Doctor Hunston," he said, "I'm sure you can understand our suspicion. You hear the dying words of a priest involved in one of the biggest scandals in goldfields history and the very next day, you cable your colleague at work from Coolgardie and ask for an extra day. It got us wondering, Doctor, it really did. You can't blame us for asking ourselves if the priest told you something."

"No I can't, but like I already said, he didn't."

Cowdray knew I was lying. He had probably interrogated Boers in the war and knew all the tell-tale signs. My face was flushed like a child's when they lie to their parents. After what Carlsson had said it was easy to imagine him using torture to get people to talk. Cowdray glanced over at Cutfield. 'Have another go,' his eyes seemed to be saying.

"Doctor," Cutfield said, with a sigh, "I would ask you one more time to search your mind and try to remember exactly what the priest told you."

My shoulders sagged.

"And I am telling you, I don't remember – he was rambling. All I heard was the febrile gibberish of a dying man."

From his reclining position, Cowdray abruptly came to the point. "Doctor Hunston. I believe the priest did tell you something that night.

I think he told you where the sacred nugget was and that you went out the very next day and located it."

I was angry now. I knew I would regret it later on, but right then it felt good.

"Believe what you want, there's no law against having fantasies."

Cowdray stood up fast, his face red with rage.

Equally riled, I approached him and put my face close to his.

"And say, hypothetically that I did as you allege, Captain Cowdray, what makes you think I would tell someone like you?"

"Doctor Hunston," Cutfield said from the other side of the room, "I will not have you speak to the Egremont mine manager in such a way."

Cowdray spoke quietly so only I could hear what he said.

"Think twice about what you say to me, for if I decide to, I can destroy you."

I remembered a story Crosbie had once told at school, about Philip of Macedon challenging the Spartans: 'You are advised to submit without further delay, for if I bring my army into your land, I will destroy your farms, slay your people, and raze your city'. The Spartans had sent back messengers with a one word reply; 'IF'.

Now I challenged Cowdray with the same laconic reply and watched the vein stand out on his forehead.

Cowdray had wanted to make me angry, and he had succeeded; it was part of his plan to force me into giving something away. And I was a bad liar.

They both clearly knew I had been on the nugget's trail and doubtless would do all they could to discover Father Long's secret.

Back in the mess I tried to roll myself a cigarette to calm my nerves, but my hands were shaking so much that the precious tobacco spilled onto the floor.

Dudley was in the British Arms, leaning casually against the bar and talking to McKay.

"The whole shit house has gone up in flames…" Dudley was saying, tapping the newspaper lying on the counter between them.

He saw the look on my face.

"What's happened, Doc?"

I didn't hold back because McKay was there, I launched straight in.

"I've just been with the bloody inquisition. Cowdray and Cutfield suspect something. They know I saw Father Long and they know I was in Coolgardie the next day. They found the telegram I sent to Poyntz. I didn't tell them anything but Cowdray knows… he's not stupid."

Dudley stared at McKay, then at me, then back at McKay again.

"I've got to tell him, Jim," he said.

McKay didn't say anything. He looked down at his wooden bar top and started to polish it. Then he gave a nod of assent.

"Tell me what?"

Dudley sighed and put down his cup of coffee.

"Tell me bloody what?" I said, more loudly this time.

He rubbed his temple on the side of the eye patch and winced.

"It's a fake," he said.

I looked at him in disbelief. There was no sign of Dudley's characteristic smile.

"What is?"

For a bizarre moment I thought he was referring to the Russian Princess's wig.

"The sacred bloody nugget… It's a fake."

"What?"

I was scarcely able to take in what he was saying.

"How on earth do you know that?"

Dudley shifted awkwardly on his stool and looked over at McKay again, who was still polishing a non-existent stain on the bar top.

"I know because I bloody painted it," he said.

I looked over to McKay for confirmation. He had stopped polishing now and was pouring out three shots. He downed his and gave another to Dudley.

"Doc…" Dudley said, drinking his shot in one go, "…what I'm saying is that in July 1898, Cookie, Mckay and I treated a broken iron cam from a stamp battery with gold paint."

"*You* were the ones who lied to Father Long!"

"Here, drink," McKay said, holding out the last shot towards me.

I took it and drank it down, still lost for words.

Beyond Dudley and McKay I caught sight of my face in the mirror behind the bar – open mouthed, wide-eyed, a look of pure disenchantment.

I sank down into one of the chairs by a table and tried to assimilate the news.

"A hoax," I said.

Lots of things made sense now; Dudley's odd silence when we had uncovered the nugget at the Wealth of Nations. He hadn't been in shock, he had feeling guilty because he already knew, and that's why he had got steaming drunk the night we had camped in the crater. Guilt.

"It was supposed to be a bloody joke," Dudley said.

He took a deep breath.

"You remember what Hoover said? How it was called 'the sacred nugget of Kanowna'?"

"Yes, so?"

"Kanowna is twelve miles away from here. Five years ago it was a town of many thousands, with rowdy hotels and a railway station at the end of a spur-line. At one time its gold was so rich that many thought it would become the leading town on the goldfields. We'd gone up there for Jim's stag night. By then the mine was cutting out and trade was quiet. We were well oiled and had worked ourselves up by talking about federation. Even had our tattoos done that night. In fact it was in the tattoo parlour that we thought up the 'Goldfields Reform League'. The way we saw it, if people drifted away, the goldfields would empty and our dreams of Auralia would die. So we decided to reinvigorate Kanowna. We guessed that rumours of a big find nearby would bring the place back to life."

I held out my shot glass.

"Another one if you please, Jim," I said.

McKay brought over the bottle and refilled it. Then he joined me at the table, taking the chair opposite.

"We found some paint in the hotel storeroom," he said. "Then we painted an old iron cam from one of the mine workings on the edge of town and carried it back into the hotel in the early hours. We were sitting there alone and drunk in the bar wondering what we were going to do with the bloody thing when the priest walks in on us. We probably would've fallen asleep and forgotten all about it if he hadn't shown up. But instead we started exaggerating and trying to impress the poor dupe. Showed him the nugget and swore him to secrecy, saying we wanted to work the claim before reporting the find. The first place that came into my mind was the 'Wealth of Nations' – nowhere even near Kanowna – that's how drunk we were. Father Long had only just arrived on the goldfields. He didn't know the Wealth of Nations had petered out years before, so he took my bullshit at face value."

"Anyway," Dudley said, "within weeks the rumours started flying of a find that was a prospector's dream-come-true. Father Long must have said something to someone about having seen it, and even though he wouldn't divulge any other details, he was pressured in the end to tell the location. You know the rest."

"Why didn't you just admit it was all a practical joke?"

"Jesus, Doc… It had gathered too much of its own momentum by then. We'd created a monster. You know what they do to people who start bogus rushes? In '95 they almost lynched a man named McCann for inventing a find. The police had to intervene – in the end he was banished from the goldfields by a tin-dish roll-up."

"A what?"

"A tin dish roll-up… a goldfields court. Roll-ups give summary justice at mining camps. When someone bangs a tin dish everyone attends a hearing. One miner is made judge. Accusers and accused are heard out and, if guilty, the offender is given until sundown to quit the field. When McCann started his bogus rush, the prospectors made an effigy of him which they hung and burnt. That was just a couple of dozen people – can you imagine what would've happened if I'd admitted it in front of six thousand diggers with pound signs in their eyes? Hungry, desperate men… Jesus, they would've torn me limb from limb."

I could see that Dudley had a fair point.

McKay started to speak again:

"Father Long was the only one with any honour. Granted, he must've mentioned seeing the nugget in an innocent aside, but he still kept good his promise... Never spilt the beans. Told the crowd the first place that sprung into his mind, which just happened to be Kanowna... probably the only place the bugger knew anyway. It was a good job he did too – because no-one would've bloody believed him if he had said the Wealth of Nations."

"He lied to protect us," Dudley said. "After the Kanowna bogus rush, I sometimes saw him in Kalgoorlie and he always looked harassed. So one night we went to the Catholic Church with the nugget hidden in a hessian bag and gave it to him. Told him what we'd done... and asked for his forgiveness. It was a humbling experience I can tell you. Long said he would hide the nugget and that we weren't to worry. I went off to the Boer War soon afterwards and never saw him again. You can't imagine how I felt when you came into the bar with your story."

"My God," I said, finally piecing the truth together. "Judging by the state of his clothes and the horse, it looks like the last thing he did before showing up at the hospital was to take the nugget out to the Wealth of Nations and bury it once and for all. He had it hidden in his lodgings all that time... probably under his bloody bed... a constant reminder that he'd lied to six thousand people. The nugget would have been like a festering sore on his conscience. When he got sick he knew he might die and didn't want it found in his room. So he took it out to the place where you said you'd originally found it. He probably perforated his bloody gut lugging it out there. Thought burying it would quell his soul in some way, but it didn't. I saw him that night. He was desperate until Rennie absolved him. I remember his very last words. He was saying: "Fools...fools." He was trying to say 'Fool's gold'."

"We should have stayed here for the bloody stag night," McKay said, rubbing his face wearily. "Would have saved everyone a whole lot of trouble."

"The trouble isn't over yet by the sounds of it," Dudley said. "Not with these two crooks on the case. If Cutfield and Cowdray find out, they'll trace it all back to us. You'll be dragged into the real court, Doc. You'll be forced to tell the authorities what you know under oath. They don't mess about when it comes to gold."

The neuralgia was going hard at him now. He reached into his pocket and took out his rum flask.

"Don't worry," I said, "I won't say anything."

It must have been my innocent expression: McKay and Dudley both started to laugh.

"No," Dudley said eventually, "I don't expect you will, but I'll bloody well know. Do you really think I'm going to sit there and watch you being harangued for something you didn't do? You're a mate, John... and mates don't shit on each other."

"Oh," I said, feeling oddly pleased to have been categorised in this way.

"And even if you do leave us out of it... they'll still discover Father Long lied to all those people and his reputation will be buggered. That's not fair. Me, McKay and Cookie will have to admit to the whole wretched affair to save both your and Father Long's reputations. Then they'll run us out of town – a tin dish roll-up to end all roll-ups."

McKay was looking worried now.

"Shite," he said.

The room filled with silence.

Dudley reached over and grabbed the copy of the *Kalgoorlie Miner* lying open on the bar. He walked across to my table and slapped the paper down.

"This is what we were looking at when you walked in," he said, rapping his knuckles on an article. "Today's paper... I imagine you haven't yet seen it. This all happened in London on Friday."

The main headline simply read:

'DOWNFALL OF THE EGREMONT'

This was followed by a series of smaller headlines – each as doom-laden as the one before:

'OFFICIAL RECEIVER UNCOVERS FRAUD – EMC DECLARED INSOLVENT'

'PANIC ON THE LONDON STOCK EXCHANGE – THIRTEEN FIRMS OF STOCKBROKERS BANKRUPTED IN DOMINO-EFFECT'

'SIR ROBERT EGREMONT ILLICITLY FIXED SHARE PRICES – CALLS FOR PROSECUTION'

Dudley sat down next to me and put his hand on my shoulder.

"Egremont will end up in jail, no doubt about it. The EMC stockholders have chosen a new man to come out here and reorganise the business. Man called Govette. Bloke with integrity, they say. He's going to clean up the mess and reform the whole thing. He won't want Cowdray in charge and I doubt if Cutfield will stay long either, not with his old chum Egremont on the rack. That's why they're both desperate. That's why they've cornered you this morning. They see the sacred nugget as their get out option. They'll want it fast. We should get you out of here, Doc. Get you far away for a while, out of their reach until Govette has cleared them out once and for all."

A shift was going on in my world and the elements were realigning themselves into a new form, with a different future, the way it had happened with Freddie in that Chemistry lesson.

"Tomorrow," I said. "I'll leave tomorrow."

"All right," Dudley said. "And don't worry, Doc, I'll think of something."

"Thanks Tom."

"That's all right, mate – since the whole thing is my bloody fault – the least I can do is help."

For the rest of the day Poyntz and I sat opposite each other at the mess table, sweating and drinking chilled Coca-Cola from the morgue and playing chess. He won two games in a row easily and the third game was going just as badly, my good pieces disappearing one by one.

Sister B sat watching us. She was next to Poyntz with her body rotated round at ninety degrees so that she was facing towards him. She would alternate her gaze between our game and then Poyntz's shoulder, as if she was playing an invisible chess match of her own, working out what move she might make to get him to notice her.

Half an hour later and I was losing four nil.

Though I refrained from saying I was leaving, I did tell them about the newspaper article and Egremont's collapse. Poyntz said that even if the EMC was bust, there would still be a job for me in the St. John of God Hospital, that the public would fund it from good works. Perhaps that was true, but it was difficult to imagine myself working here with Cutfield still around.

Sister B gave up trying to get attention from Poyntz.

"A bientôt, mes enfants," she said before leaving the mess and going back to the wards.

Poyntz was still staring at the pieces on the board.

"You okay, Jack? Cutfield and Cowdray seemed to be giving you the third degree about something this morning. I heard some of it from in here."

"It was nothing."

I sighed and moved my king back a row.

Poyntz kept his eyes on me.

"That priest who came in a few weeks back," I said. "They wanted to know if he had talked about hidden gold."

Poyntz rested his chin on his hands and tried to work out his next move.

"You mean the sacred nugget?"

"Yes, they were fairly insistent on knowing what had transpired that night. I didn't tell them, in case you're wondering."

"Just be careful with that Cowdray," Poyntz said. "He's an opium fiend."

This was news. I remembered his ratty pin-point pupils, but hadn't made the connection.

"I attended an overdose in the Chinese quarter one night… happened to see him stretched out, barely conscious on one of the other beds."

Kalgoorlie's Chinese quarter was a hotchpotch of hessian tents on the edge of town, not too far from the red light district.

"Unpredictable," Poyntz said. "The guy is literally living in a pipe dream." He moved another piece. "Check."

All I could do was move a pawn up the board away from the disaster being played out around my king.

Perhaps Cowdray had become addicted in South Africa, while recovering from a wound – it was quite common. That must have been why he had been discharged from the Army. You chose your addiction, I suppose. For Dudley it was rum, for Rennie the Holy Spirit.

"Check Mate, my friend," Poyntz said.

I made a pretend gun with my fingers and pointed it at him.

"You've turned me into the Kalgoorlie Wyatt Earp," I said.

Poyntz smiled.

"You have nothing to fear. Earp was a hell of a lot worse at the game than you, even on your bad days."

He started to reassemble the pieces on the board.

My mind was off the game and the defeat didn't register. All I could think about was that morning's interrogation. Cutfield and Cowdray had been a real double act. There would be some connection that went way back – Cowdray had probably fagged for Cutfield at school.

"What about Cutfield?" I said. "Do you think he's dangerous?"

Poyntz looked at me with his humorous blue eyes. "No. He's just a greedy asshole."

I laughed, despite my anxieties. "What a place," I said. "So much greed."

"Not everyone's greedy, Jack. Some of us are here for other things than gold."

"Aha… and would these 'other things' happen to feature a certain nurse?"

"They might…"

"You should marry her, you know, and put us all out of our bloody misery."

"Perhaps I'll do that."

"She loves you to bits, Poyntz… but if you don't marry her soon then maybe the church will."

He looked at me seriously for a moment and then changed the subject. "If you could be any chess piece on the board, what would you be?"

"A knight," I said. "I like the way they jump about the board erratically, one step forward, one step diagonal… How about you?"

"A pawn."

"Really?"

"Yep."

"How come?"

"I like the way they're on a journey and if they get to the end they can become anything they want. They are the soul of the game…"

"Sounds like something Rennie would say," I said.

Poyntz picked up one of the knights and stared at it. "You ever hear of a contrary, Jack?"

"A contrary? What's that?"

"You heard of the Cheyenne Indians, right?"

He pronounced it 'Shy-Anne'.

"Yes," I said, "I've heard of them. They fought at the Battle of the Little Big Horn with the Sioux, and wiped out Custer."

"Yep… but you won't know this. Sometimes their braves went one step further and became extreme warriors; what the Cheyenne called 'Contrary warriors'. These men did everything back to front, except when it came to fighting; they rode backwards on their ponies, walked through the brush instead of on tracks, washed themselves with dirt instead of water…even said 'goodbye' instead of 'hello'. They preferred the hard ground to a mattress, and lived by themselves away from the camp. And when they did fight, they fought alone; separate from the main body of the Cheyenne."

286

I stared at Poyntz and then back down at the chessboard.

"That's it?"

"Yep."

Poyntz saying 'yep' instead of 'yes', as if he knew it all, was irritating. It sounded like he was a smug bloody frog sitting there croaking at me.

"What exactly are you trying to say, Poyntz?"

He held up the knight and then knocked it gently against the table in time with his words. "You remind me of one."

Chapter Twenty-one

As soon as I was alone again my mood deteriorated. I was filled with a deep sense of foreboding about Cowdray. There was dangerousness about him that Dudley had missed, but Carlsson and Poyntz had both recognised. My guess was that I wouldn't need to be in hiding for days; it would be years. Cowdray was the type of man who would hound me all the way to the gates of hell. He would never give up. I had glimpsed his dark side in Cutfield's office – when he had whispered to me about destruction. The bravado I had expressed then was because my blood had been up, but now my bluster had been replaced by fear, enough to make me shudder.

It was only three in the afternoon, but crowds of people were already celebrating New Year's Eve. The entire adult population of the town already seemed to be drunk. Rough, loud and uninhibited, it was these same people who would crucify Dudley if they ever found out what he had done with that iron cam.

There hadn't been a hotter day since my arrival; it was at least one hundred degrees in the shade. The bunting over Maritana Street was 'gum tree' green and 'wattle' gold, the colours of the new Australia. The next day – 1st January, 1901 – all five states were amalgamating into one single country and the Commonwealth of Australia was going to be proclaimed.

An official banquet was being prepared in the Palace. The old Auralia Separatists were obviously attending because they had hung a great banner over the bar bearing the words: *'WE WANT THE ESPERANCE RAILWAY'*, one of their original demands for easy access to their own port.

Dudley, McKay and Cookie would all be there, comparing their tattoos over schooners of beer and crying into their drinks about 'Auralia' and what might have been. By midnight their tattoos would be museum pieces.

I was on-call for the night of New Year's Eve. It was only fair – poor old Poyntz had done the whole weekend for me while I had been in Perth.

The night was busy – there was a big punch-up on Hannan Street and I sutured lacerations for three straight hours until I ran out of catgut. It was sometime in the early morning when I finally fell asleep on the chaise longue.

I woke in confusion when the door to Cutfield's office slammed shut.

The large dark shape of a man was in the room, blundering through the shadows towards me. I sat up quickly, thinking it must be another wounded miner needing my attention.

"Are you, Hunston?" said a gravelly voice.

"Yes. Can I help you?"

He stepped forward and pulled me up by the lapels of my doctor's coat, squeezing so tight that it tore at the shoulders. The man smelt of beer and tobacco.

"What the… Who the hell are you?"

Something hard slammed into the side of my head and I found myself sitting back down on the chaise longue, lucid thoughts scattered all to hell. It was a few seconds before I worked out I had been punched.

"I'm the one asking the questions," I heard him say through the darkness. "The sacred nugget… where is it?"

My vision started to come back into focus as I pieced the room back together. He had hit me so hard my brain was vibrating like a tuning fork.

"The gold… where is it?" he said again.

I staggered to my feet, my legs shaky and unreliable, like a new-born foal. "Now listen to me… I don't know what you're talking about."

Another blow impacted on the side of my skull, but this time it barely registered. I even managed to stay standing. It was as if the first punch had inoculated me against any future ones.

"I'm not going to ask you again, mate."

"GOOD, THEN I'LL GO BACK TO BED, YOU FUCKING BASTARD."

The punches had made me angry… angry and fearless. They made me not care about anything anymore. Perversely, I was starting to enjoy this; all thought for my personal safety gone.

I waited for the next blow to land, but it didn't come.

Instead the door opened and Cowdray walked in.

He switched on the light and for the first time I saw the ugly face of the man who had been hitting me. He was huge. No wonder he had knocked me senseless. Cowdray must have been hoping I would cave in to his advance guard. The big man grabbed me by the coat again and held me up for Cowdray.

"Doctor, if my acquaintance can't persuade you, then I'm afraid I'm going to have to try."

I laughed madly. "Good luck, Cowdray."

As I spoke, red spittle from my bleeding mouth flew onto the collar of his starched white shirt. It felt really good to have ruined it.

A renewed surge of anger pulsed through my veins when Cowdray pulled out a knife with an ivory handle.

Bulala – the killer… He had cut the Hula Hula Girl.

"I heard about what you used to do in South Africa," I said. "You should be in a gaol, not running a mine."

"It was a war," he said, "not a bloody debutant's ball, Hunston."

He leaned his face close and his eyes told me all I needed to know – Cowdray was high on opium and crazed with gold fever; a dangerous combination. The point of his knife pushed a small indent into my upper chest.

"Tell me, you idiot, how do you find the nugget if you kill me?"

The big man looked at Cowdray for permission to thump me again, but Cowdray lifted his hand to stop him, never taking his eyes off mine.

"Not you," he said. "I'll kill that Yankee friend of yours and his pretty little nurse girlfriend too, and then that burnout of a mine manager. Maybe you don't care about yourself but I know you care about your pathetic friends."

The options came to me like choices in a chess game; it didn't take long, because there weren't many.

Tell the truth? No way. If I told him the nugget was a fake, he wouldn't just shrug his shoulders and go home to sleep. For one thing, he wouldn't believe it. I hadn't believed it when Dudley had first told me.

The only other choice was to keep up the pretence that the nugget was real and tell him where to find it. At least that option gave me some time, assuming Cowdray and his accomplice didn't drag me out to the Wealth of Nations with them. That was a risk I would have to take. What Cowdray would do when he found out the gold wasn't genuine was anyone's guess.

"You win, Cowdray, you win," I said, trying to make my resignation sound convincing. He lowered his knife a fraction. "The priest did tell me... The sacred nugget... it isn't a myth. It's real enough..."

The big man holding me tensed up and even Cowdray's look sharpened, as if he wasn't quite expecting the answer he had been pushing for.

"And I found it too; the biggest single nugget of gold I've ever seen. It is huge. But I was alone on a bicycle and it was too big for me to bring back. I didn't know what to do with it, so I left it there. It's at the Wealth of Nations find, hidden under a stone cairn."

The big man looked at Cowdray.

"I know where it is," he said.

Cowdray smiled.

"You've done the right thing, Doctor, telling me. I just hope for your sake it's the truth…"

With a flicking motion of his wrist he cut my upper cheek, just below the left eye, only a superficial nick on the skin – a warning about what could follow. No wonder the Hula Hula Girl had kept her mouth shut.

He gestured to the big man with a nod and he finally released his grip.

Without the support I sank to the floor like a puppet whose strings had been cut.

The thug stood over me, clenching and unclenching his fists.

"What shall we do with him?"

"Leave him," Cowdray said. "There's nowhere he can go and he'll just slow us down. He won't go anywhere – not now he knows I can hurt his friends. Let's go."

I stood at Cutfield's window and watched them leave. Their horses were tethered to a pole out front. They mounted quickly and rode west down Dugan Street, the noise of the hooves muffled in the dust.

Holding onto the frame to steady myself, I stared into the deserted streets, trying to order my thoughts. I needed to make a plan. They would be a lot quicker getting to the Wealth of Nations on horseback, as opposed to bicycles. Maybe they would even manage it within a day. I had to get out of Kalgoorlie.

I gagged on the metallic taste of my own blood as the shock of the assault hit home.

Before leaving, I spoke to Sister B through her door, telling her that I had to go back to the Palace and that if there were any problems she was to get Poyntz.

Then I raced back to my room and threw a few things into my suitcase. My Gladstone was still at the hospital. Maybe Poyntz could make use of it.

Before leaving the hotel, I saw myself in the large hall mirror – blood was smeared down the side of my face from the knife wound and my left eye was almost swollen shut from the punches I had taken. I had made my choices and this was where they had taken me.

It might not be chaos at all; there might actually be a PLAN, Rennie had written in his letter.

"Some bloody plan," I said out loud.

I banged on the door of the British Arms until McKay let me in.

While he went off to wake Dudley, another wave of nausea hit me and I had to lie down on the floor. The breeze from the ceiling fan felt good but the room seemed to be spinning in sympathy with it; the after-effects of the head trauma.

Dudley staggered downstairs a minute later and I lifted my bloody and misshapen head up off the floor to look at him.

"Jesus Christ, Doc."

"Cowdray's crazy," I said. "He's gone to the Wealth of Nations. He still thinks the nugget's real, and I don't want to be around when he finds out otherwise."

Edith had woken up with all the commotion and was making coffee. She also gave me a cool wet flannel to press against my cheek.

"You've got to get out now," Dudley said. "Don't go to Perth. You'll be spotted by someone and it'll get back to Cowdray on the Mulga wire."

"The Mulga wire?"

"Bush telegraph – verbal news passed from traveller to traveller. Gossip... travels almost as fast as the Wire proper. There are too many cronies out there who would sell their mother for a shilling. He'll send someone to find you, or come for you himself, if he can."

"So where then?"

The room was silent. Dudley looked at McKay with a frown.

"Go south to Esperance," McKay said. "Catch the Cobb mail coach. No-one will expect that. In Esperance there'll be a vessel of some sort. Take you wherever you want to go."

I looked to Dudley. "It's a good idea," he said.

"Cowdray threatened to kill you and Poyntz and Sister B."

"Don't worry, John. He won't do that."

"I heard he was good at it in South Africa. I heard that killing is a hobby of his."

This didn't seem to throw him in any way.

"Poyntz and B will be fine. I'll make sure it stays that way."

Dudley wasn't afraid at all. He sounded so certain that I believed him. Poyntz could carry on ignoring Cutfield, trying his best to heal people the way he always had, and B would have him all to herself now, without having to compete with our interminable chess games.

Dudley went back to his room to get something, leaving me alone with the McKays.

We drank the coffee and sat listening to the whirr of the fan and the sound of Dudley trudging around on the floorboards above.

Edith lifted up the flannel and dabbed at my cheek wound with cotton wool soaked in Leonora whisky.

I winced but made no sound.

McKay pulled down the Federation flag from the wall, folded it and handed it over.

"To remember us by," he said.

My souvenir inventory from Kalgoorlie: a prostitute's medallion, the chosen flag of the Auralia separatists, and a future scar under my eye from a madman's bowie knife, disinfected with whisky. That's the kind of town it was.

I put the flag in my suitcase, on top of my old Blue's blazer, the other garment that had caused so much trouble; I was sure if I hadn't worn it at Witworth Park, I would not have been in this situation.

Dudley's footsteps clumped back down the stairs.

McKay poured four shot glasses full of rum and handed them out.

"A 'wet' for the departing Pom," he said.

We all touched glasses and drank. I would miss the British Arms. It was the best of Australia – honest, friendly and unpretentious.

Outside, Dudley pointed to his Raleigh leaning up against the wall of the British Arms.

"Take it. You never know – it might come in useful."

"For what?"

"If things go bad – if Cowdray gets a sniff of where you're headed."

"I thought you said that wasn't going to happen. Anyway, what use is a bicycle going to be?"

"Jesus Christ – just take it to humour me, Doc."

I shrugged my shoulders.

"All right then, if it makes you happy."

"It does."

"What if he comes for you, Tom? He knows we're friends…"

Dudley didn't seem to hear what I was saying. He was already leaning over the back wheel and tightening up the straps which held my suitcase to the rear bracket.

"Tom – do you hear me?"

He straightened up and stared at me with the same chillingly detached look he had given the guard at the Fremantle prison.

"Don't worry about me, Doc. I can take care of myself. This is my town."

"Tom," I said again, trying to get the message into that thick skull of his. "You aren't scared there's a maniac out there with a big sharp knife?"

"No, I'm not."

That's right, I remembered, Dudley had already died. He wasn't afraid of anything.

The Cobb & Co coach station was next door to the train station, not far away from the British Arms. Dudley helped the Cobb & Co man lash the bicycle to the back of the dusty red carriage.

He handed me the leather water bladder we had used on the Wealth of Nations expedition and an army haversack.

"Here," he said, "take this too… some emergency tucker."

Inside the haversack was an iron ration and another full water container, the one with the rope webbing which he had made me drink from in Fremantle.

"I was given that drinking can by that giant Swedish bugger you met in the hospital…the one who shot my thumb off. He gave it to me out in Bloemfontein as a peace offering. Popped in to see me the other night – said you'd told him to. Anyway… you can never have too much water out in the bush, so take it."

"Thanks, Tom."

"I'll cable you at Dundas – it's the halfway point to Esperance. The coach will stop there. I'll use a decoy name in case Cowdray is checking the outgoing telegrams."

He scratched his head for a moment.

"I'll address it to 'Die Hard John'. That'd work – makes you sound like a prospector."

A strange feeling came over me, the same sort of spooky feeling I had experienced after the old nurse in the English hospital had spoken of the Grey Lady and I had believed her.

The 'Die Hards' had been the nickname for Freddie's unit – it's how he had addressed his men that day on Spion Kop during the charge; *'Come on Die Hards!'*

"What did you say?"

"Die Hard John… a decoy so nobody can track you."

"Why that name?"

He laughed to himself.

"Christmas Day last year, I met an English soldier at Cape Town. He was off the boat for a few hours before going on to Durban. There was a bit of fraternisation and we had a few. Told him about this place and the bugger kept asking all sorts of questions about the gold rush – wouldn't leave me alone. Funny bloke… enthusiastic he was. Looked like you, come to think of it… dark hair… tall. Anyway, when I asked his name he just replied 'Die Hard Fred' and laughed. Pointed to all his mates and called them out in the same way: 'Die Hard George, Die Hard Ed, this is Die Hard so-and so'. They all had the same bloody nicknames. That's the reason I remember the fella – told him he'd make a mean prospector with a name like that."

My blood ran cold when I heard Dudley's description of meeting my brother. It was almost a Holy Fear, that the plan Rennie had talked about really did exist, and that there were no coincidences. Perhaps our lives really were like a grand chess game being played out in the heavens.

Chapter Twenty-two

1st January, 1901

Cobb & Co ran a bi-weekly coach service south to Esperance via Dundas.

Just as the coach was pulling away, Dudley reached up to the window and shook my hand.

"I'll make sure nothing bad happens," he said.

I didn't have a chance to reply – we were already gathering speed along Hannan street.

I craned my neck around and saw him walking back to the British Arms in the clear light of dawn. His moleskin trousers looked baggy around his legs and his limp was more noticeable than ever.

It was the morning of the first day of the Commonwealth of Australia.

Soon a great mass of people would be pouring into Kalgoorlie on the early train for the celebrations. I hoped the throngs would distract Cowdray and give me more time.

My last sight of Kalgoorlie was the Egremont mine frame in the distance, like a dark satanic mill, poking above the tree line.

For a time, the sounds of the stamp batteries pounding the ore came through loud and clear in the quiet morning air and then even they petered out.

It felt good to be out of the city, to be in the wilderness, the 'Auralia' of Dudley's old hopes and dreams.

We trundled south alongside the telegraph, trailing out clouds of vermillion dust. I pulled down the canvas blinds and cocooned myself inside.

It was a thorough-brace coach with a suspension system of multiple leather straps holding the passenger compartment like a sling. I rocked and swayed gently and closed my eyes.

If they had ridden fast, they might be at the Wealth of Nations by now, tying their horses to the gum tree by the cairn. I could almost picture their faces as they lifted up the rocks and saw the nugget for the first time.

Cowdray was no geologist – Dudley had said it himself. At first he would not be able to tell it was a fake, but when he realised he had been duped, the humiliation would send him over the edge.

I touched the wound on my cheek. It had stopped bleeding at least. Good old Edith McKay and her Leonora Whisky swab.

The sun rose higher and the coach continued south.

At eleven o'clock, the Cobb driver stopped to let the horses drink at the waterhole, '50 Mile Soak', and again an hour later at 'Rock Soak'. Every now and then he would shout out the names of places we were passing – a slight rise called 'Mount Thirsty', then 'Lake' Cowan – a great dry salt pan waiting for the rains which would not be coming any time soon.

I was aware of differences in the flora – how the eucalyptus trees in this part of the country had glossy tan trunks, as if they had been rubbed down with boot polish. Under the strong sun their leaves glistened like the diamante jewellery the Russian Princess had worn around her neck.

It was mid afternoon when we arrived at Dundas. Like a lot of buildings out here, the post office was more of a shanty than a proper construction, its corrugated iron roof reflecting the sun back into the sky in a blaze of white light. The telegraphist barely noticed me – I was just another prospector heading for the Dundas goldfield; dirty and unshaven with a black eye and a cut from a brawl. Another lost soul with unrealistic dreams.

A telegram for 'Die Hard J' had come in and as I read it, fear clawed its way down into my guts:

'C COMING. GO EAST ALONG WIRE. EMBARK AT EUCLA. USE WATER HOLES. TRUST ME. TD'

Go east along wire. Not by coach. Not on foot. Dudley was telling me to cycle east alongside the telegraph line.

That meant riding straight out into the desert. Was he mad?

I re-read the end of the telegram: *'TRUST ME'*. I had to trust him, even though he had helped cause the biggest bogus rush in goldfields history, he was the only ally I had. Dudley had integrity – he had fought Egremont's corruption, and didn't care about his own skin. Then there was the way he had already 'died', and how he had no real fears anymore. He was my friend. How he could control my fate from Kalgoorlie was another question.

Though the prospect of riding alone across the arid wastes of Western Australia filled me with dread, anything was better than risking another meeting with Cowdray. If I continued on the coach south, all he had to do was wire ahead and arrange a little reception committee at Esperance.

I unloaded my bicycle and watched the coach depart.

The telegraphist had a map on the wall showing the telegraph line. Eucla was a settlement on the border of Western Australia and South Australia, right on the edge of the coastal sweep called the 'Great Australian Bight'. On the map, the telegraph line was marked on as dots and dashes, just like the Morse code it carried. Water holes bordered the line at intervals. I borrowed a piece of paper and a pencil and wrote down the approximate distances according to the scale:

Dundas – Balladonia	100 miles
Balladonia – Caiguna	120 miles
Caiguna – Cocklebiddy	30 miles
Cocklebiddy – Madura	50 miles
Madura – Mundrabilla	50 miles
Mundrabilla – Eucla	60 miles

"Cycling are ya?" said the telegraphist.

"Yes," I said, thinking he would have me locked up as crazy.

"I remember when Richardson did it a few years back – from Coolgardie to Adelaide. You're a professional cyclist like him, I take it?"

"Yes, that's right, from England... Remind me, how long did it take him?"

"A month, I think. Another plucky fellow called Snell did it not long after – from Menzies to Adelaide – even longer. Heard he averaged eighty miles a day. Must have riled Richardson because in retaliation the mad bugger did the whole country anti-clockwise last year... anyway... where you headed?"

"Eucla."

"Ahh... much shorter," he said, now not as impressed. "Stick to the wire. It's pretty bad just before Madura, with the sand hills – but otherwise you should be right."

Before leaving I went into the stores to top up my water flasks and buy some dried salted kangaroo meat which looked like biltong.

The telegraph line was easy to find – it ran directly eastwards from the back of the Post Office.

From the moment I left Dundas I started regretting I had shared my plans with the telegraphist. In that brief exchange in the post office I had blabbed everything. How could I have been so stupid? Cowdray simply had to ask and he would be back on my trail again. But those thoughts were soon overtaken by another concern – the flies. They knocked into my arms and swarmed around my face, blackening my vision. After swallowing some I tied a handkerchief around my mouth like an American Cowboy.

One hundred miles to the first water hole… that's all I thought about now. There was little point in dwelling on anything else.

The dry track had a firm surface, and I made good mileage on the flat terrain. Hours passed by, my shadow inching out longer in front of me as the sun slowly lowered from behind.

The telegraph line was the only discernible human impact on the landscape, my one tenuous link with the rest of the world. I found a certain comfort knowing messages were flying along those wires. Somewhere this line connected to the overland telegraph to Darwin, which then ran onto Java via a submarine cable. In Java it joined the International line and from there to the Asian mainland and Europe.

I concentrated on the riding, keeping the rhythm: pump the right leg… pump the left leg. Breathe in time with each down thrust. The fear proved a good energy source and motivation.

At sixty miles or so, my legs started to seize up so I bedded down by the track.

Dinner was kangaroo biltong and water.

After the sun went down, the cicadas started, then a while later stopped, and for a time there was total silence – no birdcalls, nothing at all. Even the flies thinned out.

In the west was an orange glow where the sun had been and soon the stars started to shine through the darkening skies. Strange little noises sounded out of the dark – clicks and croaks and scratches.

I thought about my friends in Kalgoorlie and the person who came to mind most clearly was Poyntz. It was easy to imagine him on the ward checking the temperature charts or up in the mess drinking coffee. I hoped Dudley would explain to him what had happened. Rennie would probably still be on his way to New Zealand, reading his Bible in a ship's cabin, on the upper bunk if they had one. Neither Poyntz nor Rennie knew the gold was a forgery and they wouldn't have cared anyway.

I woke at four in the morning and started off before it was light. I hoped Cowdray had kept going south to Esperance. But the doubts were creeping in again – even if he didn't speak to the telegraphist, it would be simple matter to question the Cobb & Co driver, and find out I had disembarked at Dundas with a bicycle. With that information you didn't have to be a genius to guess my plan. For all I knew he might be a few miles behind.

By sunrise I was well into my rhythm and making good mileage.

There was a harsh beauty to the landscape; it wasn't desert in the strict sense of the word – more like scrubland with clusters of blue-grey saltbushes and the occasional eucalyptus.

The silence stilled the mind.

Though my life was at stake, I could see that in other circumstances I might have enjoyed the ride.

As the sun climbed higher I tied a shirt around my head, as I had learnt to do on the ride to the Wealth of Nations, but it still felt like my brain was being hardboiled in my skull.

Sweat dripped off my nose like water from a faulty tap. It fell on the handlebars, soon evaporating into the hot dry air. Liquid was leaving me at a faster rate than I was replacing it.

I had to try and pace this, or it would end in disaster – to keep going would mean using up all the water. There was no option but to wait it out.

So in the worst heat of the day, I pulled off the track and sat in the shade of a gum tree sipping from my precious water supply. I was too tired to think about anything much – all I could feel now was a deep heaviness in my limbs. The muscles at the base of my neck and across my shoulders screamed from the hours spent in the crouched riding posture.

I opened Dudley's haversack and brought out the iron ration, a cylindrical container several inches long with the following written on the central band:

THIS RATION IS NOT TO BE OPENED EXCEPT BY ORDER OF AN OFFICER, OR IN EXTREMITY. THE RATION IS CALCULATED TO MAINTAIN STRENGTH FOR 36 HOURS IF EATEN IN SMALL QUANTITIES AT A TIME.

4OZ CONC. BEEF (PEMMICAN)
4 OZ COCOA PASTE

I ripped off the band and broke open the rations into two parts, scooping out some of the beef with my dirty fingers. It was saltier than the kangaroo biltong, but I needed the salt — I had sweated so much, my clothes were covered in a white salt powder which I could have dusted off and sent to the 'Cerebos' factory.

I ate a mouthful of the cocoa paste and washed it down with a gulp of water. Carlsson's bottle was nearly empty and so was the water bag. There was water at Balladonia, but I had no idea how far I had to go. Surely I had covered a hundred miles by now?

By my pocket watch it was five in the afternoon. I forced myself to get back on the bicycle. It was hard to persuade my body to get going at first, but the rest and rehydration had made a difference and, despite the residual stiffness in my neck and shoulders, I felt strong again. Some of the old fitness from my rowing days was returning and the muscles in my thighs tickled, as if relishing the prospect of more exercise. And at least when I rode I created my own light breeze.

I rode on into the clear night, the moon lighting up the telegraph poles in front of me in a surreal black and white world.

At one point, a Kangaroo bounded out and clipped my front wheel, before jerking away as if electrocuted. The fright gave me free energy for at least five minutes.

All this space and the imbecile creature had decided to collide with me.

I started to laugh.

I arrived at Balladonia at midnight. At least I thought it was Balladonia – a sign near the farmstead spelt out the word *'Barla-juinya'*. Close enough. It must have been the Aboriginal spelling.

It didn't matter what the name was because I found water there, in a granite rock depression – a pool as large as the one on the terrace at Witworth Park. The rock acted as a natural bowl, holding the water, unlike the surrounding porous land which held nothing but dust. I pushed my head under the surface and drank deeply. Then I filled my water bag and Carlsson's can. I stayed there by the precious water, forcing myself to drink until I thought my stomach might split open.

Dudley had told me the granite outcrops scattered throughout the region also contained 'gnamma holes' – deep narrow fissures in the rock that acted like underground water storage tanks. During the gold rush, Aboriginals, who for countless generations had used these as their source of water, had shared or revealed their locations for the sake of the desperate, thirsty prospectors. At first they had done it voluntarily, but later on, when they saw the whites draining them dry, they only gave the information after 'coercion'. One Aboriginal had been tied to a tree in the full glare of the sun and fed salted beef until he gave up his secret. In the end, all the gnamma holes had been appropriated into service by the whites.

The brick built homestead at Balladonia was surrounded on all sides by man-made stone walls that could have come straight out of the Yorkshire dales. Rock walls made sense in this landscape, largely devoid of timber, but with plenty of granite thereabouts. The telegraph wires I had been following all that day dipped into the building next to the main farm – a repeater station which passed on messages. An old wagon sat against the wall of the repeater station, like a boxer slumped against the ropes in between rounds. The iron rims were rusting and peeling off the wooden wheels.

I avoided the buildings just in case a suspicious telegrapher might decide to contact Dundas.

Using the clear moonlit night to my advantage, I set off again on the telegraph road. Fully rehydrated and with my topped-up water containers, I felt confident in tackling the next stage; 130 miles. It was possible – men had done it before – and I took comfort in the knowledge.

It was possible to get to Eucla and outrun Cowdray.

I had memorised the chart of waterholes and the distances, and then broken down the distances into smaller chunks. In the cooler night air I estimated I was doing ten miles per hour, compared to the five miles per hour I did in the light.

As long as I rested well in the heat of the day I would be able to cover the bulk of this stretch the following evening.

At three in the morning I stopped and lit a fire, heating up the last of the Pemmican beef by holding it over the flames on the end of a spiked stick. By my calculation I had ridden more than thirty miles since Balladonia.

I slept sporadically, disturbed by the pawing and scratching sounds of unknown animals attracted to the light of the fire. I would wake and listen to the wild noises with detached interest before dropping off to sleep again.

A deep growl pierced the night and I sat bolt upright.

Something large was out there now.

Then I saw it.

Not ten yards away was a hound of some kind, baring its teeth. Instinctively I threw a stick and hit the beast front on with a powerful shot that sent it yelping and whining back into the bush. Piling more wood onto the fire I ran around the perimeter of the camp beating a stick against Carlsson's can.

I listened out for several minutes, but heard nothing except the thumping of my heart in my chest. The creature had gone.

I curled up again, closer to the fire and eventually went back to sleep.

Broad daylight – the sun was already high. The fire had burnt down to glowing embers.

Cowdray was sitting on the ground three yards away.

I processed the scene in a split second.

He was holding a pistol, a Webley – the same as Freddie's – and behind him was the Aboriginal tracker, Eugene, standing so still that at first I thought he was just another blackened tree stump from an old bush fire. He was holding a piece of carved wood, some two feet in length.

I had been living in denial for the last two days, but deep down I had known it would come to this. I made a decision. I was going to be like Dudley – I was not going to be afraid.

"I told you I would find you," Cowdray said. "I'm a man of my word."

"Well done," I said, half out of sarcasm and half out of a grim acceptance.

He brought up his revolver, pointing it directly at me.

"The gold," he said. "The real gold this time, Doctor."

"It's in my bloody pocket," I said, this time with total sarcasm.

"What?"

"Haven't you worked it out yet, Cowdray?"

"Worked out what?"

"There never was any bloody gold. It was always a hoax. Some trickster painted an iron cam and that was it. The priest was hoaxed, I was hoaxed and now you've been hoaxed."

Cowdray laughed. "Come on, Doctor, you can do better than that. I didn't come all this way to be fed lies."

"I'm not lying. What you dragged back from the Wealth of Nations is all there is. A fake. You might as well turn round and go back to Kalgoorlie, because I've got nothing for you."

His expression was dark now, his laughter gone. "I'm going to count to three," he said.

He cocked the revolver.

"One."

My mind was still eerily calm. *This is it then. I might even get to see Freddie.*

"Two."

I decided to reason with Cowdray one more time. "It's the truth, I tell you... for Christ's sake man, look where we are. If it existed I would bloody tell you."

"Three."

I closed my eyes and waited for death. It wasn't cold though, not like it had been the other times death had been close. Not like in the ward that night when Freddie had died, or at the Spitz Kop.

The seconds passed and I opened my eyes again.

"You're telling the truth," Cowdray said, his expression blank.

Then a look of sheer hate came over his face, more savage even than the face of the wild dog in the night.

"I'm going to finish what I should have done a few nights ago anyway."

"What? Why?"

"Because I just don't bloody like you, Hunston."

That's right. He was Bulala – the killer.

He pointed the revolver again and pulled the trigger.

Click...

Misfire.

Cowdray frowned in confusion. "Bloody dust," he said.

Seeing my chance I sprang like a cat – entirely focussed on the revolver. Before Cowdray knew what was happening, I was over the fire in a single bound and swinging my right foot to kick the Webley out of his hand. It looped high into the air and landed several yards away. I started for it, but in a second Cowdray had reacted. He grabbed me in a hold from behind, his left arm around my neck. As I struggled to wrench myself free I felt a searing pain in my torso as Cowdray landed a punch on the right side of my ribcage.

Then there was a loud cracking sound and his grip released. I felt him sink to the ground.

Eugene was holding up the piece of carved of wood I had noticed earlier. He'd used it to knock Cowdray out cold.

Something wasn't right though.

It hadn't been a punch.

The ivory handle of Cowdray's bowie knife was sticking out of my right side at a strange angle. The bastard had rammed it in to the hilt and a steadily enlarging blood stain was appearing on my shirt.

I held the knife handle, breathing wildly and grimacing. A wave of nausea and faintness came over me and I lay down. My body was utterly bathed in sweat and I felt as though I was falling away from my surroundings.

"I'll be all right in a minute," I said. "Just give me a minute…"

I simply wanted to breathe and get the awful nausea and clammy feeling out of my system.

Amidst the panic, the cold, survival-orientated part of my brain ran a diagnostics check. I could still take deep breaths – perhaps my lung hadn't been punctured – it must have missed my heart too. I think my breastbone had broken the blade's trajectory.

Eugene stepped over the prostrate Cowdray and squatted down next to me. He didn't seem in the least perturbed by my injury.

He was throwing small stones into the bushes. He held the last one up and studied it briefly. I saw then that it was a bullet. He was throwing bullets away. Not a misfire then – Cowdray's gun had been empty all the while.

"That fella one mad bugger," Eugene said. "Was going to shoot you dead for sure…then me too. Thought I was too stupid to know. Forgot he had a knife though. Sorry about that, Doc…"

Time seemed to be slowing down.

"Dudley told me to make sure you got to Eucla alive. Don't worry. Gonna fix you with black fella medicine."

He grabbed the bowie knife by the handle and pulled it out of my torso with a swift movement.

I gasped with the pain. Blood oozed from the entry wound and dripped down into the dust. Feeling sure I would be dying in this godforsaken place, I started to think it wasn't so bad.

My mental faculties were quieting now.

It wasn't so bad.

Chapter Twenty-three

Eugene tore open my shirt, fully exposing the jagged bloody mess. The blade had entered my chest through the lower ribs and cleaved the breast bone in half. Parts of the bone were protruding from the skin like shards of ivory. They rose up and down in time with my ragged breathing. I swallowed back the rising bile.

Eugene brought out several small hessian bags and a concave piece of wood from his pack. He emptied the contents of the bags onto the wood and added water, stirring rapidly until it became a black tar-like paste. I remembered the scarred tree back in Perth and what Dudley had told me about Aboriginal medicine men mixing herbs on the bark bowl. A 'coolamon' he had called it.

Scooping up two large handfuls, Eugene smeared the mixture over the edges of my wounds, completely covering the lacerations.

"What is that stuff?"

"Black fella medicine," he said, smiling.

He re-made the fire and heated up some water in a billy, adding some leaves from another of his hessian bags and decanting the liquid into an enamel mug. He handed over the brew.

"Drink," he said.

I downed it quickly like one of McKay's shots. It had an earthy flavour, like drinking a liquid version of the red dirt.

"You'll be okay soon, Doc."

I nodded and moved my legs, scraping at the cinnamon dirt with the heels of my shoes.

Eugene pointed at paw prints.

"Dingo was here."

He was referring to the creature I had scared away in the night, the wild Australian dog.

"You bloody lucky only one of them… a pack and you would have been in big trouble."

I almost laughed. Where did my current state rate in Eugene's scale of trouble – medium?

"Listen carefully, Doc… You want to live?"

It was a not an easy question to answer.

"I don't want to die" I said after several moments.

He drilled me with his stare.

"Okay… I can fix you… but you need to listen to me. Can you do that? It's not like white fella doctoring."

I wasn't in a position to quibble. I would take whatever I could get. There was no sign of the Grey Lady yet – I still had a chance.

"Yes," I said, "I'll listen."

"Good. Forget about everything bad. Think good thoughts. You need to do this… only think about this, nothing else. Don't think about all this mess… go somewhere else and think good thoughts. That drink will help. Don't worry about your body now."

Good thoughts.

I searched my mind.

I thought of the time Freddie and I had rowed the double to near perfection. I imagined myself back in the boat, our blades cutting into the cool waters with precision. That's where I went – back to the river with Freddie.

****

We had gone rowing the morning after the formal dinner and the fight.

Just before 6 o'clock I went down to the basement, to where Freddie had fallen asleep. He was still in the bath tub, dressed in full military regalia.

"Hey... HEY!"

"Go away," he said.

I switched on the cold tap.

"Aaarggh... What the hell... I was waking up."

"Come on. I've been waiting for this for the last five years; ever since the day you left."

"What?"

"Five years since the day of our last scheduled row together, which, for various reasons never took place."

"Has it been that long?"

"Yes, it has. I've been marking time, waiting for you, Freddie... so get changed."

I threw him a pair of shorts and a spare zephyr shirt and he started to get change in silence, contrite now after what I had said.

It had always been in the back of my mind that we would row the double again. I had rowed in faster boats, rowed in the Boat Race three years running, rowed with stronger men and more talented oarsmen than my brother, but this felt like unfinished business.

It was quiet in the narrow city streets as we walked down to the boathouse. Our hangovers were not severe enough to spoil things and, as the walk warmed us up, so our collective mood improved. We hummed the ragtime tune from the night before. By the time we reached the river we were in high spirits and looking forward to the outing.

Conditions were still – the flag atop the boathouse hung close to the pole and the water was as flat as a millpond – perfect rowing conditions.

The sliding doors rumbled like distant thunder when we dragged them open. The sound disturbed the geese on the dock and they flew away to the west, the beat of their wings clipping the surface of the water for a hundred yards before they became properly airborne.

We took out the oars and set them down on the pontoon. Then we went back for the boat and brought it out on our shoulders, one of us at each end. Rolling the boat down in one smooth movement, we rested it on to the surface of the water with a gentle slap. The boat wasn't as good as our old 'Wisden', but it would have to do.

I was already smiling as I fastened my oars into the gates.

Jim the boatman arrived for work. He was standing up in a flat-bottomed tub and paddling through the mist towards us with an oar that had been sawn in half, like a Gondolier who had hit hard times. Jim lived in a small cottage down the river. As he neared, he recognised me and we exchanged brief waves.

Not only did Jim build and repair boats, but he knew how to get them to move fast through the water. He was the best oarsman I had ever known, but because he 'worked with his hands' he was barred from amateur rowing competitions. In the old days he had been a professional and would often tell me how he had matched the great Harry Searle – 'stroke for stroke' – when the Australian had visited Oxford and sculled the stretch.

Jim was willing to pass on his knowledge to anyone prepared to listen. When I arrived at University from school, I spent a whole term trying to make the 'bell note'; the ideal sound of the splash at the catch. It would only happen if the spoon gripped the water with enough bite – not too violently though, just with speed. When I got it right – perhaps one catch in ten – the boat would leap forwards without a check. Over the next two years I slowly improved on that ratio to perhaps an eight. Sometimes, when I arrived at the boathouse early, Jim would already be out sculling and I would join him. Afterwards we would sit by the potbellied stove in his workshop drinking tea, our backs steaming. I came to think of Jim as an artist, not a tradesman.

Freddie and I pushed off from the dock and paddled up and down the stretch, stopping to turn around every ten minutes. We rowed off the rust for the first couple of laps, slowly getting warm. After half an hour, the bow of the boat was cutting the water cleanly and smoothly. The mist burnt off in the sun and everything came into sharp focus.

Despite the fact we had not rowed together for five years, the outing that morning was the best we had ever had; the balance, the timing, the swing – all of it effortless. We were locked into the sounds and feel of the river. It felt easy.

I thought back to the times we had been slumped over our oars as schoolboys, dejected at yet another substandard performance. I thought of all the years we had toiled to get the boat balance right, the effort we had put in to stop our blades skipping along the water like blind men's canes. At school Crosbie would lean forward and rest his elbows on the handlebars of his bicycle, the characteristic position he adopted for coaching from the tow path. "Do another half-hour, it'll come," he would say. All those times we had been on the verge of giving up, tears in our eyes from exhaustion. Crosbie would turn his bicycle around so that it pointed back down the tow path ready for another run and we would nod back dumbly and set off again.

We had finally done it, finally had the answer from our years of sacrifice to the rowing god. That day in the double, we felt we could keep rowing forever and never tire. Two sets of snake rings imprinted on the water, the puddles our electromagnetic signature in Maxwell's force-field Universe.

Jim helped us in when we finally docked. He had been scraping some of the goose droppings from the pontoon with his oar.

"Looking good out there today, lads," he said.

This was high praise indeed.

"I never want to row again," Freddie said. "Today was perfect."

****

Western Australian Desert
1901

I awoke to a pulsating noise.

Eugene was standing over me, swinging a lasso around his head; faster so that the whirring sound reached a fever pitch, then slower so that the tone lowered an octave, then faster again. The ear-splitting din rang out around the plain and reverberated through my body with an elemental intensity. It was like the purring of a cat through a loudhailer, varying in pitch and volume.

When he finally stopped, I saw it wasn't a lasso – just a long piece of string looped through a small hole at one end of an oval shaped baton of wood.

"What's that?"

"Gayandi... telegram to the spirit world... need help from the spirits to make you better, Doc."

Cowdray was trussed up against a tree nearby. His shirt had been torn open in the earlier struggle so I could see a red rash covering his chest. He was shivering and sweating too – the unmistakable signs of typhoid fever.

I looked away. I had too much on my plate to start worrying myself about him.

Eugene rubbed his hands together fast, then clenched and unclenched them rapidly and shook them out. He started to move them up down my chest about an inch off the body, as if there was an invisible outer skin that only he could see. He did it gently and smoothly, at first moving both hands together in the same direction, then both towards one another, one from the neck down and one from the lower abdomen up, and meeting in the middle over the wound.

"What are you doing?"

"Telling the chest how it used to be, Doc. Your bones and meat have memory, I'm talking to them. Help them remember what they were

315

before the shock of the knife. Keep doing what you promised. Think good thoughts."

He began to chant in his own language.

I thought I could detect repetition, as if he was recanting a prayer of some kind over and over again. All the while he kept moving his hands back and forth over the wound, I drifted in and out of consciousness, half in life and half in death.

Every now and then he would spit onto the ground. Sometimes it looked as though he was almost vomiting up bile. Then he would start singing again.

The sun went down and still the singing went on.

I didn't wake again until the next day.

My head was resting on a blanket that had been rolled up into a pillow. I felt only minimal pain. When I dared look down, I could not believe what I saw; the bones under the tar seemed to have shifted into something like their original position.

Much later, I worked out we must have been at the camp for two weeks. I wasn't sure if it was the herbal drink he kept giving me, but all I did was sleep or lie dazed by the continually burning fire.

Like me, Cowdray lay moribund on the ground. Eugene did the basics for him – gave him water and what food he could tolerate, covered him in a blanket at night – but he didn't do any of his magic. Cowdray remained a dark presence a dozen yards away, but for the most part he was ignored by both Eugene and I. His hands remained tied.

I had thought that if the injuries themselves didn't kill me, then an infection would, but it didn't happen. At no time did I suffer any fever.

With the passing days the black compound dried out and fell away, much like an ordinary scab. Underneath was a large pale scar.

In addition to his almost miraculous healing skills, there were other things about Eugene's world that I found inexplicable.

One night – a colder one than usual – I opened my eyes to see him asleep with his bare torso lying directly on top of the burning sticks of the fire… literally, sleeping in the fire. When I woke him up, I was astounded to note that there were no burns, his bare torso unmarked. Whether this was a memory or a hallucination, I cannot say.

Eugene decided we needed Kangaroo meat: 'malu'.

He spent that afternoon making a spear from a gum tree sapling, working it through the flames of the fire to make the wood supple and then straightening out any kinks. He scraped away the bark with a sharp stone, the same way Jim the boatman had done when making new oars. Jim would drive his plane along the surface of the blade and shavings of wood would coil off and fall onto the floor of the boathouse. And like Jim had done with the oars and rowing, I was about to see just how much Eugene could get out of the object he had made. He glued a piece of sharp quartz onto the end of the spear using the sticky resin from Spinifex gum and secured it with twine.

Finally, he brought out the cudgel he had used to knock out Cowdray. "Woomera," he said. "Make spear go fast." The wide central section was decorated with a zigzag pattern and one end was rounded off with a ball of resin – a grip. The other end had a small protrusion poking out, like a tooth. In one fluid motion he picked the spear off the ground with his foot, gripping it with his toes so that he didn't even have to bend down. He rested it on the Woomera, the tooth slotting neatly into a notch at the back of the spear.

Holding a few sprigs of saltbush as camouflage with his free arm, he approached a Kangaroo two hundred yards distant, his stealth dance-like in its smoothness.

With a seemingly innocuous throw, the spear arced away and I saw how the Woomera acted as a lever to increase the speed of the spear, the same way a medieval trebuchet did when flinging rocks at castle walls.

The spear killed its prey at the first attempt.

I knew enough about a learned skill to appreciate that what I had witnessed would have taken many years of practice.

Eugene disembowelled the Kangaroo, then dug a pit in the ground using his woomera, added some large rocks and made a fierce fire in the hollow. Once it had burned down, he threw in the kangaroo and covered it with earth until only the front paws and back legs were visible.

Two hours later, he pulled the carcass out of the fire pit by its feet and announced dinner was ready. We ate as darkness fell.

It was a lot better than the dried Kangaroo biltong from Dundas, the meat surprisingly tender with a stronger flavour than beef or lamb. It smelt and tasted of the earth, but I didn't care because I was hungry.

"Good bush tucker," Eugene said. "Malu put strength in you. You heal even better now, Doc."

One day I had enough strength to stand.

I brought out Freddie's old chocolate tin and made a cigarette, smoking it in silence and watching the prone figure of Cowdray. During my slow recovery he had been going through his own crisis, barely registering our presence. Eugene had loosened his ties and made him as comfortable as possible on the dirt floor, but still hadn't tried any 'black fella' medicine on him. Most of his time was spent in tending the fire.

He was in his usual sitting position – cross legged with his feet resting on the opposite thighs. I leant back against a tree with my legs out straight.

"Thank you," I said, "for saving me."

He finished adding sticks to the fire and looked up.

"Ever since you fix me I've been watching you. I know you a good man when you gave me back the yellow rock. You and that priest fella and Dudley not like the other white fellas. Other white fellas only care about the yellow rock."

"What about the man who was with him?" I said, pointing at Cowdray.

"No man with him."

I had a good idea as to what would have happened. Cowdray would have wanted all the gold for himself. The big man who had punched me senseless was probably under the pile of rocks at the Wealth of Nations in place of the sacred nugget.

"Cowdray shows Dudley the rock in British Arms and Dudley just laughs and chips off paint. Then Cowdray goes mad and finds out from Cobb fella you gone south. Dudley tells Cowdray he'll need the Company tracker to find you. Apart from Dudley and his mate McKay, no-one else knew Cowdray was coming for you."

"Was it easy to track me?"

Eugene laughed. "Easy? I know when you got tired, when you stopped, when you take a piss, what you ate. Saw where you kneel for a drink at Balladonia." He pointed at my bicycle. "It's easy to track the white fella who goes along on one of those."

I rubbed at the scar over my sternum. Even if I had received the best care from the most skilled surgeons in England, the wounds would not have healed as fast.

"What was in this?" I said, peeling the last flecks of the dried black substance off my chest.

"Clotted blood from women's monthly bleed, and herbs."

When he saw the look on my face, Eugene burst out into laughter again, high-pitched like a Kookaburra's.

"Black fella medicine different to white fella medicine," he said. "I used spirit energy, Doc. In our language 'tumpinyeri mooroop'. Energy from the spirit world came through me, then out of my fingers and into your wound. It makes blood come to the area and heal it quick. You had to believe it would work. That's why I can't fix him..." Eugene looked at Cowdray. "He doesn't believe black fella useful for anything. That mate of yours – that Rennie fella – he always talking about that Jesus fella making people better... how his power come straight from the spirit world too."

"The holy spirit," I said.

"Yeah... but even he knew people had to believe first. Didn't work otherwise..."

The sky was lightening, but the sun had not yet risen over the horizon. Eugene was propping up my bicycle by the saddle.

"Get on your bike, Doc," he said. "Get ready to leave."

Somehow, Cowdray had freed himself from his ties and left on horseback in the night. Spiteful to the last, he had also taken Eugene's horse.

Before we left, Eugene told me to rub handfuls of dirt into my armpits and throw it back onto the ground. Unquestioningly, I did as he asked.

"Now the land knows your smell," he said. "Now the ancestral spirits know you are travelling over their land. They will protect you."

Eugene then pointed westwards and fixed me with a serious look.

"I will lead. You follow. When I am running, you do not disturb me. I will turn to you when I need to, not the other way round... Understand, Doc?"

Confused but obedient, I nodded at him, and went to ready myself on the bicycle.

Then something very odd happened, the likes of which I still find hard to reconcile, even now, in this retelling of my adventure.

Eugene ran.

And he did so with such an extraordinary swiftness that I had to pedal hard to keep up. When he ran, it was as if he was on an invisible trampoline, with an exaggerated bounding gait, covering a distance of perhaps ten feet with each stride.

Of all the magic I had seen and experienced with this Aboriginal medicine man, his running was the most incredible. Here is what was astonishing – after the first dozen miles or so, I was convinced that Eugene's feet were no longer hitting the ground, but impacting *on the air* instead, perhaps six inches above it. I blinked the sweat from my eyes to make sure I was seeing this properly. It looked real.

If anything, the farther we went, the quicker the pace, as if even his air carpet was moving towards Cowdray too.

Eugene continued his metronomic rhythm for hours without a break. When he did stop to check the tracks, he was not out of breath. He acted as if I wasn't there, half in a trance. I kept my part of the bargain and did not disturb him.

I would estimate he ran fifty miles that day.

Even I could see Cowdray's trail. He had followed the telegraph line at first, but the hoofprints had eventually veered off the track altogether.

We found the horses first.

From a distance they looked like two pale rocks; close up, like animals long dead, every drop of their body fluids sucked out by the dry air.

"Imported stock, not brumbies," Eugene said. "Not good in the heat... and Cowdray could not find more water."

Human foot prints trailed off further into the bush.

Every few hundred yards we would find a discarded piece of his clothing: a jacket, then the shirt, then the shoes and finally the trousers. The trail meandered. By the time we found Cowdray's naked corpse, we had gone in a loop perhaps three miles in circumference, almost back to the dead horses. Cowdray was not like the human being I had seen the day before, he was like one of the unwrapped Egyptian mummies I had once seen on display at the British Museum, desiccated and dry. Ants were crawling all over him.

Eugene said Cowdray had suffered a 'perish'.

"Thirsty fellas wander into the bush and walk miles back to where they started. Last thing they do is take off their clothing. Dead men are always found with no clothes after a 'perish'."

Delirious, Cowdray had wandered into oblivion. As I piled desert rocks onto his dried-out husk of a body, I found it hard not to feel pity for him, despite everything.

The sun was unmerciful and we were out of water.

Eugene walked over to a dry clay pan nearby and started to dig down with his woomera, then his hands. He unearthed a large frog which he lifted up and squeezed. A trickle of water ran from the reptile into his open mouth. When he had finished, he let the frog hop away. Then he dug out another one and gave it to me. "Water holding frog, Doc..."

It was blown out with water and it gave me enough liquid to slake my thirst. I put the frog down and it jumped away.

Eugene was looking over at the rocks where we had buried Cowdray.

"No black fella ever had a 'perish'," he said. "There's always plenty gabba if you know where to look."

Chapter Twenty-four

Ever since Balladonia, the telegraph track had been running dead straight.

After burying Cowdray, we kept heading east; by my estimate closer to Eucla now than we were to Kalgoorlie.

In the late afternoon we finally stopped and I sat exhausted, in the shade of a gum tree with my eyes closed. A warm desert wind was blowing, drying out my sweat and turning the surface of my skin to salt dust. I stayed like that for some time, totally spent, but enjoying the fact we were still and that there was no danger anymore.

After sunset the dark silhouettes of the trees stood tall in the twilight and I stayed in my place while Eugene made a fire. When night fell, the star constellations of the Milky Way spread out above me, as brightly as I had ever seen them, even in Australia. The Southern Cross was dominant – the star formation of the Federation flag so clear I felt I was on the very edge of space, that I had somehow been given permission to see things that no other white man was allowed to see.

The sky began to lighten at half past four the next morning.

"Gonna show you something special today, Doc," Eugene said. "You're gonna like it."

He didn't elaborate and we set off, not long later turning off the track northwards. After two hours – say twenty miles – we came to halt by a rocky outcrop, which stood alone on the surrounding plain. Without a pause, Eugene climbed up onto one of the rocks and swung the gayandi around his head for several minutes. Then he stood there silently as if listening out for something, before hopping back down to ground level.

I was standing next to my bicycle, still sweating, with my hands on my hips. With Eugene I was learning I didn't have to say much, and that he would tell me what I wanted to know if I simply gave him a questioning look.

"Black fella telegram," he said, by way of explanation, "asking permission to show you sacred place. This is 'bora' ground."

"Who were you asking?"

"The spirit ancestors… they said 'yes', by the way."

I kept quiet.

"Need your help, Doc."

He pointed to a log on the ground and I helped him wedge it under a great rounded boulder. After much straining, the boulder rolled away a few feet, enough to reveal a fissure between the rocks disappearing off deep underground.

I presumed it was an old gnamma hole, formed by rains beating against the limestone plateau for millennia. The Aboriginals had done well to keep this one hidden. No-one would ever find this place unless they were shown where it was.

A steady, strong gust of wind was coming out of the hole, the same way a wind signalled the approach of a London underground train.

"Cave's breath," Eugene said, his wiry hair wafting in the breeze. He wrapped a piece of cloth around a stick, gave it to me and made himself another. "For fire – to help us see. Bring your water containers, Doc."

We descended, one at a time, carefully placing our feet on ledges and rocks which jutted out on both sides of the narrow space. Some forty feet below we reached a solid floor and Eugene lit the torches with a match.

"White fellas good for some things," he said, smiling and blowing out the match.

With the fires, I could see we were in a tunnel – about head height – and that it was sloping steeply downward. Dozens of ochre hand stencils were decorating the walls. Eugene placed his hand over one.

"These very old, Doc… made long, long time ago… made by blowing paint." He pretended to blow over his hand and then lifted it away from the rock. "Like that."

I had seen children do this kind of thing at school, but then Eugene put a three-making spanner into the works of my judgmental thoughts.

"White fellas think of a painting being made here," he said, slapping his hand on the cold rock. "Black fellas think they are marking what is already there… put there by the spirits. They see the marks of another world. It's easy to see the spirits when you have no fear… and black fellas have no fear."

I held up my burning torch and stared at the handprints, trying to imagine people standing at the same rock face a thousand years before and seeing it as a window to the spirits, and not a rock face at all.

The passage narrowed and shortened in height so that after a few hundred yards we could only crouch and shuffle forward. Just when I thought there was no way to go on, it opened out again and we emerged into a high vaulted cave. When I craned my neck up to try and see where the roof was, I couldn't make it out; that's how big the space was. Only the echoes of our footsteps and voices gave more of a sense of the cave's immensity.

Because the illumination was limited, I didn't notice at first, the same way I hadn't noticed when the ship approaching Australia had slowed down, but as I swung the torch around me, I froze in astonishment.

Swathes of the cave floor and walls were streaked with a shimmering bright yellow colour. My heart thumping, I walked over to the edge of the chamber and examined the cave wall more closely. When I held the torch close up to the wall, what I saw jolted me back to something I had seen a decade before – a Van Gogh painting of sunflowers in an art exhibition in 1890.

It had been on a trip to Brussels. Freddie and I had both been there and had both been transfixed. Looking at them made you feel strange.

They made everything else in the room seem less bright. The yellow flowers seemed to be fizzing off the canvas like the paint was made of Champagne. "Says here the artist associates the colour yellow with hope and friendship," Freddie had said, managing to translate from a small sign on the wall.

My mind skipped back to the present.

"Is this…"

I couldn't say it.

Eugene was standing next to me. The torchlight reflecting off the wall turned us into yellow beings.

"This is all gold, Doc" he said. "We call it 'yellow room'."

Goosebumps travelled down my neck.

We were standing in an underground cathedral of pure gold. There was enough here to start a gold rush to end all gold rushes. It wasn't even hidden in telluride. Now I noticed nuggets of varying sizes scattered all over the cave floor. This must have been where Eugene had picked up the gold he tried to pay me with in Kalgoorlie.

"Sacred place for the black fellas… the ancestors thought the colour was pretty… made a nice light in the fires. This is place of dreaming."

"You sleep in here?"

"Nah, Doc. Dreaming is a place… another world hidden in this world. Long ago, ancestor spirits travelled the land, creating everything. When it was done they went into the land and became the landscape. They left signs all around. If you can understand the signs then you can understand the world. The dreaming is not just about the past – it's about present and the future too. Forget about time when you think of the dreaming. Your friend – he knows all about the dreaming – I see him tell other white fella about it in church."

"You mean Rennie and the Kingdom of Heaven?"

"That's right, Doc. He has his black book about the Kingdom of Heaven. For us the land is our black book. Song line runs right through here."

"Song line?"

"One song follows one story, tracks the paths the creator ancestors once took. Song lines cover Australia like a big net."

I thought about the old paths in England – the South Downs Way, the Ridgeway, the routes of the Roman Roads which had themselves been built on even older tracks. Maybe the Ancient Britons had been in touch with the land in the same way as the Aboriginals.

There was a burial mound called 'Wayland's Smithy' on the Ridgeway path, one of the pilgrims' ways trodden for hundreds of generations by the 'ancestors'. It was surrounded by oaks which kept the long grave in a perpetual twilight. It was eerie. You felt there might be ghosts there, even if you didn't believe it in other places.

"This place was made when the ancestral spirit of the goanna – the Bungarra – stole the sun. The Bungarra was so quick he took it right out of the sky and everything turned dark like night. The Bungarra brought the sun into this hole in the ground. But the sun was so powerful it turned the rock yellow and the Bungarra was so dazzled that he let the sun go. It escaped and went back to the sky and the day came back."

"A solar eclipse."

"That's the way the white fellas see it. Our stories are not just about the land, but the sun, moon and the stars too. That is what this place became – a story of the sky." Eugene pointed up at the golden wall. "Look closer, Doc."

There were hundreds of holes – man made holes – perhaps an inch or two deep. Some of the patterns looked familiar and, as I continued to study the wall, I realised it was because they were star constellations. One was Orion, and near Orion seven clustered notches representing the Pleiades. There was Lyra – the larger notch representing the star Vega. And the Southern Cross – the same constellation I had been staring up at the night before.

Several of the pictograms seemed to represent comets, with lines for the tails, their trajectories heading downwards to the floor of the cave.

"Old dreaming stories tell of rocks hitting the earth, and making big holes in the ground," Eugene said.

I was reminded of the crater Dudley, Rennie and I had camped in, near the Wealth of Nations. One of the comets was much larger than the others and the tail had been elaborated into the shape of a snake.

"This one…?"

"It came a long time ago… big hole up north where it hit."

He put two of his fingers into the notches of the comet.

"See, the eyes of the snake are the rock coming through the sky… rocks like this bring life to earth at the beginning of time – the snake is the mother and father of all forms of life… made it possible for the first ancestors to live."

We walked through into another smaller chamber, everywhere still streaked with the glitter of the underground golden reef. I felt my feet in water. Trapped in the golden bowl of rock was a large lake, of such exceptional clarity that I had walked straight into it.

"Drink," Eugene said.

By example, he dipped his hand in and scooped out a mouthful. The water was cool.

"Is this water sacred?"

"More than the bloody gold, that's for sure, Doc. Out here, without water, you die in two days. Fill your bags with it; you still got a long way to go."

By the time we left the cave and rolled the boulder back into position it was dark.

We camped among the rocks near the cave entrance and ate dried pieces of Kangaroo. Watching the fire flickering in the desert night, my mind was a blur of images – prehistoric hand prints, golden walls and crystal clear underground lakes.

"Eugene, why do you trust me?"

He nodded to himself as if he had been expecting this question.

"You fix me up good in Fremantle and I remember that. You can decide to tell other white fellas about the yellow room, but I don't think

328

you will. You know they peel the skin off the earth to get at gold. No more sky map. Song line cut. White fellas everywhere... don't even need gold for the white fellas to destroy our places – look how they blew up the rock at Fremantle."

Eugene was right. The cave was an open invitation to destruction. I envisioned the water pipe being extended out here, the sweating pipe men and the beer shacks, the hundreds of dreamers and schemers filling up the new squalid shanty town, all hoping to strike it rich. This sacred place on the song-line would become just another sudden metropolis in the bush, with typhoid fever, raw sewage and rubbish in overcrowded streets.

To the Aboriginal people the gold was irrelevant – it was just a bright yellow canvas for their star map, their version of the Royal Greenwich Observatory. It occurred to me a western 'Song line' ran through that building too: zero degrees longitude, the prime meridian.

"We look at stars like you do," I said, "in our observatories."

He smiled.

"Yeah, I saw the one in Perth... but when the white fella looks at the sky, he looks for the brightest stars and joins up the dots like a child. Black fellas look at the spaces in between the stars and we draw our stories from that. We see patterns in the dark places."

I had never heard of anyone naming the dark spaces.

Eugene took me over to a flat rock with a carving, less than ten yards from where we were camped.

"Look, Doc."

It was the carved outline of a bird with a familiar shape – I had glimpsed some real ones on the ride, bounding along through the scrub as if accompanying me.

"An emu," I said

"Yes. Now look up."

He pointed at the Milky Way.

"See it, Doc? Emu... Southern Cross at the head."

It was hard to make it out at first – but then it slowly materialised. A giant emu, stretched out horizontally in the night sky; the head near the Southern Cross, the neck bisected by the pointer stars, the body covered by the constellation of Scorpio. The legs were stretched out behind; one huge emu-shaped dark patch within the starry luminosity of the galaxy.

Eugene pointed back down at the carving.

"Sky is a calendar. Tells us when tucker is ready. When the emu in the sky sitting down," he said, holding the edge of his hand at the horizontal, "then time to collect emu eggs. When emu running in the sky," he said, moving his hand to the vertical, "then time to hunt emu… even better tucker than the eggs if you ask me."

I continued to stare up at the emu. Again, just like with the three making match, my perceptions were being altered.

At daylight, after dusting over our footprints around the cave entrance, Eugene tied saltbushes to two ropes and attached one to his belt and one to the bicycle so that our tracks were rubbed out. We travelled the two hours back south to the telegraph track and then pushed eastwards, making Caiguna by late afternoon, another forty or fifty mile day, when you took into account the extra distance we had gone north of the track.

Eugene was still running.

Going by what I had noted down in the Dundas telegraph office, we still had some two hundred miles to go before Eucla. At Caiguna we were able to buy some supplies and fill up our canteens from the waterhole. Eugene led me a few miles further east of the homestead and we set up camp off the track; I had the impression he needed to be away from any sign of settlement before he felt 'at home'.

That night, satiated on two tins of 'tinned dog' each, we settled in by the fire.

"Why do you have a western name, Eugene?"

"I was brought up on a station. Eugene Tickell is my white fella name. My other name is Tickenbutt. I'm from Esperance Bay tribe."

I remembered the cold stares the Aboriginal groups had given me in Kalgoorlie whenever I had walked by.

"What do you think of white fellas?"

He had evidently worked it all out some time ago because he answered me straightaway.

"Like I said before, some of them are decent blokes. White fellas know a lot about some things but they also know nothing at all. They invent telegraph and steamships but they also destroy everything they touch. Before the white fellas came we got water at different rocks and plenty of food too. We watch at the rocks for kangaroo and emu, and when they come to drink, we spear them there. Now near the towns we have a lot of trouble getting water. We wait for hand-outs at the condenser plants – sometimes they give us water, sometimes they don't. Things were better before. When the white fella comes, there are always so many, like a flood. Everything gets used up and spoiled."

It made me feel ashamed to hear his analysis. As a distraction I checked the time on my pocket watch. Ten o'clock.

Eugene pointed at my watch.

"White fella loves numbers... He loves to count and measure – counts his money, breaks up the day into numbers on his clocks. White fellas put numbers on just about anything. Numbers give the white fellas an order in their head of the way the world is. Before white fella come – just bush. Then they find the yellow stuff and they all come. Numbers come too... ounces of gold per tonne of rock, pounds and shillings. You live in great cities with big buildings and newspapers where fellas throw around the numbers like spears. The world of numbers destroys."

I put the pocket watch away and when he saw me do this Eugene laughed.

"Black fellas not perfect, Doc, but we learn our lessons. Long time ago, in the desert, two mobs lived near each other. Then one summer a drought dries up one mob's water. So they go to the other mob's gnamma hole. But one man doesn't want to share so he spears one of them and then gets speared in return. Many years later there is another drought and the same mob comes again. The elders remember the deaths from the stories and they decide to share the water. They celebrate and have a great feast because no-one has to die for it. We learnt our lesson long time ago, but white fellas never learn."

His talk of 'two mobs' reminded me of two rowing teams.

"Every year in England there's a boat race on the river – they are fierce rivals. One boat loses and one boat wins. Losing is not as bad as being speared, but it still hurts the losers' pride and they are sad for a while."

Eugene looked mystified.

"Why does one team have to lose? Why can't they both be equal? Then no-one is sad."

I remembered the dead heat of 1877; Grenfell's Boat Race.

"Well, once there was a race where both teams were equal. Nobody lost and nobody won."

"Ah... I understand this race... and everyone was happy?"

I thought back to Grenfell's bitterness over the result.

"No. People like to win all the time."

His smile was replaced by a deep frown.

"White fella problem. Always the winners and the losers, always wanting to win, always chase numbers."

"Over the years, it will probably all even out," I said. "Both teams will have won the same number of races."

After this we were both silent.

I was frowning now. Perhaps it hadn't been a good example – I realised I didn't like the idea of Cambridge and Oxford being equal; I wanted Oxford to win.

"Actually, the time I felt happiest in a boat wasn't even in a race," I said. "The water was good and it felt very special."

"Sacred?"

"I suppose..."

"You must have been rowing the boat on a song line."

I laughed.

"Or you had made the ancestors happy," Eugene said.

Maybe he had a point. Perhaps the River Thames was some kind of arterial song line running through the south of England. There were times when Freddie and I would joke before training that the 'rowing god' wanted us to sacrifice more hours, and there had been times, most memorably the last time we had rowed together, when the river did feel like a god with whom we were being allowed to commune. The image of our circular puddles imprinted onto the skin of the river came into my mind again: two pairs of Kekule's snake rings.

Eugene was squatting by the fire and poking at the embers with a stick, staring intently into the flames as if mesmerised. Then, using the stick, he drew two pairs of circles in the dirt, just as I had been imagining.

I started to feel uneasy.

"Snakes?" he said out loud, as if he was conferring with someone.

Now my blood ran cold.

"Don't worry, Doc," he said. "Your brother okay – the one already in the dreaming."

I shivered. Something made me stare into the darkness on the other side of the campfire. Was he talking to Freddie?

"How do you know that?"

"You were thinking about him then; he was the other fella in the boat."

"Yes… but I didn't tell you."

"Didn't have to, Doc. Your thoughts made him come here and sit by the fire."

"But… he's dead."

Eugene looked through the fire and seemed disappointed.

"Now you've made him go again."

"I don't understand… my brother is dead."

"He's as real as this bloody fire, mate."

"That's impossible."

Eugene remained silent for several seconds before speaking again.

"When Dudley told me to go with Cowdray to find you, he told me in the British Arms. On the roof there is spinning stick…"

He moved his finger around in a circular motion.

"You mean the fan propeller on the ceiling?"

"Yeah… fan propeller, made of wood."

"Yes. What about it?"

"When still, you can't see through the wood. That's your body, my body. Then Dudley switch on propeller and it goes very fast and you can see through it. It's gone. That's you and me in the dreaming. That's your brother now… everything moving faster in the dreamworld."

I stared long and hard at Eugene. I felt exactly the same as when I had stared at the old nurse at Spike Island, when she had told me about the Grey Lady, before I started to believe her. In other words, what was going through my mind was incredulity.

"Be careful what you think, Doc. Thoughts go to the dreaming like messages on the telegraph." He pointed up at the wire suspended twenty feet above us. "And thoughts come back too. Good thoughts and you get good telegraph messages back. Think bad thoughts and all you get back is bad… like that Cowdray fella. He was full of bad telegrams – impossible to fix. No bloody chance. All the magic depend on energy from the dreaming. Everything – good or bad – come from that world. You've been thinking too many bad thoughts, Doc. I saw the look in your eyes the first night I met you – you were full of them. You'd almost sung yourself, mate. Bit better now. You row in that boat for hours and get better. Same with thoughts – you need to practice with those too."

"I need to practice… *thinking?*"

"Yeah… thoughts… Kungullen."

Eugene started to talk in his own language, waving his burning stick in the air so that it made light patterns in the night.

"Kaldowamp kungullen boorala wanye tumpinyer yackatoon – always think good then life will be happy. Kungullen motong thure… Think strong and straight."

"Kungullen," I said, trying to pronounce the word the way I had heard him say it. "Kungullen…"

I remembered Freddie saying how electromagnetic thoughts could change the world, and it helped me to accept what I had been told by Eugene. I even fell asleep believing that Freddie had, in some form, visited our campfire and communicated with him.

That night though, my thoughts went astray as I dreamt of a golden city, a place filled with well-dressed crowds, impressive civic buildings, multi-coloured fountains, oysters and Champagne… a sacred city of numbers. The new city of Hunston, named after the man who had first claimed the huge reef. It would probably be the capital of the state, supplanting Perth. I even dreamt of an oil painting called: 'Hunston's Luck' depicting me standing by the rock entrance to the yellow room.

I woke at five the next morning to find that Eugene had gone. It was because he had been able to see into my dream about claiming the yellow room for myself, I was sure of it.

Next to my pack was a parcel with a gold nugget perched on top, the same nugget he had tried to pay me with in Kalgoorlie.

He had used it as a paperweight: the parcel underneath was addressed to me as 'Jack' in Poyntz's distinct handwriting.

I untied the string around the brown paper.

Inside was a tub of sand and a letter.

> *Jack,*
> *Dudley tells me I owe you one – tells me the tracker is going to give this to you.*
> *There's no time to write much, but thank you.*
> *Until we meet again, hope some Nome gold will help see you through.*
> *Yours,*
> *Poyntz*
> *P. S. I'll explain things to my fiancée*

I prised open the tub.

It wasn't sand; it was gold dust, at least ten ounces worth.

As the sun rose higher and it got lighter I scanned the horizon for Eugene but saw only emptiness.

With Poyntz's Nome gold and Eugene's nugget, I had become a moderately rich man overnight. But was it enough? There was the potential to do a lot better.

I stood with my bicycle on the track and looked west, back in the direction of the yellow room. All I had to do was ride back there, put some stakes in the ground and get rich beyond my wildest dreams. The dream was nagging at my conscience, tempting me.

Eugene's fireside philosophy had faded already and I was back in the world of numbers. Besides, he had deserted me, left me completely in the lurch. I owed him nothing.

Stake your claim, my logical mind was saying. *There's enough money in that piece of ground to set you straight for life. Ride back there and claim it, you idiot.*

I tried to justify to myself that Eugene wouldn't mind, that I would be able to control how the area was developed, keeping a part of it for the Aboriginal tribes so they could maintain some of their sacred site. It seemed perfectly reasonable to propose pulling down an entire cathedral and leaving a small side chapel to serve the same purpose. With the money I could buy them decent houses, teach them how to read and write, even build them their own hospital.

I could buy Egremont's place in England now that he was bankrupted, take guests to the underwater room and amaze them. Just thinking of the scenario thrilled me. People would pay attention to me now – my opinion would be solicited by the great and the good.

The incantations from the world of numbers continued.

Good. You're doing the right thing if you go back there. You have the right to claim it. You deserve it. You're a doctor not a crook. You can use the money for good.

I started to ride west back towards the yellow room, but within a mile a feeling of self-loathing overwhelmed me.

Kungullen – my thoughts of greed had gone out into the dreaming and come back amplified, to justify my temptation.

What if Eugene, Dudley and Rennie were right and there was some place beyond death? What if the two worlds even overlapped at certain points? The Grey Lady had been there – an unhappy ghost, trapped by the misery of her own suicide – but there all right. I had seen her and there was nothing anyone could say to convince me otherwise.

Somehow Eugene had known about Freddie the night before.

I imagined him watching me from behind one of the shabby gum trees out on the plain, waiting to see what decision I made. If I went back for the gold, he would not stop me. He would watch me destroy his song line from a distance, and then he would turn his back on the white fellas once and for all and walk off further into the interior.

It occurred to me that I was being tested.

Just a few weeks into the newly federated country of Australia, Eugene was acting on behalf of all the Aboriginal peoples, testing a representative of the white fellas to see if there was any hope for a future together, or whether we were doomed to destroy everything in our relentless pursuit of profit. For some reason the test had been laid at my door – he had asked his ancestors for permission to show me that place, spun his 'gayandi' in the air, and the ancestors had given him the go ahead, aware that it was a test. And here I was, about to trample all over that trust. If I was being tested, I was failing miserably.

Some camels were standing near to the track.

I knew what Rennie would have said: "It is easier for a camel to go through the eye of a needle, than for a rich man to enter the kingdom of God."

From his pulpit in my mind he continued: "What does it profit you if you gain the whole world and lose yourself? Get thee hence, Satan!"

I slowed the bicycle to a stop, drank some water and rolled myself a cigarette, standing there smoking it until my head cleared and my chattering mind had become as silent as the land around. At the end of the smoke, I turned the bicycle around and started pedalling towards the rising sun.

Jesus, I had almost convinced myself about staking a claim on the yellow room and it was frightening how quickly it had happened.

It was good to have the doubts back again. If a panel of experts had asked me why I turned around, I would have shrugged. I had no evidence or facts to offer them, it had just felt right. All I had to go on was a faint feeling which had persisted after all the chatter in my head had ceased. Or maybe I could have appropriated Dudley's words, bearing in mind that Eugene was a mate: 'mates don't shit on each other'.

I kept riding until my breathing became rhythmical and then, passing the spot where the camp had been the night before, I pushed onwards with renewed vigour. Travelling away from certainty and reason felt good – I was following the way of Poyntz's Contrary.

Chapter Twenty-five

That same day I made Cocklebiddy, where I was able to re-fill my water containers. The building was empty though, and with no food stores to be had, I kept going.

Madura was only another fifty miles.

I ate the last of my supplies on the ride and camped perhaps fifteen miles short of Madura. I had used up a lot of my reserves – it had been a sixty-five mile day and the hottest one I had experienced so far. My water was running low and I went to sleep hungry that evening.

There were Kangaroos all around but I could not throw a spear like Eugene. I managed to catch a small lizard, and cook it over the fire, but it wasn't enough. All Eugene had left me was the gold and you couldn't eat that.

At least I would be able to get supplies the next morning at Madura.

But Madura was more desolate than Cocklebiddy had been, and this time the water hole was empty. This was fast turning into a nightmare.

I had no choice but to ride onwards to the next waterhole at Mundrabilla, sixty miles further on. The leather bag was completely empty and I was down to Carlsson's water can – about half a pint left. I was treading the precipice of dehydration and exhaustion.

To try and get through it, I broke the distance down into ten mile goals and this strategy worked for a while.

Twenty, thirty, forty...

The heat became a living thing, sapping at my strength like a parasite, but I made fifty and cycled on.

Some time after the fifty mile marker, which in my mind signalled that I was near the end, I stopped by a scrawny tree to drink the last of the water. My tongue had almost become glued to the roof of my mouth so I had no other choice.

Where the hell was the next water station?

For a mile I cycled on, trying to get to where I needed to be, but all that did was empty the last of my reserves.

I slowed down. The pain in my limbs began to ebb away and the front wheel started veering from side to side across the track.

And then the 'perish' began; euphoria at first, a strange feeling of invincibility, as if I could keep cycling forever.

I became hypnotised by the unchanging scrub. My vision darkened around the periphery and it was as though the track lit up in front of me, like riding in a tunnel.

Too hot, I felt. So I threw off my shirt.

Then my consciousness seemed to split so that I was in two places at once, in the tunnel at ground level but also floating high above the land. Far below me, the desert stretched out like an old man's sunburnt skin. Way out to the west was the turquoise Indian Ocean, shimmering, and the curve of the earth beyond, bright against the dark backdrop of space. When I looked to the south east I could see the Great Australian Bight and the Southern Ocean and even the distant whiteness of the Antarctic.

A final wave of fatigue crashed down and I eased off the pedals and drifted to a halt. I climbed off the bicycle and leant it against a telegraph pole.

Something dark was nearby; the same cold feeling I had experienced on the ward the night Freddie had died. Not the Grey Lady herself, but the darkness she represented. Death was waiting for me to fall asleep.

Not even the flies bothered me now. They were staying well away. I lay down on the ground, my face in the dirt, so close that I could see the desert floor wasn't just sand, but thousands of tiny spiral seashells.

The silence was tomb-like.

As the darkness came closer, I began to drift off.

"Get up, John."

Someone was there.

I looked around but there was nobody. And yet there was the strongest sensation of Freddie's company. There was no doubt in my mind that he was there with me on the otherwise silent desert track.

"Come on, get up."

I listened and obeyed, managing to stand.

"Put a jacket on – you're getting burnt."

I found my Blues blazer in my suitcase and slipped it on.

"Now get back on the bloody bicycle and start riding."

I did as ordered, cycling away from the patch of dirt that until a few moments before was to have been my last resting place. As I rode, I felt Freddie with me, just as surely as if we had been rowing in the double scull together. He was just behind my right shoulder, easily keeping pace.

"Don't stop… Push on… Hang on John."

It was all quite business-like and there was little emotion. It reminded me of assisting in the operating theatre, with the surgeon giving instructions: "Cut the stitch here please, pull that retractor back there…"

"Ten more pedals… That's it… Another ten…"

This encouragement lasted half an hour or more, a constant patter of orders, as if we were in our old boat.

"It's just over this next rise… You're nearly there now… Last ten…"

Suddenly he was gone, and I was all alone again.

What little logic I had left told me it had been a hallucination, the desperate grasping of my mind looking to survive. Even so, when the voice went, I felt the absence acutely, as crushing a loss as I had ever known. I was so dejected that I almost stopped again, and the only reason I didn't was because when I looked up, I saw the tin roof of the Mundrabilla Station gleaming through the heat haze.

A man called Talbot had seen me coming from a distance and was waiting with a flask of water and some damper when I pulled up outside.

For an hour I just sipped the water and didn't say anything.

Talbot watched me the whole time, waiting patiently for me to recover.

I was the one who finally broke the silence. He had a gold nugget hanging from his watch chain and I pointed at it.

"Are you a prospector?"

"Was one" he said, "Found this in September of '92," he said. "I was the first to find gold at Coolgardie."

"They said Bayley and Ford were the first. I've seen the oil painting in Faahan's pub."

Talbot was swinging his watch chain around his finger and smiling knowingly.

"They said…"

Later, once I had rested a while and eaten, he told me the rest of his tale.

"I was in Southern Cross, fifty miles west of Coolgardie, with me two mates. We followed the track of Hunt, an old-time explorer… ended up near a waterhole at Gnarlbine rocks. Bayley and Ford were camped nearby. Bayley sometimes came over and talked to us but Ford never did; he was a cold fish. Anyway, one morning, we went out prospecting on a small rise of land and gold appeared all around us."

Talbot held up his prized specimen on the watch chain and grinned. Half his teeth were rotten, but one of them was gold.

"I picked this little beauty up off the ground that day. It's all I have left."

"What happened?"

"Well, we were novices, so wild with excitement that we didn't think to peg it out right then. Instead, we went back to our camp and slept late the next morning. After breakfast we set off to our find, but when we got there, Bayley and Ford were already pegging it out. We argued but they said it was fair game and we were three damn fools for not having pegged it the night before. Ford even took out a revolver, but Bayley told him to put it away…"

I stared wide-eyed at Talbot.

"You never bloody pegged it?"

"Never bloody pegged it," he said.

I started to laugh and he soon joined in.

Once we were laughing it took about a minute to stop and every time we did, a short silence would pass before we started again. It put me in such a good mood that I almost told him about the yellow room.

Despite his sorry tale, I admired Talbot for the way he told it with so little bitterness. Tired of the greed of the goldfields, he had come out here to run the sheep station and he hadn't lost hope.

"I don't know what I'm worth, and that's a fact. When I left England I was but 16 years old. My father gave me £8. I have that £8 yet… I'm thinking of going into property investment. My poor wife hasn't seen another white woman in four years. I want to take her to Perth one day – and we'll have a big house that looks out over the Swan River."

Talbot bristled with energy. He would get his house in Perth, I was sure of it.

I left the station at dusk and cycled for two hours before setting up camp.

The Nullarbor Plain – that's what Talbot had called the country I was now cycling through. Nullarbor was Latin for 'no trees'… Old Crosbie would have been proud of me for remembering that.

Talbot had given me two cans of 'tinned dog' to complete the journey and I ate one of them by the small fire, savouring every particle of salt.

That last night in the desert my thoughts came clearly and whole. If there was something divine out there it would have to mirror the beauty of the night sky. I wondered if small clues in the world hinted at a greater beauty in 'the dreaming': Sister B's beauty; the feel of that kiss from the Russian Princess; the way a wave broke onto the shore, the fizzing sunflowers of 'Van Goff'; the emu out in space; the way a man could turn his back on the riches of the world and move on regardless.

My thoughts retreated and the whirring sound of Eugene's gayandi took over.

I slept deeply and without fear.

The following day the track dipped down off the tableland and onto the coastal plain. The ocean was in the distance.

By the early afternoon I had reached the telegraph station at Eucla.

Inside, the station was busy, the incessant clatter of Morse code keys filling the building like the sound of the cicadas at sunset. After my desert odyssey, seeing all this life and hearing the noise was disconcerting to say the least. I gazed around trying to process it all.

The border between Western Australia and South Australia ran down the centre of the room, represented by a painted white line bisecting the long table. Two clocks on the wall ran ninety minutes apart, representing the two time zones of the states.

A clerk wearing a dark waistcoat came to the reception desk and noticed me looking at the line.

"Just a few weeks ago," he said, "before federation, the telegraphists from each state passed each other the messages through small holes in a wooden partition in the middle of the table. They even used different types of Morse code. Now the partition is gone."

I could tell that the two teams were wary of one another, still trying to come to terms with the fact that they were now citizens of the same country. All the while they kept tapping out messages on the keys. To them it was second nature, like talking out loud. They didn't hear them as random sounds with no meaning, the way I did.

"Anyway, can I help you, sir?"

"What's the date?" I said.

"It's January the twenty-fourth... Is there anything else?"

"Um yes… Are there any messages for Die Hard John?"

"Is that under D or J?"

"Try J."

He went over to a wall of pigeon holes to look for the telegram.

Twenty four days.

It was hard to believe it had been that long. I must have been a sight – I had grown a straggly beard and my clothes were so caked in dust that they could have been dropped on the ground and mistaken for it.

The clerk returned to the counter with a telegram.

It was only now that I saw he was wearing a black armband. Everyone in the room was wearing one.

"Who died?"

"The Queen," he said. "Two days ago… it came through on the wire yesterday."

Dudley's message read as follows: *'GLAD YOU MADE IT. C SACKED, P NOW BOSS. TRAVEL WELL. TD'*

There was a lot I wanted to say in return but when the clerk gave me the pencil and paper my mind went blank and all I wrote was: *'THANKS FOR ALL HELP VIA EUGENE. J'*

Great sand dunes rose up directly behind the telegraph building, threatening to engulf it.

Pulling my bicycle behind me like a reluctant child, I climbed to the top of the biggest dune and sat down to work out what to do next.

From the summit I could see a rickety wooden jetty down on the beach, straddling the white sand and the surf. Men were unloading supplies from a cargo boat and a tram was moving the supplies through the dunes to the small township of Eucla near the telegraph station.

Piles of sandalwood lay stacked on the beach ready for the vessel to take on board. A man with a clipboard was busy taking an inventory, while two lumpers lifted the bundles of wood into large crates stamped with the words: *TO ESPERANCE*.

It felt like a good time for a smoke.

I rummaged around in the haversack for the chocolate tin, but when I opened it there were only a few shreds of tobacco left, not even enough to roll a single cigarette. The last dry flakes took off into the warm breeze and for several moments I stared down into the empty tin, thinking about Freddie and all the waiting and hoping I had been doing. Wasn't that what the Count of Monte Cristo had said? Wait and hope? Rennie's prayer came to mind, one line in particular: 'lead him back from his wilderness'.

In a strange and yet beautiful way, there had been an answer out there on the Nullarbor: first my encounter with Eugene's magic and the dreaming, and then most mysterious of all, hearing Freddie's voice, *talking to me, encouraging me, helping me*. Granted, it wasn't the type of proof to sway a hard-bitten scientist in the re-telling, but it had all felt real enough at the time.

Either way, what had happened told me that Freddie's spirit lived on. God only knew how, but somehow it did.

I put the tin away and lingered on the dune awhile, gazing at the Southern Ocean.

The brilliant turquoise of the shallow water ran out for miles, only turning into a darker cobalt blue near the horizon. The coast stretched away to my left and right so that it seemed as if the entire Great Australian Bight was within my scope. Once, back in Kalgoorlie, I felt I had been in a waiting room at the very edge of the known world, but I was wrong. That place was here; this was the edge of the world and now I was about to leave for the unknown.

When I saw the crates bound for Esperance being loaded onto the boat, I wheeled my bicycle down through the sand dunes and headed towards the jetty.

Somewhere along the way, I realised I was smiling.

Author's Notes

Owing to the historical setting of *The Sudden Metropolis*, an extensive range of sources were used, the full listing of which goes on for many pages (available on my author website). For the reader's interest, some of the main references are set out below:

Philip Hoare's excellent *Spike Island: The Memory of a Military Hospital* (Fourth Estate, 2010) was the inspiration for the Hunston brothers being repatriated to that establishment and provided the factual backbone for those sections of story, including the phenomenon of the Grey Lady ghost and Queen Victoria's visit in 1900. Visiting the Royal Victoria Country Park myself afforded further details, such as the tombstone epitaphs: 'Accidentally drowned in Southampton Water' and 'Died from fever contracted in South Africa'.

Anyone who has studied chemistry will be aware of the benzene ring which Kekule discovered in 1865; his having 'dreamt up' the structure was only later revealed to a conference of German chemists, in 1890 (A. Kekule. *Benzolfest: Rede* Berichte der Deutschen Chemischen Gesellschaft, 1890, 23: 1302 – 11).

Lavina Mitton's small volume *The Victorian Hospital* (Shire Publications 2008) contains the putdown Hunston receives from the patient with the headache: 'It's the likes of me that keeps the likes of you...', as well as the types of medical equipment used at the time and the layout of wards. The BMJ article Hunston reads in the Blue Boar Club was by A. Bowlby (*The War in South Africa*, BMJ, 1900, 1610 -12). The hypothetical wording from the impending typhoid inquiry is from Parliamentary Papers Cd 453 and Cd 454 (London: HMSO, 1901).

Sir Robert Egremont is based on the tycoon Sir Whittaker Wright (1846-1904) whose country house at Witley Park Hampshire (Witworth Park in the book) was as grand as described. Today the grounds are inaccessible, but the underwater room still exists — with dramatic photographs available at:
http://sometimes-interesting.com/2015/04/22/the-conservatory-under-a-lake/. Whittaker Wright's London and Globe Corporation collapsed on 28th Dec 1900, and I have adhered to this date in describing Egremont's downfall. Quotations relating to Captain Cook's journal in Egremont's library were sourced from: *Cook's Endeavour Journal: the inside story* (National Library of Australia, 2008).

William Grenfell (1855-1945) rowed in two Boat Races for Oxford (in 1877 and 1878). Harry Mount's article - *A sporting life* (The Spectator, 16th June 2012) provided some extra colour on the man. Grenfell's wife, Ettie (1867 — 1952) was a well-known socialite and the remark that she 'told enough white lies to ice a wedding cake' was recollected in: *The Listener* (11 June, 1953). Hunston's 1896, 97 and 98 Boat Races for Oxford are based on those of an oarsman called R. Carr (Eton and Magdalen). *The Boat Race* by G.C. Drinkwater (Blackie and Son Ltd, 1939) established this fact. Dudley's later descriptions of the sculler Harry Searle were from Scott Bennett's *The Clarence Comet* (Sydney University Press 1973).

Conan-Doyle being unable to recall his favourite Sherlock Holmes story is described in: Janet Pascal's *Arthur Conan Doyle: beyond Baker Street* (OUP, 2000). Vincent Cirillo's paper, *Arthur Conan Doyle (1859-1930): Physician during the typhoid epidemic in the Anglo-Boer War (1899-1902)*, Journal of Medical Biography, 2013, 22 (1): 2 – 8), was also useful.

The Army Medical Services Museum near Aldershot had everything there was to know about the RAMC (including displays on the Boer War period with artefacts such as medals, fever charts and the coin catcher). Photographs from the booklet *Royal Army Medical Corps 1898-1998: Reflections of one hundred years of service* (RAMC 1997) inspired the Raadzaal and quartermaster scenes. The webpage http://samilitaryhistory.org/vol092sw.html detailed the Spitz Kop conditions and typhoid fever incidence rates during the summer months of 1900. Lord Wolseley's derogatory comments on sanitation were from Colonel Charles H. Melville's *Military Hygiene and Sanitation* (London, Edward Arnold, 1912) and Kipling's saying 'Bloeming-typhoidtein' on the train is taken from his poem: *The Parting of the columns* (1903).

Details of Almroth Wright and the typhoid inoculation came from Oscar Craig and Alasdair Fraser's *Doctors at War* (The Memoir Club, 2007), and Kevin Brown's *Fighting fit: Health, Medicine and War in the twentieth century* (The History Press, 2008). The statistician Pearson's findings on Wright's data were eventually published in 1904 (K. Pearson *Report on certain enteric fever inoculation statistics*, BMJ, 1904, 3:1243 – 46).

With regards to the Bloemfontein typhoid epidemic, Thomas Pakenham's *The Boer War* (Abacus, 1992) was informative, with an extract of Burdett-Coutts' article from *The Times* (27th June 1900) and examples of the red tape hampering the running of the army hospitals. It also contained a photograph inspiring Freddie's graffiti on the farmhouse wall. Emanoel Lee's *To the bitter end: a photographic history of the Boer War 1899-1902* (Butler & Tanner Ltd, 1985) mentions the 'dum dum' bullets used, complete with battlefield X-ray images. Freddie's rallying cry "Come on Die Hards" at Spion Kop is based on that by 2nd Lieutenant Bicknell (in Charles Lethbridge Kingsford's *The story of the Duke of Cambridge's Own*, Country Life, 1916). *Marching to the drums: eyewitness accounts of war from the Kabul massacre to the siege of Mafikeng* (Editor: Ian Knight, 2015 edition by Frontline books) furnished some battle scenes, and details on injuries and surgery are vividly described in: Frederick Treves's *The tale of a Field Hospital* (Cassell and Company 1900). The newspaper cutting Hunston finds on the floor was written by Winston Churchill, then a young reporter (Morning Post, 17 Feb 1900). Freddie's encounter with the Indian stretcher bearer alludes to Gandhi, their conversation inspired by Gandhi's words from 1922: 'Non-violence is the first article of my faith. It is also the last article of my creed' (In: *Oxford Dictionary of Thematic Quotations*, OUP 2000).

Cowdray's war background is founded on that of Alfred 'Bulala' Taylor – described in Lt. George Witton's *Scapegoats of the Empire: the true story of Breaker Morant's Bushveldt Carbineers* (D.W. Paterson Company, Melbourne, 1907), Dudley's on Lt. Willoughby Dowling (of the First Australian Horse), and Carlsson's on a Swedish Boer fighter interviewed by an Australian War correspondent called Hales on the shooting of Lt. Dowling during the ambush. Hales recounts Dowling's astonishing fight in *The Singleton Argus*, Dec 1st 1900. Dudley's newspaper clipping of the aftermath is by A.B. Paterson, aka 'Banjo' Paterson (*The finding of Kilpatrick* The Sydney Mail, 24th February 1900). Paterson wrote the words to 'Waltzing Matilda' in 1895.

The cranial capacity theory discussed by the racist professor in Skull alley stems from ideas in Stephen Jay Gould's *The Mis-measure of man* (W.W. Norton & Co, 1981). Aboriginals being: 'the most lowly of all living races' is a direct quote from: *Newnes Modern Pictorial Atlas* (George Newnes Ltd, 1939). Details on Java man and Neanderthal man in the novel are from Bjorn Kurten's *Our Earliest Ancestors* (Columbia University Press, 1993). Cutfield's racist views are quoted from: Henry Morris' *The History of Colonization from the earliest times to the present day* (Macmillan Company, 1900). Hunston's breakdown at the funeral was inspired by an observation on Combat Fatigue (Major Dick Winters *Beyond Band of Brothers*, Ebury Press, 2011): 'When you see a man break, he usually slams down his helmet and messes up his hair. I don't know if it's conscious or unconscious, but a soldier goes to his head and massages his head, shakes it, and then he's gone. You can talk to him all you want, but he can't hear you.'

Regarding Western Australia, *The Mile that Midas touched – the story of Kalgoorlie from 1893 to 1968* by Gavin Casey and Ted Mayman (Seal Books 1968), was an invaluable source, and it was here that I first read of the true story of Father Long, the state of 'Auralia', stock market manipulation and the hedonism of Kalgoorlie life. *The history of female prostitution in Australia* by Raelene Frances (In: Perkins, Prestage, Sharp, & Lovejoy (eds.) *Sex Work and Sex Workers in Australia*, University of NSW Press, 1994) helped set the scenes with the prostitutes, including the certificate on venereal disease being on show. An informative government website http://slwa.wa.gov.au/federation/fed/027_sepa.htm had a photograph of the separatists and a map of Auralia, both used in the book. *Gold and Typhoid – two fevers* by Vera Whittington (University of Western Australia Press 1988) supplied the table of typhoid deaths which Wright gives to Hunston, together with the descriptions of Reverend Rowe, the St John of God nurses and the hospitals. Sir John Kirwan's *My Life's Adventure* (Eyre & Spottiswoode, 1936) offered extra insights on Father Long and goldfields life. Long did die of typhoid fever, but in Perth and in 1899, a year earlier than in the story.

Facts about the Fremantle gaol and Moondyne Joe's fortified cell are from: Cyril Ayris' *Fremantle Prison – a brief history* (Freelance, 1995), as well as a personal visit to the building, now a museum. The British Arms pub was built in 1899 and operated until 1924. Said to be still haunted by Edith McKay's ghost, the building now forms part of the WA Museum Kalgoorlie Boulder, as does the Ivanhoe head frame (the 'Egremont' head frame in the novel). The museum holds information on the mineralogy of gold bearing 'telluride' and the construction of the water pipeline. Laying and jointing of the pipes did not start until March 1901 and the pipeline was officially opened on 24th January 1903.

Future US President Herbert Hoover (1874 – 1964), worked as a mining engineer in Kalgoorlie in 1898 and then again in 1901. His autobiography: *The Memoirs of Herbert Hoover: 1874 – 1930 Years of Adventure* (Macmillan Company, New York, 1951) provided information for the speech delivered by his character at the Stopes dinner. Lou Hoover's remark '…I have majored in Herbert Hoover ever since…' is genuine (Paul Boller, Jr *Presidential wives - an anecdotal history*, 1988, 2nd Edition, OUP). His earlier dalliance with a local Kalgoorlie girl is unverifiable, although a love poem supposedly written by him is displayed in the Palace Hotel today.

For Rennie's multitude of quotes and his sermon, I employed the King James Bible and *What Jesus Meant* by Garry Wills (Penguin 2006). The poem Dudley recites on the way to the Wealth of Nations is by Barcroft Boake (*Where the dead men lie and other poems*, Angus and Robertson, 1897).

Poyntz's 'Contraries' feature in Thomas Berger's *Little Big Man* (Eyre and Spottiswoode 1965) and really did exist. His criticising Hunston's bed-side manner - 'don't take away his hope' – is a quote by Sir William Osler, Professor at Johns Hopkins School of Medicine from 1893 – 1905. Poyntz's Klondike exploit is rooted in history: an avalanche on the Chilkoot trail occurred on April 3rd 1898, 'the crazy kid river pilot' alludes to Jack London (1876 – 1916) and 'Uncle William' is based on William Judge (1850 – 1899). Wyatt Earp (1848 – 1929) was in Nome at that time running a bar called 'The Dexter'.

Mention of C.Y. O'Connor being 'sung' appears in a publication written by local Aboriginal elders entitled: *Statements of significance for the Fremantle area and Registered Aboriginal sites – Cantonment Hill, Rocky Bay and Swan River* (WA Government 2016). Hunston's dreaming of aboriginals planting their flag on the white cliffs of Dover actually did occur in January 1988, the year of Australia's bicentenary. Burnum Burnum (1936-97) 'claimed' England for the Aboriginal people, saying: 'We wish no harm to England's native people. We are here to bring you good manners, refinement and an opportunity to make a 'Koompartoo', a fresh start.' (*The Oxford Dictionary of Thematic Quotations*, OUP 2000).

Equipment such as spears, coolamons and woomeras exist as artefacts in the Australian Museum in Sydney. Various websites helped with aspects of Eugene's outlook and actions, including his account of the 'world of numbers' (http://singing.indigenousknowledge.org/exhibit-4/2) and details of the 'emu in space' (http://www.atnf.csiro.au/research/AboriginalAstronomy/). Spear making and kangaroo cooking is described in W.J. Peasley's *The last of the nomads* (Eye books 2004). *Mutant Message Down Under* by Marlo Morgan (Thorsons 1995) was informative on aboriginal healing methods.

Some of Eugene's extra-ordinary powers are described in A.P. Elkin's *Aboriginal Men of High degree: initiation and sorcery in the world's oldest tradition* (first published 1945, Inner Traditions International, 1994). The ability to run for long distances at pace is called 'fast travelling'. Elkin's field notes from 1944 describe one aboriginal – a so-called 'clever man' - being 'able to cover 112km per day'. Cyril Havecker's *Understanding Aboriginal Culture* (Cosmos 1987) and *Voices of the First Day* by Robert Lawlor (Inner Traditions International, 1991) were both invaluable and among the most interesting reads in the entirety of my research. Lawlor describes the anthropological experiments with matches (the 'three making match') and Havecker much of the spirituality related in the desert scenes of the novel.

Freddie's physics lesson from 1892 centres on the findings of Maxwell (J. Clark Maxwell, *A Dynamical theory of the Electromagnetic field*. Phil. Trans. R. Soc. Lond. 1865, 155: 459-512). For the less mathematical, the BBC i-player documentary *Scotland's Einstein: James Clark Maxwell – the man who changed the world* helps. The article Freddie then finds in the school library is by: Richard Caton (*The electric currents of the brain*, BMJ, 1875, ii: 278).

Hunston's ghostly encounter with Freddie is not just fanciful thinking; the phenomenon is well-documented in John Geiger's *The Third Man factor: surviving the impossible* (Canongate, 2009). Images from the booklet *Across the Nullarbor with panorama* (Panorama Books, 1986) inspired the scenes at Barla-juina, the cave, and the telegraph office at Eucla. The Nullarbor had been crossed on bicycle by Arthur Richardson in 1896 and William Snell in 1897 and would have been an achievable feat for Hunston.

Books and the internet aside, nothing can beat visiting the place or seeing the actual objects; be it walking the shoreline at Royal Victoria Country Park, feeling the iron rivets in Moondyne Joe's gaol cell or sitting on a sand dune at Eucla – all are imbued with potential for storytelling. An old Queen Victoria chocolate tin on the shelf of an antique shop becomes an item for characters to use and cherish.

Paintings and drawings described

Taplow Court, portrait of William Henry Grenfell by Leslie Ward - pseudonym 'Spy' (Published in Vanity Fair, Dec 20th 1890).

Down on his luck, Frederick McCubbin, 1889 (Collection: Art Gallery of Western Australia).

Bayley's Luck, Gerald Walsh, 1899 (Collection: Western Australian Museum). For many years it hung in a goldfields pub (http://trove.nla.gov.au/newspaper/page/3803958).

The Doctor, Luke Fildes, 1887 (Collection: The Tate Britain, London).

Sunflowers, Vincent Van Gogh, 1888 (Collection: The National Gallery, London). This painting was at 'Les XX' in Brussels in 1890 (one of two Van Gogh sunflower paintings in that exhibition).

Appendix 1

Abbreviations Used

RAMC: Royal Army Medical Corps

MO: Medical Officer

PMO: Principal Medical Officer

BMJ: British Medical Journal

SS: Steam ship

DM: Doctor of Medicine (Oxford)

Appendix 2

Glossary of Australian vernacular circa 1900:
(From: Whittington, pp. 421 - 2)

Billy tea: tea made in water boiled in a billycan over an open fire

Brumby: a bush horse

Damper: bread without yeast baked in ashes of an outdoor fire-place

Duffer: an unproductive mine. A mining claim without gold

Jonny Cake: pieces of fried damper

Lumper: a worker on a wharf employed in loading and unloading cargo

Moleskin pants: trousers made of moleskin – a strong soft fine-piled cotton fustian, the surface of which is 'shaved' before dyeing

Mulga wire: bush telegraph or grapevine - verbal news passed from traveller to traveller

New-chum: an inexperienced newcomer

Peg a claim: to mark out a miner's claim by placing pegs at the four corners, each peg bearing the claimant's name

Perish, do a: to die

Roll-up: roll-ups administered summary justice at mining camps where there were no police or courts. To the banging of a tin dish all were expected to attend a hearing. One miner was appointed judge. Accusers and accused were heard by the assembled men. If judged guilty the accused was given until sundown to leave the field.

Sandgroper: nickname for a West Australian

Telluride: a compound of tellurium with another element - often rich in gold or silver.

Tinned dog: tinned meat – corned beef or pressed meat mixture

Tucker: food

T'othersider: pre-federation, a term used in Western Australia for a person from the eastern colonies

Wildcat: characterized by wild, irresponsible speculation. A mining company in which the management raises money, often by misleading statements

Willy-willy: in hot weather, a miniature cyclone

Wogga: a floor-covering of sewn wheat bags (or hessian bags)

'Wet': a drinking session as for a farewell

Wire: a telegram

Printed in Poland
by Amazon Fulfillment
Poland Sp. z o.o., Wrocław